I0564602

Flames of the Fire

Rebecca Lange

Published by Rebecca Lange Books, 2026.

Table of Contents

To the women whose tempers burn like volcanoes—and to the men who love them all the more because of it.

FLAMES OF THE FIRE

First edition. May 10, 2024

Second edition. January 24, 2026.

Copyright © 2026 Rebecca Lange.

ISBN: 9781957089430

Written by Rebecca Lange.

1

Ashes Don't Lie

Flames roared skyward, hungry, furious, sending towering columns of smoke twisting into the heavens, a signal of devastation visible for miles. Joy had only just crested the ridge when the acrid stench of burning timber hit her like a blow. Sharp. Suffocating. Unmistakable.

She turned in her saddle, scanning the valley below, and froze. Her breath caught, then escaped in a strangled gasp. That plume of thick, black smoke rose from the very place she feared most: her sister's homestead. Her heart nearly stopped.

"No..." The whisper dissolved on her tongue as panic surged through her veins. She dug her heels into her horse's flanks, urging it into a breakneck gallop. Wind tore at her eyes, but nothing could blur the dreadful clarity of that rising smoke.

When the homestead finally came into view, she leapt from the saddle before the animal had even slowed. What met her eyes was a nightmare stitched into waking life. Fire devoured everything, walls, beams, memories, its roar a monstrous thunder, its crackle a violent chorus of splintering timber. Sparks spun like enraged stars through the smoke-choked air.

Coughing against the searing haze, Joy stumbled forward, her voice raw with terror.

"Alice! Alice, where are you?" There was no room for tears, no space for fear. She had to find her sister, her nieces, her brother-in-law.

Her gaze snagged on a glint of metal. Tools leaned haphazardly against the fence. She seized a shovel, lifted it with shaking arms, and drove it into the nearest window. Glass exploded outward, shards scattering across the porch. Flames hissed greedily as the rush of fresh air fed them.

"Alice!" she screamed again, each strike of the shovel matching the frantic drum of her heartbeat. Then she saw it. Through the rolling black smoke in the kitchen, she glimpsed a figure sprawled motionlessly across the floorboards. Her blood iced over.

"No..." The word broke inside her as she clawed at charred boards and shattered glass, trying to force a path inside. The heat seared her face, blinding her, forcing her back. Even from that brief, terrible glimpse, she understood. Her brother-in-law was beyond saving.

Grief lunged for her throat, but she shoved it down. There would be time to mourn later. If she didn't move now, there would be no one left alive to mourn at all. Skirting the inferno, Joy sprinted toward the back of the house, her lungs burning, eyes stinging, boots slipping in the ash raining down from the collapsing roof. The washroom window, yes, behind the bedroom. If they had found refuge anywhere, it would be there. She hammered both fists against the small pane.

"Alice! Alice, answer me, please!" For a breath, there was only fire. Then, a miracle of miracles, the narrow window scraped open. "Alice!" Joy cried, a sob breaking loose as she grasped her sister's soot-blackened arms. Behind her, the shrill, terrified wails of the children tore through the smoke.

"You must get out at once!" Joy urged. But Alice shook her head violently, her hair plastered to her temples with sweat and soot.

"John is still inside. I must find him!"

"No," Joy barked, the word sharp as steel. "There's no time. Hand me the children, now!"

Hands trembling, Alice lifted her baby first. Joy pulled the two-month-old close, the child's tiny body shaking with sobs, and ran. She bolted across the blistering yard toward the pond, the heat clawing at her back like a living thing. The infant wailed as Joy laid her gently in the cool grass, safe. Safe, for the moment. She didn't pause. Didn't breathe. Joy wheeled around, sprinting back through the smoke with a single, desperate purpose: she would return for the next child, and then drag her sister to safety before the fire claimed them all.

Once they reached the pond, the two women collapsed onto the grass as if their legs had simply given out. The children wailed beside them, their cries cutting through the choking veil of smoke with shrill, terrified sharpness. Joy and Alice doubled over, coughing until their ribs throbbed and their chests felt carved open. Every breath dragged fire into their lungs, the taste of ash coating their tongues.

For a long, aching moment, there was nothing but the ragged rasp of their breathing and the frightened sobs of the little ones. Then came the crash. The sound split the air like a cannon blast. Both women whipped their heads toward the homestead just in time to see the roof give way with a deafening, fiery roar. The structure folded inward, flames leaping skyward in triumph as a storm of sparks rained down like burning snow. What had been a home moments ago, was now a collapsing skeleton of fire.

Alice screamed. It was a sound ripped from the deepest place grief could reach, raw, broken, animal. Before Joy could react, Alice lurched upright and bolted toward the inferno.

"No—Alice, no!" Joy cried, scrambling after her. She caught her sister by the arm and wrenched her backward with every ounce of strength she possessed. Alice fought her like a wild creature, striking and clawing in blind desperation, her face contorted by anguish until Joy scarcely recognized her. But she held on. She had to. Locking her arms around her sister, she dragged her close, forcing her to stop.

"Alice, look at me," Joy pleaded, her voice hoarse, shaking. She lifted trembling hands to cradle her sister's soot-streaked cheeks, bringing their foreheads nearly together, as if she could ground her by sheer will. "It's too late. Do you hear me? It's too late. He didn't make it. You can't go back in there."

For a heartbeat, Alice's eyes were wild, uncomprehending. Then she collapsed. Her sobs tore from her in violent, shuddering waves, her whole body folding inward as if grief itself were crushing her. Joy sank with her, wrapping her arms tight around her sister, whispering whatever shaky words of comfort she could muster, even though both knew the truth. No whisper, no embrace, no prayer could mend a wound like this. Not now.

At last, when Alice's sobs dulled into trembling gasps for breath, Joy guided her back to where the children huddled together in terrified misery. They reached for their mother and aunt at once, clinging with small, desperate hands.

Joy pressed a clean handkerchief into Alice's shaking palm. Alice swiped at her eyes, though fresh tears kept spilling, streaking new paths through the ash on her face. Still, through sheer force of motherly instinct, she gathered the little ones onto her lap, soothing them with soft, broken murmurs. Joy knelt beside them, lending her presence, her steadiness, her strength, because for now, it was all she had left to give.

Joy could not sit still. Grief churned inside her, boiling into a restless, jagged fury that refused to be contained. She rose abruptly, fists clenching at her sides, nails biting into her palms as if pain might anchor her. The image of John's lifeless body burned behind her unrelenting, merciless eyes.

He should have listened. Her father had warned him, had warned them both. *Don't build so far from town. Don't stake your life on a homestead with no neighbors close enough to come running when trouble strikes.*

But John had been stubborn. Proud. Determined to carve out a life on his own terms, to prove he could stand alone against the wilderness. Now that stubbornness lay in ashes. Alice was a widow. The children were fatherless. And a home, every hope bound within its walls, had vanished in a matter of heartbeats.

Joy dragged a shaking breath through smoke-scorched lungs and shook her head, tears stinging her eyes as fiercely as the ash clinging to her lashes. Yet beneath the sorrow, something else stirred. A disquiet she could not ignore.

Yes, the season was dry. Fires were always a danger this time of year. But this, this had spread too fast. Too violently. The flames had devoured the house as if it were nothing more than stacked kindling, roaring with a fury that made no sense. They hadn't needed a fire in the hearth. The days were warm. And Alice was meticulous, careful to a fault. She would never leave the stove unattended, never let an ember smolder. There had been no dry brush piled against the walls, no nearby trees close enough to carry flame so suddenly to the roof.

Joy's gaze swept the yard, sharp and searching. That was when the chill slid down her spine.

Near the wood pile, the dirt bore fresh boot prints, deep, heavy impressions pressed into the soil. Too large to be Alice's. Too recent to be ignored. Joy crouched, brushing ash aside with careful fingers. Her stomach twisted. And beneath the overpowering reek of smoke, she caught it, a faint, oily tang that did not belong. Sharp. Acrid. Kerosene, perhaps. Or something like it. Wrong.

Her jaw tightened as she slowly straightened, eyes narrowing as they lifted toward the raging ruin of the homestead. The flames crackled and leapt, consuming what little remained, as if mocking her dawning realization.

"No," she whispered, the word cold and certain. This fire had not been an accident.

Then it struck her. Her father's note. She had tucked it into her pocket, meant for John, entrusted to her with strict instructions to deliver it without delay. The thought barely had time to form before her fingers brushed the fabric of her skirt, reaching for it. Movement flickered at the edge of her vision. Her heart slammed against her ribs.

Someone moved along the far side of the barn. At first, it was only a shadow slipping through smoke and heat. Then the distinct, crouched figure of a person emerged, low, deliberate, moving with purpose. Joy went utterly still, breath locked in her throat, pulse roaring in her ears. The stranger tipped a container. Dark liquid spilled in uneven trails along the barn's foundation, soaking into dirt and timber. Joy didn't need to step closer to know what it was. Oil.

"Hey!" Her voice cut sharp and fierce through the smoky air. The figure jerked, startled, head snapping up. For one searing instant, their eyes met across the yard, cold, intent, unmistakably aware. But instead of fleeing, the intruder moved faster, splashing more oil in quick, practiced arcs.

"Stop that right now!" Joy shouted, her throat raw, the cry torn loose by fury. The stranger ignored her. Joy spun and bolted for her horse, skirts tangling around her knees as terror and rage collided inside her chest. Her hands shook, but they did not hesitate. She wrenched open the saddlebag, fumbling until her fingers closed around cold metal. Her father's revolver.

At that same instant, the stranger struck several matches and flung them through the barn's open doorway. Joy gasped. Flames sprang to life at once, racing along the oiled paths with horrifying speed. Dry hay ignited in an explosive roar, heat and light blasting outward in a violent rush. But worse than the inferno itself were the screams, the shrill, panicked whinnies of trapped horses ripped through the air, piercing Joy like blades.

"My word—no..." she choked, a sob breaking free. Exhaustion dragged at her limbs like lead, but she crushed it down. There was no time for fear. No time for despair. Her gaze snapped to the discarded shovel near the house. Joy sprinted, seized it, and plunged headlong into the choking haze of the burning barn. Flames licked close, singeing her skin, scorching her sleeves, but she hacked and shoved at blazing debris with savage determination, carving a narrow passage toward the stalls. Smoke clawed at her lungs as she battered bolts and shattered latches one after another, until each gate burst open.

The horses surged past her in a thunder of hooves, and terror, wild eyes flashing, bodies brushing close as they fled into the open field beyond. Only when the last animal had escaped did Joy stagger backward, chest heaving, vision swimming. Her whole body trembled, muscles screaming in protest. She let the shovel fall from her grasp and bent double, dragging in ragged gulps of smoke-tainted air.

Then it hit her. The stranger. Joy's head snapped up, eyes scanning the yard through the wavering heat. Fury surged hotter than the flames themselves as her grip tightened around the revolver. And there he was.

2

Someone Lit the Fuse

The stranger had nearly reached a horse tethered at the far edge of the yard. In one swift, desperate motion, he swung into the saddle, heels driving hard into the animal's flanks in a frantic bid for escape. The horse lurched forward, hooves striking sparks from the scorched ground. Joy's pulse thundered in her ears.

Fueled by fury and raw desperation, she raised her father's revolver. Her hands trembled, the weight of the weapon unfamiliar and terrible, but her aim held, locked by sheer will. She drew a breath she did not have time to spare and squeezed the trigger. The gunshot tore through the smoky air like lightning.

A ragged scream of pain followed, raw, high, unmistakably human. The rider pitched violently sideways, tumbling from the saddle to crash to the ground with a bone-jarring thud. The horse reared, shrill with panic, then broke free and bolted, disappearing in a thunder of hooves.

Joy did not hesitate. She sprinted across the yard, skirts whipping around her legs, breath shredding her throat as she ran. Heat pressed in from every side, smoke stinging her eyes, but she dropped to her knees beside the fallen figure without slowing. Grabbing a fistful of the coat, she wrenched the intruder onto their back. Her breath caught. Her eyes widened in stunned disbelief.

It wasn't a man.

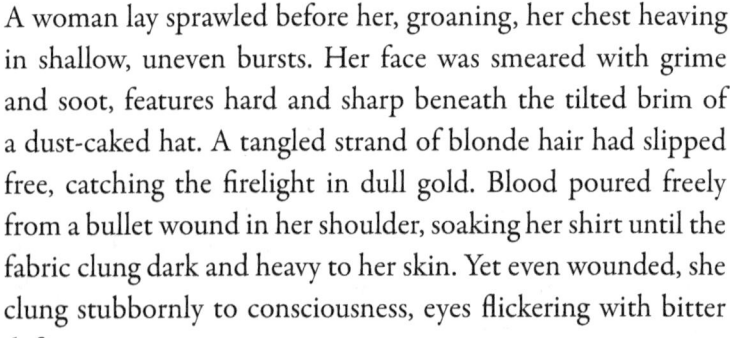

A woman lay sprawled before her, groaning, her chest heaving in shallow, uneven bursts. Her face was smeared with grime and soot, features hard and sharp beneath the tilted brim of a dust-caked hat. A tangled strand of blonde hair had slipped free, catching the firelight in dull gold. Blood poured freely from a bullet wound in her shoulder, soaking her shirt until the fabric clung dark and heavy to her skin. Yet even wounded, she clung stubbornly to consciousness, eyes flickering with bitter defiance.

"Who are you?" Joy demanded, her voice edged with a fury that shook her from the inside out. "Why did you set the fire?" She grabbed the woman's shoulder and shook her hard. When only a low groan answered, Joy's restraint shattered. Rage surged through her veins, hot and blinding. She kicked the woman's leg with sudden ferocity.

The stranger howled, unleashing a torrent of curses so vile Joy recoiled, heat flooding her cheeks. Words she would never repeat scorched the air, but they only fed the fire raging in her chest.

"Answer me!" Joy shouted, her voice cracking under the strain. The woman gave a low, rasping chuckle, lips curling in mockery despite the pain.

"Ain't none o' yer damn business."

Joy's blood boiled. "It is my business," she snapped. "You killed my brother-in-law!"

"So what?" The words slurred with cruel indifference. "We all gotta die sometime. Some jus' sooner than others." She coughed, her body shuddering violently, then fixed Joy with a hard, glinting stare. Venom dripped from every word.

"'Specially them fancy lawyers like John Haven. Oughta be glad his purty wife an' them brats ain't dead. Ain't yer kin worth nothin' anyhow."

The words lashed Joy like a whip. She trembled, not with fear, but with a fury too vast to be contained, by her small frame. With a cry torn from her chest, she seized the woman by the collar, hauled her upright, and slammed her back against a fence post. Wood rattled beneath the impact.

"You disgusting piece of prairie coal!" Joy spat, her voice shaking with righteous wrath. She shoved her again, harder, ignoring the woman's sharp cry of pain. "I swear, you will pay for this."

The stranger only scoffed, the sound weak but dripping with mockery. Then her eyes rolled back. Her body went slack. Joy released her, letting the woman crumple to the dirt in a lifeless heap. Only then did her own hands begin to quake violently as the adrenaline drained away. She turned and snatched a coiled rope from the fallen woman's saddle, clumsy but determined fingers moving fast. She bound the arsonist's wrists and ankles, jerking the knots tight, looping them repeatedly until escape was impossible. Only then did the weight of everything crash down upon her.

Joy staggered away, toward the pond where her sister and the children waited. Smoke had thickened, pressing into her lungs like a smothering blanket. She coughed hard, each breath shorter, shallower than the last. The ground tilted beneath her feet, the world swaying as a merciless ringing filled her ears.

"Alice..." she rasped, trying to call out. Her knees buckled. Fire and ash spun together, swallowing her vision, and the world went black.

It was as though someone were calling to her from a great distance, tugging her back through a thick, suffocating fog. Joy fought the weight dragging her down, struggling to surface, until another violent cough tore through her chest and wrenched her eyes open. Alice knelt beside her.

Her shoulders shook with silent sobs. Her face was streaked with soot and tears. She clutched the tiny baby girl close against her breast, while her stepdaughter clung to her skirts, wide-eyed and trembling, knuckles white with fear.

"Joy, oh, thank goodness." Alice's voice cracked, relief and grief colliding in the same breath.

Joy tried to speak and managed only a rasp. She pushed herself up on unsteady arms, every muscle protesting. Her body felt weak, her lungs raw and burning, but the sight of the smoldering ruins beyond the pond brought everything crashing back at once. The fire. The woman. John.

Her throat tightened. Without hesitation, she reached for her sister and pulled her close, holding her fiercely as Alice broke against her shoulder. Joy rocked her gently, murmuring the only words she could offer.

"It's all right. I've got you. I've got you." Her own tears burned hot behind her eyes, but she blinked them back and drew the older child into her lap as well, smoothing soot-matted curls with slow, steady strokes.

"You're safe, sweetheart," she whispered. "Auntie's here." Yet even as she offered comfort, her heart twisted painfully. Her gaze drifted to the blackened shell of the homestead, its skeletal remains still smoking against the sky. Why? Why had that woman come here, set the farm ablaze, slaughter John without mercy, and nearly killed Alice and the children? What kind of hatred burned hot enough to drive someone to such cruelty?

A faint groan snapped her from her thoughts. Joy's head turned sharply toward the bound figure near the fence. The arsonist shifted against the ropes, stirring, though her eyes remained closed. For now, she was still unconscious. And then Joy remembered. The note. Her hand flew to her pocket, fingers closing around the folded paper her father had pressed into her hand with such unusual urgency. Her pulse quickened. Had he known? Had he sensed something terrible was coming?

A chill slid down her spine. What if this wasn't only about John? What if her parents were in danger, too? Fear surged through her, sharper even than the smoke clawing at her lungs. Joy surged to her feet, startling Alice, who instinctively tightened her hold on the baby.

"We need to get back to town," Joy said, her voice trembling with urgency. "Now." Her eyes swept the yard. John's two horses were gone, scattered in panic, likely miles away by now. Only her own faithful mare and the stranger's gelding remained. The gelding hadn't bolted far, tethered and restless, tossing his head as if sensing the peril still hanging in the air.

Alice did not question her. Whether it was the terror threaded through Joy's tone or the unspoken trust between sisters, she obeyed without hesitation. Cradling her infant and calling softly to her stepdaughter, she rose and hurried after Joy.

Joy held the baby close while Alice swung herself into the saddle. The infant whimpered softly, soot-smudged cheeks pressed against Joy's shoulder, as Alice reached down to gather her daughters. Carefully, Joy passed the two girls up to their mother one at a time, steadying them until Alice had them settled as securely as possible against her chest.

As Alice shifted in the saddle, adjusting her grip, her sleeve slid back, just for an instant. Dark, angry bruises marred her arm. Finger-shaped. Unmistakable. Blooming deep beneath the skin. Alice jerked the fabric down at once, but it was far too late.

Joy's breath caught. Without hesitation, she seized her sister's wrist, firm but not bruising, and pushed the sleeve back again, her fingers tightening despite herself.

"Alice..." Her voice dropped sharp with dread. "How did you get these? Did John do this to you?"

Alice flinched as though struck. Tears welled in her eyes, spilling over before she could stop them.

"It was... an accident," she whispered. "He was stressed. He—he grabbed me harder than he meant to."

The words sounded rehearsed. Fragile. Even Alice seemed to recoil from them as they left her mouth. Joy's stomach twisted painfully. Anger flared, hot, protective, demanding, but there was no time to unearth the truth now. Smoke still clung to the air. Danger still lurked too close. Whatever that story truly held, it would have to wait.

"We'll talk about this later," Joy said firmly, releasing her sister's arm. The promise, and the warning, hung between them. She turned and sprinted for the other horse, where the unconscious arsonist still lay bound in the dirt.

With no hope of lifting the woman outright, Joy urged the gelding to kneel, then dragged the limp body across the animal's broad back. Muscles screamed as she heaved, but she did not stop. Once the horse rose again, she shoved the woman into the center of the saddle and secured her with the remaining rope, binding it tight to the horn. She checked the knots twice, yanking them hard until she was certain the prisoner couldn't slip free. Only then did Joy mount behind her.

Alice had watched in silence, her face pale but resolute, the children clinging to her as if they understood the need for stillness. Joy met her gaze and gave a single, sharp nod. No more words were needed. Together, the two sisters turned their horses toward town and rode hard into the smoke-stained horizon, leaving ashes, secrets, and grief behind them, and carrying the weight of reckoning ahead.

Dark clouds of smoke billowed into the sky, thick and rolling, and Joy felt herself teetering on the brink of collapse. The weight of the day pressed down on her chest until every breath hurt. Alice must have seen it in her face, must have felt it too, because she didn't argue when Joy urged her to stop at the café.

Joy reached for her nieces, clutching them close as Alice slid stiffly from the saddle. The children whimpered softly, clinging to familiar arms, their small bodies still trembling from terror. Joy did not release them until she was certain her sister had them firmly in her grasp and the café door had closed behind them. Only then did she gather the reins with shaking hands.

Without looking back, Joy turned her horse toward her parents' home at the edge of town. Her heart hammered so violently it stole her breath, each pounding beat echoing in her ears as though warning her to turn back. She leaned forward, gripping the saddle horn until her knuckles whitened, urging the horse faster. And then the house came into view. Already, flames clawed up its familiar walls.

"No... no, no—" The words spilled from her lips, broken and breathless. Joy leapt from the saddle before the horse had even stopped and ran. Townsmen shouted orders, forming frantic bucket lines, boots pounding the dirt as water sloshed uselessly against the growing blaze. Smoke burned her eyes as she sprinted toward the yard, but before she could reach it, the house shuddered violently. With a groan like a dying thing, it collapsed inward, sparks exploding into the sky in a shower of fire and ash. Just like John's. A scream ripped from Joy's chest, raw and agonized.

"Ma! Pa! Nooooo!" She lunged toward the inferno, driven by instinct and despair, but strong arms caught her mid-stride and hauled her back. She fought against the hold, thrashing, clawing, kicking, desperate to break free, to reach them, to do something, anything. The grip that held her was iron.

"Easy, girl," a deep voice rumbled near her ear, calm but commanding. "You can't go in there."

Joy sobbed and kicked harder, grief lending her a final surge of strength, but the man only tightened his hold, steady and unyielding.

"Listen to me," he said, his voice firm with authority, and something gentler beneath it. "You'll only burn alive. I won't let you."

At last, her strength shattered. Her body sagged, wracked with sobs, and the sheriff drew her close against his broad chest, one arm solid around her shoulders. His voice softened then, words low and sure, a steady presence anchoring her while everything else fell apart.

"Dave, there is—" the deputy began, then faltered. Through her tears, Joy recognized the younger man's voice. John's brother.

The sheriff said nothing, but the look he gave was enough. The deputy swallowed hard and turned away at once. Time blurred. When at last Joy's sobs dwindled into broken shudders, the sheriff guided her gently aside, far enough that the flames no longer dominated her vision, far enough that she could breathe without choking on smoke and despair. She lifted her head, and their eyes met. His face was etched with sorrow, lines carved deep by years of bearing witness to tragedy, but his gaze held a steady compassion that did not waver. It was the look of a man who had stood beside too many grieving souls and never turned away.

For a single, suspended breath, the chaos faded. The smoke, the shouting, the crackle of fire, all of it fell away. There was only the strength of a man who had chosen to shoulder her weight when she could not carry it herself. His faint smile was sad, almost fatherly, and the steady hand resting on her shoulder carried no promise but one. She was not alone.

"Hey, will someone get me off this damn horse?"

Joy froze. The voice cut through the smoke and chaos like a blade, cold, sharp, unmistakable.

The woman. In her grief, Joy had forgotten the prisoner entirely. Now every nerve in her body ignited at once. Fury surged, white-hot. She tore free from the arms holding her and crossed the distance in a heartbeat. Pain fueled her strength.

With a violent jerk, she dragged the woman from the saddle and sent her crashing into the dirt with a heavy, bone-jarring thud. Before reason, or mercy, could intervene, Joy seized the arsonist by the shirt and slammed her head into the ground. Once. Twice. Again.

"Why?" Joy screamed, the sound raw and ragged, torn straight from her chest. "Why did you do this? What do you have against my family?" Her hands moved of their own accord, fingers clamping around the woman's throat. The stranger choked, gasping for air, eyes bulging as Joy's rage tightened its merciless hold.

For a heartbeat, the men nearby stood frozen, stunned by the sudden ferocity of it all. Then the sheriff surged forward. He caught Joy from behind and wrenched her back, breaking her grip before the woman could lose consciousness.

"Let me go!" Joy thrashed, striking blindly, her voice splintering. "She did it—she did it!"

The sheriff did not let go. He understood this was not cruelty. It was anguish unleashed, grief stripped bare, a heart shattered beyond reason. He pinned her firmly yet carefully against his chest, powerful arms locking her fast without hurting her, absorbing every blow until her strength began to falter.

"Easy now, child... easy," he murmured, his voice low and steady near her ear. "You're safe. I've got you. Let it go."

Joy fought him with everything she had left, until she had nothing. Long minutes passed. Her struggles weakened, then dissolved into violent sobs. Her body shook as the fury drained away, leaving only exhaustion and unbearable sorrow in its wake.

"You need to make her talk, Dave," Joy cried, tears still clinging to her lashes though she fought to steady herself. Her voice shook with urgency and fury. "She's behind it. I saw her."

David Baker's expression softened at her distress, even as his jaw remained set with grim resolve.

"I'm so sorry about your parents, Joy," he said quietly. "We heard an explosion, and then another not long after. By the time we reached the house, there was nothing left to save." His gaze darkened. "Someone used dynamite."

Joy gasped, horror tightening around her throat like a vice.

"Dynamite?" she whispered. "I don't understand. John and Alice's house burned too. That woman, I watched her pour oil. I watched her set the barn on fire."

David's eyes widened sharply. Beside him, Matt, John's brother, stepped closer, his face gone ashen.

"Is everyone all right?" Matt asked, his voice faltering, already bracing for the answer. Joy shook her head, pain carving deep lines into her face.

"I got Alice and the girls out," she said, her words breaking. "But John was already gone when I reached them." Her breath hitched. "I'm so sorry. Maybe if I'd come sooner, maybe if I—"

"No," Matt said quickly, the word brittle but firm. He shook his head, eyes shining. "Don't do that, Joy. Don't you dare. You did everything you could, more than anyone could've asked."

David stepped closer then and lifted her chin gently, his calloused fingers steady beneath her jaw until her eyes met his. Around them, smoke churned, men shouted, buckets clanged, but for a moment, the chaos seemed to fall away.

"Listen to me," he said, his voice low and certain, seasoned by years of bearing hard truths. "We will find the truth. That woman will talk. And whoever set this in motion, whoever thought they could destroy your family and walk away, we'll uncover them." His hand shifted to her shoulder, firm and grounding.

"And Joy," he added quietly, "you're not alone in this, my girl. Not while I'm here."

Her chest ached with grief so deep it felt hollowed out, but his words gave her something solid to cling to, something steady in the storm threatening to pull her under. His touch held no softness meant to soothe, only strength meant to shield.

Nearby, Matt and two other men lifted the unconscious woman and hauled her toward the lockup. A doctor hurried forward through the smoke, his satchel swinging as he scanned for the wounded.

David drew Joy into a brief embrace, strong, sure, grounding, before releasing her to the physician's care. As she was guided toward the clinic, he watched until smoke swallowed her from sight, his jaw tightening with resolve. This was no accident. And David Baker intended to see justice done.

David and her father, Max, had been best friends for as long as Joy could remember, long before her own memories even began. Back in Sacramento, David had worn the badge as sheriff, a man known and respected for his steady hand, clear judgment, and unshakable sense of justice. People trusted him because he listened, because he weighed truth carefully, and because once he acted, he did so without fear or favor.

When Max chose to move his family to the quieter town of Auburn, seeking peace and a better life for his girls, David had not hesitated. He followed without question, trading city streets for dirt roads and small-town law, simply so he could remain close to the people he loved like family.

To Joy, David had always been more than a family friend. She loved him like a second father.

It was David who placed a revolver in her hands the first time she learned to shoot, his grip firm but gentle as he adjusted her stance, showing her how to line up the sights and breathe steadily before pulling the trigger.

Slow and true, he'd told her. *Never rush what matters.*

It was David who patched skinned knees and soothed bruised pride, who offered a stern word when she tested boundaries, and who gave a quiet shoulder when the weight of the world pressed too heavily on her young heart.

Whenever Max was away on business, it was David who checked in, making certain Alice, Joy, and their mother had everything they needed. Repairs were made. Wood was chopped. Worries were eased before they had time to grow. He never made a show of it. He simply appeared, steady as sunrise.

Through every season of her childhood and adolescence, through laughter and scraped knuckles, through missteps and hard lessons, through moments of grief she had not yet known how to name, David had been there. A constant. A guardian. And now, as everything familiar lay in ashes, Joy understood with aching clarity just how much that presence meant, and how deeply she would need it in the days ahead.

Since Joy was still coughing, and struggling to draw a full breath, Doc Perkins pressed a small cloth gently to her face and bade her to breathe in. The sharp tang of chloroform burned her nose, making her wince, but almost at once her lungs loosened. The tightness eased, and her ragged gasps softened into slower, steadier breaths.

"There now," the physician murmured. "That's enough." He eased the cloth away and studied her with practiced eyes before straightening. "I want you to stay here overnight, Joy," he said, his tone firm but not unkind. "You've endured more than any young woman ought to in a single day and breathing in that much smoke is no trifling matter. I need to keep an eye on you."

Joy shifted restlessly on the narrow cot, her voice hoarse and thin.

"What about Alice?" she asked. "I have to look after her, and my nieces."

"You must rest," Doc Perkins replied, lifting one bushy eyebrow in that familiar, no-nonsense way of his. "Alice is with her mother-in-law now, from what I hear, and I've no doubt that woman will tend to those girls as if they were her own flesh and blood. They're safe." His gaze softened slightly. "Right now, my concern is you."

Joy's composure shattered. "I was too late, Doc Perkins," she blurted, tears spilling hot and unchecked down her soot-streaked cheeks. "If I had just hurried, if I'd ridden faster, maybe I could have saved John."

The older man sighed, long and heavy, and pulled a chair closer to her bedside. He lowered himself into it, joints creaking in protest, and gently took Joy's trembling hand in his broad, weathered one. His face was solemn, lined with years of tending the wounded and the grieving, but his eyes held only kindness.

"Don't you go laying this at your own feet, Joy Collins," he said quietly, his voice steady as bedrock. "Whatever that woman was about, whatever evil she carried with her, she will answer for it." He squeezed her hand gently. "But you? You had no part in it. None."

Joy's shoulders shook as she tried to still her sobs.

"If anything," he went on, "you arriving when you did may well have spared Alice and those little girls from a far worse fate." His thumb brushed lightly over her knuckles, a simple, grounding gesture. "Sometimes, child, we don't get to choose the outcome," he said softly. "We only get to choose what we do with the moment we're given. And today, you met that moment with everything you had. Don't you forget that."

Joy ducked her head, overcome. Tears dripping onto the thin blanket. Doc Perkins leaned forward then, lowering his voice even further.

"Your father always said you had his fire," he added gently. "And I reckon he'd be proud as any man could be if he'd seen you today, standing your ground, protecting your kin, showing more courage than most grown men I've known." He gave her hand one last reassuring squeeze. "Don't let grief blind you to that truth, young lady."

The words settled over Joy like a warm blanket, insufficient to ease the ache, perhaps, but enough to keep her from breaking entirely.

Both Joy and Doc Perkins turned at the sudden, heavy knock on the door. The physician rose from his chair and crossed the room, opening it to admit Matt Haven. His face was pale and drawn, eyes shadowed with fresh grief that had not yet settled into anything like acceptance. Behind him stood David Baker, his expression carved from stone, jaw tight with restrained fury. The mayor followed last, shoulders slumped, looking older and wearier than Joy had ever seen him.

Joy pushed herself upright on the cot, clutching the blanket as though it were the only thing anchoring her.

"Did you get anything out of her?" she asked, her voice hoarse but sharpened by urgency. David exhaled slowly through his nose and shook his head.

"She's not easy to crack," he said. "We tried every lawful way we know to make her talk, but she clams up tighter than a bank vault." His mouth tightened. "All she's given us is a name, Brenda Garrett. And even that..." He paused, lips pressing into a thin line. "...could be a lie."

The weight of the words settled heavily over the room. David drew a breath through his teeth, then turned toward the physician, frustration edging his normally controlled tone.

"Doc Perkins, I need you to tend to that woman's wound. She took a bullet to the shoulder, and I'll be damned if she slips away before we get answers. I want her alive until we know why she came here, and who sent her."

Doc Perkins nodded once, solemn and unflinching, already reaching for his medical bag.

"I'll see to it," he said. Before leaving, he cast Joy a final glance, steady, reassuring, the silent promise of a man who had no intention of abandoning her in this storm. Then he turned and strode from the room, the door swinging shut behind him as smoke and distant voices bled in from the evening beyond.

Joy's fingers tightened in the blanket. A name, perhaps false. Two houses in ashes. And enemies still hiding in the dark. The worst of it, she knew, was far from over.

"How are you doing, Joy?" Matt asked quietly, his gaze lingering on her face with open concern.

Joy shook her head. She closed her eyes at once, as if shutting them might hold the world at bay, might keep her from having to meet anyone's gaze or answer a question she didn't know how to answer. She fought to hold back the tears, but the effort was useless. Too much had happened in a single day. Her heart felt shattered into fragments, barely held together by will alone. The three men watched her in silence.

Her face was pale beneath streaks of ash and dirt. Her cheeks were still wet with tears. Damp strands of hair clung to her temples, darkened by sweat and smoke. To them, it was painfully clear she stood on the edge of breaking, body and spirit wrung to exhaustion.

"Perhaps we should speak outside," Mayor Hershel suggested softly, lowering his voice as if afraid a harsh word might push her over that edge. Joy shook her head again without opening her eyes.

"No," she said hoarsely. "I want to hear what you have to say."

The mayor sighed. In the two years since the Collins family had come to Auburn, he had learned one thing beyond doubt: Joy Collins was stubborn to her core. If they left her behind, she would follow. He exchanged a glance with David and Matt, then nodded. They pulled up chairs and sat down. She deserved answers.

"Have you found out anything?" Joy asked.

"Not yet," Matt said, his voice rough with strain. "The fire isn't fully out. Once it is, we'll search for evidence tomorrow."

"Joy," Mayor Hershel said gently, folding his hands. "David told me John's house was burned as well?"

She nodded. "Yes. I got my sister and the children out, but..." Her voice faltered, breath hitching. She swallowed and forced herself onward. "...it was too late for John."

Then the words came tumbling out, everything. The flames cresting the ridge. The barn. The oil. The strange woman. The horses screaming. The desperate rescue. She spoke quickly, as if afraid she might not be able to finish if she stopped. When she was done, silence settled heavily over the room.

A chair scraped back across the floorboards. Though her eyes remained closed, Joy knew it was Matt who had risen, grief driving him to motion, to something physical he could control. He had lost his brother, after all.

"Pa sent me to John and Alice with this letter," Joy whispered. Her voice broke as she reached into the pocket of her dress. With trembling fingers, she withdrew the folded paper and, for the first time since the men had entered, lifted her gaze. Her eyes met David's.

He reached for her hand and gave it a gentle squeeze before taking the envelope. Slowly, deliberately, he opened it and read aloud the words written in her father's familiar hand.

John,

Someone is threatening to murder my family. Get yourself and your family out of there. Jonas Andrews will hire men to investigate.

Max

For a long moment, no one spoke. The letter hung in the air like a shadow, dark, suffocating, impossible to ignore. Joy's eyes filled again, the words blurring as they echoed in her mind. None of it made sense. Who would threaten her father with something so calculated, so merciless? And how long had the danger been creeping toward them, unseen?

Her thoughts drifted back to when her parents had first come to Auburn a little over two years earlier. They had left behind their life in the heart of Sacramento for the quiet beauty of the foothills. John and Alice had followed not long after. For Max Collins, who traveled often for his work, location had mattered little. Auburn had been chosen with care, a place of peace and promise, where they had quickly fallen in love with the land and forged friendships with the townsfolk.

After the sudden death of John and Matt's father, their widowed mother and Matt had come as well, opening a small café that soon became the beating heart of the community. What had seemed like a fresh start for all of them, safe, hopeful, filled with new beginnings, was now blackened by fire and blood. And whatever force had shattered that peace was not finished yet.

3

The Proposal in the Pew

Joy shot upright in bed, her heart vaulting into her throat as a series of explosions shattered the night. The concussive blasts rattled the windowpanes, vibrating through the walls and straight into her bones. Within seconds, the acrid stench of smoke seeped into the air, thick, unmistakable. A chill swept over her, draining the blood from her face.

No. Not again. She flung back the covers and leapt from the bed, bare feet hitting the floor as she raced to the window. Her breath caught painfully in her chest. Flames clawed skyward, casting a hellish orange glow over the street below. The café was ablaze. So was the bank beside it. Her stomach lurched violently. *Alice. Annie. Baby Ruth.*

Joy didn't hesitate. She tore from the clinic and into the night, not caring that she wore nothing but a thin nightgown. The cold bit into her skin, sharp and unforgiving, but she barely felt it. Panic drowned out everything else. She ran.

The closer she got, the louder the chaos grew, shouts, pounding feet, the crackle and roar of fire devouring wood. Smoke burned her eyes as she sprinted toward the café, only to stumble in sudden, breathless relief. They were outside. Alice and the children stood in the street, clinging to Maureen Haven as if she were the last solid thing in a world falling apart. Alice, however, was undone. She sobbed and gasped, nearly hysterical, her breath coming in sharp, panicked bursts as though her lungs refused to obey her.

Joy reached her just in time, wrapping her sister in a fierce embrace. Only then did Alice's trembling begin to ease, her face buried against Joy's shoulder. Annie cried against her grandmother's skirts, small hands clutching tight, while Baby Ruth wailed in Joy's arms, thin, desperate cries that pierced straight through her heart. Joy held them all, rocking, whispering, grounding them as best she could while fire raged behind them.

Nearby, David Baker, Matt Haven, and a determined line of townsmen battled the inferno with buckets of water and soaked blankets. They moved like a single organism, passing, shouting, dousing, refusing to yield. For hours they fought, voices hoarse, muscles screaming, smoke choking every breath.

At last, near dawn, the flames were beaten back. The café lay in smoldering ruin, nothing left but blackened timbers and drifting ash. The bank's outer walls still stood, scarred and blistered, but the interior had been gutted beyond recognition. Joy stared at the devastation. Her arms wrapped tightly around her family. This was no coincidence. No accident. Someone was systematically destroying everything they loved. And the night was far from over.

Joy stood rooted to the spot, the world tilting beneath her feet, as Matt came running toward them, his voice sharp with urgency.

"David!" he shouted. "The barred window on the prison cell's been busted open. The woman is gone!"

The words hit like a blow. Joy's hands curled into fists at her sides, nails biting into her palms as fury and dread surged through her veins in equal measure. The fire. The blood. The destruction, and now this. The woman who had brought such ruin had vanished into the night.

A murmur rippled through the gathered townsfolk, fear and anger mingling in low, unsettled voices. To ease Alice's rising panic, Doc Perkins stepped in at once. He guided her gently but firmly toward the clinic, murmuring reassurances and promising something to steady her nerves. Alice clung to Joy for a moment longer before finally allowing herself to be led away, her steps unsteady, her face drained of all color.

Reverend Alden's wife moved without hesitation. She gathered Annie and Baby Ruth into her capable arms, her voice calm and soothing as she pressed the frightened children close. With several adolescent daughters at home, girls already eager to help with little ones, the Alden household would be a place of warmth and safety while Alice recovered. Slowly, painfully, order began to reassert itself.

But the day dragged on beneath a sky still stained with smoke, the air thick with the scent of ash and loss. Auburn reeled, not only from the destruction of buildings and homes, but from the chilling knowledge that the woman responsible was once again free. Somewhere beyond the smoldering ruins, she was out there.

Joy stepped closer to her sister's mother-in-law and gently took Maureen's hand.

"I'm so sorry, Maureen," she said, her voice trembling despite her effort to keep it steady. "Once we have access to my parents' money, I'll help pay for the repairs."

Anyone watching could see how close she was to breaking, her shoulders held rigid, her jaw clenched as if sheer will, might keep her upright. Maureen stared at her with the same stunned, hollow look Matt had worn the day before. For a long moment, she seemed unable to speak. Then she swallowed and found her voice.

"Before we worry about money," she said quietly, "we need to find who's behind this." Her gaze sharpened as it settled on Joy. "And don't you dare blame yourself. You had nothing to do with any of it."

Joy's jaw set. "Alice and the girls were with you last night," she said. "I don't know what's happening, but someone is coming after our family." Her breath hitched, then steadied. "We'll leave as soon as the funerals for Ma, Pa, and John are over."

Maureen opened her mouth to respond, but David Baker had already closed the distance. He had heard enough. His hand found Joy's, warm and grounding, and he drew her into a brief embrace. It wasn't lingering or indulgent, but steady. When he pulled back, his eyes met hers, with quiet understanding before his expression hardened into resolve.

"Joy," he said firmly, "nobody's blaming you, or Alice. You belong to this town, and you belong to the Haven family. We are not going to let you wander off into danger just because someone's targeting you."

Joy shook her head, small but stubborn.

"We have relatives," she replied. "My uncle Gerald, Pa's brother, is mayor in Deer Lodge, Montana. He's our legal guardian until I come of age in a few months. He and Aunt Eliza will take us in."

David's brow furrowed at once.

"Deer Lodge is a long way off," he said. "Stagecoach travel is slow and dangerous. Robberies. Bad weather. Breakdowns. Two young women and small children traveling alone?" He shook his head. "No. I won't allow it."

He motioned Matt over and quickly explained Joy's plan. Matt didn't soften it.

"Dave's right," he said bluntly. "That'd be reckless."

Joy lifted her chin. "We'll manage," she insisted. "We don't want to be a burden to the town. And until we know why my parents, and John, were murdered, we won't stay here and wait for it to happen again."

David's hand settled firmly on her shoulder.

"You are not just leaving," he said, his tone leaving no room for argument. "Mayor Hershel and Reverend Alden are calling a town meeting this evening. We'll decide, together, what's best for you and Alice." His gaze held hers, unwavering. "And until then, we'll make certain you're protected."

Joy exhaled slowly, the weight of resistance pressing against her ribs. She did not agree, but she did not pull away either. For now, Auburn would not let her face this alone.

Joy's hands trembled as she pushed open the heavy doors of the church. Her nerves were already stretched thin, but the conversation she'd just had with the bank owner gnawed at her relentlessly. Everything her father had kept locked away—documents, records, and securities—was gone. The fire had consumed them all, along with the savings and papers of countless townsfolk. The most vital deeds and contracts were safe with her father's lawyer in Sacramento, but that knowledge brought little comfort now.

With her father gone, the truth pressed down on her like a physical weight. She was not yet of age. Alice was younger still. By law, their uncle became executor of everything, controlling access to the things Maxwell Collins had worked for. Their future, every decision, every dollar, now lay in another man's hands. Most of the family's money remained secure in a Sacramento bank, untouched by the flames, but for the present it might as well have been a world away.

They had nothing. No home. No income. No access to even the smallest coin. Joy drew in a shaky breath and stepped farther inside. The pews were filling quickly. Men and women spoke in hushed, urgent tones, faces drawn and wary. Fear rippled through the congregation like a living thing. The mayor and sheriff had not yet arrived, but their absence only sharpened the tension, leaving the air heavy with unanswered questions.

"Joy."

She turned at the sound of her name. Doc Perkins beckoned her over and guided her into a quiet corner near the wall, lowering his voice as the crowd swelled around them. His lined face was grim, his eyes dark with concern.

"After your sister's breakdown earlier," he began softly, "I examined her."

Joy's stomach tightened.

"Her body is covered in bruises," he continued, his voice barely above a whisper. "Did you know about that?"

Joy swallowed hard before nodding.

"I noticed bruises on her arm after I pulled her and the girls out of the house."

Doc Perkins leaned closer, his whisper edged with barely restrained fury.

"She wouldn't tell me how she got them. But bruises like that, scattered, some old, some new, they usually only mean one thing." His eyes locked onto Joy's. "Did John do that to her?"

The question struck like a blow, even though some part of her had already known the answer. Slowly, she nodded again.

"She didn't want to tell me either," Joy said quietly. "When I pressed her, she said he was stressed, that he just... grabbed her too hard. By accident."

The physician scoffed under his breath.

"By accident," he muttered. "Is that what she said? Hmph." His lips thinned, his eyes flashing with anger. Joy's hands curled into fists at her sides.

"I didn't know until yesterday," she said, her voice low but fierce. "If he was like that, he hid it well. We haven't had a chance to talk since everything happened, but I can tell she's covering for him." Her throat tightened. "This wasn't an accident. Not if her whole body is marked."

For a moment, they stood in silence, the noise of the church fading into the background. Anger and grief twisted between them, hot, unresolved, heavy with things that could never be said to the dead. Doc Perkins's weathered face hardened with outrage, while Joy's heart pounded with a fury she barely knew how to name.

For all John had done, or failed to do, her sister had loved him. And now Alice was left alone, his children in her arms, his shadow still clinging to her skin. Joy closed her eyes briefly, steadying herself. Whatever else came of this night, one truth was painfully clear: the fire had not only taken lives and homes, but it had also stripped away illusions.

When the last of the townsfolk had taken their seats, Mayor Hershel rose at the front of the church, his shoulders squared, David Baker standing solidly at his side like an anchor of law and resolve. The murmurs dwindled to a restless hush, though the room still hummed with grief and unease. Smoke clung stubbornly to coats and shawls, a bitter reminder of all that had been lost. Doc Perkins cleared his throat and spoke first. His eyes found Joy in the crowd, and his voice, steady, practiced, carried without effort.

"Your sister is in no condition to travel. Losing her husband and parents in a single day would cripple anyone." He paused, choosing his words carefully. "Alice is not like you, Joy.

She doesn't have your grit. With two little ones to care for, she could never endure such a journey right now."

Joy's hands tightened in her lap, nails pressing into her palms, but when she spoke, her voice was firm.

"Then we wait until she's stronger. But we must leave as soon as we're able."

A murmur rippled through the pews. Reverend Alden leaned forward, his expression grave.

"We cannot allow you two to travel alone. If anything befell you on the road, this town would never forgive itself."

Joy rose slowly to her feet. She looked around at the faces she had come to know over two short years, neighbors, friends, men and women who had shared harvests, laughter, and now loss. Compassion and worry met her gaze from every direction, tightening her chest.

"I appreciate you all more than I can say," she began, drawing a steadying breath. "I don't want to leave. But if staying here puts this community in further danger, if even one more family suffers because of us..." Her voice wavered, then steadied. "I could not bear it."

Silence spread.

"Our uncle is now our legal guardian," she continued. "He will see us sheltered until we can stand on our own feet."

The stillness that followed was thick with resistance. Men shifted in their seats. Hands tightened on the edges of pews. Jaws set, ready for argument.

"Listen," Joy pressed on. "I know your fears. I share them. But there may be a way forward." She lifted her chin. "My father worked closely with the U.S. Marshals as a judge. If we send word, I believe headquarters could assign an escort. Surely there's an officer already traveling north who could take us under his protection."

Matt Haven surged to his feet, jaw rigid.

"Why not let Alice and the girls stay here with my mother?" he demanded. "She'd never forgive herself if her daughter-in-law and grandchildren were sent halfway across the country. And you should stay too. We'll guard this town day and night if we must. We won't let this happen again."

The pews erupted at once. The blacksmith, arms crossed like iron bars, called out, "He ain't wrong. We'll stand watch in shifts. Let 'em stay put."

But Martha Grady, the shopkeeper's wife, shook her head fiercely.

"And risk losin' more of our men to bullets?" she shot back. "Ain't we put enough in the ground this year already? Joy's right, best they move on and pull the danger clear of town."

A young farmer's son sprang up, fists clenched.

"We can stand our ground. Whoever's huntin' 'em can come on. We ain't no cowards takin' cover behind womenfolk."

"Sit yourself down," his father barked, yanking him back by the arm. "Bravery's one thing, plain foolishness is another. This here's about keepin' families alive."

Voices swelled and clashed, some urging the sisters to stay, others insisting they must go. The tension snapped back and forth like a rope pulled taut, fraying under strain. Joy stepped forward, her eyes blazing.

"And put more men in the ground for our sake?" she demanded. "No. We don't know who's behind this, or how many of them there are. I won't have wives widowed and children fatherless because of us." Her voice rang through the church. "Pa would never want us to become a burden to this town." Her words cut through the clamor, silencing some, provoking others.

David exhaled hard through his nose and shook his head. For all the affection and protectiveness, he felt for Joy, her unyielding resolve drove him perilously close to exasperation. In her lifted chin, in her fearless eyes that dared any man to challenge her, he saw Max Collins's spirit blazing unmistakably through her. At last, Mayor Hershel raised both hands.

"Enough."

The room stilled.

"We will have order in this meeting," he said firmly. "Joy has spoken her piece, and this matter will be weighed carefully before any decision is made." His gaze swept the pews. "Tonight, we will hear all sides, but there will be no rash words and no promises we cannot keep."

The church quieted, though uneasily. Lamplight flickered across the rafters, casting long, restless shadows as the people sat braced, waiting for the storm of voices to rise again.

Joy cleared her throat before she spoke again, steadying herself against the tightness pressing on her chest.

"I am not saying we will stay away forever," she said, her voice calm despite the strain beneath it. "But it isn't this town's responsibility to protect and care for us."

Matt leaned forward abruptly, his hands clenched together, knuckles whitening. When he spoke, his voice was low but urgent.

"What if you and I got married?" he asked. "Would you stay then?"

The words struck her like a blow. Joy gasped, heat flooding her face as the church seemed to tilt beneath her. For a heartbeat, she could only stare at him, certain she had misheard. But the look in his eyes, earnest, desperate, pleading, told her she had not.

"Matt..." she whispered, grasping for breath. "You can't mean that."

"I do." His jaw tightened, eyes shining in the lamplight. "I've already lost John. I can't bear the thought of losing the rest of you too. If marriage is what it takes to keep you here safe, then I'll do it. You, Alice, the girls... you're all I have left of him." His voice cracked. "Don't take that away from me."

Joy's heart twisted painfully at the raw grief in his tone. She drew a slow, steady breath, forcing herself to speak with clarity rather than emotion.

"Matt, I care for you deeply," she said. "But marrying out of duty or grief won't heal anything. We both know we are not in love." Her gaze held his. "And as I've said before, I will not make myself a burden, to you, or to anyone in this town."

He opened his mouth to protest, but she lifted a hand, stopping him.

"And think of your mother," she continued softly. "She has already lost one son. What would it do to her if she believed she might lose another because of us?"

"It wouldn't be your fault," he insisted hoarsely. "But with John gone, it falls to me. Someone must look after the children. Alice can't shoulder it all alone. And Annie, she isn't even her blood."

Joy's eyes flashed, her voice sharpening.

"Alice is the only mother Annie remembers. She loves her as if she were her own. You are not suggesting tearing them apart, are you?"

Matt shook his head fiercely. Anguish etched into his face.

"No. Of course not. But if you leave, Joy... it will break my mother's heart." His voice dropped. "And mine."

Her throat tightened, but she did not look away.

"Alice lost her husband," Joy said quietly. "Every corner of this town reminds her of John, and of our parents. Once she is strong enough, she deserves the chance to heal in her own way, even if that means leaving." Her voice steadied. "She can return when she's ready. But right now, distance is the only mercy we can give her."

Before Matt could answer, Mayor Hershel cleared his throat, cutting the moment short.

"Joy," he said, "do you know if your father made any serious enemies in recent weeks or months? Judges seldom live quiet lives."

Joy let out a weary breath and lifted her shoulders in a small shrug.

"Pa never spoke much about his cases," she replied. "After we moved to Auburn, I helped him with paperwork now and then, but if he had dangerous clients, or enemies, he never mentioned them. And as far as I know, John didn't speak of his work either." She hesitated. "It's possible something happened that prompted them to move us out here, traveling between towns as judge and attorney. But if there were threats, neither Pa nor Mama ever said a word."

Matt pushed himself to his feet, jaw tight, hands curling into fists.

"Then we'll find out ourselves," he said grimly. "I'll take a few men and see if we can track down that woman we jailed yesterday. Tomorrow, I'll ride out to John's farm and search for anything that might give us a clue. We'll comb through the burned buildings here in town, too." His voice shook with barely contained fury. "There has to be something that points us to who did this."

Joy understood the fire in him all too well. It wasn't only duty driving Matt Haven forward. It was grief. And a desperate hunger for justice, for his brother, and for the parents she had loved, with her whole heart.

4

Bruises and Truth

With the café reduced to ruin, Joy and Alice took shelter at the clinic. Mrs. Alden came faithfully each day with the baby whenever it was time for her to nurse, her presence calm and reassuring. Annie, meanwhile, was lovingly claimed by the Aldens' daughters, who surrounded her with the attention and gentle care only a house full of girls could give. For the moment, at least, the children were safe, warm, watched over, and spared the worst of what had been lost. Joy, however, could not rest.

Sleep came only in fitful snatches, chased away by smoke-scented memories and the relentless drum of unanswered questions. When her lungs were strong enough to bear it, she returned again and again to the charred remains of what had once been her parents' home. Each visit nearly broke her.

Standing before the blackened shell of the house, the place where laughter and quiet evenings had once lived, left her chest aching with a grief she could scarcely contain. But she forced herself to keep moving, to keep searching. If she didn't fight, if she didn't look for answers, there would be no justice. And she owed her parents more than tears.

The devastation was absolute. Charred timbers lay collapsed upon one another, blackened stone cracked by heat, warped fragments of once-familiar belongings scattered like bones. Yet amid the ruin, something caught her eye, something untouched by flames. Her parents' buckboard stood a short distance away, packed and intact.

Joy's breath caught. Several bags of clothing and household items rested inside, carefully arranged, as though her mother and father had been preparing to leave in haste. Her hands shook as she pulled the bags aside, a strange, hollow gratitude filling her chest. She and Alice had nothing now, but the clothes they wore. This, at least, would help them endure the days ahead.

Hour after hour, Joy sifted through the wreckage, her hands blackened with soot, her throat raw from ash and smoke. Most of what she touched crumbled to nothing, falling apart at the lightest pressure, memories reduced to dust. Then her fingers brushed against something solid. She stilled, heart pounding, and carefully drew it free, coughing as ash drifted up around her. In her palm lay a small metal object. A key.

It was tiny, delicate, meant for a diary, a lockbox, something private. On its own, it seemed useless. Every book, every scrap of paper her parents had owned had been consumed by fire. And yet, something deep within her whispered that it mattered. It was the last solid thing left of her parents' possessions. Proof that something had existed beyond the ashes.

Joy closed her fingers around it, resolve settling in her bones. She would clean it, thread it onto a chain, and wear it close to her heart. Whatever secrets it had once guarded were gone now, but the key itself would remain. A reminder. Of love. Of loss. And of truths still waiting to be uncovered.

Meanwhile, David, Matt, and the others returned from their search with grim faces and heavy silence. They had scoured every corner of the jail, examined the bent bars and shattered window frame, and followed the tracks that circled the prison yard like a mocking riddle. Hoofprints led them across the hard-packed dirt beyond town, pressed deep by haste and weight. They followed those tracks until the land gave way to the creek. There, the trail vanished.

Water rushed cold and swift over stone, erasing every sign, carrying evidence downstream until nothing remained but ripples and mud. They searched both banks, probed the shallows, even rode farther along the creek's course, but the current had done its work too well. Whoever had set the fires had planned her escape carefully.

She had left nothing behind. No scrap of fabric. No broken branch. No misplaced print. No clue at all, only ruin in her wake. And the terrible certainty that she was still out there, moving unseen, waiting for her next strike.

The funeral was almost unbearable. Friends and neighbors gathered in solemn ranks, hats clutched to chests, heads bowed in reverent silence. Words of comfort were offered, prayers spoken, but grief lay heavy over everything, thick as fog, pressing down until even breathing felt like an effort.

Annie, too young to understand death yet old enough to feel its cruelty, seemed to know that her grandparents and her father would never return. She cried endlessly for her Papa, her Nana, and her Daddy. Her small body wracked with sobs that tore through the stillness like a blade. Each wail cut deeper than the last. Every sound drove Alice further into despair.

At last, she broke completely, trembling, sobbing uncontrollably, as Joy wrapped her arms around her sister and held on with everything she had. Alice clutched her like a lifeline, her grief raw and unrestrained. Watching it nearly shattered Joy's resolve, but she would not let herself fall apart. Not now. Alice needed her strength, and Joy would not abandon her to the darkness.

Still, when the coffins were lowered into the ground, Joy felt her own knees weaken. The sight of dark earth swallowing everything she had loved, her parents, her brother-in-law, was almost more than she could endure. Her vision blurred, the edges of the world wavering as her breath caught painfully in her throat. She swayed.

A steady hand came to rest at her elbow. David Baker leaned close, his presence firm and grounding, his voice low and meant for her alone.

"Take a deep breath, sweet girl," he murmured. "I've got you."

The strength in his grip, solid, unwavering, the quiet certainty in his words anchored her where nothing else could. For a moment, she allowed herself to lean into him, drawing comfort from the same steadfast presence that had steadied her since childhood. Slowly, her footing returned.

Only then did David ease his hold, stepping back just enough to give her space, his expression solemn and fiercely protective. Before he withdrew completely, he bent his head slightly and added, barely above a whisper, "Your pa would be proud of you, Joy. More than you know."

The words settled deep in her chest, aching, bittersweet, another weight to bear, but one that reminded her she was not alone, even now. And as the final prayers were spoken and the earth closed over the coffins, Joy stood straight, grief burning through her veins, resolved that she would endure, for Alice, for the children, and for the loved ones now entrusted to her memory alone.

After the funeral, Joy sent a telegram to her uncle in Montana. The reply came swiftly: her aunt and uncle would gladly open their home to her, Alice, and the children. Relief washed over her, warm and immediate, yet edged with sorrow. Leaving Auburn would mean leaving the last place where her parents' laughter still echoed in her memory. The next step was protection.

She returned to the post office, the familiar scent of ink and paper grounding her as she sat at the small table and began drafting a telegram to marshal headquarters, requesting an escort for the long journey north.

She had just set her pen to paper when the door swung open. David Baker stepped inside, dust still clinging to his coat, his hat tucked under his arm. His expression was set with purpose.

"Joy," he said, crossing the room without hesitation. "I'm glad I caught you. I've been thinking, and I've decided to move to Deer Lodge as well. I'll travel with you." He paused, watching her reaction. "There's no need to involve the marshals."

Joy froze, her pen hovering mid-stroke. Her eyes widened, and for several long seconds she could only stare at him, words refusing to form. David waited, lips curving into a faint, amused smirk.

"So," he drawled at last, tilting his head, "you've nothing to say?"

That snapped her out of it. She shot him a withering glare.

"You can't just leave, Dave. Auburn is counting on you."

"Matt's more than capable of taking over as sheriff," David replied easily. "I've got nothing tying me here anymore." His voice softened. "After my wife passed, your family became the only family I truly had. I could go back to Sacramento, live with my stepchildren, but we never shared the same bond. They were nearly grown when their mother and I married."

Joy lowered her gaze, guilt stirring beneath her gratitude.

"I just don't want you to feel obligated."

David's voice gentled, but the steel beneath it remained.

"Don't trouble yourself with that, young lady. Your pa would want me keeping an eye on you and Alice." He gave her a small, knowing smile. "You'll be safe with your aunt and uncle once you arrive, but until then, you'll need someone you trust to see you there." He adjusted his hat.

"I'll write to your uncle and see if Deer Lodge has need of a lawman. Who knows? Maybe they're in the market for a new sheriff." He winked.

Despite herself, Joy smiled. She would never say it aloud, but relief bloomed deep in her chest. The thought of leaving Auburn, of traveling so far without her parents, terrified her more than she cared to admit. She adored her aunt and uncle, but years of distance had left them strangers in many ways. Having David with them, her father's dearest friend, the man who had been like a second father all her life, made the journey feel possible.

In the days that followed, David and the men of Auburn took turns standing watch, by lantern light and dawn's pale glow, guarding the town against further attacks. Rifles rested close at hand. Horses were kept saddled. Every unfamiliar sound drew wary glances and tightened grips. The nights were long, tense, and sleepless, but no one complained. Auburn had closed ranks.

The women brought food to the watchmen, pressed warm cups of coffee into cold hands, and sent their children to bed with whispered reassurances they barely believed themselves. Shopkeepers boarded up windows. Doors were locked earlier than usual. Even the church bells seemed to ring more softly, as if mourning alongside them.

Joy watched it all with a heavy, grateful heart. This town had taken her family in when they arrived with little more than hope and good intentions. Now, in the face of fear and loss,

Auburn stood firm, steadfast, loyal, unwilling to abandon its own. The depth of that kindness settled in her chest like a quiet ache.

And yet, with each passing day, her restlessness grew. She felt it in the way her lungs tightened whenever she walked past the ruins. In the way Alice flinched at sudden sounds. In the hollow look that crept into her sister's eyes when she thought no one was watching. Auburn had become a place of ghosts, of echoes that refused to fade.

Joy longed to leave. Not because she lacked gratitude, but because she feared what staying would do to them all. She could not shake the certainty that as long as they remained, the danger, shadowing her family would linger too, circling, watching, waiting for another chance to strike. And more than that, she knew Alice needed it.

Joy did not yet know what awaited them beyond Auburn, but she knew, with unwavering certainty, that staying was no longer an option.

Two weeks had passed since the fires, yet Alice could scarcely summon the strength to rise from her bed. Most days she lay in silence, her face drained of color, eyes swollen and rimmed red from endless weeping. At times she seemed entirely hollowed out, staring at nothing, as though her spirit had wandered somewhere Joy could not follow. Only when her children were brought to her side did she stir at all.

Her arms would tighten around them instinctively, her voice softening as she murmured faint comforts, rocking the baby with gentle motions born of muscle memory. In those fleeting moments, she seemed almost like herself again. But once the little ones were carried from the room, the fragile light in her eyes dimmed, leaving only exhaustion and grief behind. Joy's heart ached every time she witnessed it.

She and Doc Perkins had quietly agreed it would be cruel to press Alice about the bruises that bore silent witness to John's harshness. Still, the knowledge gnawed at Joy. She had never suspected her brother-in-law capable of such cruelty, and the unanswered questions haunted her. Had it been a darkness that crept in only toward the end? Or had Alice borne it in silence for years, shielding both her children and her sister from the truth?

For now, Joy forced herself to remain silent. Patience, she told herself, was the only kindness left to offer. At last, when it became painfully clear that Alice was not improving, Joy asked to speak privately with Doc Perkins. Seated across from him, she clasped her hands tightly in her lap, gathering her resolve.

"I know you want Alice to grow stronger before we travel," she began, her voice low but unwavering, "but I don't think it's wise to keep her here any longer. She hasn't improved at all." Her breath hitched, then steadied. "Every street, every corner reminds her of Pa, Ma, and John. Staying here is crushing her. I don't believe she'll begin to heal until we leave this place behind."

Doc Perkins let out a long, weary sigh, his lined face heavy with compassion.

"I fear you're right, Joy," he admitted. "I had hoped that being among familiar faces might help her find closure, perhaps even give her the courage to speak of what she endured. But the

memories here do her no favors. They only deepen the wound."
He nodded slowly. "Yes... she desperately needs a change."

Relief loosened the tight knot in Joy's chest.

"Aunt Eliza and Uncle Gerald will give her that," Joy said
quickly. "They're empty nesters now, but one of their daughters
has recently returned home. Her husband is a U.S. Marshal
and gone often. She has six children, the youngest is ten. With
such a lively household, Alice will have help with the little ones
and no shortage of distraction." Her voice softened. "She won't
have to face her grief alone."

Doc Perkins studied her for a long moment, weighing not
only her words, but the strength behind them. At last, he gave
a single, firm nod.

"You've thought this through carefully," he said. "I agree.
Let's begin preparations for your departure. The sooner you
set out, the sooner Alice, and perhaps you as well, can find a
measure of peace."

Joy exhaled slowly, resolve settling in her bones. Leaving
Auburn would not erase their losses, but it might finally give
her sister room to breathe again.

Saying goodbye to their friends was far harder than Joy had
expected. Auburn had shown them nothing but kindness in
the wake of tragedy, open doors, shared meals, steady hands
when they faltered. Yet Alice's grief remained so raw, so
consuming, that staying longer would only deepen the wound
rather than ease it.

FLAMES OF THE FIRE

Joy's throat tightened as she watched Maureen Haven kneel to gather Annie and baby Ruth into her arms. The older woman clutched her granddaughters as though committing the feel of them to memory, her face lined with sorrow and fierce love. She understood, of course she did, that leaving was best for Alice now. Understanding, however, did nothing to soften the ache of parting.

Annie clung to her grandmother, sobbing into her skirts, small hands fisting the familiar fabric. Joy had to bite the inside of her cheek to keep her own tears at bay. Her family needed her steady, anchored, not breaking alongside them.

David Baker had already handed the sheriff's badge over to Matt Haven. Now he rode alongside the stagecoach, Joy's horse led close behind. His quiet vigilance and steady presence calmed her in a way nothing else could. If danger waited somewhere along the road ahead, she knew without question that David would step between it and them without hesitation.

The journey itself was exhausting. Long days jolting along rutted dirt roads left their bodies aching and their nerves frayed. Dust clung to everything, hair, clothes, lungs, until even breathing felt like work. Still, they were fortunate to have the coach to themselves for much of the journey, and that small measure of privacy proved a blessing.

The children fared better than Joy had dared to hope. They rarely fussed, their soft breathing and small, warm bodies pressed close, offering a quiet comfort that eased some of the tightness gripping her chest. At night, when the coach finally stopped and the world grew still, Joy found herself watching them sleep, drawing strength from their fragile peace.

Yet as they neared their third overnight stop, unease began to coil beneath Joy's skin. She sat rigid on the narrow bench. Her gaze fixed on the endless sweep of prairie beyond the window. Mile after mile slid past, golden grass bending in the wind, distant hills blurring into the horizon, but she scanned it all relentlessly, searching for movement that did not belong. An extra rider cresting a rise. A shape lingering too long at the edge of sight. A shadow that refused to fall behind.

The feeling sharpened with every passing mile.

Her vigilance did not go unnoticed. With the children asleep against their sides, Alice slipped her hand into Joy's, her touch tentative but searching.

"What is it, Joy?" she whispered. "Why are you so restless?"

Joy hesitated. She did not want to frighten her sister, but she would not lie.

"I don't know," she admitted quietly. "I can't shake the feeling that we're being followed. I've seen nothing clearly, nothing I can point to, but the dread won't leave me."

Alice's eyes widened, though she forced herself to remain calm.

"Perhaps it's just the prairie," she said gently. "Hours of the same view can play tricks on the mind. Maybe you're imagining it."

"Perhaps," Joy murmured, though the word carried little conviction. She slipped a hand into her pocket, her fingers closing around the small revolver she had taken from her father's belongings. The cool, familiar weight of the metal steadied her racing thoughts, grounding her in something solid and real. Whatever lay ahead, she would not be helpless. And if the shadow dogging them proved real, Joy Collins would be ready.

Her father had not chosen the weapon lightly. Years earlier, Max Collins had entrusted the task to a close friend, a skilled gunsmith whose work was known for its precision and reliability. Together, they had designed the revolver to Max's exact specifications. It was compact enough to be concealed, balanced perfectly for smaller hands, yet solid and dependable in a crisis. It had been made with Joy in mind. And David Baker had made certain she knew how to use it. Under his watchful eye, Joy had learned every detail, the measured patience of loading, the steady breath required to aim true, the discipline to fire only when it mattered. He had drilled her until muscle memory replaced hesitation, until her movements were instinctive and sure.

She had proved herself a 'natural'. Joy never missed her targets, not the distant tin cans lined along fence posts, not the paper silhouettes pinned to trees, not even the moving marks David devised once he trusted her control. Her accuracy rivaled that of seasoned marksmen, a fact that had filled both her father and David with quiet pride.

It had comforted them to know that if misfortune ever struck, if they were absent, or if her brother-in-law failed in his duty, Joy would not be helpless. She would be capable. Capable of standing her ground. Capable of protecting her mother, her sister, and her nieces. Now, as the prairie rolled endlessly past the coach window and unease tightened her chest, Joy's fingers rested on the familiar grip. Her confidence did not come from violence, but from preparation. Her father had planned for this. And she would not fail him.

Now, as the stagecoach rolled over a low rise, something faint caught Joy's eye far across the open plain. A blur. At first glance, it might have been nothing more than wind lifting dust from the earth, but it did not waver or scatter. It held its shape, a thin, steady plume rising against the distant horizon. Her breath hitched. A rider. Perhaps two.

They were too far away to make out clearly, mere silhouettes swallowed by distance, yet close enough that her instincts flared with certainty. This was no trick of light. No wandering shadow cast by the prairie sun.

Joy tore her gaze away, before Alice could notice, schooling her expression even as her pulse thundered in her ears. She forced her breathing to steady, her posture to remain calm, as though nothing at all had changed. Slowly, deliberately, her hand tightened around the revolver hidden in her pocket, fingers settling into familiar grooves.

The unease that had haunted her for miles hardened into cold resolve. Danger was no longer a feeling. It was no longer behind them. It was coming.

A silent sigh slipped from Joy's lips as her thoughts drifted, once more, to her father. Max Collins had been a true man in every sense of the word, unyielding yet fair, resolute without ever being cruel. He had been the quiet pillar of their family, a protector who carried authority and compassion in equal measure. As a judge, he bore the weight of justice with solemn care, never treating another person's fate as something to be handled lightly.

When a man's life hung in the balance, Max never rushed to judgment. He demanded every shred of evidence, examined every angle, and listened, not only to facts, but to the truths hidden between them. And whenever the law allowed it, he offered mercy. He believed, fiercely, that a second chance belonged only to those willing to change, but that redemption, however rare, was possible.

For as long as she could remember, Joy had wanted to be like him. Not a judge. That path was barred to women, and in truth she had no desire to sit behind a bench deciding whether a man lived, died, or spent his years behind iron bars. But she had inherited his spirit, his fierce protectiveness of those he loved—his intolerance for injustice, and his refusal to bend when the matter at hand truly mattered.

Alice had chosen a different life. She had married young, stepping quickly into the roles of wife and mother, finding her purpose in care and devotion. Joy, by contrast, relished her independence. She felt no urgency to wed, no longing to surrender her autonomy, and no patience for a man who would attempt to claim ownership over her will.

For a time, she had even been grateful for her brother-in-law, believing John treated Alice as an equal. That illusion had shattered. The bruises told a far different story. Alice's nature had always been gentler, inclined toward obedience, toward harmony at any cost. That softness had likely left her vulnerable to John's temper, his frustration, his cruelty. The thought twisted Joy's heart with guilt. She should have seen it sooner. She should have asked harder questions. She should have protected her sister better.

Her father, at least, had always seen her clearly. He had urged her to be strong. To stand her ground. To never allow anyone, husband, judge, or society itself, to silence her voice. From the bench, he had witnessed too many cases where women were broken by violent men, stripped of agency and protection, left powerless beneath the law's slow, grinding wheels. He had sworn his daughter would never be one of them.

So, he had trained her mind, hardened her resolve, and given her the tools to defend herself—physically and morally. Not to seek violence, but to never be defenseless. Not to dominate, but to endure. Now, as danger gathered on the horizon and the echoes of loss pressed in on her heart, Joy vowed to honor those lessons. She would be strong. She would stand. And she would never allow fear, or a man, to decide her fate.

5

The Line He Crossed

Knowing Alice had still not spoken fully about her marriage, Joy decided the time for gentleness alone had passed. She leaned forward, fixing her sister with a steady, unwavering gaze.

"Alice," she said softly, but firmly. "I know this is hard. But I need the truth, once and for all. Was John a terrible husband?" Her voice lowered. "And please... don't lie to me."

Alice released a long, weary sigh, as though the breath carried years of silence with it.

"John hardly spent time with us after we moved to Auburn," she said quietly. "He was angry when Baby Ruth was born. He wanted a boy so badly." Her mouth tightened. "Most days, I didn't even know where he was. And when he did come home..." Her voice faltered. "He drank. Whiskey. Too much of it. That's when he changed. That's when he became aggressive. Mean."

Something cold coiled in Joy's chest.

"He never hurt the girls," Alice continued. "But he took it out on me."

Joy's jaw tightened. "Did he beat you?"

Alice hesitated, then nodded faintly.

"Sometimes. Most of the time, he grabbed me too hard. Shoved me against walls." The detachment in her voice, so practiced, so resigned, made Joy's hands curl into fists.

"Please tell me you fought back," Joy pressed.

Alice shook her head. "What good would that have done? He would've only hurt me worse."

"So, you just... let him?" Joy's voice broke, disbelief and fury flashing in her eyes.

"I'm not like you, Joy," Alice whispered. "I accepted my fate. I married him willingly."

Joy stared at her. "What do you mean, willingly? Did he treat you like this before you married?"

Alice nodded. "He threatened me. More than once. Said there'd be consequences if I refused." Her voice dropped to a whisper. "I was afraid he'd hurt Annie. So, I put myself in the way, to protect his daughter."

Joy gasped. "Alice... did you ever tell Pa?"

"No." Shame flooded Alice's face. "Pa would have made a scene, and I was terrified John would follow through and take Annie from me."

"But Annie would have been safe with her grandmother," Joy insisted.

Alice let out a bitter scoff. "Safe? Maureen isn't a good grandmother. I've seen her slap Annie more than once this past year. She's been cruel to me too." Her voice hardened. "She drinks whiskey, just like John."

Joy felt dizzy. "What?"

Alice nodded grimly. "I don't know if it started after her husband died or if it's been longer, but it makes her unbearable."

Joy swallowed hard. "Is that why you didn't argue when I said we should go to Montana?"

"Yes," Alice said quietly. "I was relieved. When the café burned and Reverend Alden's wife took the girls, I finally felt they were safe. I never trusted Maureen for long."

"Why didn't you tell me?" Joy demanded. For the first time since the conversation began, Alice's eyes filled with tears.

"Because John threatened me. He swore he'd take the girls away if I ever spoke."

Joy shook with fury. "What kind of coward was that man? He sounds like nothing more than a lump of prairie coal!"

"Joy—"

"No," Joy said sharply. "I'm appalled, and furious, that we never saw it. You should have told Pa. He would have ended it immediately."

"Maybe," Alice whispered. "But who would've believed me? John and Maureen were good at pretending. To the town, they looked like saints. Even when they drank, they fooled people into thinking they were kind."

Joy's voice softened, though the fire in her eyes did not fade.

"What about Matt? Did he ever suspect? Or was he like them?"

Alice only shrugged. "I don't know. He wasn't around enough for me to tell."

Silence stretched between them. Joy studied her sister, the sorrow hollowing her eyes, the resignation etched into every line of her face. Her chest ached with grief, but beneath it burned something steadier than rage. She remembered her father's voice, stern yet gentle, teaching her as a girl that too many women suffered because no one dared to stand between them and cruelty.

Be strong, Joy. Stand your ground. Protect those who cannot protect themselves.

In that moment, she made herself a vow, fierce as any oath her father had ever sworn from the bench. Never again. No man, no matter how charming his words or how carefully he wore the mask of respectability, would ever raise a hand against Alice or the girls while Joy still drew breath.

Her father had taught her how to fight. Now she would carry that fight for them both.

Joy leaned out the window and let her thoughts race unchecked. Never in a thousand lifetimes would she have imagined John, or his mother, as drinkers, much less as abusers. The revelation turned her stomach. Men who wore civility like a well-pressed coat, who hid cruelty behind respectability, were the most dangerous of all. Her jaw clenched, fury simmering just beneath the surface.

Her mind was still churning when the soft scrape of hooves reached her ears. Her spine stiffened. The unease that had plagued her since they crested the prairie rise surged back, sharper now, undeniable. David must have sensed it too. She glimpsed him through the window as he wheeled his horse around, eyes sweeping the horizon with a lawman's instinct.

Joy started to pull her head back inside and froze. Four riders burst from behind a stand of brush and the shelter of boulders, driving hard, low over their saddles. Too close. Too fast. Her heart slammed violently against her ribs. She did not scream. She moved.

Joy shoved the softer bags, blankets, and her coat into the bottom of the stagecoach, building a crude barricade. She urged Alice down without explanation, pressing her flat against the floorboards, then pulled the girls against her, tucking them beneath the coverings until only Alice's arms and whispered prayers remained visible.

Then Joy reached for the revolver. Her father's revolver. The weight of it, solid, familiar, anchored her shaking hands. She drew it free, breath steadying as resolve locked into place. She would defend her family. No matter the cost.

Gunfire erupted almost immediately. The sharp crack of pistols tore through the air as the attackers opened fire. David wheeled his horse and returned fire at once, riding hard to draw their attention away from the coach drivers and buy them precious seconds.

The girls screamed as bullets snapped past, splintering wood. Alice crouched over them, rocking and whispering, though terror swallowed every word. Then came rifle fire. Deeper.

Heavier. Deadlier. Joy's breath ripped from her lungs as both stagecoach drivers pitched forward from the box and struck the ground with sickening finality.

"No—" The sound escaped her as a broken whisper. They were dead. One attacker leaped down and began unfastening the traces from the lead horse. Another lunged forward, reaching for the reins, trying to seize control of the coach. David fired again, Joy saw one figure crumple and fall. The stage lurched violently. Instinct took over. Joy flung herself across Alice and the children as the coach tipped, rolled, and crashed into a shallow ditch. They slammed against the side and came to a brutal stop. The world spun, then stilled. They were bruised. They were shaken, but they were alive.

Outside, shouts and scattered gunfire tore through the air, then, abruptly, everything went silent. The stillness pressed down hard. Unnatural. Worse than the chaos before it. Joy held her breath. Silence could mean retreat. Or it could mean someone was coming.

She leaned close to Alice and whispered fiercely, "Stay down. Don't move." Her ears were strained. Footsteps crunched closer. Then, the unmistakable metallic click of a hammer being cocked. Joy slid her fingers until both weapons rested within reach at her hip. A shadow slid into the open window. A man. Blinding sunlight flashed along the barrel of his gun as he aimed straight for Alice.

Joy fired. Once. Twice. Three times. The man dropped with a strangled cry, clutching his shoulder as he collapsed beneath the window. Adrenaline surged through her veins, white-hot. There was no time to hesitate. Joy kicked a seat aside, hauled herself through the low window, the coach resting on its side, and dropped hard to the ground. The air reeked of gunpowder and horse sweat. The wounded attacker groped desperately for his pistol.

Joy pivoted and brought her boot down on his hand with crushing force. He screamed, reflexively reaching for the rifle lying inches away. She ended it. Swinging the butt of her revolver with all her strength, she smashed it across his temple. His body went slack, collapsing into the dirt.

For a heartbeat, Joy stood over him, chest heaving, ears ringing with the echo of gunfire. Beyond the fallen man, shapes still moved, horses snorting, silhouettes shifting against the horizon.

The fight was not over. But this threat, this one, was ended by her hand.

Joy drew a steadying breath, forcing her trembling hands to obey. She stripped the attacker of his weapons and flung them as far from his reach as she could. A quick, practiced glance confirmed what she already suspected, her shots had struck true. Two bullets had torn through his shoulder, another through the upper leg. He would not be rising anytime soon.

Her own legs felt like water beneath her. She pressed her back against the overturned stagecoach, drawing strength from its solid frame as she fought to slow her breathing. Alice's voice carried faintly from inside, calling her name, sharp with fear. Joy did not answer. Not yet. The danger wasn't over. The crunch of footsteps confirmed it. Someone was climbing up from below the ditch.

Joy tightened her grip on her father's revolver and slid her free hand into her pocket, fingers closing around the smaller gun. She would not be caught unprepared. Careful not to fire blindly, and risk hitting David, she leaned around the corner of the coach. A shadowed figure hauled himself onto the wreck, inching toward the window where Alice and the girls lay hidden. Rage flared, hot and sudden.

Joy surged to her feet and fired. Three sharp shots in rapid succession. Each bullet struck its mark, slamming into the attacker's legs. His screams tore through the air before he pitched backward, crashing onto the rocks below with a sickening thud.

Heart hammering, Joy crept forward. She circled the wrecked coach and found him sprawled in the dirt, blood pooling beneath his head. Without hesitation, she kicked his gun into the canyon, then bent and yanked the bandana from his face. Her breath caught. Not a man. It was her, the same woman who had torched John's barn. The one Joy herself had shot before. A sharp gasp tore from her throat.

"Joy!" Alice called again, panic breaking through her voice. Joy forced herself upright and leaned into the coach window.

"I'm all right," she said quickly. "Two of them are down, and I saw David take out at least one more. Keep the girls quiet. Don't come out until I say so."

Alice's reply came in a tearful whisper.

"Be careful, Joy."

Pulling herself from the ditch, Joy scanned the road. Two attackers lay still in the dirt. Not far beyond them, David was slumped against a rock. Panic surged through her veins. She ran to him, dropping to her knees at his side. Blood stained his sleeve, but the wound was clean, a bullet through the shoulder.

"Do you need help getting up?" she asked, breathless. David shook his head grimly.

"Is your sister safe? The children?"

"They're all right," Joy said, relief flooding her voice. "Just bruised." She squeezed his arm once before rising. "I'll check the others. Make sure they're no threat." She forced herself toward the bodies. Both men lay motionless, chests still. Dead.

The finality of it hit her like a blow. Her knees buckled as the last of the adrenaline drained away, and she staggered back, sinking to the roadside. Her whole body trembled now, lungs burning as she struggled to draw breath. Then, hoofbeats. Joy's head snapped up. More riders crested the horizon, closing fast. For one terrible heartbeat, her heart seized, certain more outlaws had come. But the silhouettes were wrong. Not bandits. Indians.

David saw them too. His eyes flashed, and he motioned sharply for Joy to get back to the coach. Then, despite his injury, he vanished into the brush, concealing himself with practiced speed. Joy pushed herself upright, but the strain of everything she had endured crashed down upon her all at once. Her chest tightened painfully. Each breath came in sharp, uneven gasps. Darkness crept in at the edges of her vision. She took one step. Then another. And before she could reach the coach, her strength gave out. The world tilted, blurred, and vanished into black.

A cool, damp cloth brushed across Joy's forehead, tugging her back from the edge of blackness.

At first, everything swam, shadows without shape, voices without meaning. Then her vision sharpened, and she found herself staring up into two unfamiliar faces, dark against the pale sky. Panic flared. She tried to scramble to her feet, but a hand, gentle yet unyielding, pressed her back down.

"Please," Joy gasped, her voice raw with fear. "Don't hurt my sister. I'll go with you, just... don't touch her."

The young man's voice was calm and steady, carrying no threat.

"Your sister and the children are safe. We did not come to harm you. We came to help." He spoke perfect English. Relief warred with confusion, leaving her breathless.

"You're not with the men who attacked us?" she asked. He shook his head.

"No. We're from the Duck Valley Reservation, not far from here. We heard the gunfire and rode out to see what had happened." He gestured toward the horizon. "There's an army camp a few miles away. They'll take you in and keep you safe."

Joy exhaled shakily. "Thank you."

The young man's mouth curved into a warm, reassuring smile.

"I'm Ahote," he said before indicating to the man beside him. "This is Sam." He nodded toward two others standing nearby. "Halian and Kitchi."

"Sam isn't a Native name," Joy blurted before she could stop herself, still half-dazed. Both men grinned.

"Names change," Sam said easily. "We live close to the army now."

Ahote shrugged. "We're allowed to hunt beyond the reservation. The sergeant and captain treat our people decent."

Sam added, a mischievous glint in his eye, "I reckon Sergeant Matthews has a soft spot for Ahote's sister."

Ahote rolled his eyes but offered Joy his hand, helping her sit up carefully. When she steadied, he asked, "What is your name?"

"Joy—Joy Collins."

"Joy," Sam repeated thoughtfully, a teasing smile tugging at his mouth. "Pretty name. Means something good."

Joy swallowed hard. "My pa cared about your people," she said quietly. "He tried to help when he could. It troubled him, the way things are." Her voice wavered. "He was... a judge in Sacramento."

"Was?" Ahote asked gently, concern sharpening his tone.

Joy lowered her gaze. "He died in a fire. Along with my ma and my brother-in-law. A few weeks back."

The men exchanged looks. Sam's expression sobered.

"Was it... murder?"

Joy's breath hitched. "We think so." She told them, briefly, about the barns and houses burned, the woman she had seen setting hay alight, the ambush on the stagecoach. The words came out clipped and sharp, easier to say aloud in the open air than they had been locked inside her chest. Ahote nodded slowly.

"There's talk," he said quietly. "A judge who does right makes enemies." His eyes darkened. "We hear rumors on the reservation. People whisper about such things."

Sam's jaw tightened. "Are they coming after you? Will they follow you all the way to Montana?"

Joy met his gaze. The weight of the question settled heavily on her shoulders.

"We were headed to our uncle in Deer Lodge," she said. "But now... I don't know. What if they follow us there too?"

Ahote folded his arms, thinking.

"The army camp will give you a place to rest. Then we'll speak with the sergeant. He can advise you." His tone was practical and steady. "If you must continue, we can send a rider with word to your uncle, or to marshal headquarters." He looked at her meaningfully. "But first, you need warmth. Food. Your wounds tended. You cannot decide everything tonight."

Joy nodded, gratitude and fear braided tightly together in her chest. Around them, the prairie stretched wide and indifferent beneath the sky. Yet for the first time since the flames had stolen everything familiar, someone beyond her family had offered help without demand or suspicion. And that kindness mattered more than words could say.

The army welcomed them without hesitation. Food was pressed into their hands first, hot stew and hard bread, followed by fresh water and clean blankets. Only once the women and children were settled did the soldiers turn their attention to the aftermath of the ambush, moving with brisk efficiency born of long habit.

The two surviving attackers were carried to the infirmary, their wounds bound with professional detachment, then escorted under heavy guard to the stockade. Iron bars closed behind them with unmistakable finality, and armed sentries took their posts without a word.

Sergeant Matthews wasted no time. At Joy's request, he personally saw to the telegram she had written to her uncle in Montana. Within the hour, two soldiers were mounted and dispatched to Elko, riding hard to ensure the message would reach Deer Lodge without delay.

David's shoulder was examined next. The army doctor cleaned the wound thoroughly and pronounced it clean, the bullet having passed through without splintering bone.

"He'll heal just fine," the physician assured Joy. "Provided he rests and follows orders."

Relief loosened the tight band around her chest. With the immediate dangers addressed, Joy turned to practical matters. When she asked about the next stagecoach north, an officer informed her it would not arrive for another three days. The waiting weighed heavily, yet it also brought an unexpected gift, time. Time to breathe. Time to gather themselves, before moving on. Alice and the girls bore their bruises and shock with fragile resilience, gradually settling, beneath the watchful care of the camp. The children clung less tightly as the days passed, their sleep growing deeper, their tears fewer. Alice, though still quiet, began to eat again, her eyes no longer quite so hollow, her movements no longer so tentative.

And whenever duty allowed, Ahote and Sam rode in from the reservation. Their visits brought warmth to the camp, easy conversation, gentle humor, moments of laughter that felt almost foreign after so much sorrow. Sam teased, Ahote listened, and between them they reminded Joy of the goodness that still existed beyond grief and violence. She found herself deeply grateful for their presence. Grateful for the steadiness in their voices. For the way they asked nothing in return. For the simple truth that kindness still lived in the world, even after everything she had lost. Those three days did not heal their wounds. But they gave them strength enough to face what came next.

The evening before the stagecoach was due to arrive, Alice was settling the girls when shouts echoed across the camp. Soldiers called out warnings, someone was approaching. Joy froze, her heart leaping into her throat.

Attackers? Surely no one would be foolish enough to assault a fortified army camp, but fear did not wait for reason. Several long minutes passed before the tent flap flew open. Joy sprang to her feet, and gasped. So did Alice.

"Matt?" Joy stared at him, disbelief crashing through her. "What on earth—what are you doing here?"

Matt Haven stepped inside, his face flushed from hard travel but brightening at the sight of her.

"The army sent a telegram to Auburn. They said you were safe, but Mom was worried sick. I came as fast as I could."

Joy's pulse thundered. "You can just leave?" she demanded. "You have a whole town to look after."

His smile faded. "Your safety matters more. My deputy is in charge now. I'll be joining you the rest of the way."

"No, you won't," Joy snapped, casting a glance toward Alice. "Dave is with us. That's all we need."

"Clearly it isn't," Matt shot back. "This journey is too dangerous."

"We are not alone," Joy said sharply. "David has more than proven himself capable."

"Having another man along doesn't hurt."

"You shouldn't have followed us," she said flatly. "Your duty is to Auburn, and to your mother, not to us."

"I resigned." His tone was blunt. "And Mom's coming on the next stagecoach. She wants to rebuild the café, but she can do that anywhere."

Joy stared at him, stunned. "You resigned?" she whispered. "David barely made you sheriff! Have you lost your mind?"

Instead of answering, Matt reached for her hand and tugged her toward the tent opening.

"Matt—stop," Joy protested, but he was already pulling her outside, steering her toward a quiet corner near a fallen tree.

"Sit," he urged. Uneasy, Joy lowered herself onto the trunk. Matt remained standing, too close, his gaze intense and unblinking.

"I didn't come just because we were worried," he said, voice thick. "I came because I love you. I've loved you for two years."

Joy's breath left her. "What?"

"I tried to tell you before," he went on. "You always brushed me off. You must have known."

"I—" She swallowed. "I don't know what you expect me to say."

"How do you feel about me?"

Joy drew a slow, steadying breath. "I care about you, Matt. But I'm not in love with you. I never have been. I've always thought of you as more of an older brother."

His flinch was unmistakable. "Ouch."

"I won't lie to you," she pressed. "I won't lead you on or promise feelings that aren't there." She rose, intending to leave. That was when his arms closed around her, suddenly, crushing, dragging her hard against him as his mouth came down on hers. The kiss was rough. Demanding. Suffocating. Panic surged, stealing her breath. She shoved at his chest, but he only tightened his grip, fingers digging into her arms.

"Stop!" she gasped, twisting away. Fury exploded. Joy bit his lip and shoved with all her strength, tearing free and stumbling back, breath ragged.

"What has gotten into you?" she demanded, fists raised defensively. "You're losing control!"

His eyes were fixed on her mouth, unfocused, dazed.

"Sorry," he muttered. "I got carried away."

"You think?" Her voice shook with anger. "That was uncalled for. Completely inappropriate."

"But you kissed me back."

Her stomach lurched. "No, I didn't. I was fighting to get away."

"You're just playing hard to get."

"I am not that kind of woman," she snapped. "I told you, I don't see you that way. There is no love between us."

"I know you felt something."

"The only thing I felt was anger," she shot back. "You're confusing lust with love. Real love is nothing like what you just forced on me."

His pride hardened into resentment.

"You've never even been in a relationship," he sneered. "That was probably your first kiss."

The words cut deep, but Joy straightened.

"Yes," she said, voice trembling with fury. "And you ruined it. You took something that wasn't yours to take. My parents showed me what love looks like. What you did was the opposite."

Still, he pressed on. "I came after you," he said harshly. "I showed you how much you mean to me. And this is how you repay me?"

"Repay you?" Her temper flared white-hot. "I owe you nothing. You forced yourself on me, and now you expect gratitude? That isn't love, Matt, it's selfishness."

His expression darkened. Before she could step away, his hands seized her arms again, harder this time, fingers biting into her flesh as he pinned her in place, his grip meant to overpower rather than restrain.

"You're not listening—"

"Let me go!" she cried, panic breaking through as she twisted against him, her breath coming fast and shallow.

He lunged, dragging her back into him with brutal force. His hold bruised, his breath hot and furious against her cheek, and before she could wrench her head aside, his mouth slammed against hers in a violent, silencing kiss, rough, uninvited, meant to dominate rather than persuade. She froze for a heartbeat in shock, then fought him, shoving at his chest, her protest trapped as he tried to keep her there.

Heavy boots struck the ground behind him, slow, deliberate, closing the distance. A shadow fell over them. A thunderous voice cut through the night, cold with promise.

"Release her. Now."

Matt went still. Not because he wished to, but because he understood, in that instant, that whatever happened next would not end well for him. David Baker stood several paces away, fury carved into his face, soldiers flanking him with ready weapons. His voice was a low, lethal growl.

"If you ever lay hands on her like that again," he said evenly, "you will answer to me."

Matt froze. Slowly, he released Joy. He shot David a dark, smoldering look, but with armed men watching, he knew better. Without a word, he turned and vanished into darkness.

Joy stood trembling, her breath coming in ragged, uneven bursts. Her arms still burned where Matt's fingers had dug into her skin, the memory of his grip lingering like a bruise beneath the surface. David crossed the space between them in two long strides and placed his hands gently, but firmly, on her shoulders. The weight of his presence steadied her at once. His voice was low and sure, carrying both authority and care.

"Joy," he said quietly, "you listen to me. None of that was your fault. Not one bit."

Her lips trembled. "I told him I didn't—"

"I know," David interrupted, his tone firm but protective, his gaze holding hers so she could not look away. "I heard enough. You were clear. He ignored you." His jaw tightened. "That's on him. Not you."

Joy swallowed hard, shame and anger warring inside her chest.

"I feel... so foolish," she whispered. "I should have—"

"No." David's voice sharpened, not at her, but at the thought itself. "Do not blame yourself. You did exactly what you should have done. You set a boundary. You stood your ground. And when he crossed it, you defended yourself." He nodded once. "That took courage."

Her eyes burned, and this time she did not fight the tears. They spilled freely, hot and unrestrained. David drew her into his chest, the way her father once might have, and held her there without hesitation. His arm around her was strong, steady, unshakable.

"You're like a daughter to me, Joy Collins," he said softly. "And I will not stand by and let anyone harm you. Not Matt. Not the people who murdered your family. Not anyone."

For the first time since Matt's outburst, the fight drained from her body. Joy leaned into David's solid frame, letting his steadiness quiet the storm raging inside her. They stood like that for a long moment, the night air cool around them, the camp hushed once more. At last, David spoke again, his voice was gentler now.

"You are not alone, Joy. You never have been. You've got me." He squeezed her shoulder lightly. "And as long as I'm breathing, you'll always have someone to turn to."

Joy closed her eyes and breathed in his words, clutching them like a lifeline, a promise of safety in a world that had too often taken it away.

Matt was gone by morning. No farewell. No explanation. Only the lingering knowledge of his absence, heavy and unresolved, hung over the camp like a shadow.

Alice and Joy had spoken long into the night. Alice had overheard enough of the confrontation to understand what had transpired between her sister and brother-in-law, and once the words began, they were difficult to stop. With quiet bitterness, Alice admitted that John had begun much the same way early in their marriage, demanding, insistent, dismissive of her wishes and boundaries.

The confession troubled Joy deeply. Alice agreed with Joy's suspicion that no woman had ever truly stood up to Matt before. He was accustomed to being admired, to women withdrawing quietly when things turned uncomfortable, never to someone daring to look him in the eye and tell him his behavior was wrong.

Joy lay awake long after Alice drifted into restless sleep, unsettled by the weight of everything she had learned. So much of what she had believed about the Haven family had cracked and splintered. Matt's behavior was not an isolated misstep, but the latest fracture in a pattern she could no longer ignore. What should have been nothing more than a harmless, unspoken regard had revealed something darker beneath the surface, pride sharpened into entitlement, desire tangled with control, a temper kept hidden until it was challenged.

And then there was the loss she had not yet allowed herself to fully name. Her first kiss. It saddened her more than she wished to admit that such a moment, one that should have been gentle, chosen, and treasured, had been taken instead, forever tainted by force rather than affection.

As dawn crept across the horizon, Joy stared at the pale light filtering through the tent canvas and asked herself a question that would not be silenced. Had she been so naïve, so willing to trust, that she had failed to see the Haven family's true nature all along? The answer, whatever it was, offered no comfort.

6

Escape Without Confession

By midmorning, the sisters had packed what little they owned, and a soldier drove Alice and the girls by buckboard to White Horse, Joy and David riding watchfully alongside. The stagecoach was due in the early afternoon, and they arrived with scarcely a moment to spare.

Annie let out a squeal of delight when she spotted her grandmother already seated inside the coach. She rushed forward and clung to Maureen's side as though afraid the woman might vanish if she loosened her grip. Maureen gathered her close at once, murmuring reassurances, then looked expectantly toward Alice and Joy.

"And Matt?" she asked quietly.

Neither sister was eager to explain. With careful, measured words, they told her the truth, that Matt had kissed Joy against her will, that Joy had refused him, and that he had left soon after. Maureen's expression tightened, lines deepening around her mouth. She shook her head slowly.

"I feared something like this might happen," she admitted. "Its unfortunate Joy had to be the one to see it." After a pause, she added, "I only hope it humbles him, that he learns from it. Perhaps one day, a young lady will capture his heart properly." Her gaze softened with reluctant honesty. "But he will need to grow into the man he ought to be first."

The rest of the journey passed without incident. Three days later, the stagecoach rattled into Deer Lodge, dust billowing in its wake. Waiting along the road were Eliza and Gerald Collins, waving eagerly, faces etched with relief and concern. The moment Joy and Alice stepped down, their aunt and uncle swept them into tight, tearful embraces.

For the first time since her husband's death, Alice did not try to hold herself together. She broke down completely, clinging to Eliza as though she might never let go, her grief finally spilling free in great, wracking sobs. Eliza held her without a word, rocking her gently as though she were a child once more.

When Alice found enough composure, she introduced her mother-in-law. Joy could see the effort it cost her. Maureen explained that she would be moving to Goldcreek, where her brother and sister-in-law had settled after the gold rush. They had offered her a place until she could rebuild her café.

Goldcreek lay two hours from Deer Lodge, far enough to grant Alice a measure of peace, though Joy knew visits between the girls and their grandmother could not be avoided forever.

In the meantime, David settled quickly into his new life. Before leaving Auburn, he had quietly applied for the sheriff's position in Deer Lodge, and the timing proved providential. The aging lawman was eager to retire, and his deputy had no desire to shoulder the responsibility alone. The prison building was small but solid, with an office in front and a furnished room behind. For a single man, it was more than sufficient.

David moved in at once. And though none of them dared believe the danger had passed entirely, for the first time in weeks, Joy felt something like the faintest stirring of hope. A new place. New beginnings. And, perhaps, the chance to finally breathe again.

At the Collins home, Aunt Eliza wasted no time in taking Alice under her wing. Their cousin's six children swarmed the weary travelers at once, voices bright with excitement, hands tugging, laughter spilling freely. The house filled with life and sound, a warm tide that swept Alice along with it. For Alice, it was a balm.

She softened beneath the attention, her shoulders easing for the first time in weeks. A faint smile touched her lips as Eliza guided her indoors, the children clinging to her skirts as though she already belonged there, as though she always had.

Joy lingered on the threshold. Watching her aunt and uncle embrace her sister and nieces, seeing the easy affection of cousins and grandchildren filling the house, only sharpened the ache in her chest. The warmth that soothed Alice pierced Joy instead, a reminder of everything she no longer had. Parents. A home that was truly hers. The quiet certainty of belonging without effort. Without a word, she slipped away.

A short distance from the house stood a small horse enclosure. Joy made her way to the fence and rested her arms against the rail, gazing out as the horses trotted and snorted softly in the cool late morning air. Their steady movements, the familiar scent of hay and leather, grounded her, but only barely. She bit down hard on her lip, fighting the sobs that clawed at her throat.

For Alice's sake, she had stood tall. She had swallowed her grief and wrapped it tight, becoming the steady shoulder her sister needed to lean on. She had been strong because someone had to be. But here, alone with the horses, her strength wavered. Tears burned behind her eyes, threatening to spill. Joy knew that if she let them come now, she might not be able to stop. So, she stayed silent, gripping the fence, breathing through the ache, holding herself together by sheer will, even as tears threatened to spill.

Joy nearly jumped out of her skin when someone stepped beside her. She hadn't heard him approach. Instinctively, she closed her eyes and swallowed hard, knowing that if she looked at her uncle now, the fragile hold she had on her emotions would shatter completely.

Gerald must have sensed it, for he didn't speak at once. Instead, he reached for her hand and gently drew her against his chest.

"Joy," he said softly, his voice warm and steady, "let it out. I know you've been carrying it all inside since that terrible day. But you can't keep it locked away forever." He rested his chin lightly against her hair. "Your sister and the little ones are safe now. They're cared for. You don't have to carry this alone anymore."

His words slipped straight through the walls she'd built around her heart. With a broken sob, Joy buried her face in his shirt and wept. Gerald held her without comment, his arms firm and patient, anchoring her as the storm finally broke. He did not hurry her. He did not offer platitudes or try to mend what could not yet be fixed. He simply stayed.

When the worst of it had passed and her sobs faded into quiet, shuddering breaths, Gerald guided her to a bench behind the house, near the pond where the water shimmered in the late morning light. The air was still, the world gently indifferent to grief. He lifted her chin carefully, waiting until she met his gaze.

"You've been trying to stay strong for Alice and the girls, haven't you?"

Joy nodded, her voice barely above a whisper.

"Alice lost her husband. She's a widow with two little girls. And then Ma and Pa..." Her throat tightened. "I knew she needed someone to lean on."

Gerald sighed and drew her close again, his arm firm around her shoulders.

"Just like your pa," he murmured. "Always strong. Always putting everyone else first." He studied her for a moment, then asked quietly, "What happened to the men who attacked you on the road?"

"The army took them," Joy replied. "They've been sent to Sacramento. Pa's attorney wants them tried in court, and the stagecoach company will press charges as well."

Gerald's expression darkened. "David told me you took down two of them yourself. Is that true?"

She nodded. "I couldn't let them hurt Alice and the girls."

He let out a slow, weary breath.

"I wish I'd been there. You should never have had to face that alone."

Joy squeezed his hand. "Cousin Bridget and her children needed you here. Making that journey twice would've been too much. And David, he kept us safe. He wouldn't have let anyone truly harm us." She met his eyes. "We're here, Uncle Gerald. That's what matters."

A sad smile curved his mouth. He brushed her cheek with his roughened fingers.

"You're so much like your pa," he said softly. "He never backed down, no matter what the world threw at him."

Tears welled again, though Joy managed a faint smile. Gerald bent and kissed the top of her head.

"Are you sure it's all right for us to stay with you?" Joy asked hesitantly. "I know the house must already be full, with your daughter and her children here."

Gerald smiled kindly, though regret flickered in his eyes.

"We're glad you're here, Joy, but you're right, it will be a tight squeeze. I've made arrangements for you to stay with close friends of ours. Alice and her girls will have one bedroom, your cousin will share with her daughters, and the boys will sleep in the sitting room. There simply isn't room for everyone under one roof."

Joy's stomach sank. She hadn't even considered how small the farmhouse truly was. Now she would be imposing on strangers as well. Gerald read the thought on her face and squeezed her hand.

"I know it isn't ideal. I wish we could keep you here too. But until I can add another room, it simply isn't possible. I'm sorry."

"It's all right," Joy murmured. "Nothing about our lives is ideal right now." She drew a breath. "You and Aunt Eliza were empty nesters. It wouldn't make sense to expand the house for such a short time. I'll find work, and once I can access Pa's savings, I'll rent a place for Alice and me."

Gerald shook his head firmly.

"Your father left more than enough to care for you both," he said, his tone leaving no room for argument. "And I won't have you living on your own, not when someone has been targeting you. I'm certain your pa wouldn't have wanted that either." He continued gently, "The family you'll stay with are the Harrisons, the wealthiest family in the state. They have ample room."

Joy frowned. "But they won't want a stranger living with them. I don't want to be a burden. We're already imposing on you and Aunt Eliza."

"You are not imposing on anyone," Gerald said quietly, with unmistakable authority. "You and Alice are family, and we love you. And I assure you, you won't be a burden to the Harrisons either. Brigham Harrison himself suggested it. He and his wife, Darlene, were visiting when I received your telegram, and they didn't hesitate for a moment."

Joy shook her head slowly, still overwhelmed, but before she could protest again, Gerald continued.

"You'll meet them this afternoon. Today is the End of Summer Fest, and families from all over will be gathering in town." His voice softened. "I believe Maureen mentioned earlier that her brother and sister-in-law plan to attend and then take her home afterward. If Alice feels up to it, she should come as well. There will be friendly faces. Familiar music. Laughter." He paused. "Sometimes healing begins with being reminded that the world still turns."

Joy felt something loose in her chest, not peace, not yet, but the faintest sense that perhaps, just perhaps, they had reached a place where healing might begin.

Alice had perked up within hours of being reunited with her aunt and cousin. Bridget's children swarmed her girls with gentle attention, quick smiles, soft laughter, and small kindnesses that warmed Joy's heart. For the first time in weeks, Alice laughed, softly, hesitantly, as though she had nearly forgotten how. Color returned to her cheeks, and something long dimmed in her eyes stirred back to life. The sight eased the tight band around Joy's chest. Coming to Deer Lodge had been the right choice.

The End of Summer Fest unfolded in cheerful splendor. Tables overflowed with food, children darted between games, and music drifted through the square. Lanterns would be lit later for the evening dance, and laughter rippled through the crowd like a promise. As mayor, Uncle Gerald welcomed Joy and Alice formally, introducing them to the townsfolk with warmth and pride. Applause followed, kind, sincere, and soon the festival buzzed with easy merriment.

Joy stood with her aunt and Maureen Haven when Gerald returned, accompanied by a well-dressed couple near his own age.

"These are Darlene and Brigham Harrison," he said. Joy offered a polite smile.

"It's a pleasure to meet you, Mr. and Mrs. Harrison."

"Oh, please, Darlene and Brigham," Darlene said at once, beaming. "You'll be living with us. I expect we'll become fast friends."

Joy's smile wavered slightly. "I'm deeply grateful for your kindness, but I promise it won't be for long. I'll make other arrangements as soon as I'm able."

"Nonsense," Darlene waved her off cheerfully. "Unless, of course, you find yourself a fine young man and marry him."

The comment was delivered with such warmth that it eased some of Joy's unease despite herself. Before she could respond, Maureen stepped forward.

"Why don't you and I rent a place together, Joy?" she suggested. "Alice and the girls could live with us."

Joy glanced at her sister and caught the flicker of unease in Alice's eyes. Her reply came without hesitation.

"That won't be happening."

Maureen frowned. "Why not? It would solve everything."

"We already made arrangements," Joy replied evenly. "Our uncle is our legal guardian. Pa wanted us with his brother if anything happened."

"But you aren't even living with them."

"For now," Joy said coolly.

Maureen's mouth tightened. "I think this is ridiculous."

The tension drew curious glances. David Baker began to move closer, but Joy lifted her chin, determined to stand on her own.

"Our plans are settled, Maureen," she said firmly. "You were never meant to move here. If you don't wish to stay with your brother and sister-in-law, then return to Auburn and make arrangements with Matt."

"You have no right to tell me where to live," Maureen snapped. "I *do* have the right to be near my grandbabies."

"Near them, yes," Joy replied, her voice steady and final. "Living with them, no."

Maureen's lip curled. "You're just avoiding Matt. You embarrassed yourself turning him down, and now you're hiding."

"I already told you what happened. I turned him down because I do not have feelings for him," Joy said, her tone controlled, edged with steel. Then she deliberately softened it. "This is neither the time nor the place. We can speak of it later. You are causing a scene."

Maureen laughed harshly, brittle and sharp.

"I'm causing a scene?" Her voice rose, carrying across the square. "You led my son on. You smiled at him, encouraged him, made him believe he had a chance, and then you cast him aside and humiliated him!"

Joy did not raise her voice. She did not step back. Her hands clenched once at her sides, then stilled.

"That is not true," she said clearly. "Matt forced himself on me. He kissed me without my consent. When I tried to pull away, he became more demanding. That is the truth."

A collective gasp rippled through the crowd, followed by murmurs that spread like wind through dry grass. Maureen's composure cracked, her face twisting with fury.

"Lies," she spat. "My son wouldn't hurt a soul. You think you're better than him, don't you? Too good for a decent man because your father wore a judge's robe?" Her voice climbed, shrill now, reckless. "Your father brought this danger on all of us with his arrogance! My café burned because of him! John died because your pa couldn't keep his nose out of other men's business!"

Joy stepped forward, not in anger, but with quiet authority.

"That is enough," she said, her voice ringing clear. "You will not speak of my father that way."

Maureen pressed on. "Your father was no saint. I heard plenty of stories. He beat your mother when you girls weren't around. A drunk, just like—"

The square fell deathly quiet. Joy stepped forward again, her voice unbroken, unwavering.

"Are you certain you're not describing your son, or yourself?" she asked calmly. "My father never touched whiskey. He despised it. He never raised a hand to my mother. He was a good man." Her gaze sharpened. "Your son, however, drank heavily and beat my sister behind closed doors."

"Don't you dare—" Maureen hissed.

"I know the truth now," Joy cut in. "Doc Perkins saw the bruises. If you deny it again, I'll have him testify to it."

Maureen's face twisted. "Your sister lies. John never hurt her. And for the record, I don't drink."

Joy's eyes narrowed. She had noticed the slur, the sway. Calmly, she reached into Maureen's purse and withdrew a small flask, lifting it.

"You carry water in this?"

Maureen lunged, stumbled, and the murmurs grew louder. David stepped forward then, solid and commanding.

"That's quite enough, Maureen," he said. "Judge Collins was a man of integrity. His daughters have endured more loss than any family should." His gaze swept the crowd. "Joy Collins has shown more courage in these past weeks than most men twice her age, and she will be treated with respect."

A murmur of agreement rolled through the square. Heads nodded. Someone whispered an *Amen*. Joy felt the truth settle, not just spoken, but believed.

7

He Stood Before Her

Maureen's face flushed a furious crimson as she drew breath to unleash another torrent of venom at Joy, but before she could speak, an elderly couple stepped forward from the edge of the gathering. Their expressions were grave, etched not with anger, but with embarrassment and long-buried sorrow.

"Sister," the man said sternly. He wore a reverend's collar, and the resemblance between them was unmistakable. "It has been a long time," he continued evenly, "yet you have not changed. Go and wait with Harriet at our buckboard."

Maureen's mouth opened, then closed again. Words failed her. Under her brother's unyielding gaze, whatever fury she had summoned drained away. With stiff movements and her chin lifted in wounded pride, she turned and followed her sister-in-law without protest.

When they were gone, the reverend faced Joy. His posture softened, though regret lingered heavily in his eyes.

"You have my apology," he said quietly. "My sister's behavior is inexcusable. She has been like this for many years... ever since she married her late husband."

Joy blinked, still reeling.

"I didn't know," she said honestly. "How long has she struggled with drink?"

He sighed, the sound weary and weighted with long-held sorrow.

"From the beginning. The man she married was vile. A criminal. She eloped with him at eighteen, despite our pleas." His jaw tightened. "His crimes only came to light later, bank robberies, theft... and eventually murder."

Joy's breath caught painfully.

"He killed five men," the reverend continued. "He was sentenced to death by firing squad."

The square seemed to tilt beneath Joy's feet.

"It was your father," he went on, his voice low and measured, "who presided over his trial. Your father who judged him. And who delivered that sentence."

The world narrowed to a single, stunned breath.

"I don't remember any of this," Joy whispered. "Shouldn't it have been in the papers?"

"It should have," he replied gravely. "But his family was wealthy. Powerful. They paid the newspapers to bury the story." His gaze held hers. "Silence can be purchased, Miss Collins. Justice, less easily."

A chill slid down Joy's spine as the pieces shifted and locked into place. Could this bitterness have festered for decades beneath polite smiles and false friendship? Had resentment been the true foundation of the Haven family's closeness all along? And if so... why had John married Alice at all? The reverend inclined his head. Sympathy etched into every line of his face.

"I am deeply sorry for what your family has endured." Then he turned and followed his wife and sister, leaving Joy standing alone with the weight of the truth. For a long, suspended heartbeat, the square was utterly still, as though the town itself held its breath. Then the murmurs began.

"Judge Collins was a good man."

"I always knew he was fair."

"Miss Collins spoke the truth. You could hear it in her voice."

The whispers grew into quiet affirmations. Neighbors exchanged glances, unease giving way to understanding. One woman stepped forward and clasped Joy's hand.

"I never doubted your father's honor, my dear. He was a well-known and highly respected federal judge, always merciful, always fair," she said softly. "Do not ever doubt his honor. He would never have given you reason to."

Joy blinked hard as tears rushed unexpectedly into her eyes. A rancher removed his hat, holding it respectfully against his chest.

"Your pa gave me a fair hearing once," he said. "Could've ruined me, but he chose mercy. Don't you let poison like hers eat at you. Folks here know better."

Joy's cheeks burned, but not with shame this time. She stood a little straighter, though her hands trembled faintly. For weeks she had carried fear, doubt, and suspicion like a crushing weight. Now, at last, it lifted. The town was not turning against her. It was standing with her.

Alice slipped quietly to her side, baby Ruth nestled in her arms, Annie clutching her skirts.

"Joy," she whispered, tears shining, "Pa would've been so proud of you."

Joy pressed her lips together to keep from breaking. She bent to kiss her niece's head and drew her sister close.

"I only told the truth," she murmured. Yet inside, something steadier took root, fragile, but growing, braided tightly with her grief.

As the festival slowly resumed, people deliberately sought her out, offering condolences, quiet assurances, and promises of support. Maureen's accusations still stung, but they no longer defined the moment. Truth did.

Needing a moment to collect herself, Joy turned quickly, intent on slipping away, when her uncle's voice stopped her.

"Where are you going, Joy?"

She paused, her shoulders tightening.

"I need a little time alone," she murmured, her gaze dropping to the ground. "And... I probably shouldn't stay, not after how this escalated. I never meant to cause such a scene, especially not in front of everyone."

"This was not your doing, my dear," Brigham Harrison said gently as he stepped closer. "Every person here saw exactly what happened. That woman pushed and prodded until it boiled over."

Joy shook her head, still troubled.

"I shouldn't have let her provoke me. I shouldn't have spoken of her family's troubles in front of the whole town."

Brigham's voice grew firmer, though his eyes remained kind.

"She attacked your family's honor and slandered your father. You had every right, no, every duty, to defend him. I believe I speak for most here when I say she earned the consequences of her own words."

Joy glanced around. To her surprise, she found nods of agreement, sympathetic looks, and quiet smiles offered in reassurance. Her uncle drew her into his arms, his voice low and steady.

"Brigham is right," Gerald said softly. "You asked her to stop, more than once. She wanted a spectacle. She meant to ruin your good name. Instead, she laid bare her own."

"And made herself look entirely the fool," Darlene Harrison added, slipping a warm hand into Joy's. "She revealed far more about herself than she ever could about you. Please don't let her drive you away. We all would like the chance to know you better."

Before Joy could reply, two young women approached, curiosity and kindness bright in their faces. Brigham's expression softened as he waved them forward.

"These are our daughters, Olivia and Cathleen. They're close to your age and will help you find your footing here. Our eldest just finished law school and moved to Sacramento. And our second, Graham, should be somewhere about—"

Darlene followed his gaze, then smiled knowingly and tipped her chin toward Alice, who sat among a circle of young mothers while her girls were happily fussed over by other children.

"Your sister seems to have found her place already," Darlene said. "Why don't you let Olivia and Cathleen introduce you around?"

Before Joy could politely protest, Olivia and Cathleen each linked an arm through hers and drew her into the bustle of the festival. They guided her from one group to another, names and faces blurring together, until they reached a long table laden with pies and cakes.

"You must try this," Olivia insisted, pressing a plate into Joy's hands. "Mama makes the best apple pie in all of Montana."

Joy took a bite and could not help the soft sigh that escaped her. The flaky crust and warm, spiced apples melted together perfectly.

"Good, isn't it?" Olivia teased.

"Delicious," Joy admitted, a small smile breaking through. "I see why everyone insists it's the best."

As the sisters filled their own plates, Joy's gaze drifted beyond the table. She stilled, her eyes settling on a tall figure standing apart from the crowd.

"Who is that?" she asked softly. Olivia and Cathleen followed her gaze, identical smirks tugging at their lips.

"That's our brother, Graham," Cathleen said. Joy studied him, unaware she was speaking her thoughts aloud.

"He looks... sad."

The sisters exchanged a glance before Cathleen's tone softened.

"He is. His wife left him a few months ago. Ran off with another man. It came out of nowhere and cut him deeply."

Joy's heart twisted. "That's dreadful," she whispered, her eyes straying back to him. His hat was pulled low, shadowing his face, yet she could still make out the strong line of his jaw, the faint shadow of scruff, the broad set of his shoulders, a man marked by loss, but still solid and composed.

She wondered how anyone could walk away from something so steady. And felt, unexpectedly, a quiet stirring of sympathy take root.

"Yes, and no," Olivia said, shaking her head. "It's awful that she left him. Graham didn't deserve that. He's a fine man, a great catch. But if I'm honest, we aren't heartbroken to see her gone."

Joy turned toward her, brows knitting.

"I don't understand. Aren't you grieving for your brother?"

"Of course we are," Olivia replied softly. "We hurt for him deeply. But he's better off without her." Her voice sharpened with conviction. "She's been spoiled for as long as we've known her. None of us cared for her, but once Graham married her, we endured it for his sake."

Cathleen snorted. "Endured is generous. The way she spoke to Mama was disgraceful. I don't hold my tongue well—"

"No," Olivia cut in dryly, "you never have."

Cathleen grinned unabashedly.

"True. But every time that viper behaved atrociously and I called her on it, she'd burst into tears and run to Graham. She twisted everything, made herself the victim and him the peacemaker. She lived for manipulation."

Joy frowned, her gaze drifting again toward Graham, who still stood apart from the crowd.

"He doesn't strike me as a man easily swayed."

"He isn't," Cathleen said sharply. "Which is precisely why we cannot fathom what possessed him to marry her in the first place. They'd known each other barely three months before she ran off."

"Three months?" Joy echoed, incredulously. "Are they divorcing, then?"

Olivia shrugged. "Your guess is as good as ours. She hasn't decided. Word is she's waiting, seeing whether her new beau commits. If he doesn't, she'll come slinking back here and pretend none of this ever happened."

The bitterness in their voices was unmistakable. Joy recognized it well, the sound of people who had watched cruelty unfold and could do nothing to stop it. It reminded her of sharp-tongued women she'd known in Sacramento, women whose smiles hid barbs and whose tears were weapons. Her heart ached for Graham. From a distance, he appeared solid and self-contained, yet there was a quiet loneliness about him that tugged at her. She lingered a moment longer, then followed Olivia and Cathleen back toward their parents.

Their aunt and uncle were seated with the Harrisons, conversation flowing easily. After a time, Darlene reached out and captured Joy's hand.

"Joy," she said warmly, "this is our son, Graham."

Joy looked up, and her breath caught. His brown eyes met hers, and for an instant the festival faded into a blur of color and sound. He was even more striking up close, broad-shouldered, ruggedly handsome, his presence steady and commanding without a hint of arrogance. The smile he offered was polite and reserved, though it did not quite reach his eyes.

"It's a pleasure to make your acquaintance, Mr. Harrison," Joy said, her voice softer than she intended.

"Graham," he corrected gently. The sound of his voice, deep, even, unhurried, sent an unexpected warmth through her. She nodded, her cheeks warming, and lowered her eyes, suddenly aware of her unsteady breath. Olivia chose that moment to interject with a bright remark, drawing her brother away as he took the seat beside his father.

Joy exhaled slowly, willing her pulse to settle. She told herself it was nothing more than nerves, the residue of grief and exhaustion. Yet her heart, traitorous thing, seemed unwilling to listen.

As dusk settled over the square and lanterns were lit one by one, families began ushering their children home, promising a return for the evening dance. Laughter softened into quieter tones, and the air shifted, expectant and warm. Joy noticed her aunt and Alice gathering Annie and Baby Ruth, preparing to leave. She rose at once to follow, instinct urging her not to linger.

Before she could take more than a step, Brigham's hand closed lightly around her arm, halting her.

"Graham," his father said calmly, as though suggesting the most natural thing in the world, "why don't you ask Joy to dance?"

Joy froze. Heat rushed to her cheeks, and she shook her head quickly, flustered.

"Oh—no, please," she stammered, her hands fluttering uselessly at her sides. "You needn't feel obliged. Truly. It's quite all right if you'd rather not."

The last thing she wanted was to place him in an awkward position, or to stir emotions he might not yet be ready to face. To her surprise, Graham rose at once. This time, the smile he gave her was different. Warmer. Softer. It reached all the way to his eyes, easing something tight inside her chest. He stepped forward and extended his hand, steady and unhurried, offering no pressure, only choice.

"It would be my honor to dance with you, Miss Collins."

Joy hesitated, her heart hammering so loudly she was certain everyone could hear it. She felt the weight of every gaze upon her, Darlene's hopeful smile, Olivia and Cathleen's barely contained excitement, her uncle's quiet nod of encouragement. And Graham stood there, patient and composed, asking nothing more than a single moment. Still, one thought rang loudly in her mind.

He is still married. Her resolve wavered, caught between propriety and the unmistakable sincerity in his eyes. At last, she drew in a steadying breath. She reminded herself that this was only a dance. Nothing promised. Nothing claimed. She allowed herself a small, shy smile and placed her hand in his.

"Thank you," she whispered.

Graham's fingers closed gently around hers, not possessive, not hurried, and together they stepped onto the dance floor as the music swelled around them. Lantern light flickered across the square, casting soft gold over the gathered crowd. Two wounded hearts moved cautiously, respectfully, yet willingly, toward a moment neither had expected. And for the space of a single song, sorrow loosened its grip, giving way to something fragile and quietly hopeful.

Joy felt the weight of every gaze upon her and nearly pulled her hand away, but Graham's grip remained steady, grounding her. The moment they stepped onto the dance floor, he spun her with unexpected ease. She gasped, startled, only to find him grinning when she twirled back into his arms. The sight sent a flutter straight through her chest.

The fiddles struck up a lively country waltz, and Joy quickly realized that Graham was not only a skilled dancer, but thoroughly enjoying himself. He guided her with confident grace, anticipating every step as though they had danced together before. At the end of the set, he lifted her lightly into the air, drawing an involuntary laugh from her, then turned her once more before bowing with old-fashioned gallantry. Breathless, Joy dipped into a curtsy.

Applause rippled through the square. The sound jolted her back to herself. She looked around, startled to find that the other dancers had stepped back, forming a wide circle around them. Everyone had been watching. Graham still smiled as though he might speak, when a sharp disturbance cut through the moment. A couple, roughly her aunt and uncle's age, shoved their way forward, faces flushed with fury.

"What do you think you're doing, Graham Harrison?" the man thundered, stopping mere inches away. "You are a married man. Since when do married men dance with unmarried women who are not their betrothed?"

Gasps swept the crowd. Joy instinctively tried to step back, mortified, but Graham's arm tightened around her shoulders, drawing her protectively against his side.

"I have been unfaithful to no one," he said evenly. His voice was calm, but unyielding. "I danced with a newcomer to our community, a young woman who deserved a warm welcome. That is all." His gaze sharpened. "And let us not forget, your daughter abandoned me for another man. You and your family have no right to cast stones."

Joy looked up at him, her pulse racing. His composure, his refusal to bow beneath false shame, made her breath catch. There was strength in him, quiet and immovable. Gerald and Brigham Harrison stepped forward at once, flanking Graham. Cathleen pushed through the crowd as well, fire blazing in her eyes.

"Lydia is young," the man tried again, his voice strained. "She's still finding herself—"

"She's a spoiled, entitled brat," Cathleen snapped, cutting him off. Her voice cracked like a whip. "Are you seriously excusing your daughter running off with another man by calling it self-discovery? She's twenty-three, only two years younger than Graham. At that age, you know exactly what you're doing." Her hazel eyes flashed. "And Lydia knew exactly what she wanted, to manipulate my brother into marriage, then run the moment it suited her."

The woman shoved forward, her voice shrill.

"How dare you? You've tormented our daughter from the start."

"That's right," Cathleen shot back without hesitation. "Because she deserved it. She's deceitful, selfish, and manipulative, and I don't regret a single word I ever said to her."

"Like the abuse she suffered at your brother's hands?" the father sneered suddenly, venom dripping from every syllable. A collective gasp tore through the crowd, but the shock was not belief. Joy saw it plainly. No one accepted the accusation. Faces hardened. Murmurs rose, sharp and condemning.

"That is enough, Thomas," Gerald barked, his voice booming with authority. The crowd shifted instinctively, tension breaking for a breath. "This is a community gathering, not a public trial. You will not disgrace this town with baseless slander."

"As usual, you side with the Harrisons," Thomas spat. "You've always been thick as thieves with Brigham, so of course you defend his son and his vile daughter."

Before anyone could respond, the woman struck again, her voice climbing higher.

"And perhaps that isn't the only reason." Her gaze slid toward Joy with malicious intent. "Look at his pretty niece." She lunged.

In an instant, Graham pulled Joy fully behind him, his arm a solid barrier. Cathleen stepped forward as well, fierce and unyielding, eyes blazing like a guard dog's. The woman's face twisted with rage.

"You can shield her all you want, Graham, but the truth is plain. She's a temptress, a shameless flirt, desperate for attention. I've watched her all evening. She threw herself at you the moment she arrived. Anyone with eyes can see it!" Her lips curved in cruel satisfaction. "And considering her earlier outburst with her sister's mother-in-law, this isn't the first time she's toyed with a man's affections."

Shame flared hot across Joy's skin. Her throat tightened. But when she dared to glance around, she realized, no one was persuaded. Heads shook. Whispers rippled, sharp and condemning, directed not at her, but at Lydia's parents. Faces turned away from them in open disgust. Joy drew a shaky breath. She had braced herself for humiliation, only to find herself defended by the silent judgment of the crowd and sheltered by the unwavering strength of the man standing in front of her.

⁘

She should have left after the first argument. If Lydia's parents caught even a whisper of hesitation, they would seize upon it and twist it to suit their purposes. Yet to Joy's quiet astonishment, no one seemed inclined to take Lydia's mother seriously now. Faces in the crowd reflected disbelief rather than agreement, irritation rather than curiosity. Several of the younger folk muttered openly under their breath, their disapproval unmistakable. Still, Lydia's mother was not finished.

"I suppose Gerald has no choice but to protect her," she sneered, her voice sharp with spite. "He's simply trying to rescue her poor reputation." Her lips curled cruelly. "Not that it will hide what she truly is. For all we know, her parents never died at all. Perhaps they sent her away for being too friendly with men, perhaps even the mistress of a married one."

A shocked murmur swept through the square, this time edged with outright outrage. Several women gasped. Others stiffened, eyes flashing. Even those who had stood silent before now bristled. The line had been crossed, and everyone knew it.

"That is enough." Gerald's voice cracked through the night like a whip. His patience was gone, replaced by cold authority. The sharpness of his tone made more than one person flinch. "You are far beyond propriety," he continued, his gaze hard and unwavering. "If I ever hear you speak of my niece in such a vile, slanderous manner again, I will not hesitate to take you to court." His eyes swept the gathered crowd. "And I believe it is safe to say we have more than enough witnesses here tonight to see such a case decided swiftly and decisively."

The murmurs swelled again, this time firmly on Gerald's side. Joy stood rooted to the spot, her breath shallow, her heart aching with a mix of shock and humiliation. Each cruel word had struck like a lash. And though she could see, clearly, that the crowd was not fooled, it still hurt to be dragged into such viciousness, to have her character dissected and smeared by rumor and malice.

She had faced grief, fire, and violence with courage. But there was something uniquely wounding about being judged aloud, reduced to insinuation and slander before a crowd. Even wrapped in the protection of those who stood beside her, the sting lingered.

For a moment, she wished desperately for quiet. For the safety of anonymity. For the night to swallow the ugliness whole. And yet, beneath the hurt, something else took root. Resolve. They could speak their poison if they wished. She had learned now that truth did not need shouting to endure. Lies, no matter how loudly spoken, eventually collapsed under their own weight.

Before Lydia's mother could hurl another word of venom, Darlene Harrison stepped forward.

Her face was flushed with righteous fury, her posture so unyielding that Jane Thomas faltered a step back. No one had ever seen mild, gracious Darlene look like this, and the transformation alone was enough to silence the square.

"You are a cruel, heartless woman, Jane Thomas," Darlene snapped, her voice cutting clean as a blade. "And I find it no mystery whatsoever that your daughter turned out exactly as she did. The only temptress this town has ever endured was your spoiled child."

A hush fell.

"Lydia was a practiced flirt," Darlene went on, unrelenting. "A schemer well versed in the art of seduction, not only with my son, but with the man she ran off with. She was never worthy of Graham. Not for a single day."

Jane Thomas's cheeks burned scarlet, her lips trembling with outrage. The shock rippling through the crowd was palpable. No one could recall a single moment when Darlene Harrison had ever raised her voice before, and the weight of her words struck harder for it.

"How dare you—" Jane began.

"Oh, spare me your outrage," Darlene cut in sharply. "I have bitten my tongue long enough. I will not stand by while you lash out at a young woman who has done you no wrong."

Her gaze flicked briefly to Joy, then returned, blazing. "Your daughter is narcissistic, selfish, and deceitful. And you are a gossip who cannot bear to see anyone else shine."

Murmurs rippled outward.

"You attack Joy because she is everything Lydia is not, kind, sincere, and honorable. Your daughter leaves wreckage wherever she goes. And one day, she will face the consequences of that. Frankly, I look forward to it."

The crowd held its breath. Jane Thomas looked ready to shriek, her composure fraying.

"The only reason we allowed Lydia to marry your son," she hissed, "was because he ruined her reputation. She told us how he lured her into his bed and—"

"Enough!" Cathleen Harrison's voice cracked through the square, sharp with fury. She looked ready to launch herself forward, but Graham moved first. He stepped fully in front of Joy, his body a shield, his arm tightening around her waist. His expression was dark, controlled, and utterly merciless.

"I will not allow you to slander me," Graham said evenly. The calm authority in his voice sent a visible shiver through the onlookers. "I never compromised your daughter. Not once. Lydia never even allowed me to kiss her."

Gasps erupted.

"But I was not the only man she deceived," he continued, eyes locked on Jane. "Nor the only one she manipulated with her tale of being accosted and left with child."

Shocked whispers spread instantly. Joy caught sight of several young men nodding grimly, faces tight with recognition.

"That is why I married her," Graham said, his voice hardening. "Because she claimed to be desperate. A week after the wedding, she suddenly informed me she had 'lost' the child."

Darlene, Brigham, and the sisters exchanged stricken glances. This truth was new, even to them.

"That is absurd!" Lydia's father barked.

"Is it?" Graham challenged, coolly. "I have proof. A letter Lydia wrote to a friend, boasting of her deception. She dropped it outside our house. When I confronted her, she resorted to her usual theatrics, but I was finished. Not long after, she ran off with the governor's son. I can only imagine what lies she fed him."

"You threatened her!" Jane shrieked. "She had no choice but to flee!"

Graham scoffed. "Lydia was the one who always wielded threats. She deceived me from beginning to end." His gaze sharpened. "Tell her this: she need not trouble herself about me again. Divorce papers will be sent. And if you are so devoted to her, perhaps you can find her and deliver them."

Jane gasped, but rallied quickly, venom rising once more.

"Admit it," she spat. "You wanted to be rid of her. And now here stands Miss Collins, most conveniently placed. A new distraction. Look at you, clutching her like a prize. She's your next toy, and you can barely hide the hunger in your eyes."

Graham laughed—low, dangerous.

"You think me so weak?" he thundered. "Yes, Joy is beautiful, far more so than Lydia ever was, but beauty is not what draws me to her." His arm tightened protectively. "She has honor. Integrity. Kindness. Qualities your daughter has never possessed."

"Mind your tongue about your wife!" Lydia's father snapped, fists clenching, yet he hesitated. Graham stood taller, broader, and no one doubted who would prevail.

"We'll tell Lydia, and the world, that you couldn't keep your hands to yourself," Jane hissed. "That you openly kissed the mayor's niece."

Graham's lips curved into a slow, dangerous smile.

"Then let us give them something *true* to talk about."

Before Joy could protest, or even draw breath, he pulled her fully into his arms, tipped her chin upward, and kissed her. Not a stolen kiss. Not a careless one. But a bold, deliberate declaration, passionate, unmistakable, and witnessed by the entire town. The square fell into stunned silence as Joy's world narrowed to the strength of his hold, the certainty of his choice, and the undeniable truth that whatever came next... nothing would ever be the same again.

The instant Graham's lips brushed hers, a shock rippled through Joy from head to toe. It was as though her body reacted before her mind could catch up, her breath hitched, her pulse leapt, and a fluttering swarm of butterflies burst to life in her stomach. His hands rose to frame her face, large and warm, his touch unexpectedly gentle. The heat of his palms seeped into her skin, and where his fingertips rested, every nerve seemed to spark awake, humming with awareness.

When his kiss deepened, unhurried, deliberate, her knees weakened. She swayed toward him without meaning to, drawn by the solid reassurance of his hold, by the way he kissed her not with haste or hunger, but with steady intent. For a heartbeat, she wanted nothing more than to give in to that strength, to let herself rest in the safety of his arms and forget the chaos that had brought them here.

The world blurred. The crowd's sharp gasps, Lydia's parents' furious protests, even her uncle's anxious watchfulness faded into distant noise. There was only Graham, his presence firm and unwavering, his mouth on hers as though she were precious, as though she mattered enough to be defended and chosen without hesitation.

And then anger flared. Hot and sudden, it cut through the haze of warmth like a blade. This was not how it was meant to be. This was not hers. The kiss had not been born of quiet affection or mutual consent. It had been wielded, a declaration, a challenge hurled at his enemies. He had taken something that could have been tender, private, and turned it into spectacle. The sting of that realization warred violently with the dizzying sweetness he had awakened inside her.

Her heart thudded painfully against her ribs as she stood suspended between two instincts, one urging her to melt into his embrace, the other demanding she reclaim herself. She would not be anyone's weapon. Not even his.

The young people near them erupted into cheers and applause, laughter and exuberant whoops echoing across the square. A few clapped Graham on the back. Others grinned openly at Joy, delight flashing in their eyes. It was as though the tension had snapped all at once, releasing the crowd to raucous approval.

Lydia's parents, by contrast, stood rigid, faces flushed a furious, mottled crimson, their expressions dark as thunderclouds heavy with rain. Before Joy could gather enough breath, or indignation, to scold Graham for what he had done, he shifted smoothly, stepping squarely between her and the Thomases. One hand settled at her back, not possessive but shielding, guiding her behind the solid breadth of his frame as though instinct had taken over.

"Let me make myself perfectly clear, Mr. and Mrs. Thomas," Graham said. His voice was calm, measured, yet edged with steel, each word carrying across the square with unmistakable authority. "Miss Collins has done absolutely nothing wrong. I asked her to dance. She accepted. At no point did she seek my attention, encourage it, or behave in any manner unbecoming of a respectable young woman. She is new to Deer Lodge, will be living beneath my family's roof, and I find it disgraceful that you would slander her character so publicly." He paused just long enough to meet their glares, unflinching, his jaw set hard.

"And as for your accusations of faithlessness," he continued, his tone sharpening, "you would do well to remember that it was your daughter who abandoned me for another man. She left only after I finally saw through her lies and manipulations."

A low murmur rippled through the onlookers.

"Lydia never wanted a husband," Graham went on, bitterness threading his words. "She wanted a name. A position. My father's money. From the day we wed, she refused to share my room. She refused even the courtesy of a kiss, or holding hands. I was foolish enough to believe time might soften her heart." He gave a short, humorless scoff.

"She desired the privileges of marriage without its bonds, its duties, or its honesty. She wanted security without sacrifice. And I will not allow her failures to be laid at Miss Collins's feet."

The Thomases gasped, outrage splintering across their faces, indignation simmering like a volcano on the brink of eruption. Graham did not wait for it. With a decisive turn, he clasped Joy's hand firmly in his, his grip sure and anchoring, and drew her away from the crowd. Stunned and breathless, she let herself be led, her pulse racing, her thoughts tumbling in wild disarray as the noise of the square faded behind them.

8

A New Place to Breathe

When they were finally out of earshot, Graham slowed, then stopped altogether. He turned to face her, his expression taut with regret.

"I am truly sorry for what I just did," he said quietly. "I should never have let my pride use you as a shield, or a weapon." He exhaled, running a hand through his hair. "I had no right to drag you into that, no matter how cornered I felt. You didn't deserve it."

He hesitated, then added more softly, "And perhaps you didn't even know the full story, though I suspect my sisters shared the worst of it. Either way, you have every right to scold me. To tear into me. I deserve it." With a weary sigh, he dropped onto a fallen tree trunk, shoulders bowed and waited.

Joy stood rooted to the spot, still reeling, from the kiss, from the venom hurled at them, from the way he had stood before the entire town without flinching. She had been prepared to unleash her anger, to give him a sharp, well-earned rebuke. But seeing him like this, deflated, contrite, stripped of bravado, stole the words from her. Slowly, she sat beside him, folding her hands in her lap as she searched for the right balance between honesty and grace.

"I was furious with you," she admitted softly. "And part of me still is. But... I can understand why you did it. Irrational as it was, you were cornered." She glanced at him. "And you finally stood up for yourself." She hesitated, then added gently, "I had no idea Lydia's parents lived here. Or that they would attack you so viciously, in front of everyone."

He let out a breath and scrubbed his hand down his jaw.

"Lydia and I never should have married," he said. "I saw the warning signs even before the vows. But the harder my family pushed back, the more stubborn I became." His mouth tightened. "Foolish pride." His voice dropped. "Yes, I'm still hurt. But not in the way people think. I never truly loved her."

Joy turned fully toward him.

"I hoped," he went on quietly, "that if we built some kind of friendship, love might grow from it. I wanted to believe that doing the right thing, stepping up, would be enough. I was even prepared to raise her child as my own." His eyes darkened.

"But there was no child. It was a lie." His jaw clenched. "When I learned the truth, everything finally made sense. Why she kept me at arm's length. Why she never allowed our marriage to become real. And when the governor passed through town..." His mouth tightened. "She left. Without so much as a farewell."

Joy's chest tightened. "I'm so sorry," she said, and was surprised by the warmth in her own voice.

"I've indulged my self-pity long enough," Graham murmured. "Not because I miss her, but because every time I saw a happy couple, I wondered why them? Why did I try to do the honorable thing and end up alone?" He lifted his gaze to hers. "But I won't do that anymore."

"What brought the change?" Joy asked gently. He held her eyes, steady and unflinching, and something in her chest fluttered.

"You," he said simply. Her breath caught. Heat rushed to her cheeks.

"Me?" she asked. "We've barely spoken. What could I possibly have done?"

"When I saw you tonight," he said, voice low and earnest, "and realized all you've endured these past weeks, loss, danger, grief, and yet there you were. Standing tall. Refusing to be diminished..." He shook his head. "It put my troubles into stark relief. My bitterness felt small by comparison."

She broke eye contact, flustered.

"Don't belittle your pain because it's different from mine," she said quietly. "Suffering isn't a contest. Yours matters too."

He studied her, for a long moment.

"What I felt wasn't heartache," he said finally. "It was humiliation." His hand closed gently over hers, warm, steady, grounding. She drew a breath to answer, but footsteps approached. Cathleen came striding toward them, mischief dancing in her eyes.

"Mom and Dad are ready to head home."

Graham rose at once, brushing dirt from his trousers before going to retrieve his horse. Joy stood as well, smoothing her skirts, her thoughts still tangled. She caught Cathleen's knowing smirk and narrowed her eyes.

"What?" Joy asked.

"I think you arrived at exactly the right moment," Cathleen said lightly. "I haven't seen my brother look that unburdened in months. And I'm proud of him, for finally standing up to the Thomases and exposing Lydia for what she is."

Joy frowned. "But why attack him so viciously? Even if dancing was improper, that sort of cruelty was uncalled for."

"There was nothing improper about him dancing with you," Cathleen said firmly. "The Thomases believe they're untouchable. Dr. Thomas is the only physician in town, and Lydia is their spoiled only child. To them, she can do no wrong." She rolled her eyes.

"Truth is, they tolerated Graham only because he's wealthy. If my eldest brother were here, now a lawyer in Sacramento, I daresay Lydia would've fluttered her lashes at him instead."

Joy wrinkled her nose. "So, Dr. Thomas truly is the only doctor?"

"Yes," Cathleen replied. "Your uncle tried to bring others in, but Dr. Thomas bullied every last one into leaving."

Joy tilted her head thoughtfully.

"Then perhaps Uncle Gerald should hire a female doctor," she said. "A man like Dr. Thomas would never consider her a real threat."

Cathleen blinked, then grinned.

"That's... brilliant. You don't happen to know one, do you?"

"As a matter of fact, I do," Joy said, her eyes brightening. "Back in Sacramento, my parents were close friends with a physician named Dr. Marvin Preston. His daughter, Julia, studied medicine. By now she should be fully trained."

"But wouldn't she work alongside her father?" Cathleen asked.

Joy shook her head. "He has two sons who'll inherit the practice. Julia always wanted something of her own. She was raised never to shrink herself to spare a man's pride."

Cathleen laughed softly. "She sounds perfect."

"She is," Joy said with a small, conspiratorial smile. "And exactly the sort of woman who would terrify Dr. Thomas."

Minutes later, Joy spoke with her uncle in private. Gerald listened intently, his brows knitting as she laid out her concerns, Dr. Thomas's stranglehold on the town, his bullying of rival physicians, and the damage his influence had already inflicted. When she finished, he leaned back in his chair and exhaled slowly.

"You may have just given us the answer we've been praying for," he said at last. "Deer Lodge has suffered under that man's authority for far too long. If we are to grow as a town, we cannot remain hostage to a single physician and his overbearing wife."

Joy nodded. "Julia Preston won't be intimidated. She was raised by a man who taught her to stand her ground, no matter who tried to silence her."

Gerald's mouth curved into a thoughtful smile.

"Then let's give her the chance."

Joy wasted no time. That very night, she penned a careful but heartfelt letter, explaining the situation in Deer Lodge and the opportunity before her. Days later, a telegram arrived in reply, and Joy nearly laughed aloud as she read it.

Julia was eager, no, delighted. Almost gleeful at the prospect. She wrote that she had long wanted to establish her own practice somewhere she could truly make a difference, free from the shadow of her father and brothers. Deer Lodge, with its needs and its challenges, sounded exactly like the sort of place she had been waiting for. Better still, Dr. Preston would accompany her for the first week, lending his name, experience, and formidable reputation to ensure her smooth arrival.

With Dr. Preston's standing and powerful connections, even the Thomases would think twice before attempting their usual intimidation. Joy folded the telegram carefully, a quiet sense of triumph settling in her chest. For the first time in weeks, she felt she had not only survived the storm but struck back in a meaningful way. Justice, she had learned from her father, did not always arrive with a gavel. Sometimes, it came in the form of opportunity, and the courage to seize it.

Joy settled into life in Deer Lodge more quickly than she had ever dared hope. The Harrisons welcomed her as though she had always belonged among them. Darlene fussed over her with affectionate concern, pressing extra food on her plate and insisting she rest whenever Joy looked even the slightest bit tired. Cathleen and Olivia swept her into their daily escapades without ceremony, treating her less like a guest and more like a sister who had simply been away too long. Brigham offered easy, fatherly teasing, his quiet approval evident in the way he watched over her without hovering.

For the first time since the fires, Joy felt something close to safety. Real safety, not the brittle kind born of vigilance and fear, but the warmth of knowing she was surrounded by people who would not let harm reach her without standing in its way.

Even Alice began to change. The constant hum of children's laughter, shared meals, and simple routines softened her grief. She still mourned, still had moments when sorrow overtook her, but she smiled more often now, small, tentative smiles at first, then steadier ones. Joy caught her sister laughing with the children one afternoon, and the sound nearly brought her to tears. Life, slowly and stubbornly, was pressing forward.

One morning, as sunlight streamed through the windows of the Harrison house, Olivia stepped into the parlor, shaking her head in disbelief.

"Ma, Joy is at it again," she announced, amusement dancing in her voice. "She's hauling water for the laundry."

Darlene sighed, pressing her fingers to her temple.

"That girl," she muttered fondly. "I swear she doesn't know how to sit still." She rose at once, already resolved. "I'll have to remind her, again, that we hire help for that sort of thing." Yet even as she spoke, there was a smile tugging at her lips, born not of irritation but of affection. Joy Collins, with her tireless hands and refusal to be idle, was weaving herself into the fabric of their household—thread by determined thread.

Joy trudged across the yard with yet another brimming bucket, her full attention fixed on keeping every precious drop inside. She was so focused, jaw set, shoulders squared, that she nearly leapt clean out of her boots when a deep, amused voice drifted toward her.

"Why is it so hard for you to ask for help?"

She whirled around, clutching the handle tighter. Water sloshed dangerously close to the rim.

"Graham!" Her heart thudded. "You scared me."

"That," he said lazily, pushing away from the fence post he'd been leaning against, "wasn't an answer."

Late-afternoon sunlight cut across him at just the right angle, gilding his broad shoulders and catching the faint dust on his sleeves. His arms folded across his chest as his gaze flicked pointedly to the bucket straining her arms. Joy's stomach made an entirely unhelpful little flip.

"Those things aren't made for a lady to carry."

"You don't say," she shot back, arching a brow. "I assumed you were too busy admiring your fences to notice."

One corner of his mouth twitched. He crossed the distance with an easy, confident stride that made her acutely aware of how close he suddenly was.

"There are plenty of men on this ranch," he said mildly. "Why not let one of us take the burden?"

Joy lifted her chin, stubbornness flaring.

"Because I can manage just fine."

Fate, clearly amused by her defiance, chose that moment to intervene. Her toe caught on a stone. The bucket tipped. Water surged forward, sloshing straight onto Graham's boots and trousers. A horrified gasp burst from her, followed immediately by peals of laughter from the corral. Several cowboys doubled over, one clutching his side as he wheezed. Joy stared at the spreading wetness, mortification warring with a traitorous spark of mischief.

"I'm so sorry," she said quickly, then couldn't help the sweetness that crept into her voice. "I suppose you're right. It really *is* far too heavy for a little lady like me." Her lashes lifted. Her eyes danced.

Graham looked down at himself. Then back at her. Slowly, very slowly, a grin spread across his face. The sort that made Joy's instincts scream *run*.

She dipped a quick curtsy. "If you'll excuse me," she said lightly, and bolted. She made it three steps. A strong arm hooked around her waist, lifting her clean off the ground with humiliating ease.

"Graham!" she squealed as he slung her over his shoulder, her protests punctuated by his low, utterly infuriating laughter.

"Oh, don't worry," he said cheerfully as he strode toward the trough. "I'll help you."

"Put me down this instant!"

"I *am* helping." He tipped her straight into the cold water of the trough.

Joy surfaced with a sputtering gasp, hair plastered to her cheeks, gown clinging scandalously to every curve. The cowboys howled, some even applauded, as though they'd just witnessed a performance. Her cheeks burned, partly with embarrassment... partly with something far more dangerous. Graham leaned against the trough, arms crossed once more, utterly unrepentant. She scooped up water and flung it at him.

"So, this is how you treat women who carry buckets heavy with water?"

"Not for carrying it," he said, and there it was. The laughter drained from his voice, replaced by something lower. Warmer. Before she could react, he caught her wrists and hauled her out of the trough as though she weighed nothing at all. Instead of setting her down, he kept her pressed against his chest, water dripping from both of them.

Joy's breath hitched. His shirt was damp beneath her palms. She could feel his heartbeat, steady, strong, under her hands. His face hovered inches from hers, eyes darkened, unreadable.

"It wasn't the bucket," he murmured, his gaze dipping briefly to her lips before returning to her eyes. "It was the sass that came with it."

"Sass?" she whispered, her lips betraying her by parting. "Whatever do you mean?"

His thumb brushed a wet strand of hair from her cheek, lingering far longer than necessary. The playful grin softened into something far more dangerous. For one breathless moment, the world narrowed to the space between them. His mouth lowered. Her lashes fluttered shut, her heart pounding so hard she was certain he could feel it. Then, he stopped. His breath ghosted warm against her cheek. With a low chuckle that sounded suspiciously like restraint, he tapped her nose.

"Exactly."

Joy's eyes flew open, relief and sharp disappointment tangling painfully in her chest. Graham finally set her on her feet, but his hand slid slowly from her arm, leaving her skin tingling long after he stepped back.

"My word, Joy, what on earth happened to you?" Darlene gasped the instant Joy stepped into the house, water dripping from her skirts and her hair plastered damply to her cheeks. Graham followed close behind her, looking entirely too pleased with himself, like a boy who had just gotten away with mischief and intended to savor every second of it.

"Your son decided I needed a bath," Joy said dryly, not even bothering to turn around as she shot Graham a withering look over her shoulder. Darlene's eyes widened, then narrowed sharply as she rounded on her son.

"Graham Harrison! You should be ashamed of yourself. The evenings are already turning cool, and fall is nearly upon us. She could catch her death of a chill!"

Graham merely shrugged, utterly unrepentant.

"It was necessary, Mother. Someone had to teach this young lady a lesson. Her sass was getting out of hand."

Darlene planted her hands on her hips, arching a brow in pure disbelief.

"I don't believe that for a moment. Joy Collins is the sweetest, most polite young woman I have ever met. *Sass?* Honestly, Graham, you are making excuses."

Joy pressed her lips together to keep from laughing. The fierce indignation in Darlene's defense warmed her more effectively than any fire ever could. For a fleeting second, she almost forgot she was soaked through and standing in a growing puddle on the floor. As Darlene bustled off to fetch towels, muttering under her breath about boys with more muscle than sense, Joy couldn't resist. She turned just enough to stick her tongue out at Graham in triumph, her blue eyes sparkling with mischief.

His grin widened instantly, that devil-may-care gleam in his gaze sending an unexpected heat skittering up her spine despite the chill clinging to her wet gown. He leaned casually against the doorframe, arms crossed, clearly enjoying her fluster far too much. Joy huffed and swept past him toward the hallway.

"Excuse me while I change into something dry," she called over her shoulder, "before your son's *lessons* give me pneumonia."

A low, rich chuckle followed her, warm, amused, and far too pleased with himself, as she disappeared down the hall, heart thudding and lips betraying her with a reluctant smile.

"Joy," Darlene said gently but firmly, catching her arm before she could reach for yet another task, "please remember that you are part of this family. You don't need to keep finding chores for yourself."

Joy paused, her shoulders stiffening as guilt flickered across her face.

"We've hired a few young ladies from town," Darlene continued, her tone calm but resolute. "It gives them a chance to earn extra money, and many of the farming families around here struggle more than they let on. Their daughters, and sometimes even their wives, are grateful for the work. Besides, our housekeeper will be returning soon as well."

Joy lowered her gaze, twisting her fingers together.

"I'm sorry," she said quietly. "I truly am. I just... I feel guilty living here without paying for anything and not at least helping somehow." Her voice wavered. "I've never liked being idle, and I don't wish to be a burden."

Darlene's expression softened completely. She stepped closer and took Joy's hands in her own, warm and steady.

"You are not idle," she said with quiet certainty. "And you are most certainly not a burden. You became our daughter the moment we met you, Joy." Her thumbs brushed reassuring circles over Joy's knuckles. "Family doesn't keep accounts, and it doesn't demand repayment. That is not how love works. So don't you trouble yourself with such thoughts."

Joy opened her mouth, ready to protest again, but the words never came. Raised voices erupted outside. A sharp shout carried through the open windows, followed by someone calling her name, loud and unmistakable.

"Joy Collins! Come out here!"

Joy stiffened instantly. Her heart lurched as Cathleen's voice rang out from the front porch, sharp with unmistakable irritation as she argued with someone just beyond sight. Alarm flared. Joy and Darlene exchanged a single look, concern mirrored in both their eyes, before moving in unison toward the door. Skirts gathered in their hands, they stepped quickly onto the porch, bracing themselves to see what fresh disturbance had found its way to their doorstep.

"Joy Collins!" Doctor Thomas shouted again, striding toward her with open hostility. He stopped short only when Graham and his father stepped into view, flanking Joy without a word. Several ranch hands drifted closer as well, hands resting at their belts, not threatening outright, but ready. The air tightened, sharp as a drawn wire. Doctor Thomas's glare never left Joy.

"You suggested to your uncle that he hire another physician?"

Joy straightened, lifting her chin.

"I did. My father always said a little competition is healthy, even in a small town."

His face darkened to a furious red.

"So that's it. You're here to ruin Deer Lodge."

Joy gave a humorless huff.

"You believe one additional doctor can destroy an entire town?" Her eyes sharpened. "Or are you afraid you might lose a few patients?"

"Of course not," he snapped. "I have full confidence in my medical knowledge and abilities."

"Then why do you care?" she asked evenly. His lip curled.

"Because you did this deliberately, to destroy me. To chase me out. But it won't work." His voice dropped, thick with contempt. "You're a vile, selfish woman. My wife was right about you. You're only here because your reputation with men was so ruined that your parents had no choice but to send you away."

The words struck deep, sharp enough to steal Joy's breath for a moment. Pain flickered across her face, but she did not look away.

"I'm here," she said quietly, her voice steady despite the tears glistening in her eyes, "because I lost everything except my sister. My parents are dead. My home was burned to the ground. I was hunted on the road like an animal." Her gaze held his, without flinching. "I found safety here. I found kindness. Someone like you may not understand that, but I will not be shamed for surviving."

Graham's hand closed around hers, firm and grounding. Doctor Thomas sneered.

"Yes, I understand perfectly. You're using your tragedy to lure married men into your bed."

"That is enough!" Brigham Harrison's roar cut through the air like a gunshot. He surged forward, grabbing Thomas by the front of his coat and shoving him back hard enough that he staggered.

"You will not speak to Joy that way," Brigham thundered. "I know it's difficult for the likes of you to comprehend that not all women behave like your daughter, running off with the next wealthy man who catches her eye, but that does not give you license to spew such filth." His grip tightened. "Remember what Gerald told your wife. Keep spreading lies, and you will answer for them in court."

Graham stepped forward then, his expression carved from stone.

"Your quarrel is with me, Thomas, not with Joy," he said coldly. "Lydia should have had the decency to request a divorce before vanishing. Instead, she disappeared without a word.

And you've refused to tell me where she is, making it impossible to send the papers."

Thomas's eyes glittered with malice.

"I'll make sure she knows you've been unfaithful. I'll see to it she makes your life a living hell."

"She already did that," Cathleen cut in sharply, stepping forward, eyes blazing. "For months, while living under our roof. Your manipulative witch of a daughter disrupted our family enough with her lies. I, for one, am grateful she's gone."

For a heartbeat, it looked as though Doctor Thomas might spit back another insult. But the mood had shifted. Ranch hands stood rigid. Graham's stare was lethal. Brigham hadn't released his hold entirely. Doctor Thomas seemed to sense, at last, that he was badly outnumbered. With a stiff jerk, he pulled free, swung up onto his horse, and rode off without another word, his retreat swift, angry, and unmistakably defeated.

Joy let out a slow breath she hadn't realized she'd been holding. Graham squeezed her hand once more. A silent promise etched into the simple gesture.

9

A New Place to Breathe

Joy slipped away the moment the crowd's attention followed the physician's retreating figure. Her chest felt too tight to breathe, her heart aching with a hollow, unbearable longing. All she wanted, more than words could hold, was her father's arms around her, his steady strength, his quiet assurance that truth would always win out in the end. But he was gone, and the knowledge cut deeper than any insult ever could.

She ran. Down the path, past the barn, into the stables. Her hands shook as she saddled her horse, movements quick and practiced, as though muscle memory alone could keep her upright. Moments later, she was riding hard, wind tearing at her skirts, branches blurring past as she fled into the forest.

She didn't slow until the trees opened onto a vast, glassy lake, its surface catching the late sunlight like scattered gold. There, at last, the strength she'd been clinging to, gave way. Joy slid from the saddle, dropped to her knees near the water's edge, and broke apart. Great, wrenching sobs tore from her chest. She pressed her hands to her face, shoulders shaking, grief and humiliation tangling together until she could no longer tell where one ended and the other began.

Everyone in Deer Lodge was kind, so welcoming, so ready to accept her. Everyone except Doctor Thomas and his wife. Why her? Why attack her virtue so viciously when all she had done was dance? Why try to blacken her name when it was his own daughter who had abandoned her marriage for another man with money and influence? The injustice of it burned.

She was wiping at her cheeks when the soft crunch of hooves reached her ears. Joy stiffened, hastily swiping away the last of her tears before turning. Graham. He swung down from his horse and crossed the distance in long strides. Worry etched deep into his face. Without hesitation, he wrapped his arms around her, pulling her into his chest as though that was where she belonged.

"I'm so sorry," he murmured into her hair. "I'm so sorry Lydia's father keeps treating you that way. He has no right, none, to speak to you like that." His hold tightened briefly, protective, fierce. "And I should never have kissed you in front of him. I gave him more ammunition."

Joy drew a shaky breath and stepped back, though she didn't entirely leave his reach.

"He decided what kind of woman I was long before that," she said quietly. "All it took was watching me dance with you... and listening to my sister's mother-in-law." She shook her head, bitterness threading her voice. "It wouldn't have mattered what happened afterward. It won't matter what we say or do from here on out. He'll twist it however he wants. I wouldn't even be surprised if he blames me for Lydia running away next.

Somehow, I'll become the villain who destroyed his precious daughter's marriage."

Graham's jaw tightened. "I won't let that happen."

She gave a faint, tired smile. "You can't stop someone who's determined to hate."

He shook his head firmly. "Maybe not. But you don't need to worry about what the rest of the town thinks. No one here believes him. No one likes him or his wife, Joy. They've made enemies wherever they go."

She studied his face, then tilted her head.

"Have they lived here long?"

"No," he replied. "Only about two years. I believe they came from California, Sacramento or San Francisco."

Joy's brow furrowed, her thoughts turning inward.

"That's interesting." She looked out over the lake, its calm surface, a stark contrast to the turmoil in her chest. "I wonder if Julia Preston, or at least her father, knows Doctor Thomas. We met so many physicians when we lived in Sacramento. Pa seemed to collect friends everywhere he went." Her lips pressed together. "But I don't remember a doctor by that name."

Graham watched her closely, something thoughtful stirring behind his eyes.

"Then perhaps this isn't the first place he's left under a cloud."

Joy said nothing, but the idea settled deep, heavy and unsettling. She wrapped her arms around herself as the breeze rippled the water. Graham stepped closer again, not touching this time, but near enough that his presence steadied her. And for the first time, Joy felt the trembling inside her begin to ease, just a little.

Alice blossomed under the gentle, attentive care of her aunt and cousin. The grief for her parents had not vanished, nor had the ache left by John's death, but distance from the places where tragedy had struck gave her room to breathe again. Here, the memories did not press in from every corner. Slowly, color returned to her cheeks, and laughter, soft and tentative at first, found its way back into her voice. Seeing that change lifted a weight Joy had been carrying since the fires, easing the constant fear that everything depended on her strength alone.

Maureen visited only when her brother traveled to Deer Lodge, and he made certain to remain close at hand during every one of those visits. His presence alone was enough to keep Maureen on her best behavior, and for that, Joy was profoundly grateful. Alice deserved peace, not sharp words or thinly veiled accusations.

As for Joy, no amount of well-meant instruction could persuade her to sit idle in the Harrison household. Though Darlene repeatedly reminded her that chores were unnecessary, Joy insisted on tending to her own laundry and, when no one was watching, quietly took on a handful of other tasks, straightening, sweeping, mending small things that had been overlooked. Most often, however, she found herself in the stables.

There, among the familiar scents of hay and leather, she felt most at ease. She cleaned her horse's box with care, brushed and checked tack, and before long was doing the same for several of the other animals as well. The steady rhythm of the work soothed her, grounding her in a way nothing else could. She was deeply thankful she had been able to bring her own horse on the journey to Montana. The animal was more than a means of travel. It was a constant, wordless comfort in a season where so much had been lost.

Joy swung down from her horse and handed the reins to a waiting stable boy before turning toward the bank. The late-morning sun glinted off the tall windows, bright and celebratory, and for once the sight did not tighten her chest. Her uncle was already there, waiting on the steps. When he saw her, his face broke into a warm, unmistakably proud smile.

"Happy birthday, Joy." He drew her into his arms and hugged her with quiet affection, the kind that spoke of family, constancy, and unspoken reassurance. Joy laughed softly and returned the embrace.

"Thank you, Uncle Gerald."

She was just about to add something, perhaps a teasing remark about how quickly he'd said it, when a familiar, solid presence stepped in beside them.

"Happy birthday, kid," David Baker said, and before she could protest, he pulled her into a firm, one-armed hug that lifted her briefly off her feet. Joy laughed again, the sound genuine. It never failed to comfort her how natural it felt to be gathered into his embrace, as though no matter how much her world had changed, this piece of it remained steady and unmovable.

Her uncle cleared his throat, drawing their attention back. His expression shifted to something more formal, though pride still shone in his eyes.

"You are now of age, Joy," he said. "And with that comes full legal access to your parents' accounts and holdings." The weight of his words settled over her, not excitement alone, but responsibility. Joy straightened instinctively, recognizing the moment for what it was: a threshold crossed. Gerald gestured subtly over her shoulder.

"There are a few people who wished to meet you today."

Joy turned. A well-dressed gentleman stepped forward first, his manner polished and professional, a leather portfolio tucked beneath one arm. Beside him stood a handsome young man, neatly groomed and self-assured, and just behind them another gentleman, slightly younger, his expression keen with curiosity.

Joy's brows lifted a fraction as she took them in, instinctively sensing that this birthday would bring more than congratulations. It would bring answers. Decisions. And perhaps the first true step into the life, she would now have to build on her own.

"Mr. Andrews," Joy breathed when recognition struck, her hand lifting instinctively to her chest. He answered her surprise with a warm, familiar smile, the same one she remembered from her childhood.

"I suppose I should remind myself that you're a young lady now," he said lightly, his eyes twinkling, "but there was a time when I scooped you up and hugged you without a second thought whenever you and your parents came into my office." He tilted his head, amusement softening his expression. "Will you still allow an old friend that privilege? And please, call me Jonas from now on."

A faint blush crept into Joy's cheeks, touched with fond embarrassment, but she nodded all the same.

"Of course," she said, then added with a sheepish sparkle in her eyes, "as long as you promise not to scoop me up."

Laughter erupted softly around them and Jonas stepped forward and drew her into a firm, reassuring embrace, steady and familiar, carrying with it echoes of safety and continuity she hadn't realized she'd been craving. When he finally pulled back, she met his gaze and saw the levity fade. His smile softened, his eyes clouding with unmistakable grief, as though the memories they shared carried both warmth and loss in equal measure.

"I am truly sorry about your parents, Joy," he said quietly. "Your pa and I were close friends for many years. Losing him, losing both your parents, has been a hard blow."

Her throat tightened. "Thank you," she whispered, blinking rapidly. "I just... I hope we'll find out who was behind it all. Some kind of closure." She hesitated, then asked, "Have you been able to learn anything?"

Jonas released a slow breath. "Not as much as I'd like. There are questions, certainly, but answers are still elusive." He shifted, straightening slightly. "Before we speak of that, though, I should introduce you properly." He gestured to the gentleman beside him. "This is my business partner, Charles Gregory."

Charles stepped forward, impeccably dressed, his posture composed and reserved. He took Joy's hand in a firm, efficient shake.

"Miss Collins. It's a pleasure." His tone was courteous, but his expression remained neutral, professional to the core, as though he wished to draw a clear boundary from the start. Jonas then nodded toward the young man standing just behind him.

"And this is Dylan Andrews, my nephew. He's also the investigator assisting me."

Dylan inclined his head politely, a quick, genuine smile touching his lips.

"It's a pleasure to make your acquaintance, Miss Collins."

Joy returned the greeting, taking them both in. She sensed immediately the difference between the two men, Charles all precision and distance, Dylan attentive and quietly curious, but she kept her thoughts to herself.

"Shall we go inside?" Jonas asked gently. When everyone agreed, he led them into the small bank and through to a private room at the back. As the door closed behind them, Joy felt a shift in the air. Whatever awaited her now, answers, responsibilities, truths long buried, this was the moment they would begin to unfold.

10

Sweetheart Dance

After everyone had settled into their chairs, Jonas cleared his throat and folded his hands atop the desk. His tone shifted from friendly to measured, professional, grave.

"Dylan conducted a thorough investigation into the murders of your parents," he began, meeting Joy's eyes steadily. "The same applies to the arson at your brother-in-law's home and the ambush on the road to Deer Lodge. The couple responsible for setting the fires and attacking you are still in custody. They have confessed to being hired."

Joy's spine stiffened. "By whom?"

"By a man named Troy Haven."

Her breath caught. "John's father? But... I thought he was executed years ago."

"He was," Jonas said slowly, studying her reaction. "How did you come to know that?"

"I spoke with Maureen Haven's brother at the festival," Joy replied. "He told me about Troy, about his crimes, and that my father sentenced him."

Jonas nodded once. "That aligns with what we uncovered."

"But it doesn't make sense," Joy pressed, her brow furrowing. "Why would he hire killers after he was already dead? And why would he want his own son murdered? John died in the fire too."

Before Jonas could respond, Charles Gregory cleared his throat and leaned forward slightly. His voice was calm, clipped, analytical.

"That is precisely the inconsistency we are investigating. The note Dylan recovered, written instructions given to the hired arsonists, was penned recently. The ink, the paper, the phrasing all indicate it was not written years ago. Which means someone likely impersonated Troy Haven."

Joy's thoughts leapt instantly to one name. *Matt.* The realization struck hard enough to make her chest ache. She pushed the thought aside, resisting it even as it surfaced. Apart from what had happened at the army camp, she had always liked Matt. Trusted him. The idea that he might be capable of orchestrating such horror made her stomach twist, but justice mattered more than comfort. She drew a steadying breath.

"There's something you should know," she said quietly. She relayed everything, Alice's confession about John's abuse, Matt's fractured relationship with his father, and her own uneasy suspicions.

"Is there a chance," she asked finally, her voice steady despite the knot in her chest, "that Matt Haven is involved?"

Dylan and Charles exchanged a glance before both shook their heads.

"Highly unlikely," Dylan said. "From what we discovered, Matt had a deeply fractured relationship with his father. We spoke with former neighbors, extended family, and acquaintances in Sacramento. Every account was the same, Troy Haven terrorized Maureen for years, and Matt intervened whenever he could."

Charles nodded. "Multiple witnesses described Matt as protective, especially toward women and children. He despised his father."

Joy swallowed. "And John?"

Dylan's expression hardened. "Unfortunately, everything we learned about John suggests he followed in his father's footsteps. Controlling. Volatile. If what you and your sister reported is true, then yes, John perpetuated the same cycle of abuse."

Joy exhaled slowly, the truth settled like a weight.

"So, as it stands, our only confirmed suspects are the imprisoned couple... and a man who's been dead for years."

Dylan and Charles nodded in unison.

"Correct."

But Jonas did not. "I disagree," he said sharply. Both men turned toward him. "I don't believe we should rule Matt Haven out so quickly," Jonas continued, his jaw tightening. "Hatred for his father does not automatically make him incapable of using his name."

Charles scoffed. "Jonas, that's a stretch. The people of Auburn spoke highly of Matt. He had an excellent relationship with Joy's parents."

"That proves nothing," Jonas shot back. "A man can smile to one face and strike from the shadows. Pretending costs little."

Joy stiffened, unease tightening her chest.

"I'm telling you," Charles said firmly, "Matt Haven is not our culprit. By all accounts, he was respected, trusted, and deeply shaken by the fires."

"And yet," Jonas countered, eyes narrowing, "he behaved inappropriately toward Joy. He ignored her refusal. That speaks to character."

Charles leaned back, unimpressed.

"Or it speaks to grief, wounded pride, and poor judgment. His father was a monster. His brother died. He was rejected. That does not make him a murderer."

"You're excusing his behavior?" Jonas snapped.

"I'm contextualizing it," Charles replied coolly. "A man's moment of weakness does not transform him into a criminal mastermind."

Joy had followed the exchange with wide, attentive eyes. Something about it all felt... off. Though she was relieved to hear that Matt appeared, by every account, to be a decent man, she could not shake the unease coiled tight in her chest. The evidence leaned in his favor, yes, but her instincts refused to dismiss him entirely. Not yet. Instinct had saved her life more than once already, and she had learned not to ignore it.

And then there was Charles Gregory. Her gaze drifted to him, studying the rigid line of his shoulders, the cool detachment in his expression. Why was he arguing so forcefully with Jonas? They were partners, were they not? Meant to present a united front? The friction between them felt sharper than a simple difference of opinion. It carried an edge, almost personal. And why had Jonas taken on a business partner at all?

Joy searched her memory and found nothing. Her father had spoken often of Jonas Andrews over the years, with affection and respect, but never once had he mentioned Charles Gregory. Not in passing. Not as a colleague. Not even as an acquaintance.

An unsettling thought crept in, unbidden and unwelcome. Had Charles inserted himself into Jonas's firm after the murders? Had he maneuvered his way close under the guise of professional interest, or worse, had he always been there, hidden just out of view, pulling threads she could not yet, see?

Joy forced her expression to remain calm, even as suspicion prickled along her spine. She knew better than to accuse without proof. Reckless words could destroy reputations just as surely as fire destroyed homes, and she refused to become like the people who had torn her family apart.

Her gaze flicked to her uncle. Gerald had remained uncharacteristically silent throughout the discussion, his expression thoughtful, guarded. That, too, did not escape her notice.

He's weighing something, she realized. *And he isn't ready to say it aloud.* Perhaps later, when they were alone, she would ask him what he made of it all. Gerald was observant. Cautious. He would have felt the same dissonance, noticed the same fractures beneath the polished surface.

Joy drew a quiet, steadying breath. She might not yet know where the truth lay, but she was certain of one thing: she would not be blind again. Not to men. Not to motives. And not to convenient explanations. For now, she would listen. She would watch. And she would remember everything. Because somewhere within the fault lines of that conversation, the truth was hiding, and Joy intended to find it.

"Let us return to the matter at hand," Charles said abruptly, his tone crisp, his expression locking once more behind that cool, professional mask. "As far as the couple is concerned, they will be tried on the evidence already gathered."

Joy drew a steady breath. "Will I be required to identify the woman in court?"

Dylan shook his head. "No. She was positively identified by Matt Haven and Doctor Perkins. Your testimony won't be necessary in that regard."

Joy's brow furrowed. "If Matt identified her," she pressed carefully, "did either he or the couple behave in a way that suggested they knew one another? Anything at all out of the ordinary?"

Dylan and Charles exchanged a brief, startled glance. Joy scrunched her nose.

"What?"

Charles studied her for a moment, something like respect flickering in his eyes.

"We're impressed," he said frankly. "You're asking precisely the right questions. Not many young ladies, or men, for that matter, would think to examine motive and familiarity so quickly. You reason much like an attorney."

Heat rushed to her cheeks, and she lowered her gaze.

"I suppose that makes sense," she murmured. "I *am* my father's daughter."

A soft chuckle sounded. Joy looked up, surprised to see it had come from Charles. His rigid composure had eased, his mouth curved in genuine amusement.

"So," Joy asked, seizing the moment, "what happens now?"

Jonas answered, his voice grave. "We continue investigating. Until the couple is willing to talk, or make a mistake, there is only so much we can do. In the meantime, we'll inform David Baker and the Deer Lodge deputy that they must keep a close watch on you and your sister. Too many people know you survived both the fires and the stagecoach attack. Until we know exactly who is behind this, caution is essential."

The blood drained from Joy's face.

"You mean... even with Troy Haven dead and the couple imprisoned, you believe we're still in danger? That another fire, another attack, is possible?"

All three men nodded.

Her chest tightened. "Then we have to leave," she said urgently. "Immediately. We can't endanger everyone here." Her breathing turned shallow, uneven. Gerald called for the secretary, and within moments she hurried in with a glass of water. Joy drank, hands trembling, until the room steadied. Jonas squeezed her hand gently.

"Joy, we will not let anything happen to you."

Charles leaned forward, meeting her gaze squarely.

"Running will not solve this," he said quietly. "I know you're frightened but panic only helps the people responsible. We need clarity. We need time."

"I'm not afraid for myself," Joy said, her voice tight. "I'm afraid for my sister. For my nieces. For everyone who's taken us in. We brought this danger with us."

"Joy," Gerald said firmly, rising at last, "you are here because you are family. And family does not cast one another out to face evil alone."

"We would never ask you to risk your lives for us," Joy protested. "These people are ruthless. They nearly killed Maureen in another fire right after my parents, and John, were murdered."

A heavy silence followed.

Then Charles spoke again. "At present, they do not know where you are. We've alerted law enforcement along the west coast. Anyone traveling under suspicious circumstances is being questioned."

"That won't be enough," Joy argued. "Suspicion alone won't stop a determined killer."

"I'll call a town meeting tonight," Gerald said. "We'll ask everyone to stay alert. To watch newcomers."

"No!" Joy cried, springing to her feet. "That would make them targets. Alice and the girls and I will leave, tonight, if we must."

Gerald caught her arm as she tried to leave the room. Charles and Dylan stepped into her path.

"We will not allow it," Gerald said fiercely. "We end this here."

"You don't understand," Joy insisted, tears bright in her eyes. "Once they find us, they'll burn everything in their path. We left Auburn to protect people. We can do it again."

Charles's gaze locked with hers, unyielding.

"And run for the rest of your life? What happens when they catch up to you somewhere with no one to protect you? What happens if your sister or your nieces are harmed because you're alone?"

"I would die before letting that happen," Joy shot back, fury blazing.

"And it still wouldn't stop them," Charles said gently. "They would go after your sister the moment you were gone."

Her voice faltered. "Why? Why are they so relentless?"

"We will find out," Charles said solemnly, squeezing her hand. "I promise."

"But how?" she whispered. "If the couple won't talk—"

"There are ways," Dylan said reassuringly. "And I'll be staying in Deer Lodge for a while. We may even request a U.S. marshal."

Gerald nodded. "Agreed."

Joy sank back into her chair, exhausted. Only then did she notice how quiet Jonas had become. He hadn't risen when she panicked. He hadn't been the one to calm her. That role had fallen to Charles. Unexpectedly steady. Unexpectedly reassuring. Was grief dulling Jonas's edge, or was Charles simply stepping into a role he had always intended to fill?

Joy's unease returned, coiling tight. She didn't know whom to trust anymore, but she knew one thing with chilling certainty. The danger wasn't over. And somewhere... someone was still watching her.

✦

Joy drew a slow, steadying breath, then shook her head.

"I truly appreciate how determined you all are to protect us," she said quietly, "but how would we even justify the presence of a U.S. marshal, because of us? I considered requesting an escort when we traveled here, but this..." She hesitated. "This could mean protection for days. Weeks. Even for months. It feels excessive."

Charles leaned forward, resting his forearms on his knees, his expression uncharacteristically gentle.

"It isn't excessive," he said evenly. "Your father was not just any judge, Joy. Max Collins was powerful, respected federal judge, and widely known far beyond the West Coast. He earned enemies precisely because he did his duty without fear or favoritism."

Joy swallowed, her throat tightening at the sound of her father's name.

"He had the right to federal protection," Charles continued, "and that right did not end with his death. The threat against him did not die with him, it shifted. If this danger is connected to his rulings, then you and your sister remain extensions of that risk."

She looked at him, shaken. "You mean... we're still covered because of his position?"

"Yes," Charles said simply. "Your father took an oath when he became a federal judge. That oath binds the government and states in return. The law is obligated to safeguard not only its servants, but their families when retaliation is involved. You are not asking for special treatment. You are entitled to protection."

Dylan nodded in agreement. "This isn't uncommon in cases involving judicial retaliation. If anything, it's overdue."

Joy glanced at her uncle. Gerald's jaw was set, his gaze fierce with resolve.

"Your pa spent his life standing between the innocent and men like these," he said. "There is no shame in allowing the law to stand between them, and you, now."

A heavy silence settled over the room. Joy's emotions tangled together, relief, guilt, fear, and the sharp ache of missing her father all at once. Jonas rose from his chair, his expression firm, the earlier indecision gone.

"That settles it," he said. "Dylan will remain in Deer Lodge, and I will contact marshal headquarters in Helena immediately. One or two U.S. marshals will be assigned without delay."

Joy's breath hitched. She opened her mouth to protest again, then stopped. Slowly, she nodded.

"All right," she whispered. "If this is the only way to keep Alice and the girls safe... then I'll accept it."

Jonas gave her a solemn nod.

"Your father would have demanded nothing less."

As they stepped out of the bank into the crisp Montana air, Dylan slowed his stride until he was walking beside Joy. After a moment's hesitation, he cleared his throat.

"Miss Collins," he said, turning to her with a smile that held both confidence and unmistakable admiration, "I've heard there's a Sweetheart Dance in town next week. Would you do me the honor of attending with me, as my date?"

Joy stopped short. For a heartbeat, she could only stare at him, utterly unprepared. Warmth rushed to her cheeks, and she was suddenly acutely aware of the way Jonas and Charles exchanged knowing smirks just behind her.

"Well... I..." She faltered, mortified by the way the words tangled on her tongue. Drawing in a steady breath, she straightened her spine and forced herself to regain composure. "I hadn't planned on attending," she said more clearly. Dylan tilted his head, curiosity lighting his eyes.

"May I ask why not?"

She offered a small, self-conscious smile.

"The name alone makes it sound as though it's meant for couples. I assumed it wasn't... appropriate."

Her uncle let out a low chuckle.

"Nonsense," Gerald said warmly. "The Sweetheart Dance is for anyone old enough to attend. You don't need a sweetheart to enjoy good music and good company."

Joy felt their attention settle fully on her now, four sets of eyes waiting, amused and expectant. She shifted her weight, then lifted her chin, resolve quietly settling into place.

"Very well," she said at last, meeting Dylan's gaze. "I would be happy to accept your invitation."

Dylan's smile widened, unmistakably pleased.

"Then it's settled."

They began walking again, but Joy's steps felt lighter than before, her pulse quickened by something she hadn't anticipated. Still, beneath the flutter of excitement, a familiar awareness stirred—how one simple invitation had already begun to complicate the careful order she'd built around her heart.

"There is a new, and very handsome, young man in town," Olivia announced the moment she burst through the door after school, her eyes bright with mischief. Cathleen spun around at once.

"Really?" She leaned closer, then caught Joy's eye roll. "Oh. You know him, don't you?"

Joy sighed, already regretting whatever chain of events had been set in motion.

"'Know him' is a bit generous. I met him a few days ago when I was in town with my uncle and my father's lawyers. He's the nephew of Pa's attorney."

Olivia's eyes widened. "A lawyer's nephew?" She clasped her hands dramatically. "This keeps getting better."

"Oh, do tell," Cathleen pressed, grinning. "What does he look like?"

Joy opened her mouth, but Olivia beat her to it.

"Very handsome," she declared with a wink aimed squarely at Joy. "Tall. Well put together. And he has one of those smiles, the kind that makes you forget what you were about to say."

Cathleen sighed theatrically.

"Why do all the interesting men arrive when I'm knee-deep in chores and responsibility?" Then her eyes lit. "Do you think he'll ask anyone to the Sweetheart Dance?"

Joy suddenly found the floor fascinating.

"He... already did."

The room went very still. Then it exploded.

"Of course he did!" Cathleen giggled, clapping her hands. "He'd have to be blind not to ask you. Or utterly foolish."

Joy grimaced. "I think he only asked because he doesn't know anyone yet, and I happened to be standing there."

"Rubbish," Olivia said breezily. "Men don't ask women to dances, out of desperation, Joy. Especially not handsome ones."

Cathleen waved away Joy's protest.

"Details. Minor, insignificant details." She tilted her head. "Aren't you going to visit your sister and your aunt and uncle this afternoon?"

Joy nodded. "Yes."

Cathleen's smile turned positively wicked.

"Perfect. Olivia and I will come with you."

Joy frowned. "Why?"

Cathleen linked arms with her sister, eyes sparkling.

"Because I absolutely must see this mysterious young man for myself."

"And," Olivia added sweetly, "to determine whether he's worthy of escorting you to the Sweetheart Dance."

Joy groaned. "I am surrounded by traitors."

Cathleen laughed, already reaching for her bonnet.

"Nonsense. You're surrounded by sisters who fully intend to enjoy this."

Joy dismounted her horse and led it toward the hitching post in front of her uncle's house. Her thoughts already knotted with the week's events. As she reached the front path, a burst of soft laughter floated around the side of the building. Curious despite herself, she slowed and followed the sound, careful with her steps.

Beneath the rose-covered arch that marked the entrance to the garden, she stopped short. Alice stood there, her cheeks flushed, laughter still lingering on her lips, held comfortably in the arms of Dylan Andrews. His head was bent close to hers, his expression open and intent in a way Joy recognized all too well.

Something sharp and unexpected tugged at her chest. Not jealousy, precisely, but surprise, and a faint, unwelcome sting of displacement. She had not realized how unprepared she was for this sight. Before either of them noticed her, Joy quietly stepped back. Her thoughts churned, distracted enough that she failed to watch her footing. Her hip bumped the fence beside the entrance with a dull thud. She squeezed her eyes shut. Too late.

"Joy!" Dylan said brightly a moment later. She turned, schooling her features into what she hoped passed for a polite smile. Dylan released Alice at once and stepped toward her, enthusiasm undimmed.

"I'm glad to see you," he began, then plunged ahead without pause. "I know I asked you to the Sweetheart Dance, but I was hoping you'd allow me to take your sister instead. Ever since meeting her, she has quite taken over my heart."

Joy felt her stomach rebel.

Taken over his heart? He hadn't even been in Deer Lodge a full week. For a split second she nearly laughed, an incredulous, sharp sound, but caught it just in time. There was no graceful way out of this. He had put the question to her directly, and in front of Alice, no less.

"Of course," Joy said, the word coming out a shade too crisp. She folded her hands together, nails biting lightly into her palms. "If Alice wishes to go with you, I'm... delighted for you both."

Even as the words left her mouth, she knew she'd failed. The sarcasm clung to her tone like frost.

To her astonishment, Alice appeared to notice nothing at all. Her face lit with happiness as she stepped forward and wrapped Joy in a quick, grateful embrace.

"Thank you," Alice said warmly. Then she turned and hurried into the house, calling for their aunt. Joy watched her go, her smile slowly fading as the door closed behind her. Whatever else this was, awkward, ill-timed, faintly absurd, one thing was painfully clear. Once again, Joy had swallowed her own feelings so her sister could have joy.

Just as Dylan turned to follow Alice toward the house, Joy caught his sleeve.

"Dylan, wait."

He stopped, glancing back at her with mild surprise. Joy did not lower her voice.

"Listen carefully," she said, her tone calm but edged with steel. "I don't know what game you think you're playing, but if you hurt my sister in any way, you will regret ever meeting us."

For a heartbeat, he simply stared at her. Then a slow, crooked smirk spread across his face.

"That sounded almost like a threat, Joy Collins," he drawled. "You don't happen to be jealous, do you?"

She shot him a look sharp enough to cut glass.

"Absolutely not. But I *am* concerned," she replied coolly. "It isn't exactly gentlemanly to invite one woman to a dance and then cancel the day before to ask her sister instead." Her pulse raced now, not from jealousy, she told herself firmly, but from indignation. From the sheer impropriety of it. Dylan's smile remained infuriatingly intact as he stepped closer. Joy lifted a hand at once, stopping him.

"My sister has been through more than you know," she continued, her voice low and fierce. "I will not allow anyone to toy with her feelings or use her as a distraction. If your intentions are sincere, I won't stand in your way. But if you are merely amusing yourself, if you so much as *think* of breaking her heart, I swear—"

He lifted a finger and pressed it gently to her lips, halting her words mid-breath. The teasing grin vanished. In its place was something unexpectedly sober.

"I would never do that," he said quietly. "Not to your sister. Not to anyone." His voice held no humor now. "And I am sorry, truly, that the timing was so poorly handled. I didn't intend to insult you." He hesitated, then added with disarming honesty, "If I had met Alice before you, I would have asked her first."

Joy inhaled slowly. If she had been any other woman, that remark might have earned him a slap. Who in their right mind said such a thing aloud? Clearly, Dylan Andrews did not always think before he spoke. Still, she searched his eyes. What she found there was not mockery or manipulation, but earnestness, awkward, unpolished, but sincere. She lowered her hand and nodded once.

"All right," she said evenly. "Then see that you prove it."

Relief softened his expression at once, and a genuine smile followed.

"Your sister is lucky to have you," he said. "I've never met anyone so fiercely protective. And I don't doubt for a moment that if I ever hurt Alice, you'd hunt me down."

Joy's lips twitched despite herself.

"That," she said coolly, "is the most accurate thing you've said for as long as I've known you."

"He was nowhere in town," Cathleen whined the moment Joy swung down from her horse at the stables. "I searched main street twice. *Twice!* I went into every shop, hoping to at least catch a glimpse of him before the dance tomorrow."

Joy sighed as she loosened the cinch.

"You couldn't have found him there. He was at my aunt and uncle's." She hesitated, then added, "It appears he's formed rather a strong attachment to my sister."

Cathleen's jaw dropped. Even Olivia froze mid-step.

"But," Cathleen sputtered, "he asked *you* to the dance."

Joy shrugged, feigning far more indifference than she felt.

"He did. Then he asked if I would allow him to take Alice instead."

Silence followed. Then Olivia's eyes narrowed, unmistakably sharp.

"And you're... all right with that?"

Joy straightened, brushing straw from her skirt.

"We are not courting. And I made myself perfectly clear, if he hurts Alice, I'll personally see to his downfall."

Cathleen burst out laughing. "Oh, you absolutely would."

Olivia grinned. "I pity the man foolish enough to cross you."

Joy snorted softly. "As well he should." She finished tending her horse and glanced between them. "Besides, I hadn't truly intended to go anyway. Who invited you two?"

"Barry Flynn asked me," Olivia said brightly. "And Cat is going with Jonathan Whittaker."

"Barry?" Joy paused. "The sheriff's deputy?"

"Yes," Olivia replied, unbothered. "He's nearly thirty, but he's kind. Solid. And he doesn't take himself too seriously."

Cathleen waved a hand. "Jonathan has an older brother. If you'd like, I could see if he'd escort you."

Joy shook her head immediately.

"Absolutely not. I refuse to be anyone's afterthought." She hesitated, then added more quietly, "And truth be told, it's probably best if I keep my distance from dances for a while. Doctor Thomas and his... delightful wife already have more than enough lies to spread about me. No sense giving them fresh material."

Cathleen frowned. "That's not fair."

"No," Joy agreed softly. "But it *is* reality." She forced a smile and picked up her gloves. "You two go. Enjoy yourselves. Dance until your feet ache."

Olivia studied her for a moment, then squeezed her arm.

"One day, Joy Collins, you're going to dance with someone who chooses you first, without hesitation."

Joy's lips curved faintly. "Perhaps." But as she led her horse toward the paddock, her thoughts betrayed her, drifting unbidden to a certain broad-shouldered rancher with quiet eyes and an infuriatingly charming smile... and the way his hand had lingered just a second too long the last time he'd let her go.

Joy smiled to herself as she headed toward her room, Olivia and Cathleen's excited chatter drifting down the hall behind her. They were practically vibrating with anticipation over the dance that evening. She wasn't truly sorry to miss it, though she was mildly offended that Dylan hadn't had the decency to tell her sooner about his change of heart. Still, the thought of a quiet evening alone held its own appeal.

With no clear plan, she plucked a book from the shelf and turned toward the door, intending to read outside in the fading warmth of the afternoon. That was when a sharp neigh cut through the air. She paused. Her bedroom windows were thrown wide open, the late-summer breeze stirring the curtains and carrying in the scent of hay and sun-warmed earth. Curious, Joy stepped closer and parted the fabric just enough to glance outside... and promptly forgot how to breathe.

Graham Harrison stood in the horse enclosure below, astride a restless young horse. He had shed his shirt, and the sun gilded every line of him, broad shoulders, powerful arms, sweat-slicked skin gleaming as he worked to steady the animal beneath him. Muscles flexed with each controlled movement, strength and patience wrapped together in a way that made her pulse stutter. Heat rushed to her face. No, to her entire body.

Joy knew, with absolute clarity, that staring was wildly inappropriate. Entirely improper. Completely unladylike. Her eyes refused to cooperate. She watched every shift of his weight, every tightening of muscle, her heart hammering so loudly she was certain he must hear it from across the yard. Butterflies rioted in her stomach, her cheeks burning hotter by the second.

Why him? She had seen men without shirts before. John had split wood half-undressed in the summer heat. Matt Haven and half the town's young men had competed shirtless during festivals and games. None of it had ever done *this* to her. But Graham, Graham made her breath catch and her thoughts scatter. The memory of his kiss, angry, defiant, unmistakably real, flickered through her mind, igniting a warmth that curled low in her belly. Her lips tingled as if they remembered him all too well. She squeezed her eyes shut, horrified by the sudden, reckless urge to run outside and pull him down from that horse just to feel his arms around her again.

Get a hold of yourself, Joy Collins. She shook her head sharply, but when she opened her eyes, they betrayed her again, still fixed on him, still drinking him in. She shifted sideways for a better view. Her foot caught the leg of a chair. The book slipped from her fingers and hit the wooden floor with a sharp *thud.* Joy froze.

Mortified, she darted behind the curtain, heart pounding as the horse below snorted and Graham's head lifted toward the house. She pressed a hand to her chest and held her breath, acutely aware that her window was now the most suspicious place on the ranch. Before she dared a peek, a sudden knock sounded at her door.

She jumped, stumbling backward, catching another chair and nearly pitching to the floor before she righted herself with a soft gasp. Snatching up the fallen book, she collapsed into the armchair beside her bed, smoothed her skirts, and glared at herself.

Absolutely hopeless.

"Come in," she called, striving for calm. Olivia and Cathleen swept inside at once, their gazes immediately scanning the room.

"We heard something fall," Olivia said. "Are you all right?"

Joy nodded quickly, angling the book in her lap.

"Perfectly fine."

Cathleen wandered straight to the window, peered out, and waved enthusiastically.

"Oh! Graham's outside."

Joy's pulse skidded. Olivia's eyes flicked to the shifted chairs, then to Joy, one brow arching.

"Do you trip often while... reading?"

"I caught the chair leg," Joy said smoothly. "Dropped my book."

"Uh-huh." Olivia crossed the room, eyeing the book. "And you've been reading this entire time?"

"Since I came up here," Joy replied, lowering her gaze to the page. She barely had time to register Olivia's movement before the book was gently, but firmly, lifted from her hands. Joy sucked in a breath.

Olivia chuckled. "You might want to turn the book right-side up next time you pretend you've been reading for a while."

Cathleen turned, took one look, and burst into a grin.
"Ohhh."

Joy groaned and sank back into the chair, covering her face.

"I hate both of you."

Olivia winked. "No, you don't."

"And," Cathleen added brightly, "you were *definitely* not reading."

Joy peeked through her fingers, cheeks aflame. She had been caught, exposed, undone by a shirtless man and two merciless sisters. And judging by the warmth still humming beneath her skin, this was only the beginning.

Not wanting to risk an accidental, and entirely mortifying, encounter with Graham, Joy wasted no time retreating to the stables. She moved with purpose, saddled her horse, and slipped away into the forest that bordered the ranch, letting the rhythm of hooves and the whisper of pine needles beneath the breeze carry her forward. The ride helped... somewhat.

The forest was breathtaking in the late afternoon light, shafts of gold filtering through tall trees, the air cool and clean. Yet no matter how hard Joy tried to clear her thoughts, they betrayed her at every turn. Images of Graham, sunlit skin, powerful shoulders, the easy strength in his movements, insisted on returning, uninvited and persistent. Each time she shoved the memories aside, they crept back in, warmer and more vivid than before.

Pull yourself together, she scolded silently, urging her mare onward. By the time she returned to the ranch, the sun was sinking low, painting the sky in dusky shades of rose and amber. Joy paused for a moment, still mounted, simply watching the horizon as the day surrendered to evening. Only when the first stars began to blink awake did she dismount and lead her horse into the stable.

She moved through the familiar motions with care and affection, unsaddling, brushing dust from the mare's coat, wiping her down, then offering water and fresh hay. The simple, grounding tasks soothed her frayed nerves, slowing her racing thoughts. Still, she wasn't ready to face the house. Not yet.

Joy glanced around the stable, searching for something, anything, to keep her occupied until the others left for the dance. Her gaze drifted upward and landed on the narrow windows tucked beneath the roofline. They were grimy, streaked with dust and cobwebs, clearly neglected.

That will do nicely. Most could be reached from the hayloft ladder, but one window sat awkwardly in the center of the building, just out of easy reach. Beneath it, however, straw bales were stacked neatly, solid and high enough to serve as a makeshift platform.

After a moment's consideration, Joy fetched a cloth and a bucket, filled it with clear, cold water from the spring behind the barn, and drew in a steady breath. Carefully, she climbed the stacked bales, mindful not to slosh the water, and reached the top without mishap.

As she lifted her arm to begin cleaning, voices drifted in from outside, the cheerful chatter of Cathleen and Olivia, followed by the unmistakable sounds of horses and buggies arriving. Her heart gave a small jolt.

Brigham and Darlene called her name from the house, but Joy stayed silent, pressing herself closer to the window and focusing on the task at hand. Moments later, the crunch of wheels on gravel and the soft clatter of hooves faded as the carriages departed. Alone at last.

Joy let out a quiet breath of relief and turned back to the window, unaware that her chosen refuge, and her determination to avoid one man, in particular, might soon place her in far greater peril than an awkward encounter ever could.

It felt good to be alone. Most of the ranch hands had gone into town for the evening, and the few who remained were likely settled in their bunkhouses, enjoying a quiet night of cards or sleep. The ranch itself seemed to exhale, the wide land stretching beneath the deepening twilight in a rare moment of stillness. Joy welcomed it. Silence, at least, did not demand anything from her.

She dipped her cloth into the bucket again and wiped at the glass, but despite her efforts, her thoughts betrayed her, drifting, as they had far too often lately, back to Graham. A faint, traitorous shiver traced its way down her spine, and she huffed softly at herself.

Enough, she thought firmly. She truly had to get that man out of her head before her imagination ran completely amok. Olivia's voice echoed in her memory, cheerful and far too knowing. Graham had invited his cousin to the Sweetheart Dance, a young woman traveling in from Helena. The cousin, Olivia had explained, had only recently escaped a miserable courtship and needed distraction, laughter, a change of scenery. Graham, ever the dutiful family man, had agreed to escort her.

Joy tightened her grip on the cloth. It shouldn't have mattered. It didn't matter. Graham was still married, after all, no matter how fractured that marriage had become. And yet the thought of him collecting another woman from the stagecoach, even a cousin, bringing her home, offering her his attention, his easy smiles, his strength, his warmth, sent a strange, unwelcome ache through her chest.

Olivia had mentioned that he would fetch his cousin that very afternoon, that she would stay the night at the Harrison house. Joy had nodded politely at the time, even managed a smile. But now, alone in the dim stable, the knowledge lingered like a pebble in her shoe, small, irritating, impossible to ignore. She scrubbed harder at the window, as though effort alone might scour Graham from her thoughts along with the grime.

You are being ridiculous, she told herself. *Utterly ridiculous.* And yet, no matter how firmly she scolded herself, the image of him, broad-shouldered, earnest-eyed, smiling in that quiet way that made her heart stumble, refused to leave her mind.

Joy forced her thoughts back where they belonged, on the filthy window in front of her. Work, at least, did not disappoint. There was something deeply satisfying about it, about watching grime and dust give way beneath steady effort. She scrubbed until the glass caught the last slanting rays of the sun and gleamed like a sheet of amber. Only then did she climb carefully down from the stacked straw bales, carry the bucket back to the spring, and rinse her cloth in clean, cold water.

With the light fading fast, she climbed the ladder to the hayloft, her muscles pleasantly tired. She pushed the small window open and leaned out to wash the exterior. The sound of a horse snorting broke the quiet. Joy's heart lurched violently into her throat. Hoofbeats followed, measured, unmistakably close, then the familiar clatter of iron shoes against packed earth. Panic seized her.

A cowboy? she thought wildly. *Someone coming back early?*

Then she saw him. Graham. Her breath left her in a soundless gasp, and she very nearly swooned where she stood. Instinct took over. She ducked back from the window, flattening herself against the wall, clutching the cloth to her chest as though it might still her racing heart. She held her breath as she heard him enter the stable below.

His voice followed, low and gentle, as he spoke to his horse. She couldn't make out the words, only the tone. Familiar. Fond. And entirely unfair to her already frayed composure. Bootsteps sounded, moving away. She dared a cautious glance through the window and saw him crossing the yard toward the ranch house, long strides eating up the distance. Relief flooded her so suddenly her knees threatened to give out. A shaky sigh escaped her lips.

Why is he back? she wondered. His horse was still saddled. Had he forgotten something? Was he leaving again? She scrubbed the glass harder than necessary, trying to quiet the relentless questions tumbling through her mind. If he left again soon, all would be well. She could finish her work, retreat to her room, and survive the evening with her dignity intact. She was so intent on this plan that she nearly jumped out of her skin when she heard her name.

"Joy?"

Her heart slammed. She froze. She didn't answer.

"Joy?" Graham called again, closer this time. She pressed her lips together, refusing to breathe too loudly. If she stayed perfectly still, perhaps he would assume she was gone. Then another voice joined his, deep, older, edged with confusion.

"Why are you looking for Joy, Graham?" the man asked. "Isn't she at the dance like everyone else?"

Joy recognized it instantly. Horace. One of the ranch hands.

"I don't think so," Graham replied. "Cathleen said she stayed home. The fellow who asked her to the dance canceled on her."

A pause.

"Canceled?" Horace repeated, incredulous. "Why would he do that? Taken ill?"

"No," Graham said shortly. "Apparently, he invited her sister instead."

There was a beat of stunned silence. Then the cowboy's voice thundered through the stable.

"What kind of man does something like that?"

Joy clapped a hand over her mouth to stifle a laugh. Despite her nerves, despite her embarrassment, warmth bloomed in her chest. It felt oddly wonderful, dangerously so, to know someone was indignant on her behalf. Below her, Graham muttered something low and unmistakably displeased. Joy leaned her forehead against the wooden beam, smiling despite herself, her heart still pounding as the last light outside slipped fully into dusk.

11

Where Venom Belongs

Joy still couldn't fathom why Graham was back at the ranch at all. He should have been in town, at the dance, laughing with his cousin, his family, and neighbors, instead of haunting her thoughts and, apparently, her hiding place. She heard him return to the stable, the soft thud of boots on packed earth followed by the familiar jingle of tack. A moment later, his horse was led out. Joy exhaled in quiet relief.

Good, she thought. *He's leaving.* And that was when fate betrayed her, again. Her fingers closed around the bucket, but it slipped. Time seemed to slow, as it struck the wooden beam beneath her feet, tipped, and went tumbling over the edge of the hayloft. It clanged violently against the metal gate of a horse box below. The horse inside reared and neighed loudly, hooves scraping in alarm.

Joy squeezed her eyes shut. *Why does this keep happening to me?* She waited, heart pounding, for Graham to come storming back into the stable. Seconds passed. Then more. Instead of approaching footsteps, she heard the rhythmic beat of hooves retreating. He was riding away.

Joy remained frozen for several minutes, scarcely daring to breathe. Only when she was certain he was gone did she climb carefully down the ladder to retrieve the fallen bucket. The horse she'd startled fixed her with what could only be described as a reproachful stare. She huffed a quiet laugh.

"You're quite right," she murmured. "I deserve that."

Reaching into the pocket of her skirt, she found an apple she'd meant for her own horse earlier and had entirely forgotten. She held it out as an apology. The horse sniffed her fingers, considered the offering for half a heartbeat, then accepted it with a contented snort. Joy smiled, watching him chew, until boredom nudged her onward. She turned toward the stable door with the intent of refilling the bucket when someone grabbed her arm and spun her around.

A sharp gasp tore from her throat. The horse chose that moment to neigh again, which, under the circumstances, sounded suspiciously like laughter.

"Graham!" Joy blurted. "What on earth are you doing here?"

"I could ask you the same thing," he replied, towering over her, his expression a mixture of challenge and amusement. "Why aren't you at the dance?"

She yanked her arm free, heat rushing to her cheeks.

"You already know why. I'm not attending the Sweetheart Dance alone. And for your information, I was enjoying myself."

He glanced around pointedly. "Cleaning windows?"

"I find it very fulfilling," she shot back, arching a brow. "It's really none of your concern, Mr. Harrison." She paused, then added coolly, "Why are *you* here? I thought you were escorting your cousin."

He sighed, raking a hand through his hair. "She took ill and couldn't come after all. I helped set things up, then rode back to see if..." He hesitated, then met her gaze squarely. "If you might go to the dance with me instead."

Joy stared at him, speechless. Her face felt aflame.

"I—I don't think that's a good idea," she said at last, eyes dropping to the floor.

"Why not?" His voice was gentle, coaxing. She gestured vaguely at herself.

"Look at me. I'm not dressed for a dance. My hair's a disaster."

He stepped closer, too close, lifting a hand to her cheek before she could retreat.

"You look beautiful," he said simply. Her breath caught. Infuriating man.

"You haven't forgotten what happened the last time we danced together," she said quietly. "Mr. and Mrs. Thomas would seize on it. I don't want to provoke more trouble."

He exhaled, then reached for her hand and drew her into his arms.

Joy gasped. "Graham—"

"I know you feel it," he murmured, eyes dark and intent. "The same sparks I do."

"There are no sparks," she insisted, even as her pulse betrayed her. His grin was slow, knowing. He leaned down, lips hovering a breath from hers.

"Do you need reminding of that kiss?"

Her entire body went still. "You kissed me to spite your in-laws," she said, pushing against his chest. "It wasn't real."

His expression softened. He brushed a strand of hair from her face, his touch sending a tremor through her.

"It started that way," he admitted. "But it didn't end that way. You felt it. And so did I."

She closed her eyes, gathering her resolve, then opened them again.

"It isn't right. You are not free."

The words landed between them, heavy and undeniable. Graham searched her face, then nodded slowly. He bent and pressed a gentle kiss to her forehead.

"You're right."

Relief and disappointment tangled painfully in her chest.

"Of course I am," she said, lifting her chin. "We can only be friends."

He didn't argue, though the regret in his eyes was unmistakable. Instead, he pulled her into a fierce, lingering embrace, one that spoke of restraint rather than surrender.

"I wish I had met you before Lydia," he admitted quietly.

"So do I," Joy replied just as softly. "But you married her because you are a good man. You couldn't have known the truth."

They stood there a moment longer, neither quite ready to let go, the stable wrapped in dusk and unspoken longing, both aware that something powerful had begun, even if neither dared name it yet.

"So, the rumors are true."

The sharp, cutting voice sliced through the quiet like a whip. Joy and Graham both spun around, startled, their bodies instinctively separating.

"I should have known," the woman continued, bitterness dripping from every word. "I should have known you couldn't be trusted, that you'd go for the very next woman who crossed your path."

Lydia stood just inside the stable doors, her posture rigid, tears glistening in her eyes but not quite falling. Lantern light caught the sharp planes of her face, illuminating the fury simmering beneath her fragile display. Behind her loomed her father, his mouth curled into a smug, vindictive grin, as though he'd finally uncovered the proof he'd been hunting for all along.

Joy's heart lurched painfully into her throat. Of course. Of all nights. Of all places. She resisted the urge to step back, though every instinct screamed at her to put distance between herself and the venom now flooding the air. Her pulse thundered, her thoughts racing. Hadn't she endured enough scrutiny? Enough accusations? Enough cruel assumptions?

Graham's body stiffened beside her. His hand twitched, caught between the instinct to shield Joy and the need to confront the woman who had once claimed to be his wife.

"This is not what it looks like," he began, his voice low and controlled, but Lydia laughed, a brittle, broken sound.

"Oh, spare me," she snapped. "I've heard that line before. Funny how men always reach for it when they're caught."

Her father shifted behind her, satisfaction gleaming in his eyes. He took a deliberate step forward, his gaze locking onto Joy with open contempt, as though he'd been waiting for this moment.

"Well, well," he drawled. "Looks like we didn't have to wait long for the truth to come out."

Joy clenched her fists at her sides, forcing herself to breathe. She felt the familiar weight of judgment pressing down on her shoulders, heavy, suffocating, and utterly undeserved. She hadn't touched Graham. She hadn't kissed him. She hadn't crossed a single line. And yet, somehow, she was already guilty in their eyes.

I can't catch a break, she thought grimly. But this time, she refused to shrink.

Despite not knowing Lydia personally, Joy recognized the performance at once. Those tears were practiced, not born of genuine pain. Lydia was a master of manipulation, a woman who wore victimhood like a finely tailored gown and wielded it with deadly precision. Her beauty was a weapon, her fragility an act. And behind the shimmer of moisture in her green eyes' lay calculation, cold, deliberate. She wasn't heartbroken. She was laying groundwork, sowing guilt, preparing to bend Graham to her will once again.

Joy drew in a slow, steady breath. She had never understood women like Lydia, women who possessed every advantage and yet squandered it on cruelty and control. Lydia was undeniably pretty. She could have won hearts honestly, could have inspired loyalty through warmth and kindness. But there was no kindness in her gaze. Only hunger. Possession. A need to dominate every room she entered.

Her presence demanded attention, demanded to be centered, obeyed, indulged. Lydia wanted to call every shot, to dictate the narrative no matter the cost. She granted herself limitless freedom, the freedom to lie, to wound, to abandon, while punishing anyone who dared challenge her version of events. And when confronted, she did not reflect or repent. She cried. She accused. She played the martyr.

Joy saw it clearly now. Lydia thrived on being the injured party. It fed her sense of power, allowed her to twist truth into something unrecognizable while forcing others to defend themselves against lies. The victim's mask suited her. It excused her sins and transformed resistance into cruelty. And standing there in the stable, watching Lydia summon tears on command, Joy understood something else, too: this woman would never stop. Not until she had broken Graham's resolve or found someone else to control.

Graham shot his wife a withering glare.

"You are the last person who should be casting stones," he snapped, instinctively easing Joy behind him. She refused to remain sheltered. A heartbeat later, she stood at his side, spine straight, chin lifted.

"You ran off with another man after lying about everything," Graham went on, his voice hard with long-suppressed fury. "I married you because I believed you were desperate and alone. Because I wanted to help you. Not a single word you spoke to me was the truth."

Joy had to fight the urge to roll her eyes as Lydia's tears intensified on cue, spilling dramatically down her cheeks. With a practiced sob, Lydia swept dark strands of hair from her face and stepped closer, her gaze flicking between them.

"How long have you been seeing this woman?" she demanded sharply.

"What?" Graham stared at her, genuinely stunned.

"How long have you been meeting her behind my back?" Lydia pressed, her voice trembling just enough to sell the lie.

"I have never met her behind your back," he shot back. "She moved here long after you abandoned me."

Lydia scoffed. "Oh, don't insult me, Graham. You expect me to believe you've grown this close in just a few weeks? You've known her far longer than that."

Joy's hands curled into fists at her sides. There it was, exactly as she'd expected. Lydia was already recasting herself as the betrayed wife, and Joy as the scheming interloper who had ruined a marriage. Her pulse thundered, but before she could speak, Graham's expression shifted. Understanding dawned, followed swiftly by contempt.

"I see you're back to your favorite role," he said coldly. "The eternal victim."

Lydia blinked, clearly unprepared for his tone.

"It's astonishing how you manage to convince yourself you're never at fault," he continued, "when every bit of chaos follows in your wake. Every argument. Every broken relationship." He shook his head. Disgust etched deep into his features.

"Joy has nothing to do with this. She never did. Perhaps your new paramour still falls for your tears and theatrics, but I will not. And neither will this town. I made certain everyone knows you lied to trap me into marriage." His mouth curved humorlessly. "And judging by the looks on a few men's faces at the festival—I wasn't the first one you fooled."

Lydia's tears vanished in an instant, replaced by naked fury. Her face twisted as she screamed, shrill and unhinged, lunging at him with claws outstretched. Graham reacted without hesitation. He caught her wrists mid-strike, spun her effortlessly, and hoisted her up as she shrieked and flailed. Still shouting, she pounded uselessly against his shoulders as he carried her straight out of the stable, boots crunching over dirt toward the dunghill behind the barn. Even her father stood frozen, mouth agape, too shocked to intervene.

Joy watched, stunned, as Graham deposited Lydia squarely where her venom belonged. For the first time since Lydia had appeared, the air felt lighter, charged not with fear or accusation, but with the unmistakable sense that her reign of manipulation had finally, spectacularly, come to an end.

Once Graham released her, Lydia landed squarely in the foul, stinking heap behind the barn. For half a heartbeat, there was stunned silence. Then her scream split the air, sharp, unhinged, stripped of all pretenses. Rage replaced performance entirely.

She clawed herself upright, skirts smeared and ruined, her face twisted into something feral.

By then, several ranch hands had emerged from their bunkhouses, drawn by the shouting. They formed a loose semicircle, arms folded, expressions grim and incredulous as they took in the scene. Whatever Lydia and her father might later claim, there were far too many witnesses now. The truth lay exposed, ugly, unmistakable, and irreversible.

Joy remained rooted where she stood, her heart hammering. She had not expected this. Had not expected Graham to draw such a firm, fearless line. The man she had glimpsed only in flashes now stood fully revealed, unyielding, resolute, and finished with being manipulated. The realization left her shaken.

Lydia, meanwhile, had completely unraveled. She scooped up clumps of dirt and foul straw, flinging them wildly in Graham's direction, shrieking curses that no longer made any sense. None of it came close to hitting him. He didn't flinch or retreat. He simply stood there, jaw clenched, eyes cold, allowing her to expose herself fully to everyone watching.

Joy's gaze flicked to Dr. Thomas. His face had gone a dark, mottled red, fury and humiliation warring in his eyes as he watched his daughter's disgrace unfold. For a moment, she thought he might intervene, might pull Lydia away. Instead, his lips curled with something far uglier, calculation.

While Graham's attention remained fixed on Lydia's violent tantrum, Dr. Thomas abruptly turned. His boots struck the dirt hard as he stormed straight toward Joy. Her breath caught. She barely had time to steel herself before he loomed in front of her, eyes blazing with venom, the stench of rage and humiliation clinging to him as thickly as the dust on his coat.

***

She never saw it coming. There was no time to step back, no chance to brace herself. Dr. Thomas lunged and seized her by the arms, his grip iron-hard, fingers biting into her flesh as he shook her violently.

"Let go of me!" Joy gasped, terror flaring as her boots scraped uselessly against the dirt. He didn't listen. His face was twisted with hatred, spittle flying as he dragged her backward toward one of the thick wooden support beams of the barn. The world narrowed to the looming post behind her and the brutal force hauling her toward it. She knew, knew with chilling certainty, that if her head struck that beam, she might not rise again.

Gunshots cracked through the air. Sharp. Deafening. Final. Bullets struck the dirt inches from Dr. Thomas's boots, spraying dust and straw. The sound ripped him out of his frenzy. He released Joy at once and stumbled back, spinning around in shock. Joy sagged where she stood, her legs trembling so violently she nearly collapsed.

Every cowboy in the yard had their revolvers drawn now. Steel gleamed in the fading light. Barrels trained unflinchingly on the doctor. Not a single hand wavered. The message was unmistakable: take one more step, and you won't leave this place alive.

Graham was already at Joy's side. One arm wrapped around her shoulders, solid and protective, his other hand clenched at his side as if barely restraining himself from finishing what the men with guns had started. His eyes were lethal. Dr. Thomas's gaze snapped to him, fury reigniting as humiliation burned through his shock.

"You'll regret this!" he roared, jabbing a trembling finger at Graham. "You'll regret every second of it. You, and this harlot, will pay for crossing me and my daughter. Do you hear me?" His voice climbed toward a shriek. "She will never sign divorce papers. I'll bleed you dry in court. I'll take everything you own!"

Not one man flinched. Not one voice answered him. Graham didn't move. Didn't blink. He simply tightened his hold on Joy, placing himself squarely between her and the doctor, his silence far more threatening than any shouted threat.

Realizing, too late, that he was outmatched and surrounded by men who would not hesitate to defend her, Dr. Thomas spun on his heel and barked at Lydia to stop her hysterics. She was still shrieking incoherently, streaked with filth and rage, but at his command she scrambled to her feet.

Together, father and daughter fled for their buckboard, their retreat frantic and undignified. Wheels rattled violently as they tore away from the ranch, disappearing down the drive in a cloud of dust.

Only when they were gone did the tension finally break. Joy's knees buckled. Graham caught her instantly, pulling her fully into his arms this time, holding her as though he might never let her go again. His voice was low, rough with fury and fear.

"You're safe," he murmured against her hair. "I've got you. He will never touch you again."

Joy clutched his shirt, shaking now, not from cold, but from the shock of how close she had come to real danger. Around them, the cowboys slowly lowered their guns, exchanging grim looks. Whatever illusions remained about Dr. Thomas had been shattered. And Joy knew, with aching clarity, that nothing would ever be the same again.

"I can't believe I missed all of it," Cathleen announced with a broad, irreverent smirk. "I would have skipped the dance entirely if I'd known such fine drama was unfolding at home."

Joy, Olivia, and Cathleen were perched on the edge of Joy's bed, replaying the evening in breathless detail. Lamplight cast a warm glow over the room, softening the edges of what had been a frightening ordeal.

"Graham seriously threw Lydia onto the dunghill?" Olivia asked, eyes wide, still struggling to process it.

Joy nodded. "He did. One moment she was screaming, the next—" She made a helpless gesture. "It all happened so fast."

Cathleen stared at her for a beat, then burst into laughter, loud, unrestrained, and utterly unapologetic. She laughed so hard she had to clutch her sides, tears spilling from the corners of her eyes. Joy and Olivia couldn't help but join in, the absurdity of it all finally breaking through the lingering tension.

"Well," Cathleen managed at last, wiping her eyes, "she earned that landing. Thoroughly."

Olivia's smile faded into something more sober.

"This isn't over, though."

"No," Joy agreed quietly. "It's not. Her father threatened Graham with lawsuits and vengeance, and I know he'll come after me too."

"But you didn't do anything, except be there," Olivia protested.

"That's precisely the problem," Joy said softly. "I *was* there. And to people like them, that's enough. They were already trying to make me the villain, the woman who ruined their precious daughter's marriage."

Cathleen shook her head in disbelief, her earlier mirth gone.

"It's astonishing how low they're willing to sink. Lies, accusations, theatrics, it's all they have left." She leaned forward, her voice firm with conviction. "But don't you worry. We won't let them touch you. Not you, not Graham. And neither will this town."

Joy let out a slow breath she hadn't realized she'd been holding. For all the ugliness of the night, for all the danger that had brushed too close, there was comfort here, in this room, among friends who believed her, defended her, and stood without hesitation at her side.

"Joy Collins," came the warm, familiar voice the moment the stagecoach door swung open. Joy barely had time to turn before her father's old friend stepped down and gathered her into a firm, fatherly embrace. "You grow more beautiful every time I see you," he said with gentle affection.

Her cheeks warmed, and she lowered her eyes, but she returned the hug without hesitation. There was something achingly comforting in his solidity, the same steadiness she remembered from her childhood. He released her only to turn back to the coach, offering his hand first to his wife, then to their daughter as they stepped down.

Mrs. Preston didn't hesitate either. She pulled Joy into her arms, holding her close.

"We are so very sorry about your parents, dear. You know how much they meant to us."

Joy nodded, her throat tightening as she blinked back tears. Seeing them again stirred memories she hadn't expected, the sound of her father's laughter, her mother's gentle voice, evenings filled with conversation and warmth. Her uncle greeted the Preston family with a firm handshake and ushered them into his office, offering privacy and tea.

Once everyone was seated, Dr. Marvin Preston cleared his throat.

"I must admit, Joy, your letter surprised me," he said thoughtfully. "In my experience, folks in smaller towns tend to be even more hesitant about accepting a female physician. But Julia is well prepared for that sort of resistance."

Julia nodded, her expression calm and resolute.

"That I am. The prejudice against women in medicine is still very much alive."

Joy smiled at her, admiration shining in her eyes.

"You'll encounter a few narrow minds here as well, but I truly believe most people will be grateful to finally have another choice. Dr. Thomas has made himself... thoroughly unlikable."

Marvin's mouth curved into a knowing smile.

"I would very much like to meet this man," he said, winking at Joy. "I suspect we would have a great deal to discuss."

Joy's uncle let out a dry chuckle and shook his head.

"I wouldn't count on it. He seems to have taken sudden leave upon hearing of your arrival. How long he plans to be away is anyone's guess."

"What a pity," Marvin replied mildly, though the mischievous spark in his eyes told a different story. "My wife and I will remain in Deer Lodge for a week before returning to Sacramento. I would have liked the opportunity to make it clear to my colleague that any attempt to intimidate or chase off my daughter would be... ill-advised."

Julia lifted her chin, unfazed. "I can hold my own."

"I know you can," her father said fondly, then turned serious. "But I won't hesitate to involve the law if Dr. Thomas decides to become a threat. No one bullies my daughter, professionally or otherwise."

Joy felt a surge of relief and gratitude. For the first time in what felt like ages, the scales seemed to be tipping, away from fear and uncertainty, and toward justice and strength.

Just as Joy's uncle had predicted, neither Lydia nor her parents showed their faces in Deer Lodge while Dr. Preston and his wife were in town. Their absence proved a blessing, an unexpected calm that allowed everyone to breathe a little easier. More importantly, it gave Julia the opportunity to introduce herself properly to the community she hoped to serve.

She wasted no time. With her parents' quiet encouragement, Julia visited homes, spoke with families, and opened the doors of her temporary office to anyone willing to give her a chance. Word traveled quickly. She was warm and approachable, never condescending, yet unmistakably confident in her skill. She listened, truly listened, and examined her patients with a thoroughness that inspired trust.

Julia asked the questions Dr. Thomas never bothered with, explained her findings with care, and charged fair prices that never forced families to choose between their health and their supper. She was also highly knowledgeable and favored natural remedies, something Dr. Thomas absolutely despised. He relied almost exclusively on the most expensive medications, making it difficult for many in town to afford his care.

The very morning after Dr. Preston and his wife departed, Dr. Thomas reappeared in town. His return was anything but subtle. He wasted no time attempting to poison public opinion, muttering warnings about 'reckless experimentation' and casting doubt on Julia's credentials wherever he went. But his efforts fell flat. The townsfolk had seen enough of his temper, his greed, and his daughter's disgrace to recognize bitterness when they heard it. Few listened. Fewer still cared.

Julia, for her part, refused to be intimidated. When Dr. Thomas tried to undermine her openly, questioning her diagnoses or spreading false claims, she met him head-on. Calm, articulate, and armed with facts, she corrected him in public without raising her voice. Each time, she emerged unscathed, her composure only strengthening her standing within the community.

By the end of the week, it was clear to everyone: Deer Lodge finally had a physician who served its people rather than lorded over them. And no amount of spite from Dr. Thomas could change that.

12

Law Before Wrath

Since Joy and Julia had known one another since childhood, their friendship rekindled almost instantly. It felt natural, as though the years between them had simply folded away, leaving behind the same easy trust and shared understanding. They often walked home together after church, lingering beneath the tall trees, exchanging quiet observations and gentle laughter.

One Sunday, as the congregation filtered out and voices drifted toward the cemetery path, Julia suddenly slowed and slipped her arm through Joy's, tugging her a step aside.

"There's something that's been bothering me," Julia said thoughtfully. "I can't shake the feeling that Lydia looks awfully familiar. Do you think it's possible I've met her before?"

Joy frowned slightly and shrugged.

"I honestly don't know. She disappeared for several months after she ran off with the governor's son, but beyond that, I don't know much about her at all."

Julia fell silent, her brow furrowing as they continued walking. Then she stopped short, her breath catching.

"Oh. Oh, my goodness," she whispered. "I remember now. I was at her wedding."

Joy stared at her. "Julia... what are you talking about?"

"I'm certain of it," Julia insisted, her eyes wide. "One of my friends is close with Lydia's new beau, her husband now. I was visiting San Francisco at the time, and he invited me to attend as his date. I had to leave early because of a medical emergency back home, but I remember the bride clearly. It was her."

The world seemed to tilt. Joy's legs weakened, and she hurried toward a nearby bench at the edge of the cemetery, gripping the iron back as she sat down hard.

"Joy?" Julia dropped beside her, at once. "Are you all right?"

Joy nodded faintly, though her pulse thundered.

"Lydia is still married to Graham Harrison."

Julia recoiled. "That's—no. That's impossible."

"She never signed the divorce papers," Joy said hoarsely. "They are still legally married."

Julia stared at her, stunned. "Then how could she possibly—?"

"I think that's exactly why she married in San Francisco," Joy interrupted, her voice sharpening as the pieces clicked into place. "If she'd married here, someone would have recognized her. Someone would have asked questions. Crossing state lines was the only way to keep her lies intact." She blanched. "Which means she committed marriage fraud."

Julia shook her head slowly. "Do you think either of them, Graham or her new husband, know?"

"No," Joy said firmly. "She ran off with her new 'husband,' but everyone here believes she's merely courting him. And I'm certain she told the other man she was already divorced, or worse, painted Graham as dangerous, claimed he harassed her, and made it impossible to marry in Montana."

Julia let out a slow breath. "That is... astonishing. You warned me the Thomases lived by their own rules, but this?" She straightened, resolve hardening in her eyes. "This must end as soon as possible."

"How?" Joy asked quietly.

"Eric is studying law," Julia replied. "He began at Harvard but transferred to San Francisco to finish his studies a few months ago. If I had to wager, Lydia convinced him to transfer so she wouldn't be too far from her parents."

"And close enough to keep pulling Graham's strings," Joy muttered, her fists curling in her skirts.

"Exactly," Julia agreed. "My guess is she told Eric she was merely visiting her parents while he prepares for his final examinations. He's nearly finished, from what I understand."

"Do you know him well?"

Julia shook her head. "Not personally, but our mutual friend does. I can reach out to him easily. Eric needs to know the truth. With his education, his family's influence, and his legal standing, he could force Lydia into divorcing both men properly and at once. Graham and Eric both deserve to be free."

Hope flickered faintly in Joy's chest.

"If I write tomorrow," Julia continued, already planning, "we may see movement before Graham's birthday. The Harrisons invited me to celebrate with them, perhaps justice will arrive just in time."

Joy leaned back against the bench, her heart still racing, but for the first time in weeks, a sense of direction cut through the chaos.

"Yes," she said quietly. "Let's end her charade, once and for all."

"Betty, please add a few drops of chloroform to the cloth, just above her nose," Julia instructed calmly. The young nurse nodded at once, her hands steady as she followed the order with practiced precision. She adjusted the cloth carefully, watching the patient's breathing until it evened out, then glanced back at Julia for confirmation.

Cathleen stepped closer, a large towel folded neatly in her arms. Her expression was focused, with intent, though a flicker of excitement stirred beneath the surface. Julia met her gaze and gave a small, reassuring nod.

"As soon as I make the incision," Julia said evenly, "Betty will lift the baby out and hand the child to you. Be ready."

Cathleen swallowed and nodded again, tightening her grip on the towel. She was acutely aware of the gravity of the moment, of how much trust was being placed in her hands. Yet beneath the nerves was something else entirely: awe.

She watched Julia move with quiet authority, every motion deliberate, every decision measured. Since Julia's arrival in Deer Lodge, Cathleen had been captivated by her, by her confidence, her knowledge, and her unwavering calm in moments that would have sent most people into panic. Not long after that fascination took root, Cathleen had gathered the courage to ask if Julia might train her as a midwife. To her delight, Julia had agreed without hesitation.

"You've the right temperament for it," she had said simply. "And the willingness to learn."

Now, standing at her side, Cathleen felt the full weight of that opportunity settle upon her. This was no longer curiosity or idle interest. This was responsibility. Purpose. Julia glanced at her once more, her expression softening just a fraction.

"You're doing well," she murmured, just loud enough for Cathleen to hear. The words steadied her hands and her heart alike. Whatever happened next, Cathleen knew one thing for certain, this was where she was meant to be.

The baby's cry split the air the moment Julia lifted her free, sharp and indignant, the unmistakable sound of life. Cathleen reached out at once, her heart surging as she gathered the tiny, squirming bundle into her arms. She wrapped the infant securely in the towel and hurried to the small table nearby, where a bowl of warm water, clean cloths, and instruments waited.

Her hands trembled only slightly as she began to clean the baby, wiping away blood and fluid with gentle, practiced motions. The cries softened to ragged whimpers, then settled into a thin, persistent protest that made Cathleen's chest ache with wonder and fierce protectiveness.

"Betty, another bottle of alcohol," Julia said briskly without looking up. "I need to disinfect before stitching."

"Yes, Doctor," the nurse replied, turning toward the cupboard. The moment shattered into chaos. Glass exploded with a sharp crack, the sound echoing off the walls like a gunshot. Everyone froze. Shards skittered across the floor. Betty gasped, instinctively lifting her hands, still clutching the bottle of alcohol. A thin string dangled from its neck, trailing back to the remains of a second bottle smashed at her feet. For one heartbeat, there was stunned silence.

Then Julia looked up with alarm. White vapor curled upward from the broken glass, creeping along the floor like fog. A harsh, biting smell burned the air, stinging eyes and throat alike. Julia's face drained of color.

"That's hydrochloric acid," she said sharply. "Cathleen, out! Take the baby out now. Betty, we must move the patient. Immediately!"

"But she hasn't been stitched yet!" Betty protested, panic flaring in her eyes.

"There's no time," Julia snapped. "Move!"

Cathleen didn't hesitate. She gathered the baby tighter against her chest and fled the room, coughing as she went, the infant's cries muffled against her shoulder. Behind her, Julia and Betty worked in frantic unison, lifting the unconscious woman from the operating table onto the waiting bed. Blood stained the sheets as they covered her quickly with a blanket and rushed her into the second operating room across the hall.

Julia spun back into the contaminated room, holding her breath as long as she could. She threw open the windows, cold air rushing in, then grabbed instruments, thread, anything she could salvage to finish the operation next door. Her sleeve caught the edge of the table. The bottle of chloroform tipped.

"No—!" Julia lunged for it, but it was too late. The glass struck the floor and shattered, sharp and final, and the sickly-sweet fumes burst upward in a suffocating wave. Julia staggered back, coughing, her vision blurring. "Help!" she tried to call, but the word barely left her lips. Darkness closed in swiftly, mercilessly. Julia collapsed to the floor as the room filled with fumes, the echo of breaking glass still ringing in her ears.

Cathleen peered into the room, but the acrid stench stopped her cold. Her eyes burned instantly, her lungs protesting even from the doorway. She recoiled, heart hammering. A moment later, Nurse Betty burst through the haze, her face pale, eyes wide with fear.

"We must get her out of there. Now."

Cathleen nodded, forcing herself to think past the panic clawing at her chest.

"I need to finish stitching the incision," Betty continued urgently. "If I don't, the patient will bleed to death. You must pull Dr. Preston out, but don't breathe the fumes. They can be fatal. Hurry."

Cathleen's pulse thundered. She snatched several of the cloth diapers she had prepared for the baby and pressed them over her nose and mouth, layering them thickly before drawing a steadying breath and tying them securely behind her head. Then she stepped back into the room.

The fumes were overwhelming. Her eyes stung, tears streaming instantly as she dropped to her knees beside Julia. She slipped her arms beneath the doctor's shoulders, braced herself, and dragged her backward, inch by agonizing inch, until she could get a proper grip beneath Julia's arms. With a grunt of effort, Cathleen hauled her clear of the shattered glass and into the hallway.

She kicked the door shut with her heel and staggered back, lungs burning. Julia lay motionless on the floor.

Cathleen didn't allow herself to stop. She sprinted into another room, grabbed a thick blanket, and rushed back, shoving it hard against the gap beneath the door to seal it off. Only then did she glance down, and her stomach twisted. Blood seeped through Julia's clothing. Shards of glass glittered against the fabric, some embedded deep.

"Oh no..." Cathleen whispered, fear tightening her throat. They needed help. Immediately. She bolted out of the clinic, skirts flying, scanning desperately until she spotted two familiar figures.

"Sheriff Baker! Barry!" she shouted. "I need your help, at once!"

One look at her blood-smeared apron was all it took. They rushed toward her without a word. As they moved, Cathleen explained in short, urgent bursts, barely slowing her stride. When they reached Julia, still unconscious, the men exchanged a grim look before carefully lifting her and carrying the young physician into the room Cathleen indicated. Betty appeared moments later, breathless but composed, her hands already moving with purpose. The two men withdrew, knowing there was nothing more they could do for the moment.

"We need to get her clothes off and remove any glass still lodged in her skin," she said. "I've stitched the patient, but someone must stay with her. She cannot move when she wakes."

Cathleen nodded, swallowing hard. "I'll stay with the mother and baby. I'm not trained for this."

"That's the right call," Betty said, already turning. Cathleen hurried with her, grabbing clean linens, antiseptics, and bandages along the way. Thankfully, both operating rooms were fully stocked. There would be no need to return to the poisoned room.

As Betty set to work, tending Julia's wounds, Cathleen slipped away to the recovery room, where the young mother lay pale but alive, her baby bundled safely nearby. Only then, only once everyone was accounted for, did Cathleen allow her shaking hands, to still. Julia had saved countless lives. Now it was their turn to save hers.

Julia stirred with a low, pained moan as consciousness crept back in. Her head throbbed dully, her limbs heavy and uncooperative. She tried to shift and hissed as sharp pain flared across her back and shoulders.

"Easy," Betty said at once, her voice calm but brisk. "Don't move."

Julia realized she was lying on her stomach. The air was cool against her skin, and every breath carried a faint sting. She became dimly aware of careful hands working methodically along her back and arms.

"Glass," Julia murmured, the word rough in her throat. "The bottles—"

"Yes," Betty replied. "You were cut when they shattered. I'm removing the fragments now." She worked swiftly, practiced and steadily. "Most of the wounds are shallow. Your clothing took the worst of it. A few will need stitches, but you'll heal."

Julia let out a slow breath, relief and anger tangling in her chest.

"The patient?"

"She's stable. You saved her life." Betty paused just long enough for the words to sink in. "I finished closing the incision. Cathleen stayed with her and the baby. They're both safe."

Julia closed her eyes briefly, tension draining from her shoulders. *Thank goodness.*

"What happened after I fell?" she asked quietly. Betty told her everything, about the fumes, the rushed evacuation, Cathleen dragging her from the poisoned room, the sheriff and Barry carrying her to safety. Julia listened in silence, her jaw tightening with each detail. When Betty finished securing the last bandage, she straightened.

"I'll stay with you until you're settled. Once I'm certain you're stable, I'll send Cathleen back in."

Julia nodded, but her hands curled slowly into fists against the sheet as the nurse moved toward the door. Another accident, she thought grimly. Another coincidence, far too convenient. Willard Thomas. The name burned in her mind with absolute certainty. This had not been chance or carelessness. It had been calculated. Someone had meant to incapacitate her. Perhaps even kill her.

If she had been alone... if Cathleen and Betty hadn't been there... if help hadn't come so quickly, the outcome could have been catastrophic, not only for the mother on the table, but for Julia herself.

Her jaw set, resolve hardening beneath the lingering ache in her body. Thomas had crossed a line. Whatever game he thought he was playing, it was no longer petty rivalry or professional jealousy.

It was war.

It didn't take long before the young physician was back on her feet. The new mother was recovering well, her color returning steadily, and the baby, strong-lunged and healthy, had already become the pride of the household. Outwardly, all appeared calm again. But inside the clinic, Julia Preston paced the front room like a caged animal.

Her steps were measured, back and forth across the worn wooden floor, hands clasped behind her as she replayed the events repeatedly. Too precise. Too deliberate. What had happened in the operating room had not been chance, nor clumsiness, nor the result of poor storage. Someone had meant it to happen. Willard Thomas.

Once more, he had crossed a line, and this time, the consequences could have been fatal. The front door opened, and Cathleen entered first, followed closely by Joy, Uncle Gerald, and Sheriff Baker. The concern on their faces mirrored the storm raging inside Julia.

"What exactly happened?" Dave asked, his brow furrowed. Cathleen had given him only the barest explanation, enough to summon him quickly, but not enough to paint the full picture. Julia stopped pacing and faced them, her jaw tight as she recounted the incident in detail: the tied bottles, the shattered glass, the acid fumes, the chloroform spilling across the floor. As she spoke, her hands curled into fists at her sides.

"This was no accident," she said flatly. "Someone deliberately tied the two bottles together, knowing exactly what would happen when one was pulled free. That kind of reaction doesn't occur by coincidence. Whoever did this, understood chemistry. Understood medicine."

Silence followed her words, heavy and unsettled.

Dave broke it first. "You believe it was Dr. Thomas."

Julia let out a short, humorless scoff.

"Of course it was. Who else would risk something this dangerous?" Her eyes flashed. "He knows precisely what hydrochloric acid does when exposed like that. He knew the layout of my clinic, knew when I'd be operating, and knew how to turn it into a death trap." Her voice hardened.

"The only thing stopping us from arresting him is evidence. Unless someone saw him sneaking into my clinic, he'll deny everything, and he'll get away with it."

Joy's hands tightened together. "So, he nearly killed you, and a patient, and there's nothing we can do?"

"Not yet," Julia replied grimly. Gerald dragged a hand down his face, breathing out sharply.

"This is spiraling out of control. We cannot wait until someone is killed before we act." He straightened, resolve hardening in his posture. "I'll be calling a town meeting.

Everyone deserves to know what's happening, and that we're taking this seriously."

Joy tilted her head. "Dr. Thomas and his wife will attend?"

"They will," Gerald said. "And I want him to hear it plainly, that Deer Lodge will not tolerate intimidation, sabotage, or threats to life. Not from him or anyone else."

He turned to Dave. "Sheriff, it's time you had more help. Recruit a few good men from town as deputies. We need eyes everywhere, people we trust. I'll also be speaking to the marshals. They need to stay involved."

Dave nodded slowly. "I agree. We can't afford to be reactive anymore."

"I'm sure Dylan Andrews would be more than willing to serve as a deputy while he's here," Joy added, her tone steady but firm. "He already knows the situation, and he won't look the other way."

A murmur of agreement followed. Julia finally exhaled, some of the tension easing from her shoulders, not because the danger had passed, but because she was no longer facing it alone. Whatever Willard Thomas thought he was doing, he had underestimated one thing. Deer Lodge was done being silent. And this time, they were ready.

After her uncle and the sheriff had taken their leave, the clinic grew quieter, the tension settled into a low, uneasy hum. Joy turned back to Julia, studying her friend's pale face and the rigid way she held herself.

"Are you all right?" Joy asked softly. Julia nodded, though her jaw remained clenched.

"Physically, yes. But I'm furious." She exhaled sharply. "That man nearly killed someone today. Nearly killed me. And he did it with calculation."

Joy folded her arms, unease tightening in her chest.

"I don't understand him. If he's so unhappy here, if the town has turned against him, why doesn't he just leave? A man with his education could start over in another town. He could apply at a hospital, build a new practice somewhere else. Why stay where he's clearly no longer wanted?"

Julia's eyes darkened as she considered it.

"Because this was never just about medicine."

Joy frowned. "What do you mean?"

Julia paced a few steps, then stopped, her voice lowering.

"Men like Willard Thomas don't walk away when they lose favor. They dig in. Deer Lodge is the one place where he once held power, absolute authority over life, death, and reputation. Being forced out would mean admitting defeat. To him, leaving would be humiliation."

A chill crept up Joy's spine. "So, he'd rather destroy everything around him than surrender?"

"Yes," Julia said bluntly. "And there's more. If he leaves now, under a cloud of suspicion, it follows him. Other towns will ask questions. Hospitals will want references. Here, he can still pretend he's the wronged party, the persecuted physician driven out by gossip and meddling women."

Joy's hands curled into fists. "So, he stays, lashes out, and tries to scare us into backing down."

"Exactly." Julia met her gaze. "He's not fighting to stay in Deer Lodge because he loves it here. He's fighting because he refuses to lose."

Joy swallowed, her thoughts turning grim.

"Then he won't stop. Not on his own."

"No," Julia agreed quietly. "He won't. Which means we must be smarter, faster, and united." She gave Joy a thin, determined smile. "The good news is, he's already making mistakes. Dangerous ones."

Joy straightened, resolve hardening in her chest.

"Then we'll be ready when he makes the next one."

And in the silence that followed, both women understood the truth they had not yet spoken aloud: Willard Thomas was no longer merely a problem. He was a threat.

That afternoon, the adults of the small town crowded into the meeting hall, the air thick with heat, sweat, and barely restrained fury. Benches scraped loudly across the floor as men and women packed in shoulder to shoulder, their murmurs already sharp with accusation before the meeting had truly begun.

Joy sat beside her aunt, her spine straight, her hands folded tightly in her lap. Across the room, Willard Thomas stood rigid, his jaw clenched, his wife and daughter hovering near him like coiled vipers. Gerald rose and struck the gavel once. The sound cracked through the hall, but it did little to quell the anger simmering beneath the surface.

"As many of you are already aware," he began, his voice calm but firm, "there was a deliberate act of sabotage at Dr. Preston's clinic earlier today. A newborn and two women nearly lost their lives."

That was all it took. The room erupted.

"That was Thomas's doing!" a farmer shouted, leaping to his feet, his face red with rage. He jabbed a finger across the hall. "We all know it was him!"

A wave of applause and angry agreement thundered through the room. Willard Thomas sprang up, his chair clattering backward.

"You have no right to accuse me!" he bellowed. "There is no proof, no evidence whatsoever, and—"

"Order! Order!" Gerald roared, slamming the gavel down hard enough to splinter the sound through the uproar. "Sit down, Dr. Thomas!"

The noise ebbed only slightly, voices still snapping like sparks in dry grass. Gerald waited, his jaw tight, until he could be heard again.

"Dr. Thomas is correct about one thing," he said evenly. "There is, at this moment, no direct evidence tying him to what happened today."

A chorus of protests surged up at once.

"That's nonsense!"

"Everyone knows it was him!"

"You'd have to be blind not to see it!"

Gerald lifted a hand. "I understand your anger. Believe me, I do. What occurred today was reckless, malicious, and could have ended in death. We will not dismiss it, and we will not ignore it."

The room gradually quieted, townspeople leaning forward, listening now.

"To that end," Gerald continued, "Sheriff Baker and Deputy Flynn will be recruiting additional men to serve as deputies. We will increase patrols, keep watch over the clinic, and ensure that no one moves about this town unnoticed with harmful intent. Whatever threat is among us, it will find Deer Lodge far less welcoming from this day forward."

Murmurs of approval rippled through the crowd.

"What happened today," Gerald added grimly, "could have cost two women their lives, and a child's. There will not be a repeat."

But the farmer who had spoken earlier was not satisfied. He surged to his feet again, fists clenched.

"We all know it was Willard Thomas!" he shouted. "So why are we dancing around it? Why don't we run him and his wife, and that terrible daughter, out of town? Or better yet..." His voice dropped into something ugly and dangerous. "... hang him and be done with it."

Joy and Julia exchanged a quick, uneasy glance. The meeting was slipping beyond control. Gerald struck the gavel again, but the sharp crack was swallowed by rising shouts. Several men surged forward, grabbing Willard Thomas by the arms, already hauling him toward the aisle as if the matter were decided.

Before anyone could stop her, Joy sprang onto the bench she had been sitting on and put two fingers in her mouth.

A loud, piercing whistle cut through the chaos like a blade. Silence fell instantly. Every head turned. Every eye fixed on her.

"Listen," Joy said, her voice clear and steady despite the pounding of her heart. "I understand how you all feel. I'm not saying Willard Thomas is innocent. But you cannot hang a man simply because you believe he's guilty. What if you're wrong?"

"We're not wrong!" another farmer shouted. "He's been poison to this town ever since he arrived. The Thomases only care about themselves."

A rumble of agreement rolled through the room.

"That still isn't reason enough to kill someone," Joy shot back. "You don't want blood on your hands. I admire that this town stands up against evil, but acting on rage alone will only destroy what you're trying to protect. You must work together to find a just solution. Dr. Thomas is innocent until proven guilty. That principle must apply to everyone, or it means nothing at all."

Willard let out a harsh scoff. "I don't need someone like you defending me," he spat. Before Joy could react, one of the men shoved him hard against the wall.

"You're lucky she has more sense than the rest of us," the man growled, to loud applause. "If it were up to us, you'd already be swinging from a tree." He wasn't finished. "And you don't even deserve Joy Collins speaking on your behalf. You've treated her like filth from the moment she arrived. You blame her for your daughter's spoiled behavior, for every misfortune you face. Lydia left a good man because she was never told no. Your family is toxic to this town, but that is not Joy's doing."

Willard twisted free and snarled, "Joy Collins brought this trouble here! She convinced her uncle to hire that woman—Miss Preston. She made eyes at my daughter's husband and had him kiss her while Lydia is still married to him. That is adultery, at the very least!"

"It is *Dr. Preston* to you," Julia snapped, stepping forward, her voice sharp as steel. "I was trained exactly as you were. Your prejudice does not diminish my skill."

"And stop slandering Joy," Graham said, his voice dark with fury as he moved to her side. "I kissed Joy. She did not encourage it. Lydia is the adulterer, not her."

Willard sneered. "She's living under your roof. No one knows what goes on behind closed doors. For all we know, you're consummating every night."

A collective gasp of disgust swept the room. Graham moved faster than anyone could react. His fist connected with Willard's face in a sharp, brutal arc, sending the older man crashing to the floor. Before Willard could scramble up, Graham seized him by the shirt, ready to strike again.

"Graham!" Joy forced herself between them, her uncle and the sheriff right on her heels. She looked up at Graham, her blue eyes fierce but pleading.

"He isn't worth it," she said quietly. "Don't give him that power over you. He has nothing left but bitterness and lies."

Something in her gaze reached him. Graham's chest heaved, but his grip loosened. He stepped back, jaw tight, fists clenched at his sides. When Willard opened his mouth again, Gerald moved instantly, placing himself squarely in front of Joy.

"Shut your mouth, Thomas," he said coldly. "I am finished with your attacks on my niece's virtue. As promised, I will contact my lawyer, and everyone in this room will serve as witness."

"Hear, hear," echoed from all sides. The tension was unmistakable now. One more word, and no one would stop what followed. Gerald's voice cut through the room once more, resolute and final.

"You will stop blaming others for your own actions. There is nothing improper between Graham Harrison and Joy Collins. Accuse them again, and I will see you banished from this town before the courts ever convene. We extended welcome. You rejected it. We are under no obligation to endure your disgrace forever."

A low murmur of agreement swept the hall. Willard shot Gerald a venomous look, but before he could speak, the mayor had already turned back to the assembly.

"Sheriff Baker and Deputy Flynn have selected several men to serve as deputies," Gerald announced. "Any able-bodied man of age who wishes to volunteer is welcome."

The meeting did not end peacefully. But it ended united.

13

Lessons in Rope and Restraint

Joy remained silent on the ride back to the ranch, her gaze fixed on the darkening horizon. The rhythmic clatter of hooves and wheels did nothing to still the storm inside her. Every member of the Harrison family noticed her withdrawal, the way her shoulders curled inward as though she were bracing against an unseen blow, but out of quiet respect, no one pressed her. Not yet.

When they arrived, Joy slipped down from the buckboard and made straight for the house, intent on retreating to the safety of her room before the tears she was holding back betrayed her. She had nearly reached the staircase when a gentle but firm hand closed around her arm.

"Joy," Darlene said softly, stopping her. "Please, share with us what is troubling you. Don't keep it locked away. You are family now."

Joy's breath hitched. Tears welled instantly, blurring her vision, and she nodded mutely as Darlene guided her into the sitting room. The others followed without a word. They settled around her, Cathleen and Olivia nearby, Brigham lowering himself onto the sofa beside her. He wrapped an arm around her shoulders and pulled her close in a quiet, fatherly gesture that made her chest ache.

She lifted her tear-filled eyes to his face, and for a fleeting moment, the resemblance to her father struck her so keenly it stole her breath. The same steadiness. The same quiet strength. The same way of offering comfort without judgment. Something inside her loosened, and the tears finally spilled freely down her cheeks.

Darlene knelt in front of her and took her hands—warm and reassuring.

"Is this because of the awful things Dr. Thomas said earlier?" she asked gently. Joy nodded, her voice trembling as she spoke.

"I don't understand why he attacks me like that. I know I shouldn't let it get to me. I try not to, but it hurts. Why would he accuse me of something so vile? Of adultery?" Her voice cracked on the word. Brigham exhaled slowly and drew her closer, his arm firm around her back.

"Because he sees you as a threat," he said quietly. "You are everything his daughter is not."

Joy looked up at him, startled.

"You are kind-hearted, loyal, and determined," Brigham continued, his voice steady and sincere. "You are confident without being cruel, strong without being hardened. You love deeply and fiercely. Anyone can see it in the way you protect your sister and your nieces, how you shoulder burdens without complaint, how you put others before yourself. Lydia, on the other hand, has chosen to live as a victim, no matter the cost. Her world revolves around herself alone."

Darlene nodded in agreement.

"You never made your life here about you, Joy. Not once. From the moment you arrived, you were thinking of Alice, of the girls, of how to keep others safe. Lydia only values relationships as long as she remains the center of them. And as for Willard Thomas..." Her expression hardened. "He attacks your virtue because it's the only thing he thinks he can tarnish. He has nothing real to use against you, so he reaches for lies. He hopes that by striking at your character, he can make others doubt you, because he knows the truth is known only by those close to you."

Joy swallowed hard, the knot in her chest easing just a little.

"But you don't need to fear that," Cathleen said, leaning forward with a warm, reassuring smile. "The people of Deer Lodge see you for who you are. They care for you. They trust you. Dr. Thomas, his wife, and his daughter have lost every scrap of credibility they ever had. No one takes their poison seriously anymore."

Olivia nodded emphatically. "You belong here, Joy. Fully. Completely."

Joy closed her eyes as fresh tears slipped free, but this time, they weren't born solely of pain. Wrapped in the steady presence of the Harrisons, she felt something she hadn't allowed herself to feel in a long while. Safety. Belonging. Family.

"Gerald, Dave, Dylan, what are you doing here?" Brigham asked, genuine surprise in his voice as he ushered them inside.

"We need to talk," Gerald replied gravely. "Specifically, about Dr. Preston. Something about this whole situation doesn't sit right with me, and we don't know how freely we can speak in town anymore."

Brigham's expression hardened at once.

"Then you came to the right place. Come in." He led them into his study, the familiar room heavy with leather, books, and the quiet authority Brigham carried so naturally. Graham and Joy followed, exchanging a glance before taking seats near the fireplace. Once everyone had settled, Gerald cleared his throat.

"We spoke with nearly half the town tonight," he began. "No one saw anything suspicious. No strangers. No unusual noises. And yet someone managed to get into Dr. Preston's clinic without difficulty." He shook his head. "That troubles me."

Silence followed as each person turned the problem over in their mind.

Joy broke it. "Aren't the two marshals supposed to be keeping an eye not only on Alice, but also on Julia and her clinic?" she asked carefully. "How could they have missed something like that?"

Dylan straightened slightly. "There are many ways someone could sneak into the clinic without being noticed," he said, clearly bristling at the implication. "It doesn't necessarily mean the marshals failed in their duties."

Joy's brows drew together. "But if patrolling the area is part of their responsibility, then they should have been close enough to notice something. That's literally their job."

Dave shifted in his chair, sensing the tension.

"With the additional deputies we've sworn in, it'll be much harder for anyone to cause trouble going forward," he said. "Extra eyes. Extra boots on the ground."

Several heads nodded, but Brigham did not look convinced.

"I agree with Joy," he said at last, his tone firm. "Those marshals don't strike me as particularly invested in what's happening here. Every time I'm in town, I see them leaning against buildings, laughing with pretty young women, far more than I see them patrolling."

The words settled heavily in the room. Joy hesitated, then spoke again, her voice quieter but no less pointed.

"Or perhaps Dr. Thomas has convinced them to look the other way. Or pays them to."

The reaction was immediate. Dylan stared at her.

"Are you suggesting my uncle hired marshals who can be bought?" His voice sharpened with offense. Joy didn't rise to it.

"I thought Mr. Gregory was supposed to contact marshal headquarters."

"He was," Dylan admitted after a moment. "But Uncle Jonas insisted on handling it himself. I don't think he trusts Charles much."

Joy shook her head slowly.

"Then maybe working together wasn't the wisest decision. Business partners should be aligned, especially in matters like this."

Dylan exhaled. "My uncle never liked the arrangement. From what I understand, it was your father who encouraged them to work together."

Joy blinked. "My father?" She fell silent, absorbing that, then suddenly stiffened as another thought struck her. "What if the two marshals aren't real marshals at all?"

The room erupted in startled reactions, sharp intakes of breath, chairs shifting. Dylan's irritation vanished, replaced by shock.

"What do you mean?" Gerald asked, studying her closely.

"I mean," Joy said steadily, "Willard Thomas has shown us repeatedly that he will do anything to maintain control. If he has connections, and I believe he does, it isn't impossible that he manipulated the situation and placed impostors here. Men pretending to be marshals."

The idea hung in the air, chilling in its plausibility.

"That would be easy enough to verify," Gerald said at last, his voice calm but grave. "Dylan, do you know which headquarters your uncle contacted?"

"I assume Helena," Dylan replied slowly. "But Sacramento or San Francisco are also possibilities."

Dave nodded. "I can ask them tomorrow, casually. Badge numbers. Assignments. They won't think twice about answering."

"But we must be careful," Brigham said, leaning forward. "If they *are* impostors, or compromised, we don't tip our hand."

"Exactly," Gerald agreed. "We keep this quiet for now. If Thomas is behind this, we need to understand why he's escalating, and how far he's willing to go."

Joy folded her hands in her lap, unease curling in her stomach. Whatever they were facing now felt larger than petty vendettas or wounded pride. Someone, somewhere, was playing a very dangerous game.

Although the situation with Dr. Thomas had not yet erupted into open violence again, the damage to his standing in Deer Lodge was unmistakable. Word traveled fast, and most townsfolk openly blamed him for the incident at Julia Preston's clinic. One by one, his patients stopped coming. Mothers chose Julia without hesitation, farmers sought her careful hands, and even those who had once defended Willard Thomas quietly crossed the street rather than greeting him.

He had already lost many of his patients over the past months, but after the town meeting, he found himself nearly without work at all. The rejection ate at him. Rather than reflect on his own actions, he stewed in bitterness, directing all his rage toward Joy and Graham. In his mind, they were the architects of his ruin, never once considering that his own cruelty, arrogance, and threats had driven the town away.

The response from Deer Lodge was swift and decisive. Dozens of men volunteered to serve as deputy sheriffs, determined to protect their families and their town. With so many eyes watching, Willard Thomas and his family could no longer approach Dr. Preston's clinic unnoticed. Anyone lingering too long or behaving suspiciously was questioned at once. The clinic, once a target, became one of the safest buildings in town.

And yet, despite the hostility, the Thomases did not leave. Their stubborn refusal unsettled everyone. A man with no patients, no allies, and no goodwill would have had every reason to move on, yet Willard remained, tight-lipped and simmering, his wife equally withdrawn, Lydia lurking like a shadow along the edges of town.

It left the people of Deer Lodge uneasy. If pride alone were the reason, surely it would have broken by now. The question whispered in homes and on street corners was the same: What truly kept the Thomas family in Deer Lodge?

One Saturday afternoon, as Joy was tightening the cinch on her saddle, she sensed someone approaching. Most of the ranch hands had already gone into town or retreated to their bunkhouses, and Cathleen and Olivia were both away on dates, leaving the yard unusually quiet.

She glanced up just as Graham came closer, an easy, dashing smile playing on his lips. Warmth rushed to her cheeks at once, but she steadied herself and waited, pretending to be far more absorbed in her task than she truly was.

"Do you have any plans this afternoon?" he asked casually.

She shook her head. "I was just going to ride out for a bit. Why?"

"I was wondering..." He hesitated just long enough to make her curious. "Would you be interested in learning how to use a lasso, and maybe a little about breaking in a horse?"

Joy stared at him, momentarily speechless.

"I—I don't understand."

He chuckled softly. "It hasn't exactly gone unnoticed how much you enjoy watching when my father and I work with the horses, or when the hands practice roping cattle. I thought perhaps you might want to learn yourself. Was I wrong?"

Her head shook at once. "No, not at all. But I have no experience. And..." She bit her lip. "That's men's work, isn't it? I don't want to make a fool of myself, or have anyone laugh."

His grin softened into something gentler, more reassuring.

"That's exactly why I asked now. There won't be an audience, and I promise you, I won't laugh. As for it being men's work, well, tradition doesn't make it law."

Her face brightened, delight flickering across her features before she could hide it. She swung up into the saddle out of habit, but Graham lifted a hand.

"Not yet. We'll start with the lasso first. Come, behind the barn. There are a few old tree stumps that make perfect practice targets."

Joy followed him, her heart beating just a little faster than usual. He demonstrated several times how to coil the rope, how to hold it just right, how to let the loop fly without forcing it. He made it look effortless.

When he finally handed her the rope, nerves fluttered through her. She wanted to do well, desperately, but she also knew this wasn't something one mastered on the first attempt. Her first few throws fell short or collapsed in awkward loops, earning her a sympathetic smile rather than mockery.

"You're overthinking it," Graham said gently. After a moment, he stepped closer, then closer still, until he was standing right behind her. His arms came around her, guiding her hands, adjusting her stance.

The nearness of him, made her breath hitch. She could feel the solid strength of his frame, the flex of his muscles as he moved, the faint, clean scent of leather and soap and something unmistakably *him*. Concentration became a losing battle.

If only you weren't so impossible, she scolded herself silently. A flicker of anger stirred beneath the warmth, anger at Lydia, at the tangled situation that kept them suspended in this fragile in-between. If not for her, Graham and Joy might have stood on honest ground, free to explore what had been simmering between them from the start.

She clung to the hope that Julia's letter had already reached the right hands, that the truth about Lydia's double life would soon surface and end the charade once and for all. For now, though, Graham's voice was low at her ear, his hands steadying hers, and the rope sailed forward, this time catching the stump cleanly. His pleased laugh sent a thrill through her.

"There," he murmured. "See? I knew you had it in you."

Joy smiled, breathless, knowing full well that the lasso was only part of what she was learning that afternoon, and that the greater danger lay not in the rope, but in how quickly her heart was learning to follow his lead.

14

Explosion in the Pasture

She heard Graham's deep voice murmur her name and looked up, startled. Their faces were suddenly only inches apart, and the sparks that flared between them sent a tremor through her. Graham leaned closer, instinctively drawn, but Joy dropped her gaze at once, forcing herself to focus on the lasso instead of the man behind her, the man who was steadily unraveling her composure.

After guiding her through a few more throws, he finally stepped back and let her try on her own again. She took a steadying breath, lifted the rope, and promptly lost control of it. The lasso slipped from her hands and looped neatly around Graham instead of the tree stump. Heat flooded her face.

"Oh, Graham, I'm so sorry."

But he only laughed, a rich, unrestrained sound. Seeing her crestfallen expression, he moved closer again, gentling his tone.

"That was quite good. If the rope hadn't slipped, you'd have caught the stump dead on."

"You really think so?" she asked, hopeful despite herself.

"I do." His hand rose, brushing her cheek with tender familiarity. The explosion of butterflies reminded her exactly why she needed distance, why she could not let him get this close. She swallowed hard.

"Maybe... maybe we should stop for today," she said softly. "It'll be dark soon."

His gaze never left hers. "There's still time for more lessons," he replied evenly. Then, with a glint of mischief, he added, "And if you ever need to catch a person with a lasso, this is how it's done."

Before she could protest, he stepped back, flicked the rope, and in seconds Joy found herself neatly bound, her arms pinned at her sides. She gasped as he drew her toward him.

"Well," he murmured, his voice low and rough, "what am I to do with you now that you're my prisoner?"

Her heart thundered so loudly she was sure he could hear it. He lifted her chin, forcing her to meet his gaze, trapping her not with rope, but with his eyes.

"Perhaps a kiss on the eyes," he whispered, brushing his lips gently over her eyelids. "Perhaps a kiss on the cheeks."

Goosebumps raced along her arms and spine.

"Perhaps a kiss on the nose."

Her breath hitched. Every sensible thought screamed at her to stop him, yet when his mouth hovered near hers, her resolve wavered.

"Perhaps," he breathed, "a kiss on those soft lips—"

His kiss stole her breath and scattered her thoughts to the wind. For one dangerous moment, she wanted nothing more than to melt into him, to answer his kiss with all the longing she had kept tightly caged. But reality surged back with painful force. She pushed against him, gasping for air.

"This isn't fair," she said shakily. "Please... stop torturing me. We can't do this. You're still married, Graham." She couldn't look at him. She felt his gaze on her all the same. Then his fingers found her chin again, lifting her face. The moment their eyes met, tears spilled free.

"Please don't," she whispered. "It isn't right. I—I want to be with you too. I want to kiss you back. But we would regret it. I'm trying to be strong, for both of us, and you're making it so very hard."

He exhaled slowly, released the lasso, and pulled her into his arms. She cried against his chest, hating that Lydia still held this power over them, still stood between what they could be.

"I'm sorry, Joy," he said quietly. "I keep telling myself the marriage was never real, that it makes this all right. But you're right. Forgive me for making this harder than it already is." He paused, a trace of bitter humor in his voice. "Perhaps Mrs. Thomas was right, men are weak." He kissed the top of her head and stepped back. Joy wiped her tears quickly and lifted her chin.

"As much as I hate that Lydia is doing this on purpose," she said firmly, "I won't give her or her father the satisfaction of turning me into an adulteress. She thrives on being the victim."

He nodded, thoughtful, restrained once more. After a moment, he offered her a small, earnest smile.

"Come," he said. "Let me show you how to break in a horse."

The second lesson proved far harder than Joy had expected. It quickly became apparent that men held a clear advantage, stronger builds, greater leverage, the ability to force a horse through sheer power when needed. But Joy was nothing if not determined. She gritted her teeth and tried again and again, refusing to be discouraged.

Each attempt ended the same way. The horse bucked, twisted, and sent her flying within seconds, but every single time, Graham was there, steady hands catching her before she could hit the hard ground. Still, she barely lasted a heartbeat in the saddle, before being unseated again, her pride bruised far more than her body.

As the sun dipped below the horizon, the air cooled sharply. Once more, Graham lifted her into the saddle, and once more, she was thrown and caught almost immediately.

"That's enough for today," he said at last, his tone gentle but firm. Then, with unmistakable confidence, and just a hint of swagger, he added, "Let me show you one more time how it's done."

Joy stepped aside, folding her arms as she watched him mount the horse. The animal immediately protested, tossing its head and stamping its hooves in open defiance. Of course, Graham stayed on far longer than she had, his balance impressive and his control undeniable, but the horse was clearly determined to prove a point. One powerful buck later, Graham went sailing straight into a large mud puddle. Joy stared for half a second in stunned silence. Then she burst into helpless laughter.

Graham pushed himself upright, dripping and spattered with mud, and raised an eyebrow at her. A slow, confident grin spread across his face.

Oh no. Joy didn't wait to see what he would do next. She spun on her heel, scrambled over the fence, and sprinted toward the house as fast as her legs would carry her. She had a respectable head start, but it didn't matter. Graham's long strides closed the distance in seconds. He caught her just as she reached the door.

Before she could protest, she was swung over his shoulder, and he took off toward the lake behind the house. Her heart nearly leapt out of her chest.

"No, please, don't throw me in there!" she begged, laughing and breathless all at once. He didn't so much as slow down. With a triumphant shout, he jumped straight into the water with her, muddy clothes and all.

Joy resurfaced sputtering, hair plastered to her face. When she wiped the water from her eyes, Graham's equally soaked, and entirely unapologetic, face was right there, wearing a sheepish grin that sent her heart fluttering despite herself. She splashed him once in protest and swam for shore.

He beat her there and hauled her out with ease, his hands warm and strong as he pulled her close. She gasped, breathless in more ways than one.

"That was not fair," she accused.

"You laughed at me," he countered.

"And you bragged about your skill at breaking horses," she shot back, meeting his gaze squarely. "I believe the animal merely wanted to teach you a lesson."

"Is that so?"

She nodded, lips twitching. His grin softened, turning unmistakably fond, and he tapped her nose lightly.

"Well then," he said, "I suppose I was only teaching you a lesson of my own, about the consequences of letting your sass get out of hand."

She shook her head, though the warmth in her cheeks betrayed her. With a soft smile, she turned toward the house, suddenly keenly aware of her soaked clothes, and of how close she'd been to losing herself in him once again. It was time to change into something dry.

Joy rode into town two days later, the familiar streets stirring a quiet ache of longing in her chest. She hadn't spent proper time with her sister and nieces in far too long, and she missed her aunt and uncle as well. Since her cousin and the children had returned to Helena, her cousin's husband now stationed there, the house felt strangely hollow, its once-lively rooms echoing with absence.

Joy had suggested moving in to keep Alice company, but her uncle had gently refused. It was better, he'd said, if the sisters did not share the same household. At the time, she hadn't argued, yet the words lingered now, heavy with meaning she hadn't fully understood then.

When she arrived that afternoon, she greeted her aunt and embraced her sister, but it quickly became apparent that Dylan was there as well. Alice's attention barely strayed from him, her laughter lighter, her smiles brighter whenever he spoke. By now, it was common knowledge in town that the two adored one another. A proposal felt less like a possibility and more like an inevitability. Her uncle soon called her into his office, closing the door behind them with deliberate care.

"I finally heard back from the marshal headquarters in Helena," he said gravely. Joy's posture stiffened.

"And?"

"The two marshals stationed here both claimed that was where they were sent from," he continued. "But Helena denied dispatching anyone. Apparently, shortly after Jonas Andrews contacted them about protection for you, they received a second telegram, also sent under Jonas's name, but it originated here, in Deer Lodge."

Joy's brow furrowed. "I wonder who would do such a thing," she murmured, though dread was already tightening its grip on her chest. Her uncle nodded slowly.

"I spoke to Johnny at the post office. Asked if he remembered sending the second telegram. He did."

"And the person who sent it was Willard Thomas," Joy said flatly. Her uncle shook his head.

"No. According to Johnny... it was Dylan."

The room seemed to tilt.

"What?" The word barely made it past Joy's lips as the blood drained from her face. Her knees weakened, and before she could stop herself, her uncle was at her side, guiding her into a chair and pressing a glass of water into her trembling hands. Her stomach churned violently.

Dylan. The man who had sworn he meant no harm. The man who had promised, solemnly, that he would never be the cause of Alice's heartache. Joy took a shaky sip of water, breathing slowly, deliberately, until the spinning eased and the room steadied once more.

"Have you... have you asked him about it?" she finally managed. Her uncle shook his head.

"Not yet. I only received the confirmation earlier today. Knowing you'd be visiting, I asked Dave, Brigham, and Graham to come as well. I want witnesses. And I want your input, whether you believe him, once he speaks."

Joy nodded, though her throat felt tight. A heavy knot settled in her stomach, twisting painfully. If Dylan was involved, if he had deceived them all, it would devastate her. But worse... it would shatter Alice. She closed her eyes for a moment, pressing her fingers together, willing herself to be strong. Whatever truth awaited them, she had to face it.

A knock sounded at the front door. Joy's heart began to race, each beat echoing too loudly in her ears. The truth was only moments away now, and she found herself wishing, desperately, that she could slip out the back, mount her horse, and ride far from the answers she feared were waiting inside.

＊

Joy glanced up when the three men entered the room. They all moved toward her at once, concern etched into their faces, and she realized her cheeks must still be drained of color. Questions hovered on their lips, ready to spill, but she lifted a hand, stopping them before a single word could be spoken. Until she understood what was truly happening, she didn't want to be pressed about her emotions. She needed clarity before comfort. Her uncle and Dylan entered the office moments later.

"What's going on?" Dylan asked at once. "Did you finally hear back from the marshals?" His gaze swept the room and stalled when he found everyone staring at him. Gerald nodded gravely and recounted what he had discovered, each detail landing heavier than the last. When he reached Johnny's statement, Dylan went pale.

"I swear I didn't do that," he said sharply, shock ringing in his voice. "I never sent a telegram. Not to anyone."

"Unfortunately," Gerald replied evenly, "at this moment it is Johnny's word against yours."

Joy studied Dylan closely. His reaction didn't feel rehearsed or defensive. It was raw, startled, and deeply unsettled. If he was lying, he was an exceptional actor. She drew in a steadying breath and spoke.

"Is there a chance Johnny was pressured? Threatened... or blackmailed?"

Her uncle fell silent, considering.

"It's possible," he admitted slowly. "But if that's the case, how do we get the truth? If Johnny was threatened, he may be too afraid to speak freely."

"What if we promise him protection?" Dave offered. "His family too. Get them out of town until this is over."

Dylan nodded quickly, relief and resolve mixing in his expression.

"That could work. Charles Gregory is experienced with witness protection," he added. "He could arrange for Johnny to be transferred to another post office temporarily and place someone else here. His family could be relocated immediately."

Gerald nodded. "The U.S. Marshals are already sending men to arrest the two impostors. We'll keep that part quiet until it's done."

Joy's worry didn't ease. "And if Johnny still refuses to tell us who really sent the telegram? We may all suspect the same person, but without proof, he'll deny everything."

"Johnny said the original telegram was destroyed after it was sent," Gerald replied. "So, handwriting won't help us."

Brigham exhaled slowly through his teeth.

"Then we take whatever Johnny is willing to give us."

Gerald stood. "Agreed. We'll speak to him immediately. Dave, Dylan, you're coming with me. Once we've spoken to Johnny, we'll send a telegram to Mr. Gregory right away."

Both men nodded, already moving toward the door. They wasted no time, the weight of urgency pressing them forward. Brigham and Graham stepped closer to Joy once the room had emptied.

"Are you all right?" Graham asked quietly. She nodded, pressing her hand to her chest.

"Now that I know Dylan had nothing to do with it, yes. When Uncle Gerald first told me..." Her voice faltered. "I thought my heart would stop."

Brigham rested a reassuring hand on her shoulder.

"We'll get to the bottom of this. Whoever is pulling these strings won't get away with it."

Joy hoped he was right. For Alice's sake, and for all of theirs, she prayed the truth would come swiftly.

After hours of pressure and careful questioning, Johnny finally broke. He admitted that it had not been Dylan who sent the telegram, but no matter how hard they pressed, he refused to reveal who had. Fear was written plainly across his face, the kind that came from threats too real to ignore.

Charles Gregory acted at once. Within days, Johnny was transferred to a different post office under an assumed assignment, his family relocated alongside him and placed under quiet protection. It wasn't justice, not yet, but it was safety, and for now, that would have to suffice.

A few days later, life at the Harrison ranch took on a brighter tone. Brigham and Graham decided it was time for Joy's first true cattle-catching experience. Graham had practiced with her every day since her lasso lesson, patiently correcting her grip, her swing, her timing. By now, she could hit a fence post with remarkable accuracy, the rope snapping tight with confident precision. Even Brigham had raised an impressed brow more than once.

They began just as planned, Joy tossing the lasso again and again at a sturdy fence post while mounted, her movements smooth and assured. Only when both men were satisfied did they guide her toward the open pasture where the cattle grazed.

Brigham rode on one side of her, Graham on the other, close enough to intervene if needed, but careful not to crowd her or undermine her confidence. They wanted her to be safe, yes, but more than that, they wanted her to know they trusted her.

Joy's face was radiant as they broke into a fast ride, the wind whipping her hair loose from its pin and laughter bubbling from her lips. It felt exhilarating, freeing, to race across open land with nothing but skill and instinct to rely on.

At first, Brigham and Graham threw their lassos at the same steer she aimed for, ensuring she wouldn't be jerked from the saddle if the animal bolted. They practiced like that for some time, the rhythm of the chase becoming familiar, her confidence growing with each successful catch. At last, Graham reined in his horse and met her gaze, pride shining plainly in his eyes.

"I think you're ready," he said.

Brigham nodded. "Your next one is yours alone."

Joy swallowed, her heart pounding, but not with fear. With determination burning bright in her eyes, she nudged her horse forward, lifted the lasso, and swung.

Fury and hatred churned in the heart of the watcher. Concealed deep within the shadows of brush and trees, the intruder remained perfectly unseen, breath held, eyes fixed on the scene unfolding below. A single, deliberate nod was given, barely perceptible, toward another hidden figure nearby. The response came instantly.

A thunderous explosion ripped through the air, rattling the ground beneath their feet and shattering the fragile calm of the afternoon. Birds burst from the trees in a screaming cloud, and the echo rolled across the land like a warning bell.

From the darkness, the first figure smiled, slow, cold, and vicious. Then, as chaos erupted beyond the tree line, the shadow slipped back into the wilderness, vanishing without a trace.

Joy had barely managed to swing the lasso over the steer's head when the world seemed to explode around her. A deafening blast thundered from somewhere nearby. The ground convulsed beneath her as dirt and rocks were hurled skyward, only to rain back down in a violent spray. Her horse reared and lunged, eyes wild with terror, while the cattle surged forward in blind panic.

"Whoa—!" Joy cried, but the rope went taut in her hands. The sudden jerk wrenched her sideways. She was ripped from the saddle, her body slamming hard into the earth. Pain exploded through her as she hit the ground and rolled onto her side, the breath knocked clean from her lungs. The rope dragged her several brutal feet before instinct took over and she released it, the fibers tearing at her palms as she let go.

Tears burned her eyes as agony flared through her shoulder, sharp, relentless. Her hands throbbed, blood already seeping where the lasso had bitten into her skin. Grit clung to her clothes, her hair, her lashes.

Still, she clenched her teeth. She would not lie there. She would not give whoever had done this the satisfaction. Gritting through the pain, Joy planted her palms against the ground and tried to push herself upright, but the moment she moved, her shoulder screamed in protest. A strangled gasp escaped her lips, and she nearly collapsed again, her vision blurring as the pain surged. Something was terribly wrong.

Graham and his father could do nothing to stop it. The explosion had startled their horses, just as violently as it had spooked the cattle, the animals rearing and sidestepping in blind panic. For precious seconds, all Graham and Brigham could do was fight for control, hauling hard on the reins as their mounts threatened to bolt.

"Easy—easy!" Graham barked, forcing his horse to wheel back toward the chaos. By the time they managed to steady the animals, Joy was already on the ground. Shouts rang out across the pasture, sharp, frantic voices carrying over the thunder of hooves and bawling cattle. Dust hung thick in the air as several ranch hands came tearing toward them, spurring their horses hard, fear and urgency written on their faces.

"Explosion!" one of them shouted. "Over there, by the fence line!"

Graham's heart slammed against his ribs as he urged his horse forward, eyes locked on the crumpled figure in the dirt. Nothing else mattered now.

226

Joy made another determined attempt to stand just as Graham and Brigham reached her. They reined in hard, vaulted from their saddles, and were at her side in an instant. One look was enough to tell them how badly she'd been hurt.

Her blouse was smeared with dirt and blood, the fabric torn at the shoulder where jagged holes revealed angry cuts beneath. When they helped her upright, her knee buckled without warning, and she would have collapsed entirely if Graham hadn't caught her. Her leg was scraped and bleeding, her knee already swelling, and the sharp intake of breath she tried, and failed, to hide told them the pain was far worse than she let on.

"We need Dr. Preston. Now," Brigham said grimly. Graham nodded and slid an arm around Joy's uninjured side, drawing her carefully against his chest. The moment her weight shifted, a soft whimper escaped her lips. Her eyes fluttered shut, her face pale, but both men knew she was enduring far more agony than she was willing to admit.

"Easy, Joy," Graham murmured, his voice low and steady despite the fury roaring through him. "I've got you."

Joy sagged against him. A ranch hand rode up at a gallop, skidding to a halt nearby.

"Is everyone all right?"

"No," Brigham snapped, already slipping into command. "The explosion caused Joy to be thrown from the saddle. You—ride to town and fetch Dr. Preston. Don't waste a second. The rest of you, spread out. Whoever did this is still close. Search the tree line, the hills, everywhere."

The cowboy nodded sharply and wheeled his horse around, spurring it hard toward town. Graham eased Joy into his father's arms just long enough to mount his own horse, then immediately took her back, cradling her securely against him. With one last look at the chaos left behind, he urged his horse forward.

They rode hard for the ranch, dust flying beneath pounding hooves, Graham's jaw set, his arms tight around the woman he cared for, while behind them, men fanned out across the land, hunting a shadow that had just declared war.

"Oh, my goodness, what happened?" Darlene cried when the front door flew open and Graham strode inside with Joy limp in his arms. He didn't slow. He didn't answer. He took the stairs two at a time and carried Joy straight to her room. Her head lolled weakly against his shoulder, her face pale and drawn, strands of hair plastered to her damp forehead. Darlene, Cathleen, and Olivia followed close behind, skirts gathered, fear etched across their faces. Brigham came in last and shut the door behind them.

"There was an explosion near the cattle run," he said, his voice tight with restrained fury. "Joy was thrown from her horse and dragged before she could free herself."

Darlene pressed a hand to her mouth.

"Oh, Joy... my poor girl."

Graham laid her gently on the bed, easing her down as though she were made of glass. When he pulled his hands away, blood was already staining his fingers. His jaw clenched hard.

"We sent a cowboy to town for Dr. Preston," Brigham continued, lowering his voice as if afraid to startle Joy. "But we can't wait for her. Darlene, Cathleen, Olivia, you'll need to start cleaning the wounds right away."

Cathleen swallowed and nodded, already rolling up her sleeves. Olivia hurried to fetch clean water and cloths, her earlier laughter from the day erased entirely. Darlene smoothed Joy's hair back with trembling hands.

"We'll take care of her," she said firmly, maternal resolve sharpening her fear. "You go."

Brigham turned to his son. "Come. We're going back out. Whoever did this is still out there, and I intend to see that he's found."

Graham hesitated, his eyes lingering on Joy, on the shallow rise and fall of her chest, the pain lines around her mouth. His hands curled into fists at his sides.

"I won't be far," he murmured, more to Joy than anyone else. Then he forced himself to step away. The men turned and left the room, the door closing softly behind them. Darlene took a steadying breath.

"All right," she said, her voice gentle but commanding. "Let's get to work. Julia will be here soon, but until then, Joy is ours."

Cathleen and Darlene worked together with quiet urgency, their movements careful and reverent as they loosened the buttons of Joy's blouse and eased the fabric away from her injured shoulder. The cloth stuck in places where blood had already begun to dry, and each time it pulled free, Joy whimpered softly, her brows knitting even though her eyes never opened.

"Oh, Joy... I am so sorry," Darlene whispered, her voice breaking despite her efforts to remain steady. She dipped a cloth into the basin of warm water Olivia had prepared earlier and gently dabbed at the dirt and blood marring Joy's skin. The wounds were worse than they had first realized, angry cuts and abrasions, some already swelling, others still bleeding. When Darlene followed with alcohol, Joy sucked in a sharp breath and let out a low, pained cry, her body tensing beneath their hands. Cathleen swallowed hard, blinking back tears.

"She's trying so hard not to scream," she murmured. "She always does that, tries to be brave for everyone else."

The sound of hurried footsteps on the stairs made all three women look up at once. Relief washed over them as a firm knock sounded at the door. Julia Preston entered moments later, her expression focused and composed, her nurse Betty close at her side with a medical bag already in hand. One quick glance at Joy was enough for Julia to assess the situation.

"Thank you," she said briskly but kindly. "I'll take it from here."

Darlene hesitated, her hand still resting protectively on Joy's arm, but Julia met her gaze with quiet assurance.

"You've done exactly what she needed until now."

Reluctantly, the three women stepped back and left the room.

*

Julia moved to the bedside at once.

"Betty," she said calmly, all trace of emotion replaced by clinical precision, "place a few drops of chloroform on a cloth and hold it gently over her nose and mouth. Just enough. She's already been through more pain than any person should bear."

Betty nodded and obeyed without hesitation. As the cloth was lowered, Joy's breathing slowly evened out, the tension easing from her face. Julia watched closely, counting each breath, then set her jaw with quiet determination.

"All right," she murmured. "Now we can help her properly."

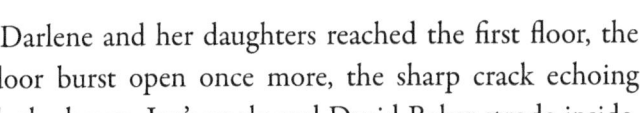

When Darlene and her daughters reached the first floor, the front door burst open once more, the sharp crack echoing through the house. Joy's uncle and David Baker strode inside, their faces tight with urgency.

"How is she?" Gerald demanded at once.

"Julia is with her now," Darlene answered, pressing a hand to her chest as tears welled in her eyes. "She looked terribly battered, though. I've never seen wounds like that on anyone."

"Who could have done this?" Olivia whispered, her voice trembling. "Someone had to sneak onto the ranch on purpose. This wasn't an accident."

"I hope they hang that swine," Cathleen snapped, fists clenched at her sides, fury blazing in her eyes. She moved to the window just as figures appeared outside. Graham and Brigham were riding in, hard, several cowboys close behind them. Between the men was another shape, someone being forced along. Cathleen squinted, her pulse quickening.

The door flew open again, and Graham shoved the captive forward into the house. The moment the light hit his face, a collective gasp rippled through the room. Olivia turned deathly pale.

"We found him hiding in the bushes," Brigham growled, his voice thick with outrage and bitter disappointment. Cathleen stared at the man in disbelief.

"You?" she shouted. "You're the sheriff's deputy!"

"You mean he *was*," Graham said coldly. Dave stepped forward without hesitation and snapped the cuffs around the man's wrists. Barry kept his head down, his jaw clenched, refusing to meet anyone's gaze.

"We also found this," one of the ranch hands said, stepping in briefly to hold up a folded note before dropping a pair of saddlebags onto a chair. He left as quickly as he'd come, the tension in the room nearly suffocating. Gerald surged forward and grabbed Barry by the front of his shirt.

"Who paid you?" he demanded. "Why would you let anyone turn you into a criminal?"

Barry said nothing. Dave shook his head grimly.

"We'll have to speak to his family. Maybe they'll answer the questions he won't."

"No, please," Barry blurted suddenly, lifting his head at last. Panic flared in his eyes. "Leave my family out of this. They had nothing to do with it."

"Then tell us why you tried to kill Joy," Gerald snapped, his voice shaking with restrained fury.

Barry swallowed hard. "I wasn't trying to kill her. I swear it. They wanted me to, but I couldn't." His voice broke. "I threw the dynamite away from her. I made sure of it."

"Who are *they*?" Dave pressed.

Barry shook his head again. "I can't say."

"We need names," Graham said, stepping closer, his tone dark and dangerous. "This ends now."

"You can't stop it," Barry muttered. "Too many people are involved."

Gerald's expression hardened. "Is your family in danger?"

Barry nodded, his shoulders slumping.

"They threatened my parents. And when I hesitated, they burned down my sister's house. She lives just outside Helena."

A stunned silence followed.

"This is monstrous," Gerald barked, slamming his fist into the doorframe.

"We'll notify Dylan and Charles immediately," Dave said, his voice rough with anger. "Barry's family will be placed under protection. And *you*," he added grimly, tightening his grip on the prisoner, "are going straight to a cell."

Barry nodded once, hollow-eyed. He knew there was no escaping what he'd done.

Gerald dragged a hand through his hair and began pacing the length of the sitting room, his boots thudding heavily against the floor. The front door had barely closed behind Dave and the disgraced deputy when the full weight of it all seemed to settle over the house.

"Whoever is behind this," Gerald said at last, his voice tight with contained fury, "has more power than we first imagined. Power enough to threaten decent folks from our town, people who've lived honest lives, and frighten them into lying, into harming their own neighbors." He stopped abruptly and turned back toward the others. "That kind of fear doesn't come from a petty grudge."

Brigham nodded slowly, his jaw set. "It's taken on a life of its own. I won't deny that Willard Thomas has been the spark behind much of the unrest here, but this..." He gestured toward the door, toward the memory of Barry's confession. "This goes far beyond one bitter doctor with a bruised ego." He exhaled heavily.

"It almost feels as though the trouble we've had with Willard is only one thread in a much larger web. Too many things are overlapping, the attacks, the fires, the sabotage, the threats against Joy and her sister. None of it feels random anymore."

Gerald's eyes darkened. "Exactly. Someone is pulling strings, and Thomas may be shouting the loudest, but I'm no longer convinced he's the one holding them."

A hush fell over the room as the realization sank in. Whatever force had set its sights on Joy and Alice was not finished. And it was far more dangerous than any of them had dared to believe.

15

A Puddle for a Viper

Joy's injuries healed quickly under Julia's careful, tireless care. The young physician had been as appalled and outraged as everyone else when she learned what had happened, and who had been responsible. Joy, by contrast, had been left mostly stunned. The sheer cruelty of it still felt unreal.

Her aunt and sister came every day, rarely missing a visit, and Joy found unexpected comfort in those quiet hours together. Laughter returned in small doses. So did a sense of belonging. By the time her shoulder was fully healed, her strength, and her impatience, had returned in full.

She was more than ready to throw herself back into ranch life: breaking horses, practicing with the lasso, riding hard and fast until the wind chased the lingering fear from her chest. But not one of the Harrisons would allow it. Nor would her aunt, her uncle, or Julia, who fixed her with a physician's glare and reminded her that healing did not mean reckless.

When Joy finally ventured into town again, she was greeted warmly on all sides. Smiles, handshakes, and quiet words of relief followed her wherever she went. Dylan stopped her near the square and assured her Barry's family was safe, though

Barry himself remained behind bars. Dave caught up with her outside the general store.

"Joy, it's good to see you out and about again," he said warmly, pulling her into a fatherly embrace. She returned it with a genuine smile. "I was hoping to speak with you," he added more carefully. "Barry's been asking to see you. He's beside himself with guilt and wants to talk, if you're willing."

Joy hesitated. Did she truly want to face the man who had nearly killed her? Dave seemed to sense her uncertainty and squeezed her shoulder gently.

"You don't owe him anything. Even he knows that."

She nodded, but something inside her shifted. Avoiding the truth wouldn't bring her peace.

"All right," she said quietly. "I'll talk to him."

Barry rose from the stool in his cell the moment she entered. His eyes were rimmed red. His posture slumped with shame.

"Thank you for coming," he said hoarsely. "I know I don't deserve it. I was terrified for my family. I didn't know what else to do."

Joy swallowed hard. "My family is safe now. So is yours. Tell us who's behind this."

For a long moment, he said nothing. Then he sighed.

"Mrs. Thomas," he blurted quietly. "She paid me."

Joy and Dave both sucked in sharp breaths.

"She's been sneaking onto the ranch, watching you and Graham," Barry continued. "She hates you, blames you for everything that's happened to her daughter. All of them do."

Joy shook her head slowly. "I never thought she'd go that far."

"She wasn't the one threatening my family," Barry added quickly. "Those came in anonymous letters. Same message every time. If I talked, they'd kill them and frame me."

Joy felt cold all over. Then Barry reached into his pocket.

"There's something else." He handed Dave a folded note. Dave read it aloud.

Willard,

We've tried to locate the deed to Max Collins's land and the contracts he signed, whatever Troy hid there, but we've had no luck. Jonas Andrews's firm claims they know nothing. Perhaps his daughter has it.

Jack

The room seemed to tilt. Joy sank back in her chair, breathless.

"They're after Pa's land."

Dave's jaw tightened. "And whatever Troy Haven hid there."

She shook her head slowly. "I've never seen a deed or contract. I assumed it was kept at the bank, or in Pa's office, or with Jonas. But Auburn burned. The house is gone. And Jonas swore he doesn't have it."

Dave exhaled sharply. "Then finding it is our priority. If we can secure it first, sell the land to someone outside this mess, we take away their motive."

Joy stared at the note again, her pulse thudding.

Who was Jack? What had Troy hidden? And how far were they willing to go to claim it? Whatever her father had uncovered before his death, it was still casting a long, and dangerous, shadow.

When Joy stepped out of the sheriff's office into the bright afternoon sunlight, her thoughts were a tangled knot she couldn't untie. So, Willard Thomas was connected, somehow, to her parents' deaths. Not directly, perhaps, but entangled in the web that had destroyed her family. The question was how to prove it. He claimed Sacramento or San Francisco as his former home, yet no one seemed able to place him there with certainty. Had he known her father at all? Or had he simply been drawn into Troy Haven's orbit later, following the promise of gain like a vulture scenting carrion? Joy rubbed at her temple as she walked, barely registering the bustle of the street around her.

"Joy! Stop a moment."

The call broke through her thoughts. She looked up just in time to see a familiar wagon rolling toward her. Maureen sat beside her brother on the bench, her posture stiff and watchful. In the back of the wagon sat Matt Haven.

Joy slowed, startled more than pleased. For a heartbeat, she simply stared. The last thing she wanted was another confrontation, another tangled exchange of half-truths and accusations. Her gaze flicked to Matt, then slid away again.

She offered Maureen the barest nod, polite, distant, final, and without waiting for them to draw nearer, crossed the street briskly. The bell above the general store door jingled as she slipped inside, leaving the buckboard, and the past it represented, behind her.

Inside, the familiar scent of coffee and dry goods wrapped around her, but her pulse still raced. Whatever truth lay ahead, she knew one thing for certain: The Haven family, in all its forms, remained far too close for comfort.

———

"Joy Collins!"

The sound of Lydia's voice, sharp, oily, and unmistakably unpleasant, reached Joy the moment she stepped fully into the general store. She halted mid-stride. Lydia stood near the back, her posture rigid, her green eyes fixed like claws. The instant Joy turned, Lydia abandoned whatever pretense of shopping she'd been maintaining and strode forward.

"How odd to see you here," Lydia said, her lips curving in a brittle smile that never reached her eyes. Joy didn't miss a beat.

She rolled her eyes and replied coolly, her voice carrying just enough for others to hear, "Yes. Imagine that. Someone shopping... in a store."

A ripple of quiet laughter passed through the room. Someone near the counter snorted outright. Lydia's expression didn't soften, if anything, it hardened.

"If you think you're amusing," Lydia snapped, "you are very much mistaken. What are you still doing here? It's long past time for you, to leave this town, and especially the Harrison ranch. You don't belong there."

Joy turned fully toward her now, irritation settling like armor across her shoulders.

"Neither do you," she shot back. "You made that perfectly clear when you ran off with another man. And in case you haven't noticed, Graham isn't taking you back. No matter how hard you try, your manipulations aren't working anymore."

Lydia's smile twisted, venomous and satisfied.

"They're working well enough to keep you apart," she hissed. "And I'll make certain he'll never be free to marry you, or anyone else."

Joy stepped closer, her eyes narrowing. Her voice dropped, quiet but lethal.

"Even people like you eventually get what they deserve. You may think you hold the upper hand right now, but it won't last."

Lydia stiffened. "Is that a threat?"

Joy tilted her head slightly. "You tell me. You're the one who's been issuing threats, against a man who tried to help you, despite how utterly undeserving you were. He simply realized too late what a conniving, poisonous snake you truly are."

The words struck home. With a shrill screech of rage, Lydia lunged, clawing for Joy's hair. Joy reacted instantly. She sidestepped, caught Lydia by the arms, and before anyone quite understood what was happening, drove her forward with controlled force.

Gasps echoed through the store as Joy propelled her straight through the open doorway. They hit the steps in a tangle of motion. Joy released her grip at precisely the right moment. Lydia stumbled, flailed, and went down hard into a broad, sloppy puddle of mud at the base of the steps.

Laughter erupted. Loud, unrestrained, and merciless. Even Joy couldn't suppress a smirk.

Lydia scrambled upright, her dress ruined, her hair plastered to her face, her fury incandescent. She surged toward the steps again, but several young men stepped forward at once, forming a solid, protective barrier in front of Joy.

"Be grateful it was only a mud puddle," Joy called out clearly, her voice ringing across the storefront, "and not the dung pile on the Harrison ranch."

The laughter doubled. Someone wiped tears from their eyes. Someone else clapped. Lydia screamed, stamped her foot in pure frustration, and flung wild glares at everyone in sight, but the town had already moved on. No one was intimidated. No one was impressed. Lydia Thomas stood alone.

Joy had just turned back toward the entrance of the general store when someone clasped her arm. She halted and turned, finding herself face to face with Matt Haven.

"Matt." Her tone was flat, guarded.

"Joy, can we talk?" His voice was hesitant, as though he already knew she might refuse.

"I don't see why we should," she replied coolly. "I believe we said everything that needed saying the last time we met." Her posture was rigid now, her expression closed. Maureen stepped closer, her hands clasped together in a pleading gesture.

"Please," she said softly. "Give him a chance to speak, Joy."

Joy exhaled slowly, the patience she had left wearing thin.

"Fine," she said at last. "What is it you want to say?"

Before Matt could answer, Joy noticed movement from the corner of her eye. Lydia, still streaked with mud, had decided the moment wasn't dramatic enough without her. She stepped closer, clearly unable to resist.

"Well, isn't this interesting," Lydia called out loudly. "Is that the young man you led on?"

Joy closed her eyes for a brief second, then opened them again. Matt glanced toward Lydia, brow lifting.

"What happened to her?"

"I threw her into a mud puddle," Joy replied evenly. Both Matt and Maureen stared at her in disbelief.

"You?" Maureen blurted.

"Yes," Joy answered, irritation flashing now. "Why is that so hard to believe?"

"Why?" Matt asked.

"Because she keeps attacking me and my character," Joy said, her voice steady but edged with steel, "and I am finished tolerating it."

"You are trying to steal my husband!" Lydia shrieked, drawing the attention of everyone nearby. Joy drew in a deep, controlled breath, refusing to rise to the bait. She turned back to Matt, pointedly ignoring Lydia.

"What is it you wanted to say?"

Matt hesitated, clearly unsettled.

"You're not even going to defend yourself?"

Joy's eyes hardened. "I see no reason to. If you choose to believe her, that is entirely your decision. But either tell me what you asked to speak about, now, or I'm leaving."

She didn't raise her voice. She didn't need to. The line had been drawn.

Matt was left speechless for a moment. Joy had always carried herself with quiet confidence, but this was something different, sharper, steadier. The time she had spent in Deer Lodge, and perhaps even more so the trials she had endured since the loss of her parents, had forged something unyielding within her. She was no longer willing to be targeted, diminished, or spoken down to. He studied her now, really looked at her.

There was vulnerability in her eyes, pain she did not bother to hide, but beneath it burned a fierce resolve. She stood her ground not out of arrogance, but out of necessity, as someone who had learned the cost of silence and the danger of yielding to cruelty.

In that instant, Matt had no doubt. The mud-streaked woman shouting behind them had wronged Joy, deeply, and whatever line Lydia had crossed, she had crossed it once too often.

"Can we talk somewhere in private?" Matt asked quietly, his gaze searching Joy's face. Before she could answer, Lydia lunged back into the conversation, her voice sharp and shrill.

"There's no need for privacy. We already know the truth. That little hussy played you and is now setting her sights on my husband."

Maureen flinched, the color draining from her face. It was painfully clear she recognized Lydia's outburst as something she had unintentionally enabled. Joy turned slowly, fixing Lydia with a steady, unimpressed stare.

"Why don't you leave? I believe clean, dry clothes are in order," she said coolly. "This has nothing to do with you."

Lydia scoffed. "You made it everyone's business when you paraded around town acting as though you were courting Graham, even though he is still married to me. I think I have every right to witness this."

Heat flared in Joy's chest, but her voice remained controlled.

"I am not courting Graham. And I would advise you to stop throwing stones while sitting in a glass house, Lydia. It wasn't I who ran off with another man and abandoned my husband." The words landed clean and sharp. Joy's hands clenched at her sides. She was exhausted, exhausted by the accusations, the manipulations, the endless performance of victimhood. For a fleeting moment, she was tempted to drag Lydia back to the mud puddle and finish what she had started earlier. But she mastered herself, refusing to give Lydia the satisfaction.

By now, several townsfolk had gathered, drawn by raised voices and unmistakable tension. Though no one stood on Lydia's side, the attention itself was mortifying. Joy lifted her chin, refusing to shrink beneath it.

"Now," she said, turning back to Matt, "you wanted to talk."

Joy noticed her fatherly friend standing a short distance away, having clearly witnessed the entire exchange. As he stepped closer, an idea sparked in her mind.

"Sheriff Baker," she called out suddenly, her voice clear and unwavering as she fixed her gaze on him. "I would like to turn myself in."

A hush fell over the small crowd.

"I physically attacked Lydia Thomas," Joy continued evenly, "and threw her into a mud puddle."

For a moment, Dave Baker stared at her. Then his lips twitched, betraying the smile he was desperately trying to suppress. A ripple of soft chuckles passed through the onlookers. Anyone who had followed the argument knew exactly what Joy was doing. The sheriff stepped to her side, squaring his shoulders and slipping seamlessly into his role.

"In that case," he said in his deep, authoritative voice, "I am ordering you to march straight to my office, Miss Collins." He cast her a stern glance worthy of the badge he wore. "You and I are going to have a very serious discussion."

Despite the severity of his tone, he gave Joy the smallest nod, just enough to let her know he understood. She inclined her head in return, then turned briefly toward Matt and Maureen.

"Please come with me," she said quietly. When Lydia, still streaked with mud and outrage, tried to follow, Dave stepped directly into her path.

"There will be no need for you to come, Mrs. Harrison," he said firmly, placing pointed emphasis on her married name. "I have this situation fully under control. Since Miss Collins has admitted her wrongdoing, your testimony will not be required."

His gaze flicked pointedly to Lydia's soiled dress.

"I suggest you take this opportunity to clean yourself up. Good day." Without waiting for a response, he turned, took Joy's arm, and escorted her to his office. The door closed behind them a moment later, leaving Lydia standing in the street, muddy, furious, and utterly dismissed.

The moment the door closed behind them, Dave's stern expression melted away. He let out a hearty laugh and pulled Joy into his arms, giving her a warm, fatherly hug.

"That was incredibly clever of you, Joy," he said, shaking his head in admiration. "Quick thinking, too. You handled that perfectly."

Joy grinned, some of the tension finally leaving her shoulders.

"What else was I supposed to do? Lydia wouldn't leave me alone."

Dave chuckled, then turned serious as he faced Matt.

"Before I step aside and let the two of you talk, there's something you need to understand." He gestured vaguely toward the street outside. "About that woman."

Matt nodded, attentive.

"You've already witnessed a glimpse of her temperament," Dave continued, his tone firm. "But I don't want you walking away from this thinking poorly of Joy because of anything Lydia has said or done."

He briefly explained Lydia's history with Graham, her manipulations, her refusal to take responsibility for her own choices, and the way she and her parents had repeatedly attacked Joy's character to shift blame away from themselves. Maureen listened in growing discomfort. When Dave finished, she shook her head slowly.

"I am so sorry, Joy," she said, genuine regret in her voice. "If I had known my presence, or my actions back then, would cause you this much trouble, I would have done things differently. But at the time, I was only thinking about myself and Matt. And being drunk certainly didn't help matters."

Joy waved her off gently. "It's all right. They would have found a way to turn me into a villain regardless."

Matt exhaled sharply, disbelief written all over his face.

"So, Lydia truly ran off with another man," he said incredulously, "and then had the audacity to accuse you of adultery for nothing more than dancing with her husband?"

Joy gave a small, weary shrug. "Lydia is always the victim. Anyone who doesn't play by her rules becomes the enemy."

Matt nodded slowly, then straightened, his expression sober.

"Listen," he said quietly. "I won't take up much of your time. I just wanted to apologize."

Joy looked at him, surprised by the earnestness in his voice.

"For the way I treated you after I followed you," he continued. "I realized too late that I spoke to you the same way my father spoke to everyone, with entitlement, with anger, and without respect. I'm not proud of that." He swallowed.

"You never met my father, but he was a cruel man. I promised myself long ago that I would never become like him.

The fact that I lashed out at you the way I did... it showed me I still have work to do. And I intend to do it." The sincerity in his eyes left no doubt that he meant every word.

When Joy mounted her horse to ride home, her thoughts refused to settle. The conversation with Matt and Maureen had brought a measure of relief, yet it hadn't erased everything that had happened. Trust did not return at once, especially not after so much pain, suspicion, and betrayal. She wanted to believe they were sincere. Truly, she did. But a thread of doubt lingered. Matt had moved in with his aunt, uncle, and mother, yet he had been careful not to share his long-term intentions. Joy understood caution, she lived with it daily now, but uncertainty had become something she could no longer ignore.

She was just leaving the edge of town, riding at an easy pace, when a sharp voice called her name. Joy closed her eyes briefly. For one reckless second, she considered pretending she hadn't heard, but she knew avoidance would only invite worse trouble. With a quiet sigh, she turned her horse to face the man striding toward her with unmistakable fury.

"Joy Collins," Willard Thomas barked before he was even close. "Care to explain why you shoved my daughter into a mud puddle? What are you, five years old?"

Joy scoffed, her patience evaporating.

"That accusation is rich, coming from *you*. Lydia throws tantrums whenever the world doesn't bend to her will. I am tired of you and your family harassing me and spreading lies. Your daughter attacked me. I defended myself."

"You are a vile, nasty woman," he snarled. "You've caused nothing but trouble since the day you arrived in Deer Lodge, and I swear you're going to pay for it."

Joy's spine stiffened. "I think it's long past time that you and your dreadful daughter answered for your behavior. Leave me alone, and we won't have a problem."

She turned her horse, intent on riding away, but before she could move, Willard lunged forward and grabbed her, yanking her violently from the saddle. Joy gasped as she hit the ground. She struggled, but his grip was crushing, fingers digging painfully into her arms.

"Let go of me," she demanded, her voice shaking with rage.

"I'll teach you some manners!" he shouted, raising his hand.

The instant his grip loosened, Joy reacted. She reached into her pocket, drew her small pistol, and slammed it hard against the side of his head. Willard staggered backward with a cry, clutching his temple and swearing loudly.

Men rushed toward them at once, several townsfolk and Dave Baker among them. Dave took in the scene in a single glance and wasted no time. He seized Willard and snapped handcuffs around his wrists, ignoring his protests.

"What are you arresting me for?" Willard shouted. "That woman attacked me!"

Dave's expression was cold. "I saw everything. You assaulted her. She defended herself."

Willard sneered. "I suppose you're one of her many admirers, then? Isn't she a bit young for you, Baker?"

Dave stepped closer, his jaw clenched.

"Say one more word, Thomas, and I'll knock you out cold before I drag you to the cell."

A murmur rippled through the gathering crowd.

"Why don't we just chase him out of town?" someone called. "We've tolerated that family far too long."

Several voices rose in agreement. Dave tightened his grip on Willard's arm.

"For now, a night in a cell will do him some good," he said grimly. "But don't worry, your chance to be rid of him may not be far off. Men like him never change."

Joy stood quietly beside her horse, shaken but unbroken, her gaze steady as Willard Thomas was hauled away at last.

16

Stolen in Broad Daylight

J oy remained shaken long after the confrontation, though she took great care not to let it show. The image of Willard Thomas's rage, his hands on her arms, the violence in his eyes, lingered in her mind far longer than she wished. Still, she said nothing. She did not tell her uncle. She did not tell the Harrisons. Joy knew it would only ignite another storm, more anger, more protectiveness, and more confrontation. Deer Lodge already simmered with tension, and she refused to be the spark that set it ablaze again. Besides, Dave had intervened swiftly, and half the town had witnessed what happened. The truth was already out there, carried on the tongues of those who had seen Willard's cruelty for themselves.

And more than that, Joy was tired. Tired of defending herself. Tired of being blamed. Tired of her name becoming a battlefield for other people's bitterness and malice. So, she held her silence close and carried the weight alone, the way she had learned to do since losing her parents. She told herself she was safe now, that the worst had passed, but deep down, she knew better. This was not over. And the quiet she chose was not weakness but resolve.

Graham turned twenty-six a few days later, and despite everything that had transpired, his family was determined to mark the occasion with warmth and dignity. His mother and sisters decorated the long table on the front porch with fresh linens, flowers, and carefully arranged dishes. Lanterns hung from the beams, ready to be lit once dusk fell, and for a moment, the ranch felt almost peaceful again.

Joy's aunt and uncle arrived along with a handful of close friends and neighbors, laughter and polite conversation filling the air as everyone took their seats. Joy chose her place carefully, settling as far from Graham as possible. It was not avoidance born of indifference, but caution. Every look, every shared smile could be twisted into another accusation by Thomas' family, and she refused to give them fresh ammunition.

The meal had barely begun when the rhythmic creak of wheels reached them. Conversation faltered. Forks paused midair. Cathleen, Olivia, and Joy exchanged a knowing glance. Every soul at the table understood the omen at once.

The carriage drew to a halt, and moments later Willard Thomas stepped forward, Lydia at his side, accompanied by an older gentleman dressed in the somber finery of a lawyer. The tension thickened instantly.

"Graham Harrison," Willard announced, his voice cutting through the stillness. "We are here to discuss what is going to happen between you and Lydia, and whether a divorce will be granted."

Brigham rose from his chair, his expression hard.

"Thomas, you are interrupting a family celebration. You can return another time."

"Oh, of course," Lydia said sweetly, her tone dripping with false civility. "It *is* Graham's birthday, after all." Her eyes flicked pointedly toward Joy before returning to Graham. "How curious that you celebrate without your wife."

"She was never a wife in anything but name," Graham snapped, all restraint gone. "And even that title was built on lies."

Willard turned sharply to the attorney beside him.

"Did you hear that, Mr. Jordan? He admits it freely. He married my daughter for the wrong reasons, only to get his hands on her money."

Graham barked out a humorless laugh.

"What money? You can't claim a dowry when you insisted, we pay for everything."

"That's enough," Brigham thundered, stepping forward. "Your daughter has taken advantage of every person she's encountered." He cast a pointed glance at the attorney. "I'd advise caution, sir. I doubt Willard Thomas has any intention of paying your fees."

Mr. Jordan stiffened, unease flickering across his face, but Willard merely scoffed.

"We are here to make an offer," Willard said coldly. "Lydia will agree to the divorce, provided Graham compensates her for half the value of this ranch."

"Have you lost your mind?" Graham shot back. "Your daughter married me under false pretenses. She will never have a claim to this land."

"Watch your mouth when you speak of my daughter!" Willard roared. Graham seized him by the shirt in an instant, fury blazing. Brigham and Joy's uncle rushed forward, pulling him back, while Mr. Jordan hurried between them, raising his hands.

"You can expect a lawsuit of considerable magnitude," the attorney snapped, regaining his composure. "This violent outburst will be included."

Before anyone could respond, another carriage approached. Brigham exhaled sharply.

"What now?"

Joy's gaze remained fixed on Lydia and her father. The moment the newcomers drew close enough to be recognized, the color drained from Lydia's face. Even Willard looked shaken.

"Graham," Lydia said quickly, panic creeping into her voice. "Before any agreement is made, I must retrieve some important documents from the room I stayed in."

"You will not step foot inside this house again," Graham said coldly. "We packed everything and sent it to your parents."

Lydia and her father exchanged a look and began to edge backward, only to stop short when Joy stood and stepped calmly into their path.

"You're not leaving already, are you?" Joy asked evenly, her voice steady despite the storm raging around them. "Not when there's still so much left to discuss."

The silence that followed was charged. And for the first time, Lydia looked truly afraid.

The approaching carriage came to a halt, and three figures stepped down. Brigham rose at once, surprise, flickering across his face before he offered Julia a warm, welcoming smile.

"Dr. Preston, welcome. I'm glad you could make it to Graham's birthday celebration," he said. Then his brow furrowed slightly. "Forgive me for asking, but who is accompanying you?"

Julia's gaze moved deliberately to Lydia and her father before she answered, her voice calm but resolute.

"This is Eric Gardener, and Judge William Lawson. Eric is Lydia's husband."

A collective gasp rippled through the gathering. Chairs scraped, forks clattered, and stunned murmurs erupted around the table. No one, no one at all, had known. Except Joy.

The color drained from Lydia's face. She and her father tried to push past Joy, but she did not move. Joy's uncle, Dave, and Brigham stepped in instantly, blocking their path. At the same moment, Eric strode forward and seized Lydia by the arms.

"Is it true," he demanded, his voice shaking with restrained fury, "that you are married to Graham Harrison?"

"Eric—" Lydia began.

"You told me you were a widow," he cut in sharply. "You swore you'd been a widow for two years. Everything you ever said to me was a lie, wasn't it?"

Tears welled in Lydia's eyes, but Eric did not soften.

"Judge Lawson," he said, turning away from her, "I request our marriage be annulled immediately. And unless Mr. Harrison wishes to remain bound to this woman, I ask that their marriage be dissolved as well."

"You can't do that!" Lydia shrieked, hysteria bleeding into her voice. "I told you I was a widow because Graham abused me. I had to make you believe I was dead!"

Eric stared at her in disbelief, then scoffed.

"You lie every time you open your mouth. If Graham was so dangerous, why are you here? Why did you return to this town at all?"

She had no answer.

"I'll tell you why," he went on coldly. "You came back to manipulate him. You thought you could wring something from a divorce settlement, and if I hadn't discovered the truth, you would have done the same to me."

Lydia broke into sobs, but no one stepped forward to comfort her. Eric turned back to the judge.

"Let's be done with this."

"Your Honor," Willard burst out, "both men are lying. They forced my daughter into marriage!"

Judge Lawson fixed him with a piercing stare.

"Mr. Thomas, I strongly advise you to remain silent. The evidence before me is more than sufficient. Your daughter committed marriage fraud, and you aided her in doing so. You should both consider yourselves fortunate that immediate annulment is the only consequence being pursued. Either man could demand her arrest."

"You're only doing this because I'm a woman!" Lydia cried, her voice cracking. "I have no way to defend myself!"

"That argument will not work here, Mrs. Gardener," the judge replied coolly. "If anything, your gender has spared you harsher consequences. A man would already be in a jail cell."

He signed a document, then turned to Graham.

"Do you wish to remain married to this woman?"

"Absolutely not," Graham answered without hesitation.

"Then present your marriage record."

Graham rose. "I can also provide a letter Lydia wrote shortly after our wedding. In it, she admits she manipulated me by falsely claiming she was with child by another man. She later bragged about lying again, saying she lost the child, when she was never pregnant at all."

The judge shook his head in disgust.

"I will take that letter as well. Let me be clear, Miss Thomas, this record will remain on file. If you attempt marriage fraud again, you will be imprisoned and tried."

"I will not sign anything!" Lydia sobbed.

"Very well," Judge Lawson said evenly. "Sheriff, arrest her."

Lydia gasped, panic overtaking her as Dave stepped forward.

"She will remain in custody overnight and be transferred to the women's prison in Sacramento."

"Daddy!" Lydia cried, clinging to her father.

"Mr. Jordan, do something!" Willard snapped at the attorney, who had stood silently throughout.

"There is nothing I can do," Mr. Jordan replied stiffly. "Mr. Gardener brought a sitting judge. The rulings are binding."

Judge Lawson folded his hands.

"So, Mr. Thomas, will your daughter sign the papers and comply, or will she face trial?"

Willard's jaw tightened. He knew the game was over.

"What do you want?" he demanded through gritted teeth.

Eric shrugged. "I want her gone. She is to stay away from me, my family, and our acquaintances. And she will return everything I purchased during our marriage."

The judge noted it and turned to Graham.

"She, and her family, are to leave Deer Lodge permanently."

Willard's face twisted with rage. "We are not leaving. You cannot make us."

Joy's uncle stepped forward, his voice controlled but lethal.

"You and your family have terrorized this community for over two years. You drove physicians away, attempted to sabotage Dr. Preston, and relentlessly harassed my niece, who came here only after her parents were murdered. Two weeks ago, someone caused an explosion on the Harrison ranch, nearly killing her."

"You caught the culprit," Willard snarled. "It was the deputy sheriff."

"Yes," Gerald replied coldly. "And he admitted he was hired. While I believe in innocent until proven guilty, that courtesy has been exhausted in your case. You have attacked my niece's character, endangered lives, and poisoned this town long enough."

The silence that followed was absolute. And this time, no one doubted whose reign had finally ended.

Joy and Dave exchanged a quick, knowing glance. They had never told her uncle what Barry had confessed, doing so would have placed him and his family in immediate danger, but it was clear Gerald had reached the same conclusion on his own. He may not have known that Jane Thomas was the one pulling the strings, yet his instincts had led him straight to the heart of the truth.

Judge Lawson cleared his throat, the sound cutting through the tense silence like a blade. "I've heard quite enough," he said coolly. "You will agree to the terms and sign the papers, or I will have the young lady arrested immediately. And let me be perfectly clear, if anyone present has evidence of criminal conduct against either of you, I will not hesitate to order your arrest as well."

Lydia turned slowly to her father, disbelief written plainly across her face. For a fleeting moment, she seemed convinced he would rescue her, argue on her behalf, spin one last tale in her defense. Instead, Willard muttered a string of curses under his breath, his jaw tightening.

"Just sign the damn papers," he snapped. Lydia recoiled as though struck. She opened her mouth to protest, but her father seized her arm and shoved her forward. Trapped and humiliated, she had no choice. With shaking hands and a look of pure fury, she scrawled her name across the pages.

Eric took the pen next without hesitation and signed. Graham followed, his expression grim but resolute, as though a crushing weight was finally lifting from his shoulders. Judge

Lawson added his signature last, sealing the document with unmistakable finality. A collective breath released around the table, relief, disbelief, and vindication tangled together.

"You have two days," the judge said briskly, setting the papers aside. "Two days to pack your belongings and leave Deer Lodge. If you wish to sell your property, that may be handled through legal counsel. But make no mistake, you will not set foot in this town again. Is that understood?"

Willard and Lydia nodded stiffly, their faces twisted with hatred and wounded pride. Judge Lawson rose to his feet.

"I will remain in Deer Lodge until you are gone," he continued evenly. "If you violate any of these terms, if you cause a disturbance, issue threats, or so much as breathe another insult toward the mayor's niece, you will be arrested immediately. Every person present is a witness, and I will not hesitate to call upon them." He lifted his hand and gestured toward the path. "You may go."

Willard turned sharply, dragging Lydia with him, while their attorney followed behind, pale and resigned. Whatever schemes they had brought with them had collapsed entirely, leaving behind nothing but consequences, and a town finally free of their shadow.

The moment the carriage vanished beyond the line of trees, the tension that had gripped the ranch shattered. Cheers erupted from every corner of the porch and yard, laughter, applause, and relieved exclamations spilling freely at last. It felt as though the very air had lightened, as if Deer Lodge itself had finally exhaled.

Judge Lawson watched the celebration with an indulgent smile, clearly amused by the sudden transformation from courtroom solemnity to outright jubilation. When Brigham invited him to stay and join the festivities properly, he accepted without hesitation. Eric, the governor's son, did as well, his expression calm but visibly relieved now that the truth had finally come to light.

Graham sought out Julia first. He pulled her into a grateful embrace, his voice thick with sincerity as he thanked her again for her courage, her persistence, and the role she had played in bringing everything into the open. She brushed it off with a wry smile, but her eyes shone with quiet satisfaction.

When Graham looked up, his gaze found Joy's across the porch. For a heartbeat, the noise around them faded. Relief, admiration, and something deeper passed between them, unspoken, but unmistakable. He offered her a smile lighter than any she had seen from him before, free of shadows at last.

The celebration resumed with renewed energy, food passed around, stories retold with dramatic flair, laughter ringing long into the evening. More than once, someone declared that this birthday would be remembered for years to come. And everyone agreed. It hadn't just been a birthday celebration. It had been the day the truth won, and the day a long, dark chapter finally came to an end.

Deer Lodge celebrated, too, when word spread that the Thomas family was leaving for good. Relief swept through the town like a long-awaited sunrise. Doors were left open again, laughter lingered in the streets, and for the first time in years, the community felt whole, peaceful, unburdened by suspicion and fear.

Judge Lawson kept his word. He remained until Willard Thomas, his wife, and Lydia were well and truly gone. Before their departure, he warned them one final time, cool, firm, and unmistakably clear, that any attempt to interfere with Deer Lodge again would bring consequences far more severe than those they had already faced. They left under that shadow, and no one doubted they would think twice before ever returning.

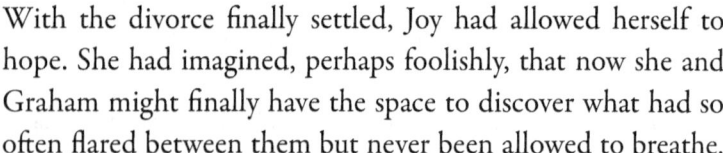

With the divorce finally settled, Joy had allowed herself to hope. She had imagined, perhaps foolishly, that now she and Graham might finally have the space to discover what had so often flared between them but never been allowed to breathe. Instead, he began to pull away.

At first, she told herself he simply needed time, to adjust to being free, to process the wreckage Lydia had left behind. She gave him space. Patience. Understanding. But days passed, then weeks, and his distance only deepened. He buried himself in ranch work, stayed out late, and, most painfully, began asking women from town out on dates.

The message became impossible to ignore. Her heart cracked beneath the weight of it, the hurt, sharp and relentless. Anger followed close behind. It felt as though he had toyed with her feelings, as though the stolen kisses and charged glances had been nothing more than indulgences while he was trapped in a marriage he despised. The thought burned.

She wanted to leave, wanted desperately to move in with her aunt and uncle, but with Alice living there, she knew it would only complicate things further. What made it worse was that nothing else had changed. Darlene still treated her like a daughter. Brigham still offered quiet encouragement and steady kindness. Cathleen and Olivia still pulled her into conversation and laughter, still loved her fiercely. Surrounded by warmth, Joy felt unbearably alone.

Day by day, she withdrew. She avoided Graham whenever she could, slipping away when he came home, choosing silence over the ache of watching him laugh with someone else. She practiced the skills he had taught her behind the barn when no one was looking, working until her muscles burned just to bleed off the tension coiled in her chest. She took on every chore she could find, rode for hours through open fields and forests, anything to keep her thoughts at bay.

But nights were merciless. In the quiet dark, everything she had buried clawed its way back. She cried into her pillow until exhaustion claimed her, waking each morning with swollen eyes and a heart that felt a little more splintered than the day before. She had been welcomed into Deer Lodge with open arms. She had found safety. Belonging. Family. And yet she had never felt so utterly alone.

Normally, she would have gone to Alice. She would have confessed everything, jealousy, hurt, the humiliation of wanting someone who so clearly did not want her back. But Alice was radiant these days, wrapped in happiness with Dylan, and Joy could not bear to dim that light. So, she swallowed her pain and told herself to endure.

She heard Darlene trying to reason with Graham once, her voice tight with concern. He brushed his mother off. Cathleen argued with him one night, voices raised, sharp with anger, but nothing changed.

Joy was grateful they tried. Truly. But she wanted no pity. If Graham did not choose her because of his own free will, she wanted nothing from him at all. Still, the sense of betrayal festered. When she noticed he was spending more time with Julia than with anyone else, she began avoiding town altogether. She rode farther each day, stayed gone longer, but the loneliness followed her like a shadow.

Her appetite vanished. Her cheeks grew hollow, her smiles rare and fragile. Those who loved her noticed. And Joy, strong, resilient Joy, felt her heart edging dangerously close to breaking.

Darlene Harrison grew increasingly alarmed as the days passed. The lively young woman who had once filled the house with quiet laughter and purpose now seemed to fade before her eyes. Joy moved through the ranch like a shadow, polite, helpful, always composed, but the light in her eyes was gone, replaced by a brittle reserve that worried Darlene far more than tears ever could.

Her aunt and uncle shared the concern. Gerald noticed how Joy lingered less during meals, how she excused herself early or claimed she wasn't hungry at all. His wife watched her hands tremble ever so slightly when she poured tea, saw the way she flinched at kindness, as though it cost her something to accept it. Together, they tried, gently at first, then more earnestly, to draw her out. Every attempt met the same quiet wall.

Joy smiled when asked how she was, offered a carefully practiced assurance that she was fine, and then deftly changed the subject. If pressed, she grew guarded, her tone polite but distant, retreating behind a calm that allowed no cracks. She thanked them for their concern, insisted she simply needed time, and made it clear, without ever raising her voice, that she would not be coaxed into revealing what she so carefully kept buried.

Darlene tried a mother's approach, offering warmth and reassurance without question. Gerald attempted reason and gentle honesty. Even Alice, sensing something amiss, reached out with sisterly affection. None of it worked.

Joy carried her hurt alone, convinced that speaking of it would only burden those she loved, or worse, expose how deeply she had been wounded. And so, she endured in silence, while those who cared for her most could only watch, helpless and aching, as the young woman they loved withdrew further into herself

One morning, after riding into town, Joy reined in before the general store. She swung down from the saddle and was about to head for the entrance when a sudden, violent commotion shattered the quiet. Shouts, the crack of gunfire, and then her sister's voice, raw with terror.

Joy froze. Heart hammering, she slipped into the shadow of a nearby hedge and crept closer, careful to keep herself hidden. What she saw made her blood run cold. Four men surrounded Alice. One tore the baby from her arms while another fired into the air, then into the ground near the feet of the men who rushed forward to help. Two townsmen went down, wounded but alive, their cries of pain cutting through the chaos. Alice screamed, reaching helplessly as the men mounted in a blur of movement. In seconds, they were gone, hooves pounding, the stolen child clutched against one rider's chest as they tore out of town.

For a heartbeat, Joy stood paralyzed, caught between the instinct to run to her sister and the knowledge that every second mattered. Women were already converging on Alice, wrapping her in their arms. Men shouted for the sheriff. Someone sprinted for Dr. Preston. That was all Joy needed to see.

Jaw set, she turned back to her horse. With swift, practiced motions, she buttoned her long leather coat, pulled her hat low to shadow her face, and swung into the saddle. She kicked her heels in, urging her mount forward before doubt could take root. She passed the clinic just as Julia burst through the door, medical bag in hand. The physician spotted Joy and called after her, alarm sharp in her voice, but Joy did not slow. She could not. There would be time for explanations later, if there was a later at all.

Once clear of town, she rose slightly in the saddle and scanned the open land ahead. There, dust on the horizon. The unmistakable line of riders fleeing hard and fast. Relief and fury surged together.

Keeping to the cover of trees and low ground, Joy followed, careful to stay far enough back to remain unseen. She had no plan yet, no certainty of what she would face. Only one truth steadied her hands on the reins and drove her forward. She would bring her niece home.

⁓

"My baby... my baby..." Alice sobbed, her entire body shaking as though the world had split open beneath her feet. She clawed weakly at the air, her knees buckling until her aunt and uncle reached her at the same moment Dave and Dylan did. Arms wrapped around her, holding her upright as the horror of what had just happened rippled outward.

The news spread through Deer Lodge like wildfire: Alice's baby had been taken. Men poured into the street from every direction, faces grim, hands already reaching for reins and rifles as the sheriff called for volunteers to ride after the kidnappers.

Julia moved with swift authority. She knelt beside Alice, murmuring calm assurances while instructing the nurse to prepare something to steady her nerves. Then she turned sharply toward the wounded men lying on the ground, blood darkening the dirt beneath them.

"Get them to my clinic. Now," she ordered. "Carefully. Do not let them walk."

Several uninjured townsmen sprang into action at once, lifting the injured and carrying them away as fast as they dared. At the edge of the gathering, Dave was already issuing commands, dividing the volunteers into groups, assigning directions and responsibilities with practiced efficiency. Horses were brought forward, saddles tightened, weapons checked. The air was thick with urgency. Julia stepped up beside him, her face pale but resolute.

"You need to leave immediately," she said, her voice tight with worry. "Joy rode out of town just moments after it happened. I saw her pass the clinic at a full gallop. She's gone after them."

"What?" The word tore from several mouths at once. Graham went rigid. Brigham swore under his breath. For a heartbeat, shock rooted them in place, then instinct and fear snapped them into motion.

"She shouldn't be out there alone," Graham said, already swinging into the saddle.

"There's no time," Brigham growled. "We track them and catch up."

Within moments, horses thundered forward. Graham, Brigham, Dave, Dylan, and a handful of hardened ranch hands followed the fresh hoofprints cutting sharply away from town and vanishing into the shadowed forest beyond.

The women left behind clustered together, hands clasped, eyes fixed on the trees as the riders disappeared, each one silently praying they would reach Joy in time, and that the child would be returned before darkness fell.

17

No Names, Only Shadows

Joy was far ahead of the men from Deer Lodge. She kept herself hidden, riding off to the side, never close enough to be seen, yet never losing sight of the kidnappers. She did not know what she would do if she truly caught up to them, only that stopping now was not an option. She trusted her instincts, riding on nothing but determination and the quiet hope that the right idea would come when she needed it most.

The trail led through dense brush and narrow, treacherous passages. The men changed direction several times, doubling back and cutting sharply through the forest, and Joy mirrored every move with care. Relief washed over her when they finally slowed, then stopped altogether. They chose a clearing to make camp.

Within minutes, a fire crackled to life. Rain began to fall, light at first, then steadier, turning the air cold and raw. Joy watched from the shadows as the men unpacked food, and several bottles of whiskey. Her hands curled into fists. That was when she saw it.

One of the men carried a cradle board strapped to his back. Her breath caught painfully in her chest. This had been planned. Deliberately. Baby Ruth lay nestled inside, mercifully asleep. Joy swallowed hard. If the child woke up and began to cry, everything would become far more dangerous. She forced herself to think.

They hadn't seen her during the attack in town. To them, she would be nothing more than a lone woman, harmless, insignificant. If she played it right, they would underestimate her. Joy smeared dirt across her cheeks and hands, dulling her appearance, then mounted her horse again and rode slowly toward the camp. Wet leaves muffled the sound of hooves, though the occasional snap of a twig gave her away.

The men sprang to their feet, guns drawn. Joy reined in calmly, her heart hammering as she came into view.

"Who goes there?" one of them demanded. When they saw her, petite, alone, unarmed, the tension visibly drained from their stances. Weapons were lowered, then holstered.

"Sorry," Joy called out, keeping her voice low and steady. "Saw your fire and figured I'd warm myself a spell. Been in the saddle for hours."

They exchanged glances. One of them shrugged.

"Come on over."

The ease with which they accepted her presence confirmed what she already suspected: these were not masterminds. They were hired hands. Fools paid to do someone else's dirty work. Joy dismounted and stepped toward the fire, holding her hands out to the warmth. She was searching for the right words when a soft whimper drifted from the cradle board. Her chest tightened.

"You hauled a baby along with you?" she asked casually. "So, who's the lucky pa?"

None of them answered at first. Finally, one shrugged.

"Ain't ours. Just deliverin' her to her folks."

The baby stirred again, the whimper edging closer to a cry.

"Where you from?" another man asked.

"Oregon," Joy said without missing a beat. "My folks tried to shove me into a marriage I didn't want. I lit out instead. Ain't got no intention of marryin' a fool."

Her defiance amused them. Grins spread as whiskey bottles were lifted.

"A feisty one," the man with the cradle board said, chuckling. Baby Ruth began to cry. Soft at first, then louder, more insistent. One of the men groaned and snapped at her to be quiet. Joy scoffed, unable to hide her contempt.

"What kind of jackass thinks hollerin' at a baby helps?"

"Oh yeah?" one sneered. "You got a better idea?"

"I do." She didn't hesitate. "Give her to me."

To her astonishment, the man unbuckled the cradle board and handed it over without question.

Joy cradled her niece against her chest, murmuring softly, rocking her with practiced ease. Within moments, the cries faded into quiet breaths. Ruth slept again. Low whistles followed.

"You got younger kin?" one of them asked.

"No," Joy said evenly. "But my sister does. And bein' a woman helps."

The rain intensified, drumming against leaves and earth. Joy scanned the clearing and spotted a cluster of pine trees nearby, their thick branches sheltering the ground beneath. She wrapped Ruth in part of her coat and laid her gently on a bed of moss, fashioning a small shelter with a branch and the remaining fabric. More whistles.

"Smart one," a man said, flashing a grin full of rotten teeth. "Care for a drink?"

Joy tugged up a thin smile. "No thanks. Still got miles to cover. Gotta keep my wits about me."

They laughed and drank more, growing slower, hazier. Joy turned away, suppressing a shudder of disgust, and then she saw her chance. Several whiskey bottles sat dangerously close to the fire. Carefully, casually, she nudged the nearest one into the flames. Then another. No one noticed. She retreated as if checking on the baby, quietly leading her horse away toward the pines. She tied the animal securely to a tree farther back, knowing the coming explosions would spook the untethered horses but leave hers safe. Her pulse raced as she stepped into the shadows. Now, all she had to do was wait.

"I think we lost the trail again," Dave said, leaning low over his horse's neck as he searched the rain-soaked ground for hoofprints nearly swallowed by mud and leaves. Joy's uncle rode beside him, jaw clenched, eyes sweeping the forest with restless vigilance. Graham and Brigham flanked them, Dylan and two other men from town riding close behind. Every one of them carried the same gnawing tension, fear for the stolen baby, and an even sharper dread for Joy, who had ridden after the kidnappers alone.

Dave was just about to dismount, hoping a closer look might reveal a hidden track, when the air shattered. An explosion tore through the forest. Then another. Shouting followed, sharp and panicked, the sound ricocheting off the trees, far too close for comfort. Dave's head snapped up.

"That came from ahead!"

No one waited for orders. They drove their heels into their horses' sides and surged forward as one, branches whipping past, rain stinging their faces. The forest blurred as fear lent speed to man and beast alike. Every thought narrowed to a single, desperate truth. Whatever was happening, Joy was there.

Joy had been waiting for the moment, had counted on the distraction, but when it finally came, it still caught her by surprise. The first explosion ripped through the damp forest, a violent crack that echoed through the trees. Just as she'd anticipated, the kidnappers' horses screamed and bolted, reins snapping loose as they vanished into the undergrowth.

Her own horse shied hard and bucked once, hooves striking sparks against stone, but Joy kept a firm grip on the reins, murmuring soothing words until the animal realized there was no immediate threat and stilled beneath her.

Baby Ruth woke instantly. Her cries tore through the air, panicked, shrill, and desperate. Joy's heart clenched. She scooped her niece up and pressed her close, rocking her gently despite her own shaking hands.

"Hush now, sweetheart," she whispered, her voice trembling but steady. "I've got you. You're safe." It took a moment, but the baby's screams softened to hiccupping sobs, then finally quieted as Joy continued to rock her. Rain plastered Joy's hair to her face, her clothes clung cold and heavy to her skin, but she barely noticed.

As soon as Ruth was calm again, Joy grabbed her coat and wrapped the child carefully inside it, cocooning her against the chill. Joy herself was shivering now, teeth chattering, but she would gladly endure the cold if it meant keeping her niece warm. She swung back into the saddle, holding Ruth securely against her chest, and turned her horse toward the trees, ready to disappear into the forest, when shouting erupted behind her.

Joy twisted in the saddle, heart leaping, and stared back toward the campsite just as riders burst through the brush. Men from Deer Lodge, Dave, Graham, Brigham, and others, stormed into the clearing, guns drawn, voices sharp and commanding.

"Hands up! On the ground—now!"

Disoriented, half drunk, and still reeling from the explosions and fleeing horses, the kidnappers froze. Confusion flickered across their faces before survival instinct took over. One by one, they dropped to the muddy ground, hands raised, fear finally overtaking bravado.

Within minutes, the men from Deer Lodge had them restrained, handcuffs snapping shut, ropes cinched tight. The threat was over as quickly as it had begun. Only then did the rescuers begin to look around wildly.

"Joy!" someone shouted. "Where's the baby?"

Joy urged her horse forward, emerging slowly from the trees. Rain streaked her face, her hair hung loose and dark around her shoulders, and she cradled Baby Ruth protectively against her chest.

"I'm here," she called, her voice hoarse but steady. Relief swept through the clearing like a physical force.

It was Graham who saw her first. He was beside her in an instant, boots splashing through the mud, as he closed the distance. Joy had barely dismounted and settled her niece back onto the moss when he pulled her fiercely into his arms, crushing her against his chest. Relief flooded his face, then irritation—sharp and unmistakable. He caught her by the arms, holding her at arm's length as his jaw tightened.

"What were you thinking?" he demanded. "Why would you do something like that, go after those men on your own? Do you have any idea how dangerous that was?"

Joy hadn't expected the hug. Hadn't wanted it. She'd frozen at first, stunned by the sudden closeness, but the moment his scolding began, something in her snapped. She wrenched herself free of his grip, her eyes blazing.

"Why do you care?" she shot back. "Why are you suddenly so concerned about my welfare?" Her voice trembled with restrained fury. "I've been doing everything on my own these past few weeks, Graham. You didn't care then, so don't start pretending now."

"Joy—" he began, but she cut him off without hesitation.

"I saw those men take my sister's baby," she said, her voice hard and unwavering. "I wasn't going to stand around waiting for volunteers while they disappeared into the wilderness. I knew every minute mattered. So, I did what I had to do."

The others reached them then, Brigham, Dave, and her uncle. One after another, they pulled her into firm, fatherly embraces, relief evident in every touch.

"That was incredibly risky, Joy," her uncle said once they released her. His expression was grave, and both Brigham and Dave nodded in agreement. Joy let out a slow breath.

"I know how it looks," she admitted, her tone calmer now. "But I followed them carefully. I had hours to think things through. I realized quickly they weren't nearly as clever as they wanted to seem, and the amount of whiskey they carried certainly helped."

Dave frowned thoughtfully. "Then how did the explosions happen?"

She explained everything, the bottles, the fire, the damp ground, the distraction. How she'd waited. How she'd protected Ruth first and foremost. How she'd planned her escape in case no one came after them. When she finished, silence settled over the clearing. They simply stared at her. Joy folded her arms and rolled her eyes.

"Do you believe me now when I say I didn't take unnecessary risks? I wasn't trying to be heroic. I didn't fight them. I didn't try to overpower anyone. All I wanted was to get my niece back, alive and unharmed."

Dave finally cleared his throat, shaking his head in disbelief.

"Joy Collins, you are a remarkable young woman. I never doubted your intelligence, but this…" A faint smile tugged at his mouth. "This proves just how sharp your mind truly is. Truth be told, if a man had followed those kidnappers, he likely would have rushed in headfirst and gotten himself killed. You, on the other hand, used patience, observation, and strategy."

She shrugged, lifting her niece and drawing Baby Ruth close to her chest once more.

"I didn't know if anyone was coming after us," she said quietly. "I couldn't count on being found. So, I did the only thing that made sense." She looked down at the sleeping child in her arms. "I took responsibility."

Joy kept her distance from Graham on the ride back to town. She rode a little behind and off to the side, her gaze fixed straight ahead, unwilling to invite another confrontation. Thankfully, the men were occupied guarding the kidnappers and ensuring none of them even considered escape, and Graham, though visibly restless, didn't try to approach her again.

When they rode into Deer Lodge, the town seemed to pour into the streets. Doors flew open. Women rushed from porches. Men spilled out of shops and saloons. Cheers erupted the moment the battered, handcuffed kidnappers came into view. Relief, outrage, and triumph blended into a single, overwhelming roar. Alice broke free from the crowd the instant she spotted them.

"Joy!" she cried, running full tilt toward her sister. Joy barely had time to dismount before Alice reached her, gently but urgently pulling Baby Ruth into her arms. The infant stirred, then settled again, safe and warm against her mother's chest.

"My baby," Alice sobbed, clinging to her child as though afraid she might vanish again. Dave and several of the men immediately led the kidnappers away, ensuring they were securely locked up before returning to Gerald and Joy. The crowd lingered, hushed now, waiting, watching. Once Alice had calmed enough to speak, she turned to her uncle, her eyes red and swollen but filled with gratitude.

"Thank you, Uncle Gerald," she said softly. "Thank you for bringing my little girl back to me."

Gerald shook his head firmly.

"Don't thank me, or any of us." He turned and placed a hand on Joy's shoulder. "It was your sister who rescued Baby Ruth. By the time we arrived, Joy had already created a distraction and would have escaped with the baby even if we'd never shown up. All we did was arrest the men responsible."

Silence swept through the street. All eyes turned to Joy. Shock rippled through the crowd as the realization settled. Murmurs followed, astonished, reverent. Joy felt heat rush to her cheeks and lowered her gaze, suddenly unsure what to do with so much attention.

Her aunt stepped forward first, wrapping her in a fierce embrace. Joy swallowed hard, but it was Alice who broke her completely. Alice crossed the last few steps and pulled Joy into her arms, holding her as tightly as she dared, careful not to jostle the baby.

"Thank you," Alice whispered, tears streaming freely now. "Thank you, Joy. I love you so much."

Joy closed her eyes, her own tears finally spilling as she returned the embrace.

"And I love you," she murmured back. For the first time since the chaos began, her heart eased, if only a little.

Eliza Collins insisted that everyone who had ridden out after the kidnappers join them for supper, refusing to take no for an answer. It was her way of grounding the day, of turning fear and chaos into warmth, gratitude, and togetherness.

The house filled quickly with voices, boots, and the scrape of chairs. Plates were set, food carried in, and for the first time since the kidnapping, a fragile sense of safety settled over the room. Joy, however, kept her distance from Graham. She took a seat at the far end of the table and focused on helping where she could, not because she was angry, though part of her was, but because she simply had no strength left to be lectured. Not tonight. Not after everything. As people were just about to sit down, Dylan gently touched her arm.

"Joy, may I speak with you for a moment?"

She followed him into a quieter corner of the room, her expression guarded but attentive.

"I want to ask your sister to marry me," he said quietly. "I had planned to wait. I wanted to be certain the threat hanging over you and Alice was truly gone. But today..." He exhaled slowly. "Today terrified her. It terrified me. I want to take her somewhere safe. Somewhere we can start without looking over our shoulders."

Joy stared at him, stunned, not only by the timing, but by the weight of the moment.

"Shouldn't you ask my uncle for his blessing?" she asked after a moment.

"I will," Dylan assured her at once. "But you are her older sister. Your opinion matters deeply to both of us. I needed to know if you would be all right with it."

Joy studied him, searching his face.

"What's your plan?"

"We'll keep the wedding small. Quiet. Only those who absolutely need to know will be invited. I don't want anyone watching Deer Lodge to have the slightest idea where I'm taking Alice and the girls, or when."

Her throat tightened. The thought of her sister leaving, of the house growing even quieter, sent a sharp ache through her chest. Yet she knew, without question, that this was the right decision.

"I don't ever want to see her go through something like today again," Dylan added softly. Joy blinked rapidly, fighting tears.

"Promise me you'll keep in touch," she said, her voice barely above a whisper. "As much as possible."

He nodded without hesitation and squeezed her hand.

"I promise."

She took a steadying breath, then gave him a small, brave smile.

"You have my blessing," she said. "Just... take good care of Alice."

"I will," he replied, his voice firm with sincerity.

As Dylan stepped away, Joy remained where she was for a moment, gathering herself. Her heart ached, but beneath the ache was relief. Alice would be safe. And that, above all else, mattered most.

Joy spent the rest of the evening lost in quiet reflection, her attention drifting in and out of the conversations around her. Laughter filled the room, plates were passed, and the tension of the day slowly softened, but her thoughts remained elsewhere. She noticed Dylan drawing her uncle aside, the two of them speaking in low, serious tones. Gerald's expression shifted from concern to contemplation, then finally to approval as he clasped Dylan's shoulder in a firm, meaningful way.

Not long after, Dylan approached Alice and asked if she would join him for a short walk.

Joy watched them leave, her heart twisting with a blend of relief, worry, and a bittersweet ache she couldn't quite name. She kept herself busy clearing dishes and helping her aunt, but her gaze drifted repeatedly toward the door.

When Alice and Dylan returned, there was no mistaking what had happened. Alice's face was radiant, her eyes bright, her smile soft and almost disbelieving, as though she feared happiness might vanish if she examined it too closely. She caught Joy's gaze across the room, her expression brimming with gratitude and love. Joy smiled back, warmth spreading through her chest. Whatever uncertainties lay ahead, at least tonight had brought one moment of undeniable joy.

No matter how often Joy turned the events over in her mind, the answer refused to reveal itself. She replayed every moment, every shouted word, every terrifying second, searching for a thread that would connect it all, but nothing fit. Her thoughts returned, repeatedly, to Willard Thomas. He was the obvious choice. He had proven himself capable of cruelty, manipulation, and vengeance. Yet the more she considered it, the less sense it made. What would he gain from kidnapping a child? Terror, yes, but leverage? Against whom, and to what end? The idea left a hollow unease in her chest. A child was not a pawn in a game of pride or revenge, not even for a man as twisted as Willard Thomas. Or so she hoped.

Joy stared out into the darkened yard, the night wind brushing softly against the windowpane, and felt the weight of a truth she could not yet name pressing in on her. Someone had planned the kidnapping. Someone had paid for it. And whoever it was, they had been willing to put an innocent life at risk to achieve their goal. That realization unsettled her more than any single suspect ever could.

Graham left shortly after supper, his departure unremarkable to everyone else, and painfully noticeable to Joy. When she stepped outside a short while later, preparing to head home, her breath caught. In the fading light, she saw him walking away from town with Julia, their hands entwined as they strolled down the path together, their silhouettes close and familiar.

The sight struck deeper than she cared to admit. She turned toward her horse, focusing on the simple, grounding motions of leather and reins, when Brigham appeared at her side.

"Shall we ride home together?" he asked gently. Joy nodded, grateful for the reprieve from words. He helped her into the saddle with the same quiet care he always showed her, then mounted his own horse. They rode side by side in companionable silence, hooves thudding softly against the earth, the evening air cool against her flushed cheeks. After a time, Brigham cleared his throat.

"Joy," he began, his voice careful, "Darlene and the girls have been watching you these past few weeks. All of us have. And we're worried about you. You're not happy, and it breaks our hearts. Don't you want to tell me what's been troubling you?" He glanced at her, but Joy kept her gaze fixed ahead, the path blurring slightly as her eyes stung. She knew if she looked at him, really looked, it would all come undone. The tears, the hurt, the disappointment she had worked so hard to bury would spill before she could stop them.

The Harrisons had given her more than shelter. They had given her warmth, belonging, a sense of family she hadn't realized she'd been starving for. She loved Darlene and Brigham deeply, far more than she would have thought possible when she'd first arrived at Deer Lodge. Cathleen and Olivia had become sisters to her in every way that mattered. But Graham... Graham had shattered something inside her.

Joy closed her eyes briefly, steadying herself. She couldn't tell Brigham the truth, not without placing him in an impossible position. She refused to make him choose sides or confront his own son on her behalf. And she certainly couldn't confess how foolish she felt for believing Graham's feelings mirrored her own.

She hadn't meant to fall for anyone. Yet, little by little, Graham had worn down her defenses with his smiles, his attention, his stolen moments and half-spoken promises. She had believed there was something real between them, had trusted the way he looked at her, the way his touch lingered. And then, the moment his divorce was final, he had pulled away as if none of it had mattered. Had she only been a distraction? A temptation he indulged in while he was bound, only to discard once he was free?

Brigham was still watching her, patiently waiting. Joy drew in a slow, measured breath.

"I appreciate you and your family more than I can ever put into words," she said quietly. "But I'm afraid this is something I have to face on my own."

He frowned. "Sometimes sharing the burden makes it lighter."

She shook her head. "Not this one. Talking about it would only make it harder."

Brigham sighed softly, frustration and concern warring in his expression, but he respected her answer.

"Is there anything we can do for you?"

Her throat tightened. Tears threatened, but she kept her voice steady through sheer will.

"You already are," she said. "You welcomed me. You made me part of your family. I'll always be grateful for that."

They rode on in silence after that, the unspoken weight between them heavy, yet wrapped in care, understanding, and a love that asked for nothing in return.

Joy went to bed with her thoughts still churning, the events of the day refusing to settle. No matter how exhausted she felt, sleep remained just out of reach. The same question circled endlessly in her mind: who had been behind the kidnapping? Dave had tried everything he could, but the men had given him nothing of value. They claimed they were only hired hands, doing a job for someone else. No names. No faces. Just shadows.

She lay staring at the ceiling when a sudden, unwelcome thought struck her so sharply she sucked in a breath. What if it was Matt and Maureen? Joy pushed herself upright in bed, her heart beginning to race. What if their apology had been nothing more than a performance? What if they had hired those men to take Alice's baby, just long enough to frighten her into leaving Deer Lodge? Maureen had always been manipulative, always convinced she knew what was best for everyone else. But then another question followed just as quickly. What about Annie?

If this had truly been about reclaiming Alice, or controlling her, wouldn't they have taken both children? Why only Ruth? Unless... unless Annie simply hadn't been there. Joy frowned, piecing it together. Alice hadn't taken Annie with her to the store that morning. The men could only take the child who was present. Her pulse quickened as the theory took shape. Perhaps the kidnapping had never been meant to be permanent. Perhaps it had been a warning. A message. Come back to us, or worse will follow.

Joy swung her legs over the side of the bed, restless energy flooding her. The more she examined the pieces, the less coincidence felt like coincidence. Patterns were emerging, dark and deliberate. There was only one way to know the truth. She would go to Goldcreek.

The decision settled over her with unexpected calm. She would ride there herself and confront Matt and Maureen face-to-face. Watch their reactions. Listen to their answers. If they were innocent, she would see it. And if they weren't, she would know that too. She would leave at first light.

Joy knew better than to tell anyone of her plan. They would try to stop her, to protect her, to remind her of the dangers she had already faced. But she could not live with the uncertainty gnawing at her. She needed answers.

Maureen's brother was a decent man. If things turned unpleasant, he would not allow his sister or nephew to harm her. That knowledge steadied her. At last, with her course set and her resolve firm, the tension in her body eased. Joy lay back down, pulling the blanket close as her thoughts finally quieted. This time, sleep came quickly, deep and dreamless, carrying her toward morning and the confrontation she knew she could no longer avoid.

18

She Left Without a Word

J oy slipped out of the house before dawn, moving as quietly as a shadow. The ranch still slept, wrapped in the hush that came just before morning, and she was grateful for it. She had no desire to explain herself or be talked out of what she was about to do. The stable greeted her with the familiar scents of hay and leather. She saddled her horse quickly, her movements practiced and deliberate, and within moments was riding away from the ranch, the sky just beginning to pale along the horizon.

Although she had never been to Maureen's brother's home, Joy knew exactly where she was headed. Her brother had once given her careful directions, in case she, or Alice, wished to visit Goldcreek. At the time, the information had seemed inconsequential. Now, it felt providential.

The ride took several hours. The air was sharp with cold, biting at her cheeks and fingers, but Joy welcomed the sting. It kept her alert, anchored her in the present, and left little room for fear or second-guessing. She rode steadily. Her thoughts fixed on the questions waiting for her at the end of the road.

By midmorning, the small settlement of Goldcreek came into view. Compared to Deer Lodge, it was quiet and modest, a handful of buildings gathered close together as if for protection against the vast wilderness surrounding them. Smoke curled lazily from a few chimneys, and the town was just beginning to stir.

Joy slowed her horse as she reached the edge of town, scanning her surroundings. She found the house almost immediately: a simple, well-kept home set beside a small church building, just as she had been told. Its whitewashed walls and tidy yard spoke of order and respectability, which only tightened the knot in her stomach. She reined in and sat there for a moment, steadying herself. Whatever answers awaited her inside that house, she was here now. And she would not turn back.

By the time Joy slipped out of the house, Graham and his father were already at the barn, tending to the morning chores. The sound of hoofbeats drew their attention, and both men paused as she led her horse from the stable. Graham's brow furrowed. Curiosity shifted quickly to irritation when he realized she was saddling up with purpose and riding out without a word. He watched her disappear down the drive, his jaw tightening.

"Where on earth is that girl off to now?" he muttered under his breath. Brigham felt no such annoyance. Instead, a familiar unease settled in his chest. Joy had been quiet, withdrawn, and distant for weeks, and something about the way she rode off alone, before anyone else was awake, set his instincts on edge.

Without wasting time, the two men saddled their horses. Brigham moved with urgency, then handed the reins to Graham and strode back toward the house. Darlene was already awake. She looked up the moment he entered, reading his expression at once.

"Joy's ridden out," Brigham said quietly. "Alone."

Darlene's face paled. She stepped outside just in time to see her husband and son mount their horses and spur them forward, following the faint trail Joy had left behind. She clasped her hands together, worry tightening her chest as she watched them ride off. Whatever Joy was running toward, or away from, Darlene feared it wasn't something that could be easily mended.

Joy dismounted and secured her horse to the fence post before forcing herself toward the front door. Her legs felt unsteady, not from the long ride, but from the weight of what she was about to ask. She knocked firmly. The door opened almost at once, and Maureen's brother stood there, blinking in surprise.

"Miss Collins," he said, clearly taken aback. "This is unexpected. Please, come in. We're just about to have breakfast. Won't you join us?"

"No, thank you," Joy replied quietly. "I won't be staying long."

He frowned. Concern slipped into his expression.

"You rode several hours to get here. You can't possibly be planning to turn around immediately."

She nodded. "I am."

By then, Maureen and Matt had stepped closer. One look at Joy's pale face and drawn features seemed to alarm them. Matt reached for her arm instinctively.

"Come on," he urged gently. "At least sit down. Have some breakfast."

Joy pulled her arm free. "I'm fine. I only came to ask one question." She drew in a steadying breath. There was no graceful way to do this, no softening the blow.

"Did you, or your mother, hire men to kidnap Baby Ruth?"

The words landed like a gunshot. Maureen and Matt stared at her in utter disbelief. For a long moment, no one spoke. Matt was the first to find his voice.

"Alice's baby was kidnapped," he said slowly, incredulity edging his tone, "and you think we had something to do with it?"

"I don't know what to think anymore," Joy replied, her voice tight. "Four men rode into town yesterday, took my niece out of my sister's arms, shot people who tried to stop them, and vanished. I can't make sense of it, and I can't think of many who would have a reason."

Maureen's hand flew to her mouth. Matt and her brother exchanged a glance, part shock, part hurt. Joy exhaled, rubbing her temples.

"I don't want to accuse you unfairly. But after everything that's happened, I'm still trying to understand who I can trust. I wondered if you might have tried to force Alice's hand, blackmail her into moving in with you, or something similar."

Maureen swallowed hard. "What happened to Ruth?" she asked urgently. "Was she found?"

"Yes," Joy said at once. "She was returned to Alice unharmed."

Relief washed over their faces, though the tension remained. Matt cleared his throat.

"I won't pretend that accusation doesn't hurt," he said quietly. "It does. But I understand why you'd be wary. I swear to you, Joy, we had nothing to do with it." He held her gaze, searching her face. Joy looked past him at Maureen's brother, who nodded gravely.

"It's the truth," he said. "They've been honest with me, about everything. My sister has been sober, truly sober. And Matt would be a fool to involve himself in something so vile. He was sheriff in Auburn. He knows exactly what a crime like that would mean."

Joy hesitated. "And you're certain? They couldn't have slipped away without you noticing?"

The reverend shook his head.

"I trust them now. If John were still alive..." He paused, sorrow darkening his eyes. "Then yes, I would believe him capable of such a thing. But not Matt. Not my sister."

Joy's shoulders sagged slightly.

"Then I'm sorry. Truly. I didn't come here to wound you, only to find the truth. I shouldn't have been so blunt."

Maureen stepped forward and offered a small, understanding smile.

"Don't apologize. If it had been my child, I would have asked the same question."

Joy turned back to the reverend, her expression troubled.

"You really believe John would have done something like that?"

Before he could answer, Maureen nodded, pain etched across her face.

"Yes. As much as it hurts to say it about my own son, yes. He was far too much like his father, charming on the surface, cruel and manipulative in private."

Silence settled between them.

"Do you have any idea who else might be behind it?" Matt asked finally. Joy shook her head.

"None. My first thought was Willard Thomas but kidnapping a baby makes no sense. He knows the slightest misstep now would land him in prison." And yet, the unease in her chest told her the truth was still out there, waiting to be uncovered.

After that was finally out of the way, Joy accepted their invitation to join the family for breakfast. Though relief settled in her chest now that her fears had proven unfounded, a lingering guilt remained for having accused them at all. Still, she was grateful, deeply so, that she had been wrong.

As they sat down at the table, Matt mentioned casually that he planned to take over the livery in Deer Lodge, and that he also intended to work as a blacksmith. Joy stared at him, surprise plain on her face.

"But you know nothing about being a blacksmith."

Matt grinned, clearly enjoying her reaction.

"That's not true. I learned the trade before we moved from Sacramento to Auburn. I did it in secret, because my father was never supposed to find out. I apprenticed under a very talented blacksmith, and I loved the work."

Joy blinked. "Your father wouldn't have allowed it if he'd known?"

Matt shook his head. "Never. My father only respected what he considered prestigious occupations, doctor, lawyer... and, apparently, criminal." His mouth tightened briefly. "Anything else was beneath him."

"That's awful," Joy murmured.

"Troy was a terrible man," Maureen's brother added quietly. "He cared for no one unless they were useful to his crime family. To this day, we don't even know how many people belonged to it, or how many were ever brought to justice."

"You never met his family either?" Joy asked, turning to Maureen. Maureen shrugged, her expression somber.

"No. He never introduced me to anyone. Only people as corrupt as he was, were allowed into that circle. Since Matt wanted nothing to do with it, Troy mostly ignored him. But John..." Her voice faltered. "John fit every expectation Troy had for someone he wanted to groom."

The silence that followed was heavy, but it carried a strange sense of clarity as well. Whatever shadows Troy Haven had cast over their lives, Joy could see now that Matt was determined to step out of them and build something honest of his own.

When Joy was getting ready to leave, she happened to glance out the sitting-room window and promptly rolled her eyes. Down the road, unmistakable even at a distance, were Brigham and Graham.

"Is there any way for me to return home without using the main road," she asked, "at least for a little while?"

Maureen's brother looked at her in confusion.

"Why would you want to avoid the main road? It's the safest and easiest way back."

Joy sighed, then pointed out the window and briefly explained why she had no desire whatsoever to ride toward Deer Lodge with Graham in tow. Her explanation earned knowing grins all around.

"Well," the reverend said after a moment, "there is a narrow passage behind our stable. It's completely hidden from the main road by trees and thick brush. It will lead you back to the road after several miles, you won't miss it once you're on it." He turned to Matt. "Why don't you fetch Joy's horse and bring it into the barn so she can leave without them noticing?"

Matt nodded at once and disappeared outside. Joy offered the reverend a grateful smile before turning to her sister's mother-in-law.

"If you're serious about starting a new café," she said gently, "please wait until all this remaining trouble has settled. I would hate for you to lose another home and business because of the chaos we're still dealing with."

Her concern was met with a warm, understanding look, one that reminded Joy she wasn't quite as alone in all of this as she sometimes felt.

After Maureen's brother pointed out the hidden passage, Joy found it without any trouble. The narrow trail wound through thick stands of trees and brush, muffling the sound of hoofbeats and keeping her well out of sight. It felt oddly comforting to ride unseen for a while, wrapped in quiet, the solitude giving her thoughts room to settle.

Before long, the path widened and curved gently back toward the main road, just as he had promised. Joy emerged from the shelter of trees and shrubbery and guided her horse forward, the familiar stretch of road leading home at last. Drawing a steady breath, she nudged her heels lightly against her mount's sides. She turned her face toward Deer Lodge and rode on.

Graham and Brigham lingered at the edge of the road. Their attention fixed on the house. When Matt stepped outside and led Joy's horse toward the barn, they exchanged a brief, puzzled glance but remained where they were, certain she would appear at any moment. She didn't. After another hour passed, Brigham finally exhaled and nudged his horse forward.

"We should ask after her," he said quietly.

A firm knock echoed through the house. It wasn't long before Maureen's brother opened the door.

"May I help you?"

Brigham tipped his hat politely. "Forgive the intrusion, Reverend, but we're looking for Joy Collins. She lives with us, and we followed her to be sure she was safe. She's still visiting with you, isn't she?"

The reverend hesitated, his expression shifting to mild dismay.

"Oh. I'm afraid not. She already left, about an hour ago."

Graham's jaw tightened. "How would she have left without us noticing," he demanded, irritation flashing in his eyes, "and more importantly, why would she do that?"

The reverend lifted an eyebrow, his tone dry.

"I believe that would be because of you."

"Because of us?" Brigham echoed, genuinely confused. The older man nodded.

"She happened to see you through the window and said, and I quote: 'I have no desire to get another lecture from Graham.'"

Brigham dropped his gaze at once, biting back a grin. Graham, however, could only stare at the reverend, color creeping into his cheeks.

"She asked about an alternate path that would lead her back to the main road," the reverend continued evenly, "and after Matt brought her horse into the barn, she left."

Graham wisely held his tongue, though his rigid posture and clenched jaw made his simmering frustration unmistakable. Brigham thanked the reverend, tipped his hat once more, and guided his horse away. Moments later, father and son mounted up and rode back toward the ranch, the silence between them heavier than before.

"Joy, where on earth have you been?" Darlene exclaimed the moment Joy stepped through the door. She crossed the room in two strides and pulled her into a tight, motherly embrace. "We've been worried sick. And where are Graham and my husband?"

Joy returned the hug briefly, then sighed.

"They're probably on their way home by now. I'm sorry for scaring you, Darlene, truly. There was something I needed to take care of, and I didn't want to make a fuss over it."

Darlene studied her face, clearly unconvinced but relieved to see her safe. Cathleen folded her arms, her expression serious.

"And why did you go by yourself?" she asked. "You could have asked Graham to go with you."

A short, bitter scoff slipped from Joy before she could stop it.

"I'm not bothering Graham for anything anymore. He keeps himself quite busy, with work and his lady friends, and when he does come after me, all I get is a lecture and a scolding." The words came out sharper than she'd intended. Realizing it too late, Joy pressed her lips together, wishing she could pull them back.

Cathleen and her mother exchanged a brief, knowing glance. Joy noticed it and felt a flicker of regret, but exhaustion, and emotion, won out.

"I'll be in my room, if that's all right with you," she said quietly, forcing a smile that didn't quite reach her eyes. "The ride was long, and I'm very tired." Before anyone could protest or ask another question, Joy turned and hurried up the stairs. She retreated into the safety of her room and closed the door behind her, leaving the unspoken worries, and the growing tension, lingering in the air below.

◆

"Whoa," Cathleen said softly once Joy's footsteps had faded upstairs, "that sounded like some serious jealousy."

Darlene didn't answer right away. Instead, she crossed the room, took Cathleen by the hand, and guided her into the large armchair by the window. She sank down beside her daughter with a weary sigh, her expression troubled.

"I don't think what we just heard was jealousy alone," she said at last. "There's a great deal more beneath it. That young woman is deeply hurt."

Cathleen nodded, irritation flashing across her face.

"And honestly, I don't blame her. Graham and Joy were thick as thieves. Anyone with eyes could see the chemistry between them, it was intense. He made her believe he had feelings for her. Real ones. And then, the moment the divorce was final and he was free, he turned his full attention to the girls in town and left Joy standing there like she never mattered." She shook her head, clearly upset.

"I can't think of a single thing Joy could have done to drive him away like that. They didn't quarrel, at least not that I know of. If anything, she's been bending over backward to give him space. He's a fool, an absolute fool, if he lets her slip through his fingers."

Darlene rested her elbow on the arm of the chair, her brow furrowed in thought.

"I don't know what happened between them, or what made Graham turn away so suddenly. But Joy's reaction tells me one thing for certain, he never gave her an explanation. He never tried to tell her why."

Cathleen exhaled sharply. "And instead, he's been taking Julia out, and a few other girls too. That must feel like a slap in the face. No wonder Joy is pulling away."

Her mother nodded slowly, sorrow and concern woven together.

"We can only hope Graham knows what he's doing and has truly thought this through." Her gaze drifted toward the staircase. "Joy is a remarkable young woman, strong, loyal, and kind. If he's missed his chance with her by betraying her trust and hurting her like this, then yes..." Her voice softened, but the judgment remained unmistakable. "...he really is a fool."

Joy had locked herself into her room. She heard Graham long before he reached her door, his boots struck the steps to the upper floor in long, angry strides that left no doubt about his mood. When he knocked, it was sharp and demanding.

"Joy, open the door."

"No."

"I want to talk to you."

"But I don't want to talk to you. Go away."

The knock came again, harder this time. The handle rattled as he tried the door and discovered it was locked.

"We need to talk," he insisted, his voice edged with frustration.

Joy didn't move. She sat rigidly on the edge of the bed, staring at the door as though sheer will might keep him on the other side. He knocked once more, but she remained silent until he spoke again.

"Why did you take off by yourself, again? Why do you keep doing things that are dangerous and foolish?"

A bitter scoff tore from her, sharp in the quiet room.

"I don't answer to you, Graham Harrison," she shot back. Her voice trembled, not with fear, but with restrained anger.

"Damn it, Joy, we just wasted hours coming after you. You owe us an explanation," he argued loudly.

"I didn't ask you to follow me and waste your time," she snapped. "Now go away."

Silence fell on the other side of the door, heavy, taut, as though he were weighing his next words. Joy pressed her lips together, bracing herself. She had drawn her line, and for once, she had no intention of stepping back.

Her stubbornness drove him mad. With a sharp growl of frustration, Graham slammed his palm against the wall, the impact echoing through the hallway, before turning and storming down the stairs. Brigham stepped closer at once.

"Did she talk to you?"

"No." Graham raked a hand through his hair, pacing like a caged animal. "She's so dang hard-headed I could strangle the girl."

Cathleen, who had been watching the exchange with simmering anger, stepped forward.

"Have you asked yourself what the problem is, Graham?" she snapped. "Because I believe it's you."

He halted mid-stride and stared at her.

"How am I the problem?"

"Oh, I don't know," Cathleen shot back, her voice rising. "Maybe because you made her believe you cared about her, then abandoned her the moment the divorce was final. And now the only time you show any concern is when she does something on her own and might get hurt. But do you show her you care? No. You scold her. You lecture her. I don't blame Joy one bit for not wanting to talk to you."

Graham's jaw tightened. "I have a perfectly reasonable explanation for my behavior."

"Really?" Cathleen crossed her arms, her eyes blazing. "Do tell, big brother. I'd love to hear what you consider reasonable."

The room fell silent. Graham clenched his fists, clearly preparing to argue back, but when he glanced at his mother, he found no comfort there. Darlene's expression mirrored Cathleen's, hurt, disappointment, and quiet reproach. Without another word, Graham turned on his heel and headed for the door.

"My point exactly, Graham," Cathleen called after him as he stepped outside. "Instead of explaining yourself or fighting for the best girl you'll ever meet, you just run away."

The door closed behind him with a solid thud, leaving the accusation hanging heavily in the air.

Brigham shook his head as he stepped outside. He hated tension within his home, especially the kind born of silence and wounded pride, but he understood why emotions were running so high. Too much had happened. Too many hearts were bruised.

He followed his son to the far fence line, and found him sitting astride the rail, elbows braced on his knees, staring out at the restless horses that still needed breaking. Graham didn't look up as Brigham came to stand beside him, but he didn't move away either. Brigham laid a steady hand on his son's shoulder.

"You can't keep shutting everyone out, Graham. I don't know what's gotten into you, but you need to talk to Joy. If your heart belongs to Julia Preston, then you owe Joy honesty. Make things right with her."

Graham exhaled sharply. "It's not a good time."

Brigham gave a soft, humorless huff.

"It will never be the perfect time, son. And the longer you wait, the worse it gets. Joy is pushing you away more every day. And every time you lecture her, every time you scold her instead of listening, you lose a little more ground with her."

"She could get herself hurt," Graham shot back. "Or worse. She goes after criminals, chases answers on her own, and doesn't think twice about the danger."

"Yes," Brigham agreed quietly. "And why do you think that is?"

Graham frowned but said nothing.

"You were her closest friend for most of the time she's been here," Brigham continued. "You were her anchor. And then, all at once, you were gone. Suddenly, you had eyes only for other women, and Joy was left wondering what she'd imagined and what had been real."

Graham shifted, his jaw tightening.

"She feels betrayed," Brigham said gently. "And she feels terribly alone. She's about to lose her sister to marriage and distance. She keeps her grief, her fear, and her heartache locked away, no matter how hard we try to reach her."

"Then why won't she talk to you?" Graham demanded, irritation flashing. "She knows she can trust you."

Brigham sighed. "Because she refuses to speak ill of you. You're our son. She won't put us in the position of choosing sides."

Graham scoffed. "If you know all this, why do you keep trying to get it out of her?"

"Because I want her to feel safe enough to come to us," Brigham answered firmly. "Even if that means hearing things that hurt. Joy has carried far too much on her shoulders since the death of her parents and her brother-in-law. Yes, she has her aunt and uncle nearby, but she doesn't open up to them either." He paused. His gaze was fixed on the distant hills.

"I truly believe Joy still thinks she's a burden. That her presence brings trouble. And so, she tries to handle everything on her own, no matter the cost."

Graham rubbed his face with both hands.

"Her stubbornness is driving me out of my mind."

"That same stubbornness is what's keeping her standing right now," Brigham replied. "Promise me you won't lecture her again. Worrying is one thing. Concern is understandable. But the way you've been speaking to her, those sharp words, that tone, its pushing her further away."

He turned fully toward his son.

"You need to talk to her. Truly talk to her. And if you've decided there is no future for the two of you, then you owe her the truth. Not silence. Not avoidance."

Graham said nothing. Brigham's voice softened, but his words did not.

"If we aren't careful, one day she'll be gone."

Graham snapped his head up. "Gone? What do you mean, gone?"

"She won't stay if she believes her presence puts us, or this town, at risk," Brigham said gravely. "She's voiced those fears to her uncle before. And I don't think they've ever left her heart."

"She wouldn't just leave," Graham argued. "I mean... yes, she's reckless at times, but where would she even go?"

Brigham met his gaze steadily.

"Don't underestimate her, Graham. Joy would walk straight into the mountains alone if she thought it would protect the people she loves. I could see her living in a hunting cabin, cut off from everyone, just to remove herself as a threat."

The words landed hard.

"And if that happens," Brigham added quietly, "you'll have to live with knowing you helped push her there."

Silence stretched between them, heavy, unforgiving, as the unbroken horses shifted restlessly in the distance, wild, waiting, and no longer willing to be ignored.

19

The Missing Hours

The dreaded day of her sister's departure arrived far sooner than Joy was ready for. Only three days after she had confronted Matt and Maureen about the kidnapping, Alice and Dylan were married. They gathered at the Harrison ranch for a quiet, carefully planned ceremony, small by design, secret by necessity.

Maureen's brother officiated, his calm presence lending the moment a solemn grace. Alice had insisted that Maureen and Matt be invited. She could not bring herself to leave without her mother-in-law knowing the truth, and the fact that Maureen's brother was a reverend only strengthened her resolve. Despite the fear and urgency that surrounded it, the wedding itself was beautiful.

Alice glowed with quiet joy, her smile soft but unwavering, and Dylan looked at her as though the world had narrowed to her alone. Annie clung happily to his hand, and Baby Ruth rested peacefully in his arms, already at ease with the man who had so willingly claimed them both as his own. It was impossible not to feel hope, even amid so much uncertainty. Dylan promised they would return to Deer Lodge once the threat against Alice and Joy was finally extinguished, or, at the very least, that they would visit whenever it was safe to do so.

Joy smiled and nodded, but her heart ached all the same. She hated seeing her sister leave. The finality of it pressed hard against her chest. And yet, beneath the sorrow, there was relief too, relief that Alice and the children would no longer be exposed to danger, no longer living beneath the shadow of threats and violence.

When the time came to part, Dylan helped Alice into the carriage with gentle care. Two U.S. marshals, *the real ones this time*, climbed aboard as well, assigned to protect the young family on their journey. Everyone hoped that the secrecy of the wedding, combined with their quiet departure, would finally sever, whatever dark thread had been tightening around Joy and her sister.

Alice had written letters to her friends in town, explaining why she had left without farewell. Her aunt promised to deliver them once enough time had passed, once it was safe.

As the carriage stood ready to depart, Dylan stepped toward Joy. Without warning, he pulled her into a tight embrace.

"Don't trust my uncle," he whispered urgently, so low no one else could hear. "Communicate with Charles. He can be trusted."

Joy stiffened, the words sinking in like a stone dropped into still water. Before she could ask what he meant, or why, he released her, met her stunned gaze, and gave a subtle nod, as though sealing a pact he could not explain. Then he turned, climbed onto the carriage, and took his seat beside Alice. Moments later, the wheels began to turn.

Joy stood motionless as the carriage disappeared down the road, her heart heavy with loss, and now burdened with a warning she did not yet understand but knew she could not ignore.

After the carriage disappeared down the road and the last well-wishers drifted away, a heavy quiet settled over the ranch. Joy stood staring at the empty stretch of land where her sister had vanished from sight, her chest aching with a loneliness she could barely name. Her uncle stepped closer and rested a gentle hand on her shoulder.

"Why don't you stay with us for the night?" he said softly. "And if you like... you could move in with us now. The house will feel terribly empty without Alice and the girls."

For a moment, Joy was tempted, more than tempted. The thought of leaving the Harrison ranch, of escaping the tension with Graham and the constant ache of his indifference, tugged at her heart. Being with her aunt and uncle felt safe, familiar, and comforting. But the temptation faded almost as quickly as it came. She worried about their safety. Too much had already happened. Too many threats still lingered unanswered. The Harrison ranch, with its hands, cowboys, and constant activity, was far better protected than her aunt and uncle's quiet home. Trespassers there would not go unnoticed, or unpunished.

"I can't move in," Joy said gently, forcing herself to meet her uncle's eyes. "Not yet. I don't want to put you at risk."

He studied her for a moment, clearly understanding her reasoning even if he didn't like it. His expression softened.

"Then at least stay with us tonight," he urged. "It's going to be awfully empty with Alice and the girls gone."

That, Joy could not refuse. She nodded, emotion tightening her throat, then hurried upstairs to gather a few belongings. Moments later, she found herself seated beside her aunt and uncle in their carriage, the familiar creak of the wheels carrying them away from the ranch and toward a house that already felt quieter than it ever had before.

As the carriage rolled forward, Joy stared ahead, bracing herself for the night to come, and for the growing sense that everything in her life was shifting, whether she was ready for it or not.

The house felt unnervingly still when Joy stepped inside. The familiar rooms echoed with a quiet that pressed in on her, as though the walls themselves were holding their breath. She knew it would take time to grow accustomed to her sister's absence, to the missing laughter of the girls, to the small, everyday sounds that had once filled the space, but the silence felt heavier than she had expected. And she knew, without a doubt, that her aunt and uncle felt it just as keenly.

Joy crossed the sitting room slowly. Her footsteps muted against the floor. She turned toward the bedroom her sister had occupied, intending to leave her things there for the night and perhaps gather herself before rejoining her aunt and uncle.

She never made it. Arms wrapped around her from behind without warning, iron-strong, merciless. Before she could cry out, a rough cloth was crushed against her mouth and nose. The sharp, bitter scent hit her instantly.

Joy thrashed, clawing blindly at her attacker, her heart hammering as panic surged through her. She tried to scream, but the sound was smothered before it could form. The room tilted sickeningly as her vision blurred, her strength draining far too quickly, her limbs growing heavy and unresponsive. The last thing she registered was a single, crushing realization. She had been followed. Then the darkness closed in, swift and absolute, and everything went black.

Joy opened her eyes slowly, disoriented. Darkness pressed in on all sides, yet faint voices drifted through the air, familiar voices. The Harrisons. Her heart skipped painfully.

Where am I? She pushed herself upright, a dull ache pulsing behind her eyes. The room was dim, the curtains drawn tight across the window. She rose on unsteady legs and crossed the floor, her movements sluggish, as though she were wading through water. When she pulled the curtains aside, dusk spilled in, washing the room in fading gold and gray. Recognition struck instantly. Her room. At the Harrison ranch. A chill slid down her spine.

How did I get here? She pressed her fingers to her temple, willing her thoughts to organize themselves. She had gone with her aunt and uncle. Hadn't she? She could picture climbing into the buggy, could almost feel the worn leather beneath her palm, yet when she tried to follow the memory further, it frayed and dissolved, leaving nothing but static. Her limbs felt heavy. Her thoughts slow. As though she had slept far longer than she remembered. Or not slept at all.

"What happened?" she whispered. The room offered no answer. Joy moved to the desk, her fingers fumbling until they closed around the matchbox. She struck one, then another, until the lamp flared to life. Warm light spilled across the familiar furniture, the neatly folded blankets, the chair by the window. Everything was exactly as it should be. That frightened her more than disorder ever could.

Had she imagined it? Had there been another attack, or was her mind betraying her? The bitter truth pressed close: she could no longer trust her own memory. Voices rose downstairs, drawing her from the room. Her pulse quickened as she stepped into the hallway and followed the sound. The Harrison family sat together in the sitting room, relaxed, at ease.

"Oh, Joy, you're up?" Darlene said at once, smiling warmly as she rose. "Did you have a good nap?"

Joy stopped short. "A... nap?"

"Yes," Darlene replied gently. "We thought you'd fallen asleep."

Joy turned slowly to Brigham. "Didn't I leave with my aunt and uncle earlier?"

He shook his head, calm and untroubled.

"No. You decided against it. You said you felt dizzy after they left and wanted to lie down for a bit. When we hadn't seen you for a couple of hours, we assumed you were resting."

Her mouth went dry.

"So... Uncle Gerald and Aunt Eliza are all right?"

"Of course," Darlene said quickly. "They're perfectly fine. And they understood. After all that's happened, they didn't want to pressure you into staying."

"Hmm," Joy murmured. But nothing about it felt reassuring. Before anyone could ask more questions, she turned and slipped outside. Cool evening air brushed her face, sharp and grounding. Her thoughts raced now, no longer sluggish but razor-edged. None of it made sense. She didn't remember feeling dizzy. She didn't remember deciding to stay. And she was certain, absolutely certain, that she had gone with her aunt and uncle. So why was there a hole in her memory? And far more unsettling still... Why would the Harrisons lie to her?

To quiet the confusion churning inside her, Joy forced herself to focus on the last clear words spoken to her before Alice and Dylan had left. *Don't trust my uncle.* Dylan's warning echoed in her mind, sharp and unsettling. What had he meant by that? Had her father's longtime friend and attorney been involved in the threat that had shadowed her and her sister for so long? Had her father suspected something, known something, long before his death?

Her pulse quickened as another possibility surfaced. What if her father had left her more than that brief note addressed to John? He had always been careful. Methodical. If he feared someone might search their home, or even Jonas's law office, he would never have hidden anything important in an obvious place. And suddenly, another memory stirred: the way he had insisted she take her saddle and bags when he sent her to her brother-in-law's house. Not suggested. Insisted.

A sharp sense of urgency took hold. The saddlebags.

Joy hurried across the yard, the cool evening air brushing against her skin, and slipped into the stables. The familiar scent of hay and leather grounded her as she found her saddle resting exactly where she had left it, the bags tucked neatly beside it. She searched them carefully, at first, her movements slow and deliberate, her breath held. Nothing.

Disappointment threatened to overwhelm her, until her fingers brushed along the outer seam of one bag. There, barely noticeable unless one knew precisely where to look, was a small incision. So slight it could easily have been mistaken for wear. Her heart began to race. Carefully, she slid two fingers into the narrow opening and felt something thin and folded. She eased it out, her hands trembling as she unfolded the paper. She recognized the handwriting instantly. Tears blurred her vision.

With darkness settling fully now, Joy grabbed a lantern from the barn and lit it before carrying it to the front porch. She sank into a chair, the soft glow of the flame illuminating the page. The note was brief, but its weight was crushing.

Joy,

I don't know what will happen in the next few days or weeks, but I've made numerous enemies over the past few years. In case I don't make it out of this alive, I gathered documents, newspaper articles, and other pieces of evidence and placed them in a metal box.

FLAMES OF THE FIRE

I hid it beneath your uncle's front porch steps when I visited a week ago. It is concealed among bushes and weeds. Inside a stone box I built there. Your uncle does not know about it. I fear I am running out of time.

Take care of your sister and mother. I love you.

Pa

Joy pressed the note to her chest as a quiet sob escaped her. How she missed him, his steady presence, his warm, reassuring hugs, the long conversations filled with quiet wisdom. And now this. The note made one thing painfully clear: her father had never expected her mother to die. Anger and grief tangled inside her, but beneath them burned something stronger. Determination.

She wanted, no, needed, to ride straight into town and retrieve the metal box he had hidden. The truth was finally within reach.

She glanced toward the darkened horizon and hesitated. Night had fully settled in. As she sat there weighing her options, another memory surfaced, sharp and vivid. The day Lydia and her father had stormed the Harrison ranch, demanding their price, Lydia had been frantic about something she claimed she had forgotten. At the time, it had seemed like one more manipulation.

Now, it felt like something else entirely.

What if the Thomas family had known about the evidence? If they were connected to her father's death, if they feared what he had uncovered, then anything hidden on this ranch would be the last place anyone would suspect. No one would imagine her father, or the Thomases, had concealed proof beneath the roof of people who had nothing to do with his past. Joy's grip tightened on the lantern. The answers were closer than ever.

Joy quickly folded her father's note and tucked it deep into the pocket of her dress, her fingers lingering there for a heartbeat, as though drawing strength from it. Lantern in hand, she crossed the yard toward the small guest house tucked behind the main building. She had never had reason to enter it before, but now every instinct urged her forward.

The little structure stood quiet and dark, its outline barely visible against the night. As she drew closer, she noticed the curtains in the front room were drawn tight, an odd detail, considering no one was supposed to be staying there. Her steps slowed. Reaching the door, Joy lifted the lantern slightly and glanced to the side, toward the washboard nailed against the exterior wall. Cathleen had once mentioned, almost in passing, that the spare key was hidden behind it. Joy reached for it, her fingers brushing the cool wood. Then she froze. The door wasn't locked. In fact, it stood slightly ajar.

A chill crept up her spine, prickling her skin. That wasn't right. The guest house was always locked when unoccupied, Darlene was particular about such things. Joy's grip tightened around the lantern handle as a quiet warning bell rang in her mind. Something was wrong. Holding her breath, she stepped back just enough to steady herself, every sense suddenly alert.

Whatever awaited her inside, she knew one thing for certain, this was no coincidence.

Her heart hammered so loudly she was certain it would give her away as she slipped into the narrow, dark hallway of the guesthouse. The lantern's glow barely pierced the shadows, but it was enough to reveal the source of the sharp, suffocating scent that hit her at once. Crude oil.

It saturated the air, heavy, unmistakable, clinging to the walls and pooling across the floor near the entrance. Joy's stomach clenched. Someone had deliberately spilled it, enough to ensure that once a flame touched it, the entire place would be engulfed within seconds.

What are they doing?

She forced herself to breathe slowly and took another careful step forward, placing her boot down with painstaking caution. From deeper inside the guesthouse came the faint scrape of fabric against wood... then a muted grunt. Someone was inside.

Joy edged closer to the corner of the hallway, her pulse racing. She leaned just enough to peer into the room beyond. A figure stood there, partially hunched, a burning torch clutched in one hand. The flickering light cast wild shadows across the walls as the person shoved a mattress aside with impatient force, clearly searching for something hidden beneath it. The oil-soaked floor glistened ominously, waiting to ignite at the slightest misstep.

Joy's breath caught in her throat. As the figure turned, the torchlight illuminated her face, sharp features, narrowed eyes, a mouth twisted with fury and desperation. Lydia. The realization struck like a blow to the chest. Joy's fingers tightened around the lantern handle as cold clarity settled over her. Lydia wasn't here by accident. She wasn't vandalizing out of spite. She was searching for something. And once she found it, or failed to, Joy had no doubt what Lydia intended to do next.

Joy's mind snapped into sharp focus. There was no time for hesitation, no room for fear. If she delayed even a moment, Lydia could flee. or worse, set the guesthouse ablaze and take half the ranch with it.

She withdrew at once, easing backward the way she had come, careful not to make a sound. Only when she was safely outside did she turn and move quickly. She set the lantern down beside the building, shielding its flame from view, then bent and snatched up a fist-sized rock from the ground. With practiced urgency, she shoved it into the pocket of her dress and sprinted toward the barn. Her boots pounded softly against the packed earth as she reached the water trough. She seized a large bucket, plunged it into the cold water, and hauled it up with both hands, muscles straining as the weight sloshed dangerously close to the rim.

Don't spill it. You'll only get one chance. She forced herself to slow and steady her breath and turned back toward the guesthouse. Each step was deliberate now, measured. The bucket trembled slightly in her grasp, but she held it firm, refusing to lose a single drop of what might be her only safeguard. As the dark outline of the guesthouse loomed ahead, Joy's pulse thundered in her ears. Whatever Lydia intended to do inside that oil-soaked building, it would end here, one way or another.

Lydia was clutching some sort of folder when Joy reached the room again. Instinctively, Joy knew the papers inside were important, important enough that Lydia did not want them destroyed or soaked. Instead of dousing her immediately, Joy chose a different tactic. She slipped the rock from her pocket and hurled it down the hallway toward a closed door at the far end. It struck the wood with a sharp, echoing crack.

Lydia whirled around, startled, a shrill gasp tearing from her throat. She flung the folder toward the corner of the room, where Joy guessed a desk or small table stood, and raised the burning torch higher, its flame flickering wildly.

"Who is there?" Lydia called out, her voice trembling, fear flashing unmistakably in her eyes.

Joy remained perfectly still, hidden in the shadows, her grip tightening on the bucket. She waited, counting the seconds, until Lydia edged closer, drawn by equal parts curiosity and panic. That was the moment.

Joy lunged forward and hurled the water with all her strength. It drenched Lydia from head to toe. The torch sputtered once and died, plunging the room into darkness. Lydia shrieked, choking and stumbling backward, disoriented and blinded. Joy did not hesitate. She snatched the heavy blanket from the bed and flung it over Lydia's head and shoulders, wrapping it tight and twisting it around her arms before the other woman could recover.

Lydia screamed, high, frantic, piercing, but Joy braced her feet and dragged her backward, hauling her out of the guesthouse and into the open air. The commotion brought an immediate response. Ranch hands came running from the barn, followed closely by Darlene, Brigham, and Cathleen, all of them wide-eyed and alarmed. Joy released Lydia, who tore the blanket away and staggered upright, only to freeze when she realized she was surrounded.

"Well," Brigham said grimly, stepping forward, "look who we have here." He turned to one of the men. "Dallas, take her into town. She's to be arrested at once. I'm certain Judge Lawson will be delighted to see her again."

Lydia erupted into sobs and furious protests, thrashing and screaming, but the cowboys showed no mercy. They restrained her quickly, tying her hands as she continued to wail and curse. Joy didn't wait. She rushed back into the guesthouse, her heart pounding, retrieved the discarded folder, and returned moments later, clutching it to her chest.

She explained everything, what she had seen, Lydia's frantic search, and the overwhelming stench of crude oil soaking the entryway. Darlene pressed a hand to her mouth, while Brigham shook his head slowly, fury and disbelief darkening his expression. Whatever Lydia had been after, one thing was now unmistakably clear. She had been willing to burn the place down to get it.

"I am just glad Graham and most of the cowboys left earlier to take the cattle to Helena," Brigham said quietly. He dragged his hand down his face, the strain of the past minutes finally catching up with him. "If he had been here and seen Lydia, I don't know what he would have done."

Darlene nodded, her expression pale.

"Neither do I. This situation could have turned far worse."

Joy said nothing. Her hands were still trembling as she carried the folder upstairs to her room. She closed the door behind her and crossed to the window just in time to see Dallas and two other cowboys hoist Lydia onto the back of a wagon. Lydia thrashed and screamed, her fury unrestrained, until the men tied her down. Then the wagon lurched forward and rumbled toward town.

Joy exhaled slowly, her shoulders sagging as a fragile wave of relief washed over her. At least Lydia was gone. She turned away from the window, intending to rejoin the others downstairs, when a thunderous boom shattered the night. Joy froze. Another explosion followed, then another, sharp, violent cracks that echoed across the valley. She spun back to the window, her heart already racing, and stared in horror as flames leapt high above the treetops in the direction of Deer Lodge. An angry orange glow stained the darkening sky, pulsing and alive. Her breath caught painfully in her chest.

"No..." she whispered, dread flooding her veins. *Uncle Gerald. Aunt Eliza.* The realization struck with crushing force, and her heart slammed against her ribs as terror eclipsed every lingering trace of relief.

Joy was out of her room and racing across the yard within seconds. Panic lent wings to her feet. She tore toward the stables, her pulse pounding in her ears, and flung the saddle onto her horse with shaking hands. Around her, Brigham, Cathleen, and the ranch hands were doing the same, the air thick with urgency and shouted commands. Moments later, they were galloping hard toward town.

As Deer Lodge came into view, her worst fears were confirmed. Two separate fires raged against the darkening sky. One blazed at Dr. Preston's clinic, townsfolk already forming frantic lines to pass buckets of water. The other, far worse in Joy's eyes, consumed the familiar shape of her aunt and uncle's home.

"No... no, no..." she whispered, horror clawing at her throat. Joy broke away from the others and spurred her horse straight toward the Collins house. She leapt from the saddle before the animal had even come to a full stop, screaming for her aunt and uncle, her voice rising toward hysteria. Heat scorched her face as she rushed the front steps, intent on bursting through the door despite the flames licking along the porch.

Strong arms seized her from behind and yanked her backward. Joy fought wildly, sobbing, gasping for air as panic overwhelmed her. Then, suddenly, her strength gave out. She collapsed against the chest of the man restraining her, burying her face into his shoulder as she shook with sobs. A steady hand stroked her hair, and a calm, familiar voice spoke close to her ear.

"Your aunt and uncle are safe, Joy," Sheriff Baker said gently. "They weren't harmed."

She lifted her head slowly, her eyes wild as she searched his face.

"Are you sure?" she choked out. He nodded without hesitation.

"I swear it."

Her knees nearly buckled with relief. "Then why—why is their house—?"

"We anticipated something like this might happen," Dave explained quietly. "We didn't expect it to be today, and we didn't expect the clinic to be attacked as well, but we discussed the possibility with Charles Gregory and Dylan days ago. Charles urged your aunt and uncle to spread word that you would be staying with them once Alice moved out."

Joy stared at him in disbelief.

"Why would they do that? Why would they sacrifice their home?"

Dave's expression softened.

"Because lives matter more than buildings. As your father's relatives, they were targets too, and with you and your sister involved, even more so. A house can be rebuilt. People can't."

"But everything they owned... everything they worked for..."

"They packed what mattered most and sent it with Alice and Dylan," he said gently. "The rest can be replaced." He lowered his voice further, his eyes sweeping the chaos around them. "They're in a secure location and will remain there until this is finished. For now, you must act heartbroken. Whoever is behind this needs to believe they're dead."

Joy swallowed hard, forcing herself to breathe.

"Earlier... I was certain I left with them. I thought I was staying the night."

Dave nodded. "That was part of the plan. Charles suspected the town was being watched. Julia slipped behind you and pressed a cloth soaked in chloroform to your face."

Her stomach twisted. "So, I wasn't imagining it."

"No. Once you were unconscious, your uncle and I wrapped you in blankets and kept the cloth in place so you wouldn't wake. We loaded you onto a buckboard hidden by the trees near the house. No one saw a thing."

"And you brought me back to the Harrison ranch?"

"Yes. Your aunt and uncle followed moments later, the same way. Charles arranged for two U.S. Marshals to be on standby, one of them is your aunt and uncle's son-in-law."

Joy blinked, overwhelmed. "They rescued them?"

"They did."

"Has anyone been caught?" she asked, fear creeping back into her voice.

"Only Lydia," Dave said grimly. "She's in custody now, and as soon as Charles sends more marshals, she'll be transferred to Sacramento. We won't take any chances this time."

Joy turned back toward the burning house, her chest aching. Relief, grief, and fury warred inside her as the truth settled in. The fire was real. The danger was real. And the game had just become far more deadly.

20

No Goodbyes

"Sheriff Baker," one of the townsmen called out, hurrying toward them. His face was pale in the glow of the flames. "We just discovered that Dr. Thomas's abandoned house is on fire as well. There was no explosion, someone set it quietly. The structure's already collapsed."

"Damn it," Dave muttered, fury flashing across his features. He spun on his heel and followed the man at once to assess the damage.

Joy stayed where she was, rooted in place, watching as her aunt and uncle's home finally gave way. The roof sagged, then collapsed inward with a roar of sparks. Her chest tightened painfully. Beneath the shock and grief, one thought pressed insistently at her mind, the metal box her father had hidden. It was still there, buried beneath the porch. But she would have to wait until the fire was fully extinguished and the ground had cooled before anyone could even think of searching. Footsteps approached behind her.

"Are you all right, Joy?" a familiar voice asked gently. She turned to find Julia at her side, soot smudging her sleeve, exhaustion etched across her face.

Joy nodded slowly. "Just... shocked. And you?"

Julia let out a tired sigh. "I was fortunate. The clinic suffered only minor damage. The fire was caught almost immediately, people acted fast. I believe it was meant as a distraction more than anything else."

Joy exhaled shakily. "That makes sense."

"I heard Lydia was arrested tonight."

Joy nodded. "Yes. She tried to retrieve documents she had hidden on the ranch. I caught her before she could escape, and the cowboys tied her up. She was moments away from setting the guesthouse on fire." Her jaw tightened. "I'd wager anything her father, and whoever else is involved, set the fires in town while Lydia slipped onto the ranch. Willard Thomas would never have allowed her to return to Deer Lodge without a plan or protection." She paused, piecing it together aloud.

"The fires weren't just about killing me or my aunt and uncle. They were meant to draw attention away from the ranch, to give Lydia time to get in and out unnoticed. Unfortunately, unless someone saw Willard himself, we can't prove it."

Julia nodded grimly. "He likely didn't do it himself. He never does. He hires others, keeps his hands clean, at least in his own mind."

Joy's hands clenched at her sides.

"I hope we find every single person involved. I want justice, for what they did tonight... and for the murder of my parents."

Julia stepped closer and wrapped her arms around her in a tight embrace.

"You will get justice," she said firmly. "They're growing reckless. Lydia was warned never to return to Deer Lodge, and she ignored it, believing herself untouchable. That arrogance got her caught. Mistakes like that are the beginning of the end."

Joy leaned into the hug, drawing strength from her friend as the fire crackled behind them, destructive, yes, but no longer hidden.

By the time Joy returned to the ranch, exhaustion weighed so heavily on her that she no longer thought about the folder she had taken from Lydia. Her limbs ached, her mind throbbed, and every step felt like wading through water. She washed, changed, and collapsed into bed. Sleep claimed her almost instantly. The knowledge that at least one culprit had finally been caught soothed something deep within her, granting her a fragile sense of peace she hadn't felt in a long while.

She woke early the next morning, the gray light of dawn barely touching the horizon, and rode back into town at once. Rain had fallen steadily through the night, and the fires were fully extinguished. The air still smelled of wet ash and smoke, but the danger had passed. With her heart pounding, she went straight to her uncle's ruined house and searched beneath the porch, just as her father had described. The metal box was there.

Her breath caught as she pulled it free, rain-soaked soil clinging to the cold surface. She cradled it for a moment, emotions swelling in her chest, before tucking it securely away. She was just about to mount her horse when a familiar voice called out behind her.

"Miss Collins!"

She turned to see the telegraphist hurrying toward her, reins in hand. It looked as though he had intended to ride out to the ranch but spotting her in town had clearly changed his plans.

"Two telegrams just came in for you," he said, handing them over before tipping his hat and heading back toward the post office.

Joy opened the first with trembling fingers. It was from Dylan, brief but reassuring. He, Alice, and the girls were safe. Relief washed through her, easing a tight knot she hadn't realized was still lodged in her chest. She unfolded the second telegram. It was from Charles Gregory.

Joy,

I was contacted by the sheriff in Helena. One of the men responsible for the fires in Deer Lodge was arrested after getting drunk at a saloon on the road to Helena and bragging about his involvement. Meet me at the sheriff's office in Helena tomorrow.

Charles

Joy inhaled slowly, steadying herself. Could justice truly be moving this quickly? Hope stirred, cautious, but undeniable. She folded the telegram and tucked it away as resolve settled in its place. She would see this through to the end.

Without telling anyone about her plans, she mounted her horse and rode back to the ranch. When she arrived, Darlene and the housekeeper were already hard at work, washing blankets and anything else that had been soaked in crude oil, determined to ensure the guesthouse wouldn't accidentally go up in flames.

Joy greeted them quietly, then slipped away. She retrieved the folder she had taken from Lydia and made her way to the barn, choosing a quiet corner where the scent of hay and leather wrapped around her like a shield. Settling onto a bale, she opened the folder with reverent care. At last, she would learn everything her father had uncovered, and perhaps, finally, understand why he had been silenced.

Her father had been meticulous, painstakingly so. As Joy sorted through the contents of the metal box, she discovered his diary at the very bottom and realized he had documented everything twice: once in official records, and again in his own hand.

Relief washed over her. It meant she could share portions of what she uncovered with Charles without surrendering every piece of evidence she possessed. As much as she wanted to trust the young attorney, too much had happened. Too many people her father had once trusted had betrayed him. She was no longer willing to place blind faith in anyone. She began to read.

> *I met Troy Haven shortly after he robbed a bank. I presided as judge over his trial, and the jury found him guilty. He was sentenced to several years in prison. Someone helped him escape.*

Not long after, he robbed another bank and stole gold from politicians under the guise of business dealings. When several men tried to intervene, he shot and killed them. He was tried again and executed.

He never revealed where he hid the money or gold. Despite countless searches, it was never found. After Troy's death, I received multiple death threats. I initially assumed John was behind them.

Joy gasped, her breath hitching painfully. Her father had suspected John, her own brother-in-law, so early? The realization struck her like a blow to the chest. This must have been shortly after Alice married him. Dread pooled in her stomach as she turned the page.

Newspaper clippings followed. Articles chronicling Troy's crimes and execution, until she reached another trial, one accompanied by her father's personal notes.

<u>*The case of Gary Norton.*</u>

It was one of the most horrific trials of my career. Innocent young women were ravished and brutally murdered by a man who can only be described as demonic. Gary Norton was sentenced to execution. Before it could be carried out, someone freed him.

After months of searching, he was found in a town not far from Auburn, where he murdered two more young women. I was contacted by the sheriff and informed him I would send U.S. Marshals to retrieve Gary and carry out the sentence.

Gary bragged endlessly about his crimes and claimed his brothers would free him again. The men of that town, outraged, took justice into their own hands and hanged him. The newspapers blamed me. They falsely claimed I authorized vigilante justice, which I did not.

However, I later learned that John Haven reached the town before Gary's death. Witnesses stated he encouraged the men to go through with it.

Joy closed her eyes and inhaled sharply. John had been an attorney. He had no authority, none, to give such advice or encouragement. The picture forming before her was unmistakable. Her late brother-in-law had been deeply involved in his father's criminal dealings, far more than she had ever suspected.

Her hands trembled as she continued. Among the documents were anonymous death threats, but also letters offering bribes. Her pulse quickened. Who had tried to bribe her father? And why?

The answer came swiftly.

The Case of Dr. Vernon Lance

Dr. Vernon Lance was accused of deliberate malpractice resulting in a patient's death. His medical license was revoked, and he was dismissed by the hospital board. The patient's family sued him, but during the trial, he disappeared. Months later, he was discovered practicing medicine without a license in small towns, treating the poor. At first glance, it appeared charitable. Further investigation revealed the truth.

Patients who could not pay were punished. Medication was withheld. Newborn babies were taken from impoverished mothers and sold to wealthy families unable to conceive. He charged exorbitant sums and amassed significant wealth.

When an affluent family uncovered the truth, authorities were alerted. Dr. Lance escaped once more and has not been found. I assume he changed his name again, as well as the names of his wife and daughter.

Joy nearly fainted. Dr. Willard Thomas wasn't Willard Thomas at all. He was Vernon Lance.

Her mind reeled. Everything snapped into place, the obsession with babies, the kidnapping attempt, the desperation for money after being cast out of Deer Lodge. Selling children had always been his method. Her chest tightened as she read the final pages.

I became curious. Troy, Gary, and Vernon were uniquely monstrous, driven by greed, power, and cruelty. Further research revealed they were brothers. Troy and Vernon claimed to be orphans and were adopted as teenagers, hence the different surnames.

Their biological father owns a vast, hidden estate in the Sacramento Mountains. I believe they are paid by powerful politicians to 'remove problems.' In return, laws are passed that benefit the Norton family. I suspect Jonas Andrews is also a brother, adopted under a different name. I have asked Charles Gregory to infiltrate Jonas's law firm.

If I do not survive, contact Judge William Lawson. He is aware of this investigation and has connections in high places, good people who will protect him.

Joy's fists clenched as tears spilled freely. Jonas Andrews. Her father's friend. His attorney. A traitor. Possibly her parents' murderer. She closed the diary and opened the folder Lydia had tried to retrieve. Inside lay the final proof, adoption records, name changes, forged documents. *Troy.*

Vernon. Jonas—born Thatcher. And another brother: *Nigel.* Nigel was likely the one now imprisoned. Which explained Charles's urgency. Jonas would try to free him.

One thing was painfully clear: Joy could no longer stay in Deer Lodge. Vernon was still at large. Jonas had not yet been exposed. And she had no idea how many men still served their father's criminal empire.

As she returned the documents to the metal box, it slipped from her grasp and spilled across the floor. She knelt quickly, gathering the papers, until one final article caught her eye.

The History of Auburn.

Gold. Her father's land lay near the Auburn Ravine. Her breath caught. John had purchased parcels along the ravine.

Why? Had Troy hidden the stolen gold there, mistaking the land for John's? Had the Haven house been burned in a frantic attempt to retrieve it? Her heart pounded.

What if Troy had written to John before his execution? What if Matt or Maureen had hidden the letter? What if John only discovered it shortly before the fires? What if the café hadn't been burned to hurt Alice, but to destroy evidence?

This was bigger than anything she had imagined. Joy sat back on her heels, shaking. She needed Charles. Immediately. And then, justice.

Joy returned to her room and packed two traveling bags along with her saddlebags, folding each item with deliberate care, as though the simple act of neatness might keep her emotions in check. When she was finished, she tucked everything into the back of her closet, hidden beneath spare blankets and dresses. If anyone asked, she would smile and say nothing was amiss. Then she sat on the edge of her bed for a long moment, staring at the floor.

She had made her decision. Rather than leave at once, Joy chose to spend the remainder of the day with the Harrison family. It felt important, necessary, to savor their company while she still could. A quiet, treacherous thought slipped into her mind, one she refused to linger on for long: *I may never see them again.* If she were killed before all of this was over, at least her final memories would be warm ones.

The evening passed gently. There was laughter, shared stories, familiar routines that suddenly felt precious beyond measure. Each smile from Darlene, every teasing remark from Cathleen and Olivia, struck Joy's heart with a bittersweet ache. She realized just how deeply she loved them, and how profoundly she would miss them. There was no turning back now.

As the hours slipped by, Joy became aware of something else, something subtle, yet unmistakable. Brigham was watching her. Not in an obvious or intrusive way, but with a quiet vigilance that hadn't been there before. When she moved from room to room, he always seemed to be nearby. When she stepped outside, he followed a few moments later under some harmless pretense.

Only then did it truly sink in. Most of the cowboys, and Graham with them, had gone on the cattle drive to Helena. Brigham had stayed behind. It hadn't taken a genius to understand why. He was guarding her. The realization caught her off guard and tightened her chest. Brigham and Darlene were worried, terrified even, that she might leave without a word. They were trying to protect her in the only way they knew how. The knowledge touched her deeply. Yet it changed nothing.

Joy knew with aching certainty that the only way to truly keep them safe, the Harrisons, her aunt and uncle, her sister's family, everyone she loved, was to remove herself from the equation entirely. If she remained in Deer Lodge, the danger would follow. So, she smiled. She laughed.

She allowed herself to be part of the family for one more evening. And all the while, her resolve hardened. Soon, she would leave the ranch. Soon, she would leave Deer Lodge. And she would do it not because she didn't love them, but because she loved them too much to stay.

Joy woke up before dawn. The house lay wrapped in sleep. For a long moment, she remained perfectly still, listening to the familiar creaks and sighs of the old ranch house, committing every sound to memory. Then she moved. She knew without question that Brigham would never allow her to leave if he saw her packed bags. He would ask questions, demand answers, and most likely refuse to let her go at all. So, she worked quickly, and silently.

The rope she had brought up the night before lay coiled beneath her bed. Joy tied it securely to the handles of her two traveling bags, testing the knots twice before easing them out through the window on the far side of the house. Her heart hammered as she lowered them slowly, inch by inch, careful not to let them scrape the wall or rustle too loudly.

A soft whisper of movement told her they had landed safely in the thick bushes below. She released the rope and let it slide down after them. There were no windows beneath hers on that side of the house, and the shrubs were dense enough to conceal anything short of a wagon. No one would notice. Only then did she allow herself to breathe.

Joy slung her saddlebags over her shoulder, gave the room one final look, and slipped quietly down the stairs. The kitchen fire crackled softly. Darlene was already awake, tending the hearth. She turned at the sound of footsteps and smiled warmly before pulling Joy into a gentle, motherly embrace.

"Good morning, dear."

Joy returned the hug, holding on a heartbeat longer than usual, then stepped back before emotion could betray her. Brigham entered moments later, fastening his vest as he joined them.

"I'll be riding into town," Joy said carefully. "I need to send a telegram to Charles. And I heard Matt Haven moved to Deer Lodge last night, he's taking over the livery and settling in. I thought I'd stop by and see how he's doing."

The lie tasted bitter on her tongue. She hated deception, especially toward people who had shown her nothing but kindness. But she knew this was the only way. Brigham studied her for a moment, his gaze thoughtful, searching. Then he nodded.

"All right. Graham should be back sometime today," he added. "He said he'd be returning with the stagecoach."

Joy's stomach tightened. The last person she wanted to see was Graham Harrison. She swallowed hard and forced a calm nod. If fate had any mercy left for her, they would miss each other entirely. She intended to leave quietly, unnoticed and without goodbyes, because goodbyes would shatter her resolve. With one last smile, she turned toward the door, determined to be seen by as few people as possible. This was the hardest part. And she could not afford to falter now.

Joy had just finished tightening the cinch when Brigham stepped into the stables and walked toward her. Her heart stuttered. For a split second, she was certain he could hear it pounding. She forced herself to remain calm, keeping her movements deliberate and unhurried as she ran a final check over the saddle. If he noticed anything, her rigid posture, the way she avoided meeting his eyes, everything would unravel.

"Joy," he said gently, stopping a few steps away. "Would you mind sending off this telegram for me while you're in town?" He held out a folded slip of paper. "I was contacted by someone in California interested in purchasing the herd of horses we're breaking in."

Relief washed through her, swift and dizzying, followed immediately by guilt.

"Of course," she replied evenly, reaching for the telegram. "I'll send it as soon as I get to town."

Brigham smiled, clearly grateful. Joy mounted her horse, adjusted the reins, and lifted her hand in a casual wave as she rode out of the ranch yard. She did not look back. Only when the stables and barn had vanished from sight did she allow herself to breathe. She slowed her horse, dismounted quickly, and hurried to the thick bushes beneath her window. Her bags were exactly where she had left them, hidden from view.

Working fast, she secured them to the saddle horn, checking the straps twice before swinging back into the saddle. Then Joy turned her horse toward Deer Lodge and rode on, her resolve hardening with every step her mount took. She had crossed the point of no return.

Joy went to the post office first and sent off Brigham's telegram, making certain it was properly stamped and handed over before allowing herself to think about anything else. Only then did she purchase a ticket to Helena. The finality of it settled over her as the clerk slid the ticket across the counter. She still had a little time before the stagecoach arrived.

Leading her horse through town, she stopped at the livery. A young man greeted her at once, and she noticed Matt and the previous owner deep in conversation inside the office. Neither of them paid her any attention, which suited her just fine. She handed the stable hand a few dollars.

"Please take my horse back to the Harrison ranch later today."

"Yes, ma'am," he replied without hesitation. Joy nodded her thanks and left quickly, unwilling to risk being seen or stopped. The stagecoach rolled in just as she returned to the post office. Instinctively, she slipped into a shadowed corner, pulling her hat lower. Only two passengers were aboard. She watched as one of them climbed down. Even before she saw his face, she knew. Graham.

Her breath caught painfully in her chest. She went utterly still, scarcely daring to move as she took in his familiar broad shoulders, the way he stood, the way he turned his head. The driver took her bags and secured them at the back of the coach, then helped her up the steps. They weren't leaving immediately, and Joy prayed silently that no one else would join them.

She settled into her seat, her heart hammering as she stared down at her gloved hands. Then she saw Julia Preston step out of the clinic. The young physician paused, glanced around, and when her eyes landed on Graham, her entire face lit up. She broke into a run. Joy watched, frozen, as Graham caught Julia in his arms and spun her around, laughing. Then, to Joy's utter shock, he stepped back and dropped to one knee.

A sound escaped Joy's throat before she could stop it. She didn't hear his words, but she didn't need to. The way Julia clasped her hands to her mouth, the tears shining in her eyes, the joyful nod, it told her everything. They were engaged. Graham rose and pulled Julia into his arms, kissing her deeply and without hesitation, as though the world belonged to them alone.

Joy's vision blurred. Her chest tightened until she thought she might suffocate. It felt as though the ground beneath her had vanished, taking her heart with it. Mercifully, the stagecoach lurched forward. As the wheels began to turn and Deer Lodge slipped slowly away, Joy finally let the tears fall. She cried silently, shoulders trembling, the ache inside her too deep for sound.

When the tears finally subsided, something else took their place. Anger. Not the wild, reckless kind, but a quiet, burning resolve. She had been used. Whether Graham had intended it, he had allowed her to believe his feelings ran deeper than they did. He had shared stolen moments, tenderness, promises left just vague enough to give her hope, and then discarded her the moment something easier appeared.

Joy did not blame Julia. She truly didn't. Julia was kind, accomplished, and deserving of happiness. But Joy knew one thing with absolute certainty. She could not return to Deer Lodge. Not until her heart had healed enough to no longer break at the sight of him.

21

The Interrogation

When Joy stepped down from the stagecoach in Helena, she paused to take in her surroundings. The town seemed larger every time she came, its streets steadily changing as new buildings crowded along Main Street. She needed a moment to orient herself before locating the sheriff's office. The hotel stood directly across from the stagecoach station. She turned to cross the street and secure a room for the night but nearly jumped out of her skin when a deep voice spoke beside her.

"Joy."

Charles stepped up next to her, catching her completely off guard. She had not expected him to be there, and her heart skipped several beats.

"I thought we were going to meet in front of the sheriff's office," she stammered, her cheeks warming despite herself. "How did you know when I would arrive?"

For the first time since she had met him, Charles wore an amused grin. It softened his usually serious features and made him unexpectedly handsome. She also noticed the scruff of a beard along his jaw, rough, unpolished, and decidedly un-Charleslike. It suited him in a way that startled her. This was a look she associated with cowboys, not attorneys. He squeezed her hand gently.

"I thought you might come with the first stagecoach. It's a long ride from Deer Lodge."

She lifted her gaze, trying to appear less flustered.

"How are you feeling?" he asked quietly.

Joy glanced around and noticed two U.S. marshals standing nearby, watchful but unobtrusive. A wave of gratitude washed over her. Charles had clearly taken precautions to ensure her safety.

"It's been a rough few days," she admitted, carefully avoiding the image of Graham and Julia. "When I first saw my uncle's house on fire, I thought my heart would stop. Thankfully, Dave Baker explained what was really happening."

Charles nodded. "I'm truly sorry we had to surprise you like that. It was a precaution, in case someone was watching you, or the town."

"I found Pa's documents," she said, lowering her voice. "His diary too. There's a great deal of evidence. It should help us bring them to justice."

"That's excellent news," he replied. "Why don't you join me for a late lunch at my place?"

Joy gasped before she could stop herself, heat rushing to her cheeks.

"Don't you live alone?"

A faint smirk tugged at his lips.

"I have a room in my aunt and uncle's house."

"They live in Helena?"

He nodded. "And my aunt is expecting us. I've also arranged for you to stay with them while you're here." His gaze flicked to the two bags beside her and the saddlebags slung over her shoulder. His brow furrowed.

"How long are you planning to stay in Helena?"

"My plans aren't exactly settled," Joy replied carefully. One eyebrow lifted.

"Joy."

The firmness in his voice made her drop her gaze.

"I won't be returning to Deer Lodge," she said quietly. "At least not until this is over."

"And where will you go?"

"I... haven't decided yet."

"You intend to leave on a whim?" His concern was unmistakable. "That's dangerous."

"I'll be careful."

"Joy—"

"My mind is made up," she said gently but firmly. "I'd also appreciate it if you didn't let the Harrisons know I'm here, or that I won't be returning."

"They don't know you left?"

She shook her head. "Brigham would never have allowed it. I won't put anyone else in danger. Honestly, I probably shouldn't even be staying with your aunt and uncle."

"You'll be safe for one night," Charles assured her. "No one will attempt anything here."

"How can you be so sure?"

"Because Helena isn't Deer Lodge. And Judge William Lawson, my aunt's brother-in-law, is currently staying with them. People know better than to cause trouble when he's nearby."

Joy blinked.

"Isn't he in Sacramento?"

"Usually. But he's visiting Helena at the moment."

For the first time since arriving, a small smile touched Joy's lips.

"That's fortunate. My father wanted me to contact him. He was aware of much of what Pa was working on."

"He's been following your case closely," Charles said. "We'll meet with him this evening." He flagged down a carriage, lifted her bags inside, and offered his hand as she stepped in. He followed, seating himself beside her. The driver waited as several wagons and coaches passed. Then raised voices erupted nearby.

Two drunken men staggered out of a saloon, shouting at one another. Joy tensed instantly. One shoved the other, who slammed into the carriage before regaining his footing and charging back. In their struggle, they grabbed the horses' reins, enraging the driver. He leapt down, shouting threats and raising his whip.

In response, one of the men drew a gun and aimed it directly at him. Joy's breath caught. She noticed Charles's hand settle calmly on the gun at his hip. The driver reacted without hesitation, lashing out with his whip. The men cursed as the horses reared and bucked violently.

"Joy, get out—now!" Charles shouted, jumping down. She stood, but at that moment two shots rang out. The horses surged forward. Joy lost her footing. Strong arms caught her.

Charles held her steady, and for a brief, suspended moment, they stared at one another, the world narrowing to the space between them. More shots cracked through the air. Charles dropped into a crouch, pulling Joy down with him, shielding her instinctively. Relief flooded her when she saw U.S. marshals rushing toward them and the sheriff sprinting across the street. For the first time since leaving Deer Lodge, Joy felt something she hadn't in days. Safe.

"Sorry about that," the carriage driver said once he glanced around and saw the two men being hauled away in irons. He shook his head. "Looks like the road's clear now. We can be on our way."

Charles offered his hand and helped Joy back into the carriage. Once they were seated, the driver clicked his tongue, and the horses finally moved, carrying them away from the commotion.

Joy exhaled slowly and shook her head, still unsettled.

"Is that sort of thing... normal here?" she asked quietly, her gaze fixed on Charles. He gave a faint shrug.

"Unfortunately, incidents like that aren't uncommon near the saloons. It's not just alcohol that makes people lose control. Gambling plays its part as well. Men lose a game, sometimes everything they own, and when pride and desperation collide, tempers ignite."

"That's heartbreaking," Joy murmured. "You'd think people would avoid such places if they knew what could happen."

"They should," Charles agreed. "But alcohol is addictive, and gambling feeds on hope. Many convince themselves it will never happen to them—that they can stop whenever they choose. It's one of the most dangerous lies people tell themselves."

Silence settled between them, heavy but not uncomfortable. Joy leaned back slightly, watching the buildings slide past the carriage window, while Charles stared ahead, his expression thoughtful.

Soon, the carriage left the busiest streets behind, rolling toward the quieter outskirts of Helena. The brief ride gave Joy a chance to take in her surroundings, the growing town, the distant hills, the sense of change lingering in the air. The frantic edge in her chest eased just a little, replaced by a fragile calm she hadn't realized she needed so badly.

"So, you are the infamous Miss Joy Collins," Charles's aunt said with a warm, welcoming smile. "I've heard so much about you and your family that I feel as though I already know you. And I am truly sorry for what happened to your parents."

Joy dipped her head, suddenly shy beneath the gentle kindness in the woman's voice.

"Thank you," she replied softly, unsure what else to say. Only then did she become aware of Charles's gaze resting on her, not intrusive, not assessing, but quietly attentive. The realization unsettled her more than she cared to admit. Until now, she had given him little thought beyond polite notice. Her mind had been consumed for months by grief, danger, and unanswered questions... and later by Graham, who had so swiftly claimed her heart only to leave it bruised and aching.

Yet standing there now, she noticed Charles in a way she hadn't before. His dark brown hair curled slightly on the sides and along his neck, as though it refused to be fully tamed. He was taller than she remembered, tall enough that she had to lift her chin just slightly when she looked at him, and he carried himself with quiet confidence that didn't demand attention but earned it all the same. His eyes, a deep blue like a mountain lake, were steady and thoughtful. And when he shifted beside her, she realized with a small start that he was broader through the shoulders than she had ever noticed, strong in a way that spoke of capability rather than vanity.

The awareness caught her off guard, leaving her faintly flustered. Joy looked away at once, reminding herself that this was hardly the time for such thoughts. And yet, the realization lingered, unwelcome, undeniable, quietly stirring something she hadn't expected to feel again so soon.

Charles's aunt showed Joy to a modest but comfortable guest room where she could wash up and collect herself. Not long after, they gathered in the dining room. Gentle conversation filled the space as plates were set on the table, and for a brief while, Joy allowed herself to simply exist, listening, responding, savoring the warmth of a home untouched by fear or suspicion. The meal was delicious, the hospitality sincere.

Once the dishes were cleared, Joy retrieved the metal box and carefully placed it on the table. She opened it with deliberate care, revealing her father's meticulous notes, letters, newspaper clippings, and the bundle of documents she had taken from Lydia. Charles leaned forward, his expression sharpening as he examined the contents.

"I'm impressed," he said honestly. "Your father was well on his way to uncovering everything."

Joy folded her hands together, bracing herself.

"Did he get close?"

"Close enough to worry them," Charles replied. "I should tell you, the Norton family abandoned their estate in the Sacramento Mountains some time ago. They've relocated somewhere closer to this region."

Joy's brow furrowed. "Why?"

"I believe your father prompted the first serious attempt to dismantle their operation," Charles said. "He urged the marshals to arrest those living on the estate, but the effort failed." He paused. "After your father's death, I asked Judge Lawson to authorize a second attempt. When the marshals arrived, the place had been cleared out. They were gone."

Joy swallowed hard. "So... they ran."

"Yes. And we're still trying to determine where they went." Charles turned his attention to the papers Joy had taken from Lydia. As he read, he let out a low whistle. "This is excellent information," he said, unmistakably impressed. "I suspected Vernon's involvement, but I had no proof. Now we do."

Joy's voice dropped. "And Jonas? He really is part of it?"

Charles sighed, the weight of the truth settled heavily between them.

"I'm afraid so. I don't know whether he had a direct hand in your parents' deaths, but I am certain he helped his youngest brother escape."

"The one who hurt and murdered women?" Joy asked quietly, dread tightening her chest. Charles nodded once.

"Yes."

Silence stretched, taut and suffocating, before he finally looked at her with quiet gravity.

"Are you ready to see and speak with Nigel Norton?"

Joy hesitated. Her pulse quickened, fear and determination warring within her. Then she rose to her feet, her spine straightening, resolve hardening.

"May I ask him questions as well?"

"You may," Charles said without hesitation. "Ask him anything you wish. I'll ensure the sheriff is present as a witness, in case he says something we can use."

Joy drew in a steadying breath. Whatever awaited her next, she would face it head-on.

The moment they stepped into the building and Joy caught sight of the man behind the bars, recognition struck her like a blow. He looked younger than Vernon, but there was no mistaking the resemblance. The same sharp lines to his face. The same cold eyes. Even a trace of Lydia in the tilt of his mouth and the arrogance in his posture.

Charles quietly pulled the sheriff aside and exchanged a few low words. The sheriff nodded once, then instructed his deputy to keep watch in the front office and ensure they were not disturbed. After that, he shut the door separating the cells from the public area.

Joy stepped closer. Nigel Norton studied her with open suspicion, his gaze crawling over her in a way that made her skin prickle.

"Well now," he drawled, his deep voice slick as oil. "Ain't you thoughtful, Gregory. Bringin' me a girl for amusement?"

"Shut your mouth, Norton," Charles snapped instantly, stepping forward. "The only reason this young woman is here is so she can look at one of the demonic scumbags responsible for murdering her parents."

Nigel's attention snapped fully to Joy. His lips curled into a vile grin.

"Aww now," he drawled. "You one o' them Collins girls, ain't ya? Still missin' yer ma an' pa?"

Joy felt the tension behind her, Charles shifting, ready to lunge, but she lifted a hand slightly, stopping him.

"Yes," she said evenly, her eyes dark and unflinching. "I am one of the Collins girls, Nigel Norton. Surprised to see me?" She tilted her head just enough to make the challenge unmistakable. "I should be dead too, you know."

For the first time, Nigel hesitated. Then he scoffed, masking it poorly.

"Truth is," he said slowly, his voice low and ugly, "yer pa weren't meant to go first. He was s'posed to sit there an' watch every soul he loved die... then we'd have finished him."

Joy's spine stiffened, fury igniting in her chest, but her voice remained dangerously calm.

"How touching. And you murdered my family because my father sentenced Troy Haven to death? Because Gary Norton was hanged after torturing and murdering innocent women?"

"That's just part of the tale," Nigel sneered.

"Then where is Vernon hiding?" Joy pressed. "Did he crawl back to your father's protection to avoid the consequences of his crimes?"

She felt Charles's gaze on her, astonishment unmistakable, but she did not look away from Nigel. She wanted him to see that she was not afraid. That she would never be his victim. Nigel's jaw tightened.

"What business you got knowin' things about my family?"

"I did my homework," Joy replied coolly. "Nobody murders my parents and gets away with it. We may not have everything yet, but you and your family will fall."

He scoffed, but before he could respond, Joy continued smoothly.

"I hear your family abandoned the Sacramento Mountains and settled somewhere in the Moors Mountain now." It was a calculated gamble. And it paid off. Nigel's eyes widened for a split second, color draining from his face before he caught himself.

"You ain't got the first notion what you're talkin' on."

"Oh, I think your expression confirmed it."

"Even if you got it right," he snarled, steady again, "you ain't never finding it, nor gettin' near it. It's guarded six ways from Sunday."

Joy shrugged lightly. "I imagine it won't take long to narrow it down. Somewhere near the Missouri River, perhaps. You need access to water, after all."

This time, there was no hiding it. Joy turned slowly toward Charles and the sheriff. Both men stared at her, stunned. Before anyone could speak, the door flew open.

"What is going on here?" Jonas Andrews barked as he stormed inside, then froze when he saw Joy. "Oh. Joy. What are you doing here?"

"I'm speaking with the man who murdered my parents."

Jonas rolled his eyes. "Charles is making a spectacle out of nothing again."

"Is he?" Joy countered, lifting an eyebrow. "Then this man didn't burn down my uncle's home, believing I was inside?"

"There's no proof—"

"He bragged about it in a saloon," Joy cut in sharply.

"That's hearsay—"

"Nigel told us where his family is hiding."

Nigel exploded. "I never said nothin' to her! She figured it on her own!"

"Guessed remarkably well," Joy said coldly.

"That's enough!" Jonas snapped, trying to regain control. "You should not be questioning a prisoner without me present. I am your lawyer—"

"No," Joy interrupted, her voice ice-cold. "Charles is my lawyer. You are a traitor. You pretended to be my father's friend while deceiving him at every turn, *Thatcher Norton*!"

The name hit like a gunshot. Jonas froze. He began pacing, muttering, denying, then his eyes flicked to Charles. Whatever he saw there made him bolt for the door. He didn't make it two steps.

The sheriff and deputy intercepted him instantly, locking him behind bars beside his brother moments later.

"You have no right to detain me!" Jonas shouted. "You have no proof!"

Joy stepped forward and calmly removed two papers from her pocket.

"Actually, I do." She held them up. "Your adoption papers, legally changing your name from Thatcher Norton to Jonas Andrews. And your birth certificate."

Silence fell. Without another word, Joy turned and walked out of the building. Outside, the air hit her like a wave. Her knees trembled, and Charles and the sheriff rushed to her side, guiding her to sit before she could collapse. When color finally returned to her face, the sheriff chuckled softly.

"Young lady, you should be in law school. That was one impressive interrogation."

Charles nodded. "I couldn't agree more. Where did you learn to do that?"

"My father taught me," Joy replied quietly, then smiled. "He said the best way to catch a liar is to surprise them."

"You should really consider law school," the sheriff urged.

Joy shook her head. "No, thank you. I'd get too emotionally invested, and I refuse to put my family in danger." She paused, then added with a sly smile, "I think I'd rather become the best female broncobuster in Montana."

Both men laughed, but they had no idea she wasn't joking.

"Miss Collins," Judge Lawson said as he entered Charles's aunt and uncle's sitting room, removing his hat with a respectful nod. "It is a pleasure to finally make your official acquaintance.

We did cross paths briefly at the Harrison ranch when I annulled the marriages involving Lydia Norton, but at the time, I could not reveal that I was already very well informed about your situation."

"I understand, sir," Joy replied quietly. He studied her for a moment, his expression thoughtful rather than cold, assessing not just her words, but the resolve beneath them.

"Charles tells me you have uncovered a considerable amount of information regarding this case."

Charles stepped forward and handed the judge the documents Joy had provided. Judge Lawson moved to the table, adjusted his spectacles, and began to read. The longer he studied the papers, the more his expression shifted, from interest, to gravity, and finally to unmistakable admiration.

After a moment, he nodded slowly.

"Max Collins was an exceptional judge," he said at last. "Everything he did was meticulously documented and thoroughly researched. He never took on a case unless he fully understood the dangers involved and was prepared to see it through, no matter the cost."

Joy's lips curved into a small, bittersweet smile. She had always known her father was remarkable in his profession. Even during the brief time after they had moved to Auburn, he had involved her in reviewing case notes and organizing documents, teaching her how to recognize inconsistencies, patterns, and the quiet truths hidden between the lines. He had trusted her mind. More than that, he had been respected, by his colleagues, by the men he worked alongside, and even by those who sought his counsel when they had nowhere else to turn.

Hearing that respect echoed now, in Judge Lawson's measured voice, made her chest ache with both pride and loss.

Judge Lawson took her hand in his, his grip firm yet gentle.

"I know this is still incredibly hard on you, Miss Collins. Losing both parents at once, especially parents as principled and devoted as yours, is a grief no one should have to carry alone. I wish there had been a way to spare you such heartache, but sometimes the cruelties of this world move beyond our control."

Joy swallowed and nodded. "I know Ma and Pa's time on this earth was up. I believe God needed them for something greater," she said softly. "But knowing that doesn't make the ache disappear. I don't think it ever will."

"No," the judge agreed quietly. "Grief rarely fades. We simply learn how to carry it." He studied her again, this time with unmistakable respect. "Everything I have heard about you tells me that you are the one completing what your father began, bringing the Norton family to justice. I am deeply grateful that Charles, Dylan Andrews, and Sheriff Baker were able to get your aunt and uncle out of their home before those criminals set it ablaze."

"So am I, sir," Joy replied earnestly.

"Why don't you tell me everything," Judge Lawson suggested, gesturing toward the chairs. "From the moment your parents passed until now. I would like to see how many pieces we can fit together."

Joy drew a steadying breath and began. She told him about discovering her brother-in-law's house in flames, about the unease that had taken root in her heart long before danger announced itself openly. She spoke of threats whispered rather than spoken, of watching shadows, of the woman she had caught attempting to set the barn on fire. She recounted, in careful detail, what she had seen, what she had done, and what had followed afterward. They spoke late into the evening.

Judge Lawson listened without interrupting, occasionally asking a precise question or jotting down a note. He did not disguise his growing admiration, not only for Joy's remarkable attention to detail, but for the clarity and courage with which she had acted under constant threat.

By the time she finished, it was clear that what impressed him most was not her bravery alone, but her unwavering resolve to protect her sister, her nieces, and everyone she loved, no matter the personal cost.

When Joy finished speaking, and Judge Lawson had asked several pointed questions to confirm details and timelines, he finally rose to his feet.

"You are a remarkable young woman, Miss Collins," he said with quiet authority. "I see both of your parents in you, but I see your father's brilliance most clearly. Anyone who knew Max Collins would recognize, without hesitation, who taught you and shaped the way you think."

Joy felt warmth rise to her cheeks and instinctively lowered her gaze, especially as she became aware of Charles watching her with unmistakable admiration. Judge Lawson's expression softened.

"I will do everything within my power to bring every person involved in this to justice," he continued. "Our next step will be to raid the Norton estate and expose the politicians who enabled them. I am convinced they are hiding far more than the crimes already uncovered. Zedekiah Norton is most likely still alive and concealed with the rest of that family. I will ensure we have sufficient U.S. Marshals, and soldiers, if necessary, to dismantle their entire operation." His voice carried steel now, and Charles nodded firmly in agreement.

Joy cleared her throat. "There is one more thing, sir," she said carefully. "I believe Troy Norton hid the money and gold he stole beneath the land where my parents' house once stood. I think that is why the house was burned down, and why so many people tried to gain control of the property. Is there a way for me to sell the land to someone trustworthy? Someone who will search it properly and return whatever is found to the banks it was stolen from?"

Judge Lawson studied her in stunned silence for a moment. "How did you arrive at that conclusion?" he asked at last.

Joy drew a breath. "When I found my father's deeds and papers, and after learning that people were searching the land, it all began to fit. Pa clearly did not trust Jonas Andrews—Thatcher Norton—to safeguard those documents, and the banks would have been too obvious a target. That's why he hid them with the rest of his evidence in the metal box." She continued, her thoughts flowing freely now, confidence strengthening her voice.

"I don't believe Troy ever told anyone exactly where the money was hidden before his execution. My father had already built the house by the time John arrived in Auburn. My guess is that Troy wrote to his son, but John only discovered the truth much later."

Before either man could respond, she pressed on.

"I think John found the letter by accident, likely at his mother's home. I believe Matt and Maureen hid it from him without realizing its importance. That would explain why the café was burned down. The Nortons were trying to destroy any remaining evidence. To me, that explanation makes the most sense." She finally looked up. Both men were staring at her in complete silence. Joy shifted uncomfortably.

"You don't agree?" she asked, suddenly uncertain. "Have I overthought it?"

Judge Lawson released a quiet breath and shook his head slowly.

"No," he said. "You have done the opposite." A faint, impressed smile touched his lips. "You are, without question, your father's daughter. The way your mind works, the connections you make, the logic you apply, it is extraordinary." He regarded her thoughtfully.

"If you ever decide you wish to study law, or even become the first female judge, I want you to come to me. I will do everything in my power to support you and make that path possible."

Joy's breath caught as the weight of his words settled deep within her. Little did either man know, however, that her path would lead her somewhere far more dangerous, and far more unexpected, than even the courtroom could offer.

22

Unreasonably
Protective

Once Joy was alone in her room, Judge Lawson's words continued to echo in her mind. They had not sounded like polite encouragement or empty praise. He had meant them. She could hear it in his voice, see it in his eyes, and that realization humbled her more than anything else.

Being compared to her father, felt like the highest compliment she could receive. She treasured it deeply. And yet, as often as people told her she would make a brilliant attorney, or even a judge, she knew, just as surely, that it was not the path meant for her. She had seen enough of the world to understand how unforgiving it could be to women who dared to step into roles men claimed as their own. She had no desire to spend her life not only battling evil but also fighting men who believed she did not belong beside them. That kind of war would drain her spirit long before it ever fulfilled her.

She admired the women who did it anyway. Julia was proof of what courage and resolve could accomplish, and Joy felt nothing but pride for women who stood their ground in a man's world and refused to be pushed aside. She would always defend them. But she had also come to understand something important about herself. She was a country girl.

Despite having spent much of her life in Sacramento, it was the move to Auburn that had awakened something in her, a deep-rooted sense of belonging she hadn't known she was missing. Deer Lodge had only strengthened that realization. The mountains, the forests, the lakes, the open skies, and the slower rhythm of life spoke to her soul in a way the city never had. People worked hard there, yes, but there was honesty in that labor, and space to breathe afterward. There was room to hear your own thoughts, to know your neighbors, to feel grounded.

This was home. And no matter where her path led next, no matter what dangers still waited in the shadows, Joy knew one thing with absolute certainty: she would never trade this life, this land, and this sense of belonging for the world she had left behind.

She opened one of her bags to retrieve her nightgown and froze. An envelope lay neatly on top of her folded clothes. Her breath caught. It had not been there before. Joy lifted it slowly, her fingers brushing over the familiar seal. Her heart began to pound as recognition struck. She knew the handwriting instantly. Her uncle's. Without sitting down, she tore the envelope open and read.

Joy,

I found out that you are in Helena. I don't have much time before we leave town, but I have more information you need. I've asked the son of a trusted friend to get this letter to you. Please meet me outside of Charles's uncle's house around midnight. I cannot be seen. Everyone believes I am dead. Do not trust anyone. And please, do not tell Charles. He does not want me to come out of hiding, but this is the only way I can get this information to you.

Gerald

The letter slipped from her fingers and landed soundlessly on the bed. Joy stared at it, her thoughts racing. It was already past eleven. Her uncle wanted to meet her in less than an hour. How did he know she was in Helena? How did he know she was staying *here*, at Charles's aunt and uncle's house? A chill slid down her spine.

She crossed the room and carefully pulled the curtain aside, just enough to peer into the darkness. The street lay quiet, wrapped in shadow. After a moment, her eyes adjusted, and shapes emerged at opposite ends of the property. U.S. marshals. Her unease deepened. Joy stepped back and retrieved the letter again, reading it more slowly this time. The urgency was unmistakable, but so was the handwriting. She had seen it all her life. Notes tucked into books. Ledgers on his desk. Letters written in a careful, familiar hand. And the seal. There was no mistaking that either.

Still, nothing about this felt right. Her uncle was risking everything by reaching out. If anyone saw him, if anyone realized he was alive, he would become a target all over again. Yet if he had gone to such lengths, the information he carried had to be important. Possibly vital. The waiting gnawed at her nerves. Midnight couldn't come fast enough, and at the same time, she wished it never would.

The street lay unnervingly still as Joy eased the door shut behind her and stepped into the night.

Too still. The faint presence she had sensed earlier was gone. The U.S. marshals who had been stationed nearby were nowhere to be seen. Whether they had been recalled or merely repositioned, she could not tell, and the uncertainty settled heavily in her chest.

Unsure where to go, or how visible she should be, Joy crossed the short distance to the low stone wall separating the Gregorys' front yard from the sidewalk and road. She perched on it, drawing her coat closer, every nerve stretched tight. The darkness was nearly complete. No moon. No lanterns. Only the vague silhouettes of trees and rooftops, swallowed by shadow. Joy forced herself to remain still, listening, truly listening, to every sound: the faint rustle of leaves, the distant creak of wood, the shallow rhythm of her own breathing.

Then she heard footsteps. Her spine stiffened. Slowly, she rose, heart pounding as a figure emerged from the darkness ahead. He moved toward her with purpose, his gait quick and deliberate. Joy strained to make him out. She saw his arm shift. He was reaching into his coat. A gun.

FLAMES OF THE FIRE

There was no time to think. The crack of gunfire split the night. Joy ducked instinctively, dropping low as shots rang out, the sound thunderous in the narrow street. A heartbeat later came a heavy thud, the unmistakable sound of a body hitting the ground. She sucked in a sharp breath, her mind scrambling to catch up with what had just happened.

Then strong arms wrapped around her waist and yanked her backward. Joy gasped and twisted, panic surging, until a familiar voice hissed close to her ear.

"Joy, don't move."

Charles. Relief crashed through her so violently her knees nearly buckled. He pulled her fully behind the stone wall, crouching low and shielding her with his body, one arm firm around her, the other ready at his side. Joy clutched his sleeve, her heart hammering as the truth sank in. Someone had just tried to kill her.

Joy's gaze drifted back to the dark stretch of road where the man had fallen. In the flickering glow of distant lantern light, she saw several U.S. marshals closing in around the motionless body. Her breath caught, a tremor running through her, and she shivered.

Without a word, Charles slipped out of his coat and draped it around her shoulders, the familiar warmth grounding her. He guided her back into the house, his hand firm at her elbow, and led her into the sitting room.

"Sit," he murmured gently. Joy obeyed, her legs unsteady. Charles crouched in front of her, meeting her eyes at the same level.

"Why did you leave the house?" he asked quietly. "Why did you put yourself in danger like that?" His expression was grave, his concern unmistakable, but there was no anger in his voice. With trembling fingers, Joy reached into her pocket and pulled out the letter. She handed it to him without a word. Charles read it once. Then again. When he looked up, her composure finally cracked.

"It's my uncle's handwriting," she whispered, her voice breaking. "And his seal. I just assumed... I thought—" Tears spilled over, blurring her vision. She clutched his sleeve desperately. "Please," she pleaded softly, "make sure the marshals didn't kill Uncle Gerald." Her blue eyes searched his face, wide with fear. Charles let out a slow, steady breath.

"It wasn't your uncle."

She inhaled sharply. "Are you sure?"

He nodded without hesitation. "Absolutely. Your uncle is not in Helena."

Joy shook her head, confusion deepening.

"Then how did I get this letter?"

"I believe it was slipped into your bag," Charles said after a moment. "Most likely during the chaos earlier, when the drunken men caused that disturbance on the street." His jaw tightened. "Whoever did this stole your uncle's seal and mimicked his handwriting. It was deliberate. Calculated." He exhaled sharply. "I should have anticipated something like this. I underestimated how far they were willing to go."

A soft knock echoed through the house. Charles rose and went to the front door. Joy listened as he spoke in low tones with someone outside, her heart pounding until he returned.

"That was one of the marshals," he said quietly. "The man is dead."

Joy swallowed hard. "Who was he?"

"The one who called himself Jack," Charles replied. "He appears to have been hired by Dr. Thomas—Vernon Norton—to locate your father's deed."

Her breath hitched. "So, he was just... hired muscle?"

"That seems likely," Charles said. "A man paid to do the dirty work while others stayed safely in the shadows." His gaze softened as it returned to her. "But it ends here. He was meant to kill you tonight. Thanks to the marshals, he didn't succeed."

Joy closed her eyes, her body finally sagging as the danger ebbed.

"One less threat," Charles added quietly. And for the first time that night, Joy allowed herself to believe it.

Joy woke early, pale morning light already slipping through the curtains. There was no rush. She had hours before the stagecoach was due to depart. Charles's aunt had thoughtfully left a bathrobe for her, and Joy slipped it on before opening the balcony door.

Cool air brushed her cheeks. Despite the lingering chill, the day was beautiful. The house sat on the edge of a lake, and from her room she could see its glassy surface reflecting the soft hues of dawn. She stood there for a long moment, breathing deeply, letting the quiet steady her restless mind. Her thoughts drifted to the night before, the gunshots, the deception, the narrow escape, but she pushed them aside almost at once. There was already too much weighing on her heart. Inevitably, her mind returned to Graham.

The betrayal still hurt. The realization that she had been used stung just as sharply. At first, she resisted the thoughts, but the longer she stood there, the clearer everything became. There was no denying that she had been drawn to him. The chemistry between them had been real. Yet as she replayed the moments they had shared, the kisses, the whispered closeness, anger slowly replaced longing. He had taken advantage of her feelings. Whether he meant to, he had played with her heart. And the speed with which his attention had shifted to Julia only confirmed it.

Joy shook her head slowly as the pieces fell into place. Graham wasn't a cruel man. But his pride, his wounded, masculine ego, had taken a severe blow after Lydia's lies and their sham marriage. Then Joy had come along. Perhaps, without even realizing it, he had needed to prove, to himself more than anyone, that he was still desirable, still capable of captivating a woman. The truth settled heavily in her chest.

She should have noticed the signs. The way he kept pushing boundaries, even after she asked him not to. The ease with which he moved on, insisting on seeing other women before settling on one. It likely never crossed his mind how deeply that might wound her. Joy inhaled slowly and closed her eyes.

Understanding it didn't erase the hurt, nor did it extinguish her anger, but it dulled the sharpest edge of the pain. It hadn't been personal. He may even have cared for her in his own way. They had simply crossed paths at the wrong time. He had been vulnerable. She had been grieving, exhausted, raw, and desperate for a friend while fighting to protect her sister.

She couldn't deny it now. She had been an easy target. Graham was handsome, charming, and attentive, and he had made her heart flutter when she was at her weakest. But with clearer eyes, she saw that what they had shared was infatuation, on both sides.

Of course she longed for a strong man beside her. For a time, she had truly believed Graham might be that man. But she would not deceive herself any longer, nor cling to the hope that had no future. Even if he were not engaged to Julia, if he were to return and profess genuine love, Joy knew the truth of her heart. She would never fully trust him again. And that knowledge, painful as it was, finally set her free.

Joy watched a small flock of ducks' glide across the lake, their wings cutting softly through the morning air before they settled onto the water, sending gentle ripples outward. She sighed again, quieter this time, as clarity continued to settle in her heart. She would never again allow chemistry alone, nor that irresistible pull toward someone, to decide whether she loved a man.

The thought carried her back, unwillingly, to Matt. To that moment, he had claimed to love her, to the entitlement in his voice, to the way he had tried to force himself on her. The realization struck her now with startling force: she had fallen into the same trap with Graham, only dressed in far gentler colors. Her mind had convinced her it was real. That what she and Graham shared was genuine affection, something deep and lasting. Yet she could no longer deny the truth, her own thoughts had betrayed her, weaving longing into certainty where there had been none.

Graham had been the first man she had truly been interested in. That alone explained so much. First feelings had a way of disguising themselves as love, especially when paired with grief, exhaustion, and vulnerability. Joy had always prided herself on being a woman guided not only by emotion, but by reason. She weighed her choices carefully, trusted logic as much as instinct. This time, however, she had let her emotions take the reins, and her mind, rather than stopping her, had followed along willingly.

Her father's voice echoed softly in her memory, reminding her of the lessons he had taught her since childhood. Decisions made purely from emotion, without the grounding force of reason, were dangerous. Hearts could be misled when left unchecked. She knew she could trust her heart, but only when it worked in harmony with her mind.

Joy loved deeply. When she gave her heart, she gave it fully and without reservation. But she wanted to love for the right reasons, not because of attraction, or timing, or loneliness, but because of respect, trust, and shared values.

As the ducks drifted peacefully across the lake, Joy straightened her shoulders. She had learned something painful, yes, but invaluable. Next time, her heart would not walk alone.

As she turned away from the balcony doors, preparing to return to her room, a soft sound nearby caught Joy's attention. She glanced up and froze. Charles stood on the neighboring balcony.

He was shirtless, his dark hair still slightly tousled, the early morning light tracing the strong lines of his shoulders and chest. The sight struck her with such sudden force that it pulled her straight back to another memory, another man, another moment she had once believed meant something more. Heat rushed to her face.

Mortified by her own reaction, Joy spun around at once and retreated through the doors, slipping back into her room as quickly as dignity allowed. She shut the door behind her and leaned against it, drawing in a slow, steady breath. Her cheeks still burned, her heart beating far too fast for such an innocent moment.

She had only seen Charles for a handful of seconds, but it had been enough. His build was strong and unmistakably masculine, his presence quietly commanding in a way that unsettled her far more than she cared to admit.

Different from Graham, she told herself firmly. *Don't compare. Don't go there.* Pushing away from the door, Joy crossed the room and began dressing with deliberate focus, determined to chase the image from her thoughts. The last thing she needed was to walk into breakfast flustered and flushed, betraying emotions she had only just begun to bring under control. She smoothed her skirt, pinned her hair with care, and took one last steady breath. Today, she reminded herself, was about clarity, not distraction.

When Joy entered the dining room, Charles was not there yet. Relief washed over her at once. The brief reprieve gave her time to steady herself and smooth the lingering flutter in her chest. His aunt had prepared a generous, inviting breakfast, the table laden with warm bread, eggs, preserves, and steaming pots of tea. She greeted Joy with a bright smile and motioned for her to take a seat.

Charles's uncle appeared moments later, his presence filling the room with easy warmth. It was the first time Joy had met him, but he welcomed her as though she were already family, offering a firm handshake and a kind word. Charles entered just as his uncle was about to say grace. Joy forced herself to lift her gaze and smile at him. The effort was successful, mostly. Heat crept into her cheeks despite her best intentions, but thankfully all eyes returned to his uncle as he bowed his head in prayer.

Once they began eating, Charles glanced at the spread and smiled.

"Thank you for cooking such a feast, Aunt Melanie."

Her face lit up. "It's my pleasure. We don't have such a beautiful guest every day, and to be perfectly frank, Joy looks as though she is in desperate need of a proper home-cooked meal."

Joy had just taken a sip of tea. She swallowed the wrong way and burst into a fit of coughing, her eyes watering as she struggled to breathe. It took a moment before she recovered enough to look up, wide-eyed, at the older woman.

"What makes you think that?" she asked, finally finding her voice. "I assure you, the Harrisons take very good care of me. I certainly don't go hungry."

"That may be," Melanie replied calmly, studying her with sharp, knowing eyes, "but have you been eating as you should? You've endured heartbreak and hardship, and you wouldn't be the first young woman to forget to nourish herself under such strain."

"I—I mean... I'm fine," Joy stammered, the blush on her cheeks deepening. Melanie arched a brow.

"If you were, you would have answered without hesitation. So, eat. And I will make sure you have a proper lunch packed for your journey as well."

Joy stared at her, utterly taken aback. She had not expected such firmness, especially from a woman she had only just met.

"But I—" she began, only to stop when Charles's uncle cleared his throat.

"Don't even try," he said gently. "Melanie won't let you leave if she's worried about you."

"Quite right," Melanie added. "Frankly, I think you should stay here a while so I can make sure you stop inventing excuses not to eat."

"I can't stay," Joy murmured, lowering her eyes. "I have to leave as planned."

"And why is that?" Melanie demanded, planting her hands on her hips. "You stayed with the Harrisons, and I see no reason you can't stay with us."

Joy lifted her gaze, her expression earnest, and resolute.

"I won't put anyone else in danger. I left to protect the Harrisons. As long as the men responsible for my parents' murder are still free, I shouldn't be near anyone."

Melanie exchanged a look with her husband and then with Charles. Both men shook their heads, clearly unhappy with her reasoning.

"Very well," Melanie said at last, her tone softening though her resolve remained unbroken. "But you will not leave this house hungry, and you most certainly will not go through the day on an empty stomach."

Joy exhaled slowly, realizing she had lost this battle entirely.

Once everyone had finished eating, they pushed their chairs back and stood. Joy turned to Charles's aunt. A deep sense of gratitude settled warmly in her chest.

"May I help you with the dishes?" she offered politely. Melanie shook her head at once.

"Absolutely not. My husband will take you into town, so you don't miss the stagecoach."

Joy smiled, touched by the certainty in her voice.

"Thank you for everything, Mrs. Gregory. I truly appreciate your hospitality, more than I can say. Thank you for welcoming me into your home."

She extended her hand, intending a proper farewell, but Melanie ignored it entirely and pulled her into a warm, motherly embrace instead. Joy stiffened for a heartbeat, caught off guard, then relaxed and returned the hug as emotion pressed unexpectedly at her throat.

"It was our pleasure," Melanie said softly as she released her. "Please be careful and look after yourself. And if you ever need a place to stay, no matter the reason, you know exactly where to find us."

Joy nodded, unable to speak for a moment. She managed a grateful smile as she gathered her things, carrying the quiet comfort of that unexpected kindness with her as she prepared to leave.

"Your bags are already on the carriage," Charles said, his smile easy and undeniably charming.

Joy blinked in surprise as he helped her up and took the seat beside her a moment later. For a heartbeat, confusion flickered, until it occurred to her that he likely needed to go into town for work.

They stopped in front of the post office, and Charles disappeared inside while his uncle kept Joy pleasantly occupied with lively conversation. The calm shattered when a stagecoach suddenly pulled up.

"I haven't even decided where I'm going," Joy said hastily, a ripple of panic tightening her chest.

"Don't worry about it," a familiar voice said beside her. She startled as Charles reappeared, shaking his head with infuriating calm. "I already took care of it."

"Took care of what?" she asked warily.

"Where we're going."

"We?" Her eyes widened. "You're not coming with me."

"Actually, I am," he replied easily, and before she could protest, he lifted her straight into the stagecoach.

Joy gasped. Charles climbed in after her and took a seat across from her. She stood at once, reaching for the door, but his arm slid around her waist and pulled her firmly back down. She shot him a furious glare.

"You cannot force me to go with you," she snapped. "And I never said you could come along."

"You didn't have to," he said evenly. "I can go wherever I choose, and I will not let you travel alone without knowing where you're going or knowing a single soul there. In case you've forgotten, there are still men out there who want you dead."

Before she could respond, he leaned out and spoke to the driver. Moments later, the stagecoach lurched into motion.

"Wait," she demanded. "Where are we even going?"

"Elkhorn."

Her jaw tightened. "I don't want you becoming a victim because of me."

"I'll be fine."

She huffed in frustration. "You are unbelievably unreasonable. Don't you have a law firm to run? How can you just leave?"

"The firm is in Sacramento," he replied calmly. "And I was never Thatcher's official business partner. Your father hired me because he knew I had potential, and because of my connection to Judge Lawson."

"And Thatcher didn't want you as a partner?"

"Oh, he did," Charles said dryly. "I just didn't want to bind myself to something I wasn't sure I wanted for the rest of my life."

She shook her head, irritation written plainly on her face. When she noticed him grinning, she nearly rolled her eyes.

"So, what's in Elkhorn?" she demanded. "Why are you taking me there?"

"It's a small mining town. My grandparents live there. My grandfather is a reverend."

Her expression flared with outrage.

"I told you I will not stay with anyone and put them in danger. I meant that."

"I know," he said, sighing softly. "My grandparents' old cabin is outside of town. They lived there before my grandfather took on his parish. Now it serves as a guesthouse when family visits. They recently renovated it."

Joy gasped. "If you think I'll stay under the same roof with you, alone, you are sorely mistaken."

His grin widened as he shifted closer, settling beside her. Her heart began to pound.

"Why not?" he asked quietly. "Do you think so little of me? Do you believe I'd behave improperly?"

She met his gaze. The teasing was gone. His eyes were serious now. She swallowed, buying herself a moment.

"I don't think little of you, Charles," she said carefully. "But it wouldn't be proper. Even if nothing happened, appearances would matter. And I won't risk your safety." Her honesty softened his expression.

"I know," he said gently. "And as much as your stubborn insistence on protecting everyone else drives me mad, I understand it. That's why I chose Elkhorn. You'll have your independence, your own space, until this is over. And I'll be close enough to step in if anything goes wrong."

At last, she leaned back, tension easing from her shoulders. "And your work?"

"Thatcher had a silent partner," Charles explained. "A retired attorney who officially owns the firm. I've already spoken with him. He has the connections to replace Thatcher without difficulty."

"And you?" she asked softly. "Don't you need employment?"

"Your father paid me well," he said. "And I've done other work. I'll manage. I only passed the bar two years ago. I'm still finding my footing."

She looked at him, startled. "Really? How old are you?"

He grinned. "How old do you think I am?"

"Well... I assumed you were in your thirties," she admitted. "You carry yourself like someone far more established."

"That's fair," he chuckled. "But I'm twenty-eight."

The conversation fell quiet. Joy turned toward the window, watching the mountains roll past as trees and open fields blurred together. No matter how far she traveled, she knew one thing with certainty. She would never tire of Montana's beauty.

23

Stubborn Meets Stubborn

When the stagecoach rolled to a stop, Joy stepped down and glanced around with open curiosity. The tiny town bustled with a quiet sort of life, though only a handful of houses and buildings dotted the landscape. Charles helped her down and waited until she turned toward him.

"There really isn't much here," she remarked.

"No," he agreed. "There are maybe a hundred people living here, if that. A few farmers live outside of town, and there's a post office, a church, and a general store. That's about it."

"Wow," Joy said softly. "I thought Deer Lodge and Auburn were small. They don't even have a sheriff or a saloon?"

Charles shook his head. "No. There's a small saloon and café at the stagecoach station in Boulder, but it's mostly for travelers." He gathered her bags along with his own and led her toward the church, which stood only a short walk from the station. As soon as they entered, he called out for his grandparents. An older couple appeared almost immediately.

"Charles! What a wonderful surprise," his grandmother exclaimed, sweeping him into a warm embrace. His grandfather followed the moment she released him. "Oh," the woman added, her eyes lighting up as she noticed Joy, "and you brought a girl! It's about time you allowed a little romance into your life instead of burying yourself in work."

Before Joy could react, she was pulled into a spontaneous hug. She froze, stunned not only by the sudden affection but by the assumption behind it. Charles, however, only grinned.

"I hate to disappoint you, Nana," he said, "but Joy Collins is a client I'm protecting at the moment, not my sweetheart."

"What a shame," his grandmother sighed dramatically. "You two would give us the most beautiful great grandbabies."

Joy felt heat rush to her cheeks as Charles and his grandfather burst into laughter.

"Forgive my wife, Miss Collins," Reverend Gregory said kindly, winking at Joy. "She's rather direct when it comes to family matters. Now that all our children are married, she's turned her attention to the grandchildren."

Charles squeezed Joy's hand briefly before turning back to his grandmother.

"I love you, Nana, but you're making Joy uncomfortable."

"I apologize," she said, not sounding particularly remorseful. "Charles has always been so serious, and career minded that I assumed his visit meant an important announcement. Come, let's go inside where we can talk." She led them into a cozy sitting room behind the church. Once they were seated, the reverend studied his grandson with curiosity.

"So, what brings you here, Charles?"

Charles explained Joy's situation and the events that had driven her from Deer Lodge. As he spoke, his grandmother's gaze softened, her eyes filling with sympathy as she looked at Joy.

"Oh, my dear girl," she said gently. "I am so sorry for all you've endured. Of course, you may stay with us as long as you like. We have a spare bedroom, and Charles can sleep in the sitting room."

Joy's cheeks warmed again, but she shook her head. Before she could respond, Charles spoke.

"Actually, Joy is hoping to stay in the cabin."

"By herself?" his grandmother exclaimed. "Absolutely not! Why would you even consider that, Charles?"

"It's what I want," Joy said firmly, straightening her shoulders. "Charles would prefer I stay with someone, but that's too dangerous. I won't put anyone else at risk while those criminals are still free."

The older couple exchanged a glance, and Charles gave a small nod.

"We can't allow you to live alone," his grandmother insisted. "This is the middle of nowhere. There's no sheriff here."

"It wasn't my idea to come here," Joy replied defensively, feeling cornered.

"She wanted to disappear on her own," Charles added. "I couldn't let her do that."

"Well, thank goodness you didn't," his grandmother said. "Why would you risk your life when you know people are after you?"

Joy rose abruptly, pacing as emotion surged.

"Because I've already lost my parents," she said, her voice trembling. "My sister is gone with her husband, and I don't even know where she is. These men burned down my uncle's house just days ago. I can't bear the thought of someone else being hurt, or killed, because of me." Her voice broke, and tears streamed freely now. "I couldn't survive that."

"Oh, sweet child," the older woman said softly, reaching for her. "None of this is your fault."

"I bring danger wherever I go," Joy continued through tears. "My aunt and uncle lost their home because of me. They were only spared because Charles planned ahead. Next time, there may not be time. I won't let good people suffer for my father's enemies." She turned toward the door, desperate for air, but Charles stepped in front of her and pulled her into his arms. She resisted for only a second before the comfort of his embrace shattered her defenses.

"You've been carrying far too much on your own," his grandmother said gently. "It's all right to let others help."

Reverend Gregory nodded solemnly. "If staying in the cabin gives you peace of mind, we'll respect that. But know this, our entire town will watch out for you."

Joy wiped her tears and managed a grateful smile.

"Thank you."

"We looked everywhere but couldn't find her." Brigham's face was drawn tight with worry now. He had feared something like this would happen, yet despite all their vigilance, Joy had still managed to slip away.

"I checked her room," Darlene added softly, the same concern etched into her features. "Most of her clothes are gone."

Brigham turned, disbelief flashing across his face.

"But how? How did she get past all of us with bags?"

"I think I know the answer to that," Cathleen said as she stepped back into the house, holding something in her hand. "I found this rope tangled in the bushes below her window."

Brigham let out a frustrated groan and struck the doorframe with his palm.

"Darn it. That girl's cleverness will be her downfall one day. I don't want anything to happen to her."

"None of us do, Dad," Olivia said quietly. "We all love her."

Brigham drew in a steadying breath, forcing himself to think.

"Maybe someone in town saw her today. I'll saddle my horse."

"Let's all go," Cathleen said at once. Darlene and Olivia nodded without hesitation.

Brigham had just stepped outside and was about to call one of the cowboys over to have the buckboard readied when a rider approached the ranch. He shaded his eyes against the sun and waited until the young man drew closer. His heart gave a sharp jolt. The second horse trailing behind was unmistakable.

"Derek," Brigham called, striding forward, his voice tight with alarm. "Where did you find Joy's horse? Is she hurt?"

Derek shook his head quickly. "No, sir. She rode into the livery early this morning, left the horse there, and asked me to bring it back to your ranch this evening."

Brigham's jaw clenched. "Did she say where she was going?"

Derek hesitated, then added, "Not to me. But I spoke with Mr. Tucker at the post office. He mentioned she bought a one-way ticket to Helena. That's all he knew."

Brigham let out a long, troubled breath and dragged a hand over his face.

"Helena," he murmured. "That doesn't help much. From there, she could go anywhere."

"Yes, sir," Derek said quietly.

"Thank you for bringing the horse back," Brigham replied, forcing steadiness into his voice. He nodded, then watched as Derek turned and rode back toward town. Brigham remained where he was, staring down the road long after the rider disappeared from view. A heavy knot settled in his chest. Joy hadn't just gone on an errand. She had left, deliberately, quietly, and without saying goodbye.

"Perhaps Charles knows where she is," Darlene suggested softly, a flicker of hope lighting her eyes. Brigham shook his head.

"I doubt it. If Joy left like this, she likely didn't tell him any more than she told us."

"What about Mr. Andrews?" Olivia offered, stepping closer. "He's been involved in all of this, hasn't he?"

Brigham's expression darkened. "Charles and Dylan, both warned us about him. They believe he can't be trusted, and that he may be involved in what's been happening."

"A traitor?" Cathleen burst out, her eyes blazing. "If he's helping to hurt, or kill, Joy, he deserves to be hanged."

"Cathleen," Darlene said sharply, catching her daughter's arm, "that's enough. We don't know nearly enough to make accusations like that."

Cathleen pressed her lips together, but the fury in her eyes did not fade. Brigham exhaled slowly, forcing himself to steady the fear clawing at his chest.

"I'll ride into town first thing in the morning and send a telegram to Charles, and to Dylan's parents as well. If anyone knows where Dylan is, it'll be them. Perhaps they can pass along a message." He turned his gaze toward the darkened horizon, unease settling heavily within him. Wherever Joy had gone, she hadn't gone lightly. And that worried him more than anything else.

"Graham, you're home late. I expected you hours ago," Brigham said as his son stepped into the house. Darlene and the girls all looked up from where they were seated, expectation flickering briefly across their faces before giving way to unease.

"I spent the day with Julia," Graham replied, shrugging out of his coat. "I proposed to her when I returned this morning." He paused, waiting for smiles, congratulations, perhaps even applause. None came. The silence that followed was thick and uncomfortable. Brigham and Darlene exchanged a brief, weighted glance. It was Cathleen who finally broke it.

"Did you tell Joy you were going to do that?"

Graham frowned. "Why would I?"

"Because," Cathleen shot back, rising to her feet, "you and Joy were inseparable before the divorce was even final. Anyone with eyes would've thought you were courting her, while you were still married."

"I never courted her," Graham said sharply. "Yes, we had chemistry. Yes, I kissed her a few times. But I never told her I would marry her."

"Oh, Graham," Darlene murmured, her disappointment unmistakable. She shook her head slowly, as though something fragile had just cracked. Cathleen stepped closer, fire blazing in her eyes.

"So, she was just a pastime then?" she demanded. "A distraction? A toy?"

"That's not fair," Graham snapped. "I never thought of her that way. We got along. I cared about her. For a while, I thought I was in love with her, but when I got to know Julia better, I realized Joy was only ever a friend."

Cathleen stared at him as though she was seeing a stranger.

"I can't believe you," she said quietly. "You let everyone in this house believe you were serious about Joy. And now you reduce it to *some chemistry*?"

"I never made her any promises."

"I doubt that," Cathleen shot back. "You've never been half-hearted about anything, Graham. You're either all in, or not in at all." She shook her head, her voice trembling now, not with uncertainty, but with fury.

"Joy probably told you to stop kissing her until you were free. And knowing you, you didn't. My guess? You told her you cared about her. Maybe even that you loved her. And if I had to guess further, you let her believe there might be a future once the divorce was final, all so you wouldn't have to feel guilty about kissing her while you were still married."

The color drained from Graham's face. The silence that followed was heavy. Condemning. Cathleen watched him closely, then spoke again, her voice low and deadly calm.

"Your face just told me everything I needed to know."

Olivia jumped to her feet, her face mirroring her sister's outrage. She was usually composed, measured, and slow to anger, especially where her older brother was concerned. Unlike Cathleen, who never hesitated to voice her opinions, Olivia often chose restraint. But this time, restraint deserted her entirely.

"You should be ashamed of yourself, Graham Harrison," she said sharply, her eyes blazing. "No wonder Joy left. She must have been deeply hurt by the way you treated her. And to anyone who watched the two of you, anyone who assumed what we all did, this looks like you used her to get back at Lydia and her family. That would feel like a complete betrayal to Joy."

Graham stiffened. "What betrayal? And what do you mean Joy left?"

Brigham let out a heavy sigh.

"Son, I know now that Charles and Dylan advised you to keep some distance from Joy for her safety, so the men who murdered her parents would continue to see her as a target. But I am quite certain they meant in public, not altogether. Not by abandoning her emotionally. And certainly not by parading your attention before other women." His voice hardened. "I asked you to speak with her after she returned from Goldcreek. You ignored me, didn't you?"

Graham didn't answer.

"You played with her feelings," Darlene said quietly, stepping closer. Her disappointment cut deeper than any raised voice. "Even if you didn't intend to, you made her believe there was something more between you."

"I never meant to hurt her," Graham protested. "I kissed her because I believed the feelings were mutual. I thought there was something real between us."

"Then you should have spoken to her honestly," Brigham replied. "No wonder she's looked so pale and unwell these past weeks. She felt lonely. And she felt abandoned by you."

"If she let herself hope for more, that isn't entirely my fault," Graham snapped, defensiveness flaring. Cathleen stepped forward, fury blazing.

"You got her hopes up, Graham. You made her believe that once the divorce was final, you and she would begin courting properly. Then the moment you were free, you tossed her aside like an old sock, as if she had no value to you anymore. And you never even had the decency to explain why you were avoiding her or that your feelings had changed. Is it really such a mystery why she left?"

His irritation sharpened, bordering on rage.

"Will someone finally tell me what you mean by *Joy left*?"

Brigham's face tightened with worry.

"Joy rode into town this morning. We haven't seen her since. We searched the ranch, and later Derek returned her horse. Apparently, she took the stagecoach to Helena."

The words struck Graham like a blow.

"When did she leave?" he asked hoarsely.

"This morning, most likely. Why?" Brigham studied his son closely.

"Oh no," Graham breathed, sinking into an armchair.

Cathleen's stomach dropped. "What did you do?"

"She probably saw me," he whispered. "When I proposed to Julia."

Silence fell.

"What do you mean?" Brigham demanded.

"I arrived on the morning stagecoach. When I saw Julia, I went straight to her and proposed."

"Outside?" Darlene asked, alarmed. "In the street?"

Graham nodded.

"Oh boy," Cathleen muttered, rubbing her temples.

"That must have been the final blow," Olivia whispered, tears brimming. "I don't think she'll come back, not even after all this is over. She might move in with her aunt and uncle. Or find someone else. Someone who truly sees her."

"I never meant to hurt her," Graham said again, his voice breaking. "I didn't even consider how my actions might affect her."

"Yes, well, you rarely do when it comes to women," Cathleen snapped, but Darlene raised a hand, silencing her.

"Listen, Graham," Darlene said gently, pulling her son into her arms. "We are happy for you and Julia. Truly. We like her very much. But you needed to understand what Joy was likely feeling. After everything she's endured, the bond she formed with you, friendship and more, meant a great deal to her. I know she would want you to be happy. But seeing that proposal..." Her voice softened. "That must have felt like a slap across the face."

Cathleen shook her head slowly. "All we can do now is hope Olivia is wrong. Because I'd miss Joy far too much."

Brigham sent out the telegrams early the following morning, his worry pressing heavily on his chest. There was nothing more he could do now but wait and hope that someone, somewhere, had seen Joy and could point them in the right direction.

Graham, meanwhile, rode into town to see Julia. He found her at the clinic and, for once, did not attempt to soften the truth or hide behind half-answers. He told her everything, about Joy, about the kisses, about the assumptions he had made, and about how abruptly he had turned away once the divorce was final.

Julia listened in stunned silence. When he finished, her shock slowly gave way to understanding. She could see now that Graham had never set out to hurt Joy, but that realization did little to ease the ache in her heart. Joy was her friend, and the thought of her riding off alone, wounded and possibly in danger, filled her with dread.

"I don't think you meant to do this," Julia said quietly at last. "But that doesn't mean she wasn't hurt by it. And knowing Joy..." She hesitated, then shook her head. "She wouldn't have left without a reason."

After Graham departed, Julia did not allow herself even a moment of hesitation. She went straight to the post office and sent off several telegrams of her own. One went to her parents, in the hope that Joy might have sought refuge with them. Another she addressed to Judge William Lawson. He was a man with influence and far-reaching connections, and if anyone could authorize or coordinate a search, it would be him.

Her parents' reply came back quickly. They had neither seen nor heard from Joy but promised to ask around and keep their eyes and ears open. Judge Lawson's response arrived hours later. He informed Julia that he was currently visiting relatives in Helena and had, in fact, met with Joy the evening before. He admitted that he had assumed she would return to Deer Lodge afterward and had been unaware of any plans she might have had to leave. However, he assured Julia that he would speak with his relatives at once and do everything in his power to discover where Joy had gone.

It wasn't the certainty Julia had hoped for, but it was something. And for now, that fragile thread of hope was all they had to cling to.

Brigham did not hear back from Charles himself, but a telegram arrived later that day from Charles's uncle instead. It explained that Joy had indeed stayed with them in Helena for one night but had left early that morning. The message continued, carefully worded, to say that he could not disclose where Joy had gone, as she had expressly asked that no one be told. There was, however, one small but vital detail at the end of the telegram. Charles had gone with her.

Brigham let out a slow, steady breath he hadn't realized he'd been holding. The worry did not vanish, not entirely, but it loosened its grip. Knowing Joy, he was certain she had intended to continue on her own, convinced as ever that isolating herself was the best way to keep others safe. The fact that Charles had refused to let her do so eased Brigham's mind more than he cared to admit.

Charles was level-headed, cautious, and deeply invested in Joy's safety. If anyone could temper her fierce independence without crushing it, it was him. Brigham folded the telegram carefully and slipped it into his pocket, offering a silent prayer that wherever Joy was headed, she would finally find a measure of peace, and that Charles would be able to protect her until this dark chapter was truly over.

"So... shall we keep looking for her?" Graham asked once they were back at the ranch. His voice lacked its usual confidence, edged instead with uncertainty and regret. Brigham shook his head slowly.

"No. It would be foolish to keep searching right now."

Graham frowned. "But what if she needs us?"

"She isn't alone," Brigham replied firmly. "Charles is with her, and I trust him. He's sharp, cautious, and far more prepared for what Joy is facing than most men his age. He won't let anyone harm her." Brigham glanced out across the ranch, his jaw tightening with resolve. "Our place is here, for now. We keep the ranch running, stay alert, and be ready. When Joy and Charles need our help to finish this, they'll know exactly where to find us."

Graham swallowed and nodded, though the knot in his chest refused to loosen. Knowing she was safe brought a measure of relief, but it did nothing to quiet the ache of knowing he had played a part in driving her away. And that, he realized, was something he would have to live with.

"Charles will take you to the cabin," Grace said firmly, her tone warm but leaving no room for argument, "but you must promise that you will join us for supper every night."

Joy hesitated. "That is such a kind offer, Mrs. Gregory, but I truly don't want to inconvenience you."

Grace smiled and gently shook her head.

"Please call me Grace, Joy. I have a feeling we will be very good friends, and before long, you'll feel like another granddaughter to us." She straightened, fixing Joy with a knowing look. "And I will not argue with you about supper. Seeing you each evening will give me peace of mind. I need to know you are safe."

She paused, then added with a soft chuckle, "That said, don't think we won't come by unannounced. And I want you coming into town whenever you can. People here should know who you are and that you're with us. Elkhorn is small, but we are a tight-knit community, and the men here are fiercely protective of their families. That will include you, young lady."

Joy nodded solemnly. "I promise. As long as it feels safe, I'll come into town and join you. And if I sense danger, I'll keep to myself and away from everyone."

Grace exhaled slowly, then nodded in approval before turning to her husband and grandson.

"All right, then." She handed Joy a small bundle. "Here are a few food items for the cabin. You can find most of what you'll need at the general store, but if you want me to teach you how to bake bread, or anything else, you just say the word."

Joy smiled. "I'm all right, Mrs... I mean, Grace," she corrected herself quickly when Grace raised an eyebrow. "My mother made sure my sister and I knew how to cook and keep house in case we ever married. Alice is better at it than I am, she's had more practice, but I know what I'm doing."

"I'm very pleased to hear that," Grace said warmly. She pulled Joy into a firm, affectionate hug, holding her a moment longer than strictly necessary. Then she and her husband stood together, watching as Joy and Charles walked away toward the waiting horses, until the trees swallowed them from sight. Only then did Grace slip her arm through her husband's and turn back toward the house, her expression thoughtful, but hopeful.

24

Cold Creek, Hot Tempers

It wasn't fully dark when they reached the cabin. The last light of day lingered between the trees, casting long shadows across the clearing. Charles helped Joy dismount, then showed her around, pointing out the small but sturdy barn beside the cabin where his grandfather's horses were kept, and the narrow, spring-fed creek winding its way through the brush behind the building.

"There's a spring just beyond those pines," he explained. "Clean water. Cold, but good." He filled a bucket and several pitchers so Joy wouldn't have to leave the cabin during the night, then returned with an armful of firewood. October nights in the mountains were already sharp with cold, and snow was never entirely out of the question.

While Charles took care of things outside, Joy made herself useful indoors. She unpacked, hung her clothes in the small closet of the larger bedroom, and built fires in both the stove and the fireplace. Warmth soon crept into the cabin, chasing away the chill, and the kettle began to sing softly as she prepared tea.

By the time Charles returned, the space felt transformed, cozy, safe, lived in. Joy was lighting the lanterns and setting them throughout the cabin, their soft glow banishing the shadows.

"The shutters lock from the inside," Charles said, demonstrating. "My grandfather insisted on it. Makes it much harder for anyone to force their way in."

Together they secured the shutters, then returned to the main room, where two armchairs sat before the fire. Joy offered him a cup of tea before he headed back to his grandparents', and he accepted. They sat in comfortable silence for several minutes, steam curling from their cups as the fire crackled. Then Joy suddenly giggled. Charles glanced at her, one brow lifting.

"I was just thinking," she said lightly, warmth creeping into her cheeks, "that we must look like an old married couple, sitting here like this."

He chuckled. "If anything, I'd say we look more like newlyweds." His teasing softened, his gaze lingering. "Are you certain you don't want me to stay? I promise I wouldn't overstep any boundaries."

Joy sighed. "I'm sure. And it isn't that I think you would do something improper, you are my lawyer, after all. It's the appearance of it. If someone saw, you leaving the cabin in the morning... and if anything were to happen to you—"

"Do you hear yourself, Joy?" he cut in, frustration edging his voice. "You're asking me to stand back when every instinct I have tells me not to. I couldn't live with myself if something happened to you."

She set her cup aside and met his gaze steadily.

"Whatever happens to me will happen," she said softly. "I won't go looking for trouble. I promise you that. But I need to stand on my own two feet. I'm not getting married anytime soon, if ever, and you will eventually return to the city, or wherever your life leads you. You deserve a future too."

He shook his head, unconvinced. She placed her hand on his arm, grounding him.

"I'm not running anymore," she continued. "I have a place of my own now. And perhaps I should even buy this cabin from your grandparents, so they aren't burdened if something happens."

"That's not necessary," he replied firmly. "The cabin is the least of anyone's worries. You should let me protect you."

Joy sighed again. "Try to understand me. I can't hide behind a man, especially not someone who isn't family. You were hired by my father for legal matters. I shouldn't have agreed to you coming with me at all."

He exhaled sharply. "Nothing would have stopped me. I would've tied you up and brought you anyway if I had to. Your father knew exactly who you were when he hired me—stubborn, fearless, and inclined to charge headfirst into danger. He wanted someone nearby who could intervene when necessary."

That did it. Joy rose to her feet, irritation flashing across her face.

"I appreciate your concern, Mr. Gregory, but I am not in need of a babysitter. If I want fatherly advice or a lecture, I have an uncle for that. Now it's late. You should go." She crossed to the door and opened it for him. His lips twitched, clearly fighting a smile, an expression that only fueled her annoyance.

"This isn't over, Miss Collins," he said quietly as he stepped past her. Joy closed the door the moment he was gone and turned the lock with finality, her heart pounding far harder than she cared to admit.

As soon as the door shut behind him, Charles let out a low, hearty laugh that echoed softly in the cool night air. He shook his head, still grinning to himself. He had met his fair share of spirited, stubborn women over the years, but Joy Collins was in a league entirely her own, a true spitfire, through and through.

He would never have guessed it at their first meeting months earlier, when she had been polite, reserved, and quietly observant, with eyes that missed nothing yet revealed very little. Back then, her strength had been subtle, folded neatly beneath good manners and careful words. Now it burned openly, sharp, fearless, and unyielding, and he found himself both exasperated and profoundly impressed.

Yes, they were in the middle of something dangerous. Yes, lives were at stake, and the weight of it pressed heavily on his shoulders. But even so, he couldn't deny it, sparring with Joy stirred something in him that he hadn't felt in a very long time. The way her chin lifted when challenged. The fire in her eyes when she refused to be managed. The fierce independence she guarded like armor. All of it made him want to meet her step for step, not tame her, not shield her, but stand beside her.

Charles glanced back at the warmly lit cabin, his smile softening. He had no intention of abandoning her to face this alone. And if pushing her buttons now and then earned him that sharp glare and flash of temper? Well... he suspected he might enjoy that far more than he should.

Joy heard his laughter through the thick wooden door and very nearly spun back around to fling it open. For half a heartbeat, her hand even twitched toward the latch. But she stopped herself.

She would not give him the satisfaction of knowing he had gotten under her skin. Instead, she squared her shoulders, returned to the small kitchen, and poured herself another cup of tea. The kettle clinked softly against the cup as she filled it, her head shaking in disbelief the entire time. She carried the tea to the table and sat, wrapping both hands around the warm porcelain as if to anchor herself.

Charles Gregory was infuriating. He had changed since the first time they met, or perhaps she admitted begrudgingly, she simply hadn't been paying close enough attention back then. His seriousness had fooled her. He had always been composed, reserved, almost severe, a man who weighed every word before speaking.

Now that they were spending so much time in one another's company, that careful sobriety had given way to something else entirely. Confidence. Quiet authority. And just enough teasing charm to make her want to throw something at his head. It unsettled her more than she cared to admit.

She didn't yet know what to make of this version of Charles, or what it might mean for the future, but at that moment, one thing was painfully clear, she was still decidedly miffed about his comment regarding her stubbornness. Who did he think he was? If anyone had a claim to that particular trait, it was him. He was every bit as obstinate as she was, perhaps more so, and the fact that he seemed entirely unashamed of it only fueled her irritation. Joy took a determined sip of her tea, staring into the dancing flames of the fire.

Very well, Mr. Gregory, she thought with a huff. *If you believe you've met your match... you may be more right than you know.*

Despite the danger that still lurked somewhere beyond the trees and mountains, Joy slept wonderfully. The cabin wrapped around her like a quiet promise, warm, solid, and safe. Every piece of furniture, every carefully placed decoration spoke of a home that had been loved for generations. For the first time in days, perhaps weeks, her mind had truly rested.

She rose early, rekindled the fire, and dressed for the day. After opening the shutters, she stepped outside and breathed in the crisp mountain air, letting the new morning greet her properly.

Drawn by the sound of running water, she wandered to the creek behind the cabin. Sunlight danced across its surface, and she smiled when she noticed fish darting through the clear water. It would make a fine supper one evening, should she feel inclined to try her hand at fishing.

Back inside, she began preparing breakfast, humming softly to herself, when a knock sounded at the door. Joy rolled her eyes automatically. No doubt Charles had come to check on her, making sure she hadn't vanished overnight. But when she opened the door, she blinked in surprise. Charles was there, yes, but he wasn't alone. His grandmother stood beside him, smiling warmly. And then Joy's heart gave an entirely unwelcome little leap. Charles wasn't wearing a suit.

He had traded polished shoes and tailored lines for boots, a worn shirt, and the unmistakable look of a cowboy. The fabric stretched across his broad shoulders, sleeves pushed up to reveal strong, muscular forearms. The scruff of beard along his jaw only heightened the ruggedness. He looked... unfairly handsome.

Joy forced her gaze away at once before her cheeks betrayed her. Clearing her throat, she stepped aside and invited them in, offering breakfast without quite trusting her voice. Neither declined. She set the table and moved about the kitchen, grateful for the distraction, and was just about to bring out the food when another knock sounded. Charles's grandfather stood at the door.

"Please excuse the intrusion," he said kindly. "I just fed the horses and will turn them out to pasture before I head back."

"Would you like to join us for breakfast?" Joy asked, sunlight catching in her eyes as she smiled. He returned her grin and nodded.

After grace was said, they ate and talked, the easy conversation filling the cabin with warmth and life. Joy hadn't realized how much she'd missed company until that moment, laughter, shared stories, the gentle comfort of voices around her. When they finished, she turned to the older couple.

"Why don't you join me for breakfast every morning?" she suggested lightly. "That way you can see with your own eyes that I'm still alive after spending the night on my own." She winked at the reverend. "Since I'm expected for supper every evening, it only seems fair."

Grace squeezed her arm affectionately.

"We would love that, Joy."

"Wonderful," Joy said, smiling. "I'll be heading into town to do some shopping."

"That's actually why we came by," Grace replied. "I thought I'd go with you and introduce you to as many townsfolk as possible."

Joy's smile widened. "I like that."

The little cabin no longer felt like a hiding place, but the beginning of something new.

Joy and Grace walked arm in arm along Elkhorn's single dusty road, Charles keeping an easy pace beside them. Grace seemed to know everyone, or perhaps everyone simply knew her. Smiles, nods, and warm greetings followed them, and Grace took clear delight in introducing Joy to each person they passed, as though she were proudly presenting a treasured newcomer to the town. Just as they reached the general store, the door swung open and several young ladies spilled out onto the porch.

"Charles! You're back!" one of them exclaimed, her face lighting up. In an instant, he was surrounded. Questions flew at him from all sides, where he had been, how long he would stay, had he come alone? A few of them leaned in closer than necessary, their laughter a little too eager, their glances lingering a little too long.

Joy slowed her steps, watching the scene with emotions she hadn't expected. An uncomfortable tug tightened her chest. Jealousy. The realization startled her. She pushed the feeling aside at once, irritated with herself. Why should she care? He had thoroughly exasperated her just the evening before. Whatever he did, and with whomever, was none of her concern.

Determined not to appear affected, she followed Grace into the store and began browsing the shelves, focusing on practical matters. She selected food staples, a few baking supplies, and other necessities she would need at the cabin.

Grace introduced her to the store owner and his wife, explaining in a few careful sentences why Joy was staying in Elkhorn, without revealing details, but making it unmistakably clear that Joy was someone the town ought to watch over.

"There's no bank here?" Joy asked quietly as she stepped beside Grace at the counter.

"No," Grace replied. "Lee Hunter, who runs the post office, orders money from various banks. Most folks keep their savings at home, and newcomers arrange things through him."

"If you find yourself short, dear, I'm happy to chalk it up for you," the store owner's wife offered kindly.

"That won't be necessary, thank you," Joy said with a polite smile. "I have enough and should be all right for a while."

The store owner glanced toward the window and chuckled.

"Looks like your grandson is a favorite once again."

Joy couldn't stop the quick, impatient glance she cast in the same direction. Outside, Charles was still engaged with the group of young women, his easy smile firmly in place. Grace laughed softly.

"If only he'd take a genuine interest in someone. And I can't blame the girls. This town doesn't have many young men of marrying age. If it weren't for the stagecoach stop in Boulder and the miners passing through, they wouldn't have a decent fellow to admire for months at a time."

"Oh," Joy murmured as she stepped closer to the window, watching Charles field their attention with practiced charm. "That must be... difficult." She wasn't quite sure whether she meant for the girls, or for herself.

An older woman approached Joy just then and struck up a friendly conversation, drawing her attention away. While Joy listened politely, the store owner's wife leaned over the counter, lowering her voice as she spoke to Grace.

"I must admit," she said with a knowing smile, "when I watched Charles and Miss Collins walk down Main Street together, I was convinced they were a couple."

Grace let out a soft sigh. "I thought the same when they arrived yesterday. But both were very quick to assure me there's nothing between them."

The woman raised an eyebrow. "I'm not certain I believe that. Your grandson is a very handsome young man, and she's a beautiful girl. They make quite the picture together."

"I won't argue with you there," Grace replied, giving the woman's hand a gentle squeeze. The store owner's wife glanced toward the window.

"To be honest, I think I even noticed her expression change when the girls surrounded Charles."

Grace's brows drew together. "What do you mean?"

"I mean," the woman said quietly, "when I stepped out onto the porch and saw our girls hurry over to him, Miss Collins didn't look pleased. Not at all."

Grace tilted her head. "You noticed that?"

"Oh yes," the woman said with a small, confident nod. "I'd even go so far as to say I caught a hint of jealousy in her expression."

Grace's lips curved into a thoughtful smile.

"How interesting." She glanced toward Joy just as the young woman finished her conversation and turned back toward them. Grace immediately smoothed her expression into one of pleasant neutrality, but her mind was already busy turning over what she had learned.

"Well, it was a pleasure meeting you both," Joy said then, a warm, genuine smile lighting her face. She turned to Grace. "Are you ready, or do you still need to do some shopping?"

"I'm quite ready," Charles's grandmother replied at once. She cast a playful wink at her friend before looping her arm through Joy's. Just then, Charles stepped into the store, still trailed by several of the town's young women. Grace smiled sweetly.

"Charles, be a dear and carry our bags for us."

"Oh no, that's quite all right," Joy said quickly, instinctively tightening her hold on her parcel. "I can manage."

Several of the young women exchanged amused glances, brows lifting in unison.

"Why wouldn't you let Charles be a gentleman?" one of them asked, half teasing, half incredulous. "Yer ma never teach you it ain't polite to turn down a man tryin' to help?"

Joy stared at her, taken completely by surprise. A ripple of soft laughter moved through Grace and the other older women nearby. Charles's gaze settled on Joy now, steady, challenging, and entirely unapologetic. Heat rushed to her cheeks, coloring them a deep pink.

"I didn't mean to be rude," Joy said hastily. "I only meant—I mean—I didn't want to inconvenience him." The words felt clumsy the moment they left her mouth. Was she trying too hard to prove she needed no one?

The boldest of the young women stepped closer and slipped her arm through Joy's, while Grace claimed the other side with evident satisfaction.

"Reckon you're from the city," the girl said kindly. "Heard tell city gals like to do everything for themselves. But out here, things run a little different. In Elkhorn, we ain't got many young men, so when one does come along, you let him act the gentleman. Give him the chance to show a little kindness."

"I haven't thought of myself as a city girl in years," Joy replied quietly.

"Well," the girl said with a friendly shrug, "some lessons stick with you. Oughta ask yer mama how she met yer pa—how he went an' swept her clean off her feet."

The words landed like a blow. Joy's smile faltered.

"My parents died in a fire a few months ago."

"Oh—oh, I'm real sorry," the young woman exclaimed, horror flooding her face. Without thinking, she wrapped Joy in a tight hug, and suddenly the others followed suit, crowding around her.

Joy felt overwhelmed, torn between the instinct to flee back to the quiet safety of her cabin and the unexpected warmth of such immediate, heartfelt concern. The store owner's wife hurried forward.

"All right now, girls, that's enough," she said gently but firmly. "You're smothering her. Remember, she's new in town, and not everyone's used to bein' hugged by strangers."

The circle loosened, giving Joy room to breathe again, her heart still thudding from the whirlwind of it all.

Joy remained quiet on the walk back, her earlier brightness dimmed to a thoughtful silence. When they reached the church, she slowed and turned toward Charles and his grandmother.

"If you don't mind," she said softly, "I'd like to be alone for a while." She reached for her shopping bag out of habit, but Charles held it back, studying her face with quiet concern.

"Perhaps being around, us, would do you good right now," Grace said gently, her voice warm but perceptive.

Joy shook her head. "I need some time to myself."

"I can bring your things by later," Charles offered. His eyes never left her, as though he were searching for some crack in her resolve. She did not look at him.

"No, thank you," she replied evenly. "It will be good for me to carry it the rest of the way. I want to bake bread later, and I'd rather have everything with me."

Reluctantly, he handed her the bag. Joy nodded once in thanks and turned away, her steps measured but purposeful as she headed toward the cabin.

Charles watched until she disappeared from view. Grace stepped closer and laid a comforting hand on his arm.

"I don't like seeing her like this," she murmured. "Something clearly weighs on her heart. But when a young woman grows quiet so suddenly, it's often because she needs space to gather herself. We must give her that."

Charles nodded, though every instinct urged him to follow Joy, to stop her, to demand the truth of what had unsettled her so deeply. Instead, he remained where he was, jaw tight, forcing himself to respect the boundary she had drawn, even as concern settled heavily in his chest.

The bag grew heavier with every step, its weight biting into her arm. Yet the effort to carry it, gave Joy something solid to focus on, something to hold on to until she reached the cabin and could no longer keep the tears at bay.

Once inside, she moved on instinct. She locked the door, set the groceries on the table, and placed the milk and butter into the icebox. Only then did her strength finally give out. She crossed the room, sank into one of the armchairs, and broke.

The sobs came hard and fast, tearing from her chest as if a dam had burst. She pressed her face into her arm, shoulders shaking. Would missing her parents ever grow easier? Some days she could breathe around the pain, almost forget it for a moment, but then there were times like this, when the loss felt as raw and violent as the day it had happened. As though a piece of her heart had been torn away, leaving nothing but an aching, hollow space behind.

The conversation at the store had reopened wounds she tried so desperately to keep closed. A careless mention of parents. A simple, innocent assumption. It had been enough to undo her.

She cried for the mother who would never again tease her in the kitchen, for the father whose steady presence had once made the world feel safe and understandable. She cried for the future they would never share, for the advice she would never again receive, for the comfort she longed for but could no longer reach.

Eventually, the sobbing softened into quieter tears. Joy drew a shaky breath and wiped at her face, grateful, deeply grateful, that Charles and his grandmother had not followed her or pressed her to speak. Right now, she needed this solitude. She needed the freedom to grieve without being brave, without being strong for anyone else.

Her thoughts drifted to Alice and the girls. She missed them terribly, missed the sound of their laughter and the comfort of knowing her sister was nearby. Yet alongside the ache came a fragile sense of relief. Alice was safe. She wasn't alone anymore. She had a good man at her side and two daughters who adored her. That knowledge didn't erase Joy's grief, but it softened it, just a little. Curling deeper into the chair, Joy allowed herself to sit with sorrow, trusting that even if the pain never fully disappeared, she would somehow learn to carry it.

Joy let herself grieve without restraint. She cried until the tears were spent and her chest no longer felt as though it might split apart. When the storm finally passed and her breathing steadied, she wiped her face, straightened her shoulders, and turned toward the work waiting for her. Bread.

The simple, familiar ritual grounded her. She measured, mixed, and kneaded, pouring her lingering frustration into the dough. There was something deeply satisfying about the physical labor, the steady rhythm of her hands, the resistance beneath her palms. With every push and fold, the ache in her chest loosened its grip, replaced by a calmer, quieter resolve.

When the bread was set aside to rise, Joy moved on to another comfort: her grandmother's biscuits. The original recipes her mother had once kept so carefully were gone now, lost to the fire, but the knowledge had survived. The motions lived on in her hands and in her memory alike. Someday, she promised herself, she would write them all down again, every loaf, every biscuit, every dish that had once made their house feel like home.

The cabin soon filled with warmth and the comforting scent of baking bread. The biscuits cooled on the table, golden and fragrant, while Joy carefully pulled the first loaf from the oven. She had just set it down when a sharp knock at the door echoed through the cabin. Startled, she jerked back. The hot pan brushed her fingers.

"Ah!" she cried, dropping the cloth as pain flared. The burn stung fiercely, sending fresh tears to her eyes, this time born of shock rather than sorrow. "You can come in," she called, striving for composure as she hurried to the washstand. She glanced around in mild panic, only to realize she'd used the last of the water earlier. With a frustrated sigh, she pressed her fingers together, breathing through the pain, and turned toward the door, hoping whoever stood on the other side would not notice the tremor still lingering in her hands.

Charles stepped into the cabin just in time to see her frantic search and the way she cradled one hand against her chest.

"What's the matter?" he asked at once, his voice sharp with concern. Joy sucked in a breath through gritted teeth, fighting the sting, and the tears threatening to follow.

"Your knock startled me. I burned my fingers."

Before she could say another word, he was already moving. Realizing there was no water within reach, Charles closed the distance between them, scooped her up without hesitation, and rushed back out the door toward the creek. Joy gasped, instinctively clutching his shoulder.

"What are you doing?" she demanded, flustered. "I didn't hurt my legs or my feet."

"But I have longer legs," he replied briskly, not slowing. He reached the creek moments later and set her down carefully, as though she weighed nothing at all. Joy plunged her burning fingers into the icy water, biting her lip as the cold bit back, sharp, painful, then blessedly numbing. She kept her hand submerged until the sting dulled, then withdrew it and wiped it on her apron, breathing a little easier.

"Let me see," Charles said immediately. Before he could reach for her, she hid her hand behind her back.

"I'm fine. You're not a doctor, and it wasn't that bad." She tried to step past him, but his arm came around her waist, stopping her short. In one smooth motion, he pulled her back against his chest and caught her wrist, drawing her hand forward. His grip was firm but careful as he examined her fingers.

"What are you doing?" she protested, squirming. "Let me go."

Her resistance earned her an infuriatingly amused smirk. The warmth of his body, the strength of his arms, the steady rise and fall of his chest behind her, all of it sent unwanted butterflies spiraling through her. When he finally released her, she stepped away at once, heart hammering.

"I just wanted to be sure it wasn't worse than you claimed," he said, his gaze lingering on her face far too long.

"There was no need," she replied stiffly. "I would have said something."

"I don't think you would have," he countered quietly. "You carry everything alone. And you always downplay the pain."

She held his gaze for a brief, charged moment, then turned and walked back toward the cabin. Charles followed. Inside, the air was warm and fragrant. He paused, inhaling deeply.

"It smells wonderful in here. I can't wait to try that bread."

Despite herself, a small smile tugged at Joy's lips.

"In fact," he added lightly, "I believe I'll start with the biscuits."

He reached for the table, and instead of swatting his hand away, she suddenly found herself caught in his arms. He pulled her close, swift and sure. Joy froze, shock flashing across her face before instinct kicked in. She struggled against him, but he didn't release her. One hand lifted her chin, forcing her to meet his gaze. Her breath caught.

His eyes were dark, searching, dangerously close, too close. She blinked and dropped her gaze, her resolve hardening even as her heart betrayed her. She would not do this again. Not after Graham. Not after everything.

"Let me go, Charles," she murmured. He tilted her chin up once more and leaned down, their lips hovering a breath apart.

"No," she said sharply, jerking her head back. "Stop. I don't want this." She pushed against his chest, desperate to put distance between them. This time, he let her go.

"Joy," he said softly. She shook her head.

"You are my lawyer. My father hired you. That's all." Her voice trembled despite her effort to steady it. "You should leave. Now."

She ushered him toward the door, and her firmness clearly caught him off guard. He didn't argue. Once outside, she shut the door and locked it, pressing her back against the wood as if it were the only thing holding her upright. Her heart thundered painfully in her chest.

"I won't let anyone hurt me again," she whispered, more to herself than to the empty room. "Men don't mean it. It's just feelings, no promises." A tear slipped free before she could stop it. It hurt because, no matter how fiercely she denied it, she knew the truth. She was beginning to feel something for him.

But she would not allow herself to follow that path. Not again. Charles would leave. Men always did. And whatever had just passed between them, whatever heat and pull had flared, it wasn't real. Just infatuation.

25

Stolen Pins, Stolen Hearts

Charles remained on the other side of the door, utterly still, his hand hovering for a moment as if he might knock again, then falling uselessly to his side. Confusion churned through him. Why had she fought him so fiercely? He replayed the moment again and again, every look, every breath, every subtle shift of her body. Had he misread the signs so completely? Or had he moved too quickly, mistaken tension and closeness for invitation?

He hadn't stepped far from the door, close enough to hear the soft, broken words she murmured to herself. They cut deeper than any accusation could have. Someone had hurt her. Badly. Enough to make her doubt not just him, but the very idea of love itself. Enough to convince her that wanting something was the same as being foolish, that trust would only end in pain. His jaw tightened.

He had seen it before, in clients, in witnesses, in women who learned too young that vulnerability came at a cost. But hearing it in Joy's voice unsettled him in a way he hadn't expected. She wasn't cold. She wasn't indifferent. She was afraid. And that frightened him more than rejection ever could.

He was certain now that she felt something too. He had seen it in the way her breath had hitched, the way her eyes had darkened before she pulled away. But whatever lay in her past had taught her that feelings were dangerous, that closeness led only to loss. Charles closed his eyes briefly and exhaled.

He could push. He knew how. Persuasion was second nature to him, he had been trained to argue, to press, to corner truth until it had nowhere left to hide. But this wasn't a courtroom. And Joy Collins wasn't a witness to be pressured or a case to be won. If he pushed her now, he would lose her. So, he forced himself to step away from the door.

He would go slowly. At her pace. He would earn her trust not with words or bold gestures, but with patience, by proving, day after day, that he wasn't going to disappear, betray her, or demand more than she was ready to give. Whatever had broken her faith in love, he would not become another reason for her to fear it. And when she was ready, if she ever was, he would be there.

Despite knowing the Gregorys were waiting for her to join them for supper, Joy could not make herself leave the cabin. Not after the almost-kiss. Not after the way her heart had betrayed her with its wild, reckless beating. She paced the main room, wringing her hands as her thoughts tumbled over one another. Facing Charles felt impossible, too soon, too raw. She had no idea how to look at him now, how to speak without remembering how close his lips had been to hers, how easily she had nearly forgotten every promise she had made to herself.

Had she led him on? Had she, without meaning to, given him hope she had no right to offer? The thought twisted painfully in her chest. A sudden, loud knock at the door made her flinch, her pulse leaping as though it might escape her altogether. She froze, staring at the wooden planks as if they might somehow give her an answer. She couldn't hide forever.

"Who is it?" she finally called, her voice steadier than she felt.

"It is Reverend Gregory," came the calm, familiar reply. Relief rushed through her so quickly it nearly left her weak-kneed. She hurried to the door and opened it, and the older man stepped inside, his presence gentle and reassuring, his warm smile easing the tight knot in her chest at once.

"I am here to pick you up," he said kindly. "You promised you would join us for supper, remember? To give my wife some peace."

Joy nodded, an excuse already forming on her lips, but one look into his eyes told her it would be useless. He wasn't there to pressure her, only to remind her that she wasn't alone. And somehow, that made all the difference.

Charles must have asked him to come, she realized. Perhaps he understood he had startled her. Perhaps this was his way of giving her space without abandoning her altogether.

"I baked bread and biscuits this afternoon," she said softly, turning back toward the kitchen. "Let me bring some with me."

Reverend Gregory's eyes brightened as he followed her gaze.

"It certainly smells wonderful in here," he remarked with a grin, then winked at her. "And your bread will go perfectly with the soup Grace made."

Joy gathered the basket, her shoulders relaxing just a little. She still wasn't ready to face Charles, not yet, but maybe soon.

They had a pleasant evening together. After the first few minutes of awkwardness, Joy found herself slowly relaxing when she realized that Charles treated her exactly as he always had, courteous, respectful, and careful not to cross any lines. He didn't look at her differently, didn't tease her, and didn't bring up what had almost happened. For that, she was deeply grateful.

By the end of the evening, she even allowed him to walk her back to the cabin. The silence between them was comfortable rather than strained, and when he left her at the door, he did so with a polite goodnight and a gentle smile, as though nothing more than friendship stood between them. It steadied her heart more than she cared to admit.

The days that followed were quiet, almost deceptively so. Joy spent most of her time with the Gregorys, joining them for meals, helping Grace around the house, and accompanying her into town whenever errands needed to be done. A few of the older women from Elkhorn stopped by the cabin with pies, jars of preserves, or simple curiosity about the newcomer living just outside town. Their kindness helped her feel less like an outsider and more like someone who belonged.

Even two of the young women who very obviously fancied Charles paid her a visit. Instead of being cold or territorial, they were friendly, curious about her story, eager to talk, and quick to include her. Their openness eased Joy's unease and helped her settle into her new surroundings far more quickly than she had expected.

A week passed. Exactly one week after the almost-kiss, Charles stopped by the cabin for his usual visit. Joy noticed the change in him the moment she opened the door. His expression was tense, his jaw set, the lightness she had grown used to absent from his eyes. Her stomach tightened at once.

"What is it?" she asked, searching his face. "Did something happen?"

Her eyes betrayed her worry, fear even, and Charles released a heavy breath before answering.

"I received a telegram from Judge Lawson," he said quietly. "The marshals and soldiers were successful. They took down what was left of the Norton family's empire."

Joy held her breath.

"Several arrests were made," he continued. "Some men resisted and were shot. Norton senior was among those killed."

A strange mix of relief and dread washed over her.

"So... what were they hiding?" she asked softly. "Was it as bad as Pa, and everyone else, suspected?"

Charles nodded grimly. "Worse. They were running a private brothel. On top of that, they were producing whiskey illegally and shipping it across state lines."

Joy swallowed hard. "That explains the need for water," she murmured. "Were Vernon and his wife, Jane, arrested?"

This time, Charles shook his head. "No. They weren't there." He hesitated, clearly hating what came next. "And... Judge Lawson said someone freed Thatcher and Nigel."

The world tilted. Joy felt the blood drain from her face as a wave of dizziness swept over her. Charles was at her side in an instant, guiding her to one of the armchairs before she could protest. He pressed a glass of water into her hands and waited, his hand hovering near her shoulder, ready to steady her if she faltered.

When the spinning eased and her breathing returned to normal, she looked up at him and forced a faint smile.

"We knew this might happen," she said quietly. "We knew they wouldn't all be caught." Her voice was steady, but her eyes betrayed the truth. "It's only a matter of time now," she added, meeting his gaze. "Until they find out where I am."

Grace and Reverend Gregory both gasped when Charles shared the contents of the telegram during supper. Grace's hand flew instinctively to her chest, her face paling as she glanced at Joy with open concern.

"Oh, my dear," she whispered. "I had hoped this nightmare was finally over for you."

The reverend remained silent for a long moment, his brow furrowed in thought, his spoon resting forgotten beside his bowl. Then he straightened, resolve settling into his features like armor. When he spoke, his voice was calm, but it carried the quiet authority of a man long accustomed to standing firm in the face of danger.

"Then we will be ready," he said. "And I will make certain the men of this town are ready as well."

Grace turned to him sharply. "You mean—"

"I do," he replied, nodding once. "Elkhorn may be small, but it is not defenseless. These families have lived off this land for generations. They protect their own." He looked at Joy then, his expression gentle but unwavering. "You are not alone here, child. Not tonight. Not ever."

Grace reached across the table and covered Joy's hand with hers, squeezing it firmly.

"Anyone who thinks they can waltz into our town and harm you will be gravely mistaken."

Charles watched the exchange in silence, his chest tight with a mix of relief and concern. He met his grandfather's eyes and gave a slight nod of gratitude. The unspoken promise between them was clear: whatever came next, Elkhorn would not turn its back on Joy Collins. Joy felt something settle deep within her chest, not safety, not yet, but solidarity.

Joy did not sleep well that night. Her mind refused to rest, circling endlessly around what might come. Strangely, her fear was not for herself. It was the thought of someone else being hurt, because of her, that tightened her chest until breathing felt difficult.

Before dawn had fully broken, she gave up on sleep altogether. The sky was only beginning to lighten when she slipped on her boots and stepped outside, the cold morning air biting her cheeks. Perhaps a quiet ride would help steady her nerves. Riding always had a way of grounding her. She hurried toward the barn and reached for the door at the exact same moment someone else did. She collided with a solid chest.

A startled scream tore from her throat. Strong arms caught her instantly, steadying her before she could stumble backward. Joy's breath hitched as she looked up, straight into Charles's face. Her cheeks flamed when she realized he was bare-chested, the early light tracing every line of muscle she had tried very hard not to think about since that morning in Helena. She stepped back at once, mortified and shaken.

"What on earth are you doing here, Charles?" she blurted, her voice trembling. "Were you sleeping in the barn?"

He nodded once, unapologetic. "It was the only way to calm my grandmother. She wouldn't rest knowing you were out here alone."

Joy stared at him, stunned. "You mean... you've been here the entire time?"

"I have."

"Why?" Her eyes flashed. "I asked you to give me space."

"And I did," he shot back, frustration sharpening his tone. "I stayed out of sight. Out of your way. But I wasn't going to let Grandma lose sleep, or leave you unprotected."

She shook her head, emotions rising too fast to contain.

"I can't believe this. Why is everyone so determined to protect me? None of you are related to me. You shouldn't have to worry about what happens to me." Her voice broke. "I should have left. I should have faced this on my own."

Charles stepped closer. "Why are you so determined to shut everyone out, Joy? Is it truly so impossible to believe that people care about you?" His voice softened. "That they... love you?"

"That isn't your responsibility—"

"Stop." His voice cut through her words. "You don't get to decide who is allowed to care. This isn't strength, it's punishment. And you're punishing yourself."

She clenched her fists. "So, I'm wrong for caring that someone else could die because of me?"

"No," he said firmly. "You're wrong for believing it would be your fault."

Silence stretched between them, heavy and unyielding.

"I don't want anything to happen to you, or anyone else," she whispered at last.

"And I don't want anything to happen to you."

"But why?" Her voice cracked. "I'm just a job to you."

His control snapped. "You were never just a job." The words tore free of him. "I stayed because I wanted to. I'm here because I want you safe, because I can't stand the thought of losing you."

"But why?" she whispered again.

"Because I love you."

The words echoed through the barn like a thunderclap. Before she could react, his arms came around her, pulling her firmly against his chest, his breath warm against her cheek as he leaned down. Panic surged.

"No." She shoved against him. "I can't." She twisted free and turned to flee, but his hand caught hers, stopping her short.

"Please," he said quietly. "Just tell me why."

She trembled. "Because this isn't real. It's infatuation. When this is over, you'll leave. You'll go back to Sacramento and find someone else."

"I already have."

Her breath caught. "I don't want to be used," she whispered, tears spilling over. "I don't have the strength for another heartbreak." She tried to pull away again, but this time he held her gently, steady, not forceful, and she broke, sobs shaking her frame.

"Why do you make this so hard?" she cried. "You have choices. Women here would gladly marry you."

"But my heart chose you."

She stiffened, then forced herself to pull back, lifting her chin, her voice turning brittle.

"I don't feel that way."

His gaze searched her face. "Is that truly what your heart says?"

"I don't trust my heart anymore."

Understanding softened his expression. "Someone hurt you."

Her voice barely rose above a whisper. "Yes." She told him then, about Graham, about hope mistaken for love, about silence where honesty should have been. About watching him propose to another woman without a word of explanation. Charles listened without interrupting, his jaw tight with restrained fury. When she finished, he lifted her chin gently.

"I am not him."

"I know," she said softly. "But I don't know how to risk believing again."

"Then let me prove it," he murmured. Before she could protest, his lips met hers, slow, warm, filled with longing rather than urgency. She resisted at first, fear warring with desire, but the kiss was patient, reverent, nothing like the ones that had once confused her. Her resolve crumbled. She melted into him, hands rising to his neck as the world narrowed to the steady beat of his heart beneath her palms.

When he finally pulled back, both of them breathless, her eyes were wide and dazed.

"That wasn't fair," she whispered. A faint smile curved his mouth.

"I've wanted to kiss you for a very long time."

Fear flickered again. "What if this ends like before?"

His hand cupped her cheek. "Then I will still fight for you. But I believe, truly believe, that we were brought together for a reason." His lips brushed hers once more, slower, deeper, and something inside Joy finally surrendered. When she pushed him back gently, it was only to breathe.

"You should probably get dressed," she said weakly. "Someone might see."

His smile turned teasing, and utterly certain.

"Then I suppose I'd better behave." He leaned close once more, his voice low. "But don't think for a moment that I intend to let you face what's coming alone."

Her heart pounded, not with fear this time, but with something dangerously close to hope.

Neither Charles's grandparents nor most of the women in town appeared surprised when word spread that Joy and Charles were now officially courting. A few of the younger women were openly disappointed, their smiles polite but wistful, yet even they accepted the news with quiet resignation. Deep down, many of them had sensed it long before the announcement was made.

Joy, however, struggled at first to trust her happiness. More than once, she asked Charles, sometimes lightly, sometimes with unmistakable anxiety, whether there was someone else somewhere. A former sweetheart. A promised bride. A wife she did not know about. Each time, he answered without irritation, meeting her questions with steady reassurance.

"There has never been anyone else," he told her firmly. "And there will not be. My heart is yours, Joy. Entirely."

Knowing his words were not merely spoken to soothe her, but rooted in quiet, unwavering truth, allowed her heart to rest a little more each day.

Charles continued sleeping in the barn, though now openly and without secrecy. With Joy fully aware of where he was, there was no need for him to slip away before dawn. He rose at a leisurely hour, often joining her for breakfast before heading into town or helping his grandparents. The simple, unhidden normalcy of it all felt like a promise in itself. Yet despite the warmth of new love, Elkhorn remained on edge.

No one had forgotten that danger still lingered beyond the ridges and trees. Men kept a closer watch. Doors were locked earlier. Horses were brought in before nightfall. The illusion of peace was carefully guarded, but never fully trusted.

Grace and Reverend Gregory spent much of their time at the cabin now, ensuring there was never reason for gossip or whispered speculation about the young couple. They were positively radiant with pride, delighted beyond measure that their grandson had finally found someone, and someone who fit so naturally into their lives.

"You were made for each other," Grace declared more than once, her eyes twinkling knowingly. Joy always tried to protest, insisting she was not truly family, but Grace merely waved her off.

"That will change soon enough," she said, as if it were already settled. Autumn deepened quickly, and with it came the unmistakable preparations for winter. The air sharpened. Nights grew longer. Frost crept into the mornings. Charles and his grandfather spent long days chopping and stacking firewood, filling the sheds behind both the cabin and the church until they were brimming. Across Elkhorn, women stocked their cupboards and cellars with dried goods, preserves, and sacks of flour. Winter in the mountains waited for no one.

Grace took it upon herself to teach Joy several new recipes, heartier stews, spiced breads, and meals meant to warm both body and soul. Joy cherished those moments, feeling as though she were reclaiming something she had lost with her mother's passing. Grace insisted she be called Nana now. Joy tried to argue, gently but firmly, but the older woman refused to hear of it.

"You are already family in every way that matters," she said with a satisfied smile.

A telegram finally arrived from Alice, and Joy read it more than once, tears blurring the words. Her sister and nieces were safe. Dylan was a devoted husband and a loving father. The knowledge lifted a weight from Joy's heart she hadn't even realized was still pressing so heavily upon it.

Rain followed in relentless sheets for several days, turning roads to muck and fields into endless stretches of mud. Instead of feeling confined, Joy found herself falling even more deeply in love with the cabin. There was comfort in the steady crackle of the fire, in shared meals, and in quiet conversations with the Gregorys that stretched long into the evening.

When the sun finally returned, drying the land and coaxing life back into the world, Joy eagerly resumed her walks and horseback rides. The mountains called to her, and she answered gladly. Charles took her to a hidden waterfall a few miles into the forest, its clear water tumbling over smooth stone in a constant, soothing rhythm. Standing there, wrapped in his coat against the chill, Joy felt something close to peace.

"There's another place I want to show you," he told her quietly. "A lake high up on the mountain. It's my favorite spot in the world. When the weather allows, I'll take you there."

The promise lingered in her thoughts like a treasured dream. She could have been entirely happy. Yet the knowledge of what still lurked beyond Elkhorn never truly left her. It hovered at the edges of her contentment, a dark cloud she could neither banish nor ignore. Joy knew too well that danger did not always announce itself before striking.

FLAMES OF THE FIRE

And so, even as love took root and hope dared to bloom again, she waited, watchful, wary, knowing that peace, for now, was only borrowed.

***

Joy had always considered washing clothes her least favorite chore. Fortunately, the outdoor stove with its large iron pot made the task a little more bearable. Charles filled the pot with water for her, and she soaked the clothes overnight in a separate tub, hoping to make the work easier the following morning. At first light, she built a fire beneath the pot, added soap and starch, and stirred the garments with steady patience until the water grew cloudy and hot. Once finished, she carried each piece to the trough to rinse it thoroughly in cold water, her fingers numbing as the autumn air crept in. A clothesline stretched from the cabin to the barn allowed her to hang everything neatly, and she worked methodically, enjoying the simple rhythm of the task. That was when she noticed the crow.

The bird landed on the ground not far from her, its glossy black feathers catching the light as it tilted its head and watched her with unnerving intelligence. Joy narrowed her eyes at it, immediately suspicious.

"Don't even think about it," she muttered. As if accepting the challenge, the crow hopped closer, then spread its wings and circled her once, twice, before landing directly on the clothesline. With swift precision, it clasped one of the clothespins in its beak and launched itself into the air, settling on a nearby tree branch. Joy gasped. Without the pin, the heavy skirt sagged and slipped, dropping straight into the dirt below.

"Oh, you wicked creature," Joy scolded, hands on her hips. "Drop that at once!"

The crow merely cocked its head and stared back at her, utterly unrepentant. When it finally released the clothespin, Joy hurried to retrieve it, but before she could rehang the skirt, the bird swooped back in and stole another pin. Again, the fabric slipped loose and fell. By the third fallen garment, Joy had reached the end of her patience.

"That's it. Absolutely not," she declared. She took down every remaining damp piece of clothing and dropped them back into the basket before the crow could claim another victory. With determined efficiency, she removed the clothesline entirely and carried it inside the cabin. The spare bedroom was quickly converted into a drying room, chairs repositioned, lines repurposed, everything safely out of reach of feathered thieves. When she finally stepped back to admire her solution, she folded her arms with satisfaction.

"Outwitted," she said firmly. Outside, the crow cawed once, almost indignantly, before flying off, as if offended by her refusal to continue their peculiar battle. Joy shook her head, a small smile tugging at her lips, and returned to her work, grateful for both a dry cabin and a small victory over nature's most mischievous observer.

26

Betrayal in the Mist

Not long after, Charles and his grandparents arrived to join Joy for breakfast. The moment she realized they were already there, a flicker of embarrassment crossed her face, nothing was prepared yet. She hurried into the kitchen at once, rolling up her sleeves and reaching for pans, determined to make up for it quickly.

Grace, however, noticed the open door to the spare bedroom. The makeshift clothesline stretched across the room, skirts and blouses hanging where bedroom furnishings should have been. She paused, took in the scene, then cleared her throat softly.

"What happened here?" she asked. Joy sighed and shook her head, frustration evident in her expression.

"I tried to hang my freshly washed clothes outside, but a crow kept stealing my clothespins. Three of my skirts fell into the dirt, and now I have to wash them all over again."

Charles grinned and glanced at his grandmother, who returned the look with a knowing wink, but unlike him, she did not laugh. Joy turned toward Charles, irritation flashing in her blue eyes.

"That's not funny, Charles," she scolded. "It's a lot of work, and now I have to do it twice."

Before he could defend himself, or tease her further, Grace stepped forward and wrapped Joy in a warm, maternal embrace.

"It *is* a lot of work," she said gently. "Why don't you go outside and rewash what the crow knocked into the dirt, and I'll prepare breakfast? You've done enough already."

Joy blinked, caught off guard by the kindness. A small, grateful smile spread across her face as she met the older woman's eyes.

"Are you sure?"

"I am," Grace replied firmly, though her lips curved with quiet amusement. Joy hugged her tightly in return, then hurried toward the door.

"Thank you, Nana," she called over her shoulder, already halfway outside.

Charles watched her go, something tender stirring in his chest, before following her, quietly this time, more aware than ever of how much she carried on her shoulders, and how fiercely she tried to do everything on her own.

***

"There is no need for you to follow me just so you can laugh at me some more," Joy said without turning around, though the tight set of her shoulders betrayed her irritation.

"I never laughed," Charles replied easily. "I merely grinned. And who said I followed you to make fun of you?" His voice dipped, playful and dangerous all at once. "Perhaps I simply wanted to steal a kiss."

She stopped short and turned to face him. Color bloomed instantly in her cheeks, though she lifted her chin in mock defiance.

"Is that so?" she countered, matching his tone while doing her best to ignore the warmth spreading through her. "Well then, I say you don't deserve a kiss after your hurtful behavior inside."

Charles nearly laughed aloud. The way she tried to scold him, bright eyes, stubborn posture, cheeks flushed pink, only made her more irresistible. Her words, however, did nothing to deter him. In one smooth motion, he caught her hand and drew her straight into his arms.

"Charles, this is not fair," she protested at once, attempting to pry herself free, though her hands lacked any real conviction.

He was as strong as he looked, and stronger than she had expected. He tightened his hold just enough to still her, then lifted her chin gently, forcing her to meet his gaze. The teasing light in his eyes darkened, replaced by unmistakable desire. Before she could form another protest, his lips claimed hers in a kiss so warm and certain it stole the breath from her lungs. It was unhurried yet deeply passionate, as though he had all the time in the world, and every intention of savoring the moment. When he finally pulled back, it was only by a fraction, his forehead resting against hers, his lips still hovering close enough to tempt her.

"I know you don't mean that," he murmured, his voice rough now. "You love it when I kiss you."

She searched his eyes, fully aware she had no defense against him, or herself. With a soft, breathless laugh, she reached up, fisting her hands in his shirt, and pulled him back down to her lips. This time, she kissed him just as fiercely, melting into his embrace without reservation. There was no denying it anymore. She was completely, hopelessly, and irrevocably in love with him.

One morning, while Joy was getting ready for the day, a knot of unease settled deep in her stomach. It was the kind of feeling she had learned not to ignore, the quiet, insistent warning that something was wrong. Outside, the sky hung low and heavy, rain drifting in and out, casting the world into a dull, oppressive gray.

She had just begun preparing breakfast when the ground itself seemed to shudder. Several loud explosions echoed through the valley, close enough to rattle the windows and send a violent tremor through the cabin. Joy gasped, her heart leaping into her throat. Without thinking, she rushed to the door and flung it open, her pulse pounding as she scanned the surroundings.

Not again. Dark smoke curled upward beyond the trees, thick and ominous, rising from the direction of the post office. Panic surged through her. She gathered her skirts and was about to run toward town when strong arms wrapped around her waist, yanking her back. Charles had just come out of the barn, his expression grim and alert.

"We have to go and help," she cried, her face drained of color. "This isn't a good sign."

"I know," he said firmly, tightening his hold just enough to keep her still. "But if this means what we think it does, you cannot run straight toward it. That's exactly how they'd want to draw you in. You must keep a cool head."

Her hands clenched against his arms.

"But what if someone is injured, or worse?" Her voice trembled despite her effort to stay calm.

"Elkhorn has been on high alert," Charles replied, his gaze fixed on the rising smoke. "Everyone knew something like this might happen. They'll split into groups, some to fight the fire, others to watch the perimeter. If this is a diversion, they'll be ready."

She swallowed hard, torn between fear and the desperate need to help. The rain began to fall again, light but steady, mixing with the smoke in the distance. Joy leaned back against his chest, drawing strength from his presence, even as her heart pounded with the certainty that whatever had just begun would change everything. And this time, there would be no pretending the danger was still far away.

"Figured as much you'd be with her, Gregory," a deep voice sneered. Joy and Charles turned at once. Only a few feet away, still mounted on their horses, sat Thatcher and Nigel Norton. Rain darkened their coats, their postures relaxed in a way that spoke not of ease, but arrogance.

Joy's breath caught when she noticed movement beyond them, several men lingering among the trees and rocks, half-hidden but unmistakably armed. Her heart lurched. They were surrounded.

"Well, not everyone is a criminal and a liar like you, Norton," Charles shot back, his voice steady but deadly calm. His gaze locked onto Thatcher with an intensity that made the air between them feel charged. "I took an oath when I became a lawyer, and I made a promise to Max Collins when he hired me. I happen to keep my promises."

Thatcher's mouth curved into a sneer.

"What do you want, Jonas, *I mean*, Thatcher?" Joy demanded, finding her voice despite the fear clawing at her chest. She leveled him with a withering stare. He scoffed openly.

"You know damn well what we're after."

"I don't," she snapped back, her tone sharp as a blade. "I know you betrayed my father, had him murdered, and now want me dead as well, for reasons you still haven't bothered to explain. But don't expect me to believe it was out of grief for your brothers. Men like you don't mourn. You calculate. Power and money mattered more to you than blood ever did."

Thatcher shook his head slowly, his expression darkening.

"You ain't got the first notion what you're talkin' on."

"I know more than you think," Joy shot back. "John didn't hesitate to betray his own uncle just to remove one more obstacle, one less man to share the stolen gold and money his father hid. That tells me everything I need to know." She narrowed her eyes. "So, tell me, how did you find me?"

Thatcher and Nigel exchanged a vicious grin.

"That part was easy," Thatcher said, smooth as oil. "We knew Gregory wouldn't let you stray far, so we went an' paid his aunt an' uncle a little visit. Funny thing 'bout pain, it loosens tongues somethin' fierce. Folks'll tell you most anything once they're properly encouraged."

Her world tilted.

"No. No!" Joy cried, horror ripping through her. She surged forward, but Charles's arm wrapped firmly around her waist, pulling her back against him.

"Let me go!" she snapped, struggling. "Why aren't you furious? How can you be so calm?"

"Because they're lying," Charles replied evenly, never taking his eyes off the Nortons. "And they know it. You think I'd leave my family unprotected? I arranged for U.S. marshals to guard the house day and night. If either of you had come anywhere near them, you'd already be in chains, or dead."

Joy searched the Nortons' faces. The flicker of rage, the split second of frustration, told her everything. They had been bluffing. Her knees nearly buckled with relief as she let out a shaky breath, leaning into Charles as the truth settled. The danger was still very real, but at least, for now, the people she loved were safe.

"Go into the barn and lock yourself in," Charles murmured urgently, so low only she could hear him. Joy shook her head once.

"No."

"Joy," he warned, his jaw tightening, "do what I'm telling you."

"No, I won't go." She pressed her lips together in defiance. Charles breathed through his teeth, fighting both frustration and fear. Instead of backing down, Joy lifted her chin and fixed Thatcher with a deadly stare.

"So, how did you *really* find me?"

The man standing beside Thatcher scoffed softly.

"You had someone follow us," Joy continued coolly, her mind racing as the pieces fell into place. "You knew the day we left exactly where we were headed. But because you were still in prison, and didn't know how much protection we had, you waited. Then your brother bribed the sheriff's deputy, got you released, and *only then* did you send men after us. Isn't that, right?"

The silence that followed was deafening. Charles didn't need confirmation. Their expressions said everything.

"If all that is true," Joy pressed, fury flaring, "why come after me at all? You could have fled and lived out whatever miserable years you had left in hiding."

"And hide out the rest of our lives?" Thatcher snapped. "Thanks to yer pa, and *you*, handin' them papers over to Judge Lawson, we're wanted damn near everywhere."

"And you think killing me will fix that?" Joy shot back, arching an eyebrow.

"It sends a message," he growled. "Anybody crosses us don't live long enough to regret it."

Joy stared at him in disbelief. How had a man with such a warped mind ever been allowed to practice law? She shook her head slowly.

"You are a fool if you believe that."

Behind her, she heard movement, boots shifting, men spreading out. The unmistakable clicks of guns being readied echoed through the clearing. The men of Elkhorn had arrived. Grateful for the backup, Joy scoffed.

"Perhaps you should have stayed away from your daddy's whiskey. Alcohol does terrible things to already feeble minds."

Thatcher and Nigel stared at her, stunned. A few of the townsmen chuckled. Even Charles had to turn away, coughing to hide his grin. But the moment passed quickly. Their shock hardened into rage. The men who had come with them stepped closer.

"Joy," Charles said sharply, his voice low and dangerous, "go. In the barn. Now."

But she wasn't finished. "I want to know why you murdered my parents," she demanded, her voice cutting through the tension like steel. "You pretended to be their friend for years. What changed?" Her blue eyes burned with icy fire as she locked her gaze onto Thatcher's face.

"Ain't gonna tell ya nothing," he sneered. "You won't be breathin' much longer, and neither will a good many of your friends."

Joy glanced around, the townspeople, Charles, the men who had come to protect her. She closed her eyes for a heartbeat. And then it hit her. The bribery notes. The threats. The tension that had haunted her father in his final months.

"You tried to bribe my father into making you a judge," she said suddenly, her voice ringing clear. "You wanted to bypass the vote because you knew you'd never earn the position honestly."

"That's ridiculous," Thatcher snapped.

"No," Joy fired back, her anger blazing. "Your father wanted you on the bench so the corruption he and his allies started could continue. You were meant to look the other way. To pardon crimes. To punish innocent people instead. And Pa refused."

"How'd you come by that?" Thatcher demanded. "Yer pa was sworn to keep his mouth shut."

"And he did!" Joy shouted. "He never told me. But I saw a letter once on his desk. I didn't read it fully, but I saw enough. You asked him to make you a judge without a vote."

The clearing fell silent. Charles, the townspeople, everyone stared at her.

"If Pa had shared his suspicions sooner," Joy continued, her voice trembling with restrained grief, "maybe he'd still be alive. But he didn't yet have proof." She fixed Thatcher with an unrelenting stare. "Did you threaten Judge Lawson after you killed my father?"

He refused to look at her.

"Did you?" she pressed. "Did you threaten him?" Again and again, she demanded it, until Thatcher snapped.

"Yes!" he roared. "An' we'll kill you, and anybody else dumb enough to stand in our way. Then we'll go after Lawson. An' if he won't bend, we'll find someone who will. This ain't over, not by a long shot."

"You are delusional," Joy shot back. "Evil never wins in the end. It may thrive for a while, but justice always comes." She clenched her fists. "So, I suppose this makes us even? You killed my father, and I made sure yours died too."

She knew she'd crossed a line. She didn't care.

"Sheriff Baker, get Joy!" Charles shouted suddenly. Joy turned, and in that split second, Sheriff Baker grabbed her legs, hoisted her over his shoulder, and ran. Gunfire exploded behind them. He burst into the barn and dropped her into a pile of hay.

"Stay here," he growled. "Lock the door once I'm out."

"Where did you come from?" Joy gasped, stunned. "How are you even here?"

"Later," he said, already backing out. "Lock it." The door slammed shut.

Joy exhaled sharply, then sprang into action. She grabbed her father's revolver from her saddlebags, climbed the stacked hay bales, and eased open the loft window just enough to slip the barrel through. From above, she had a perfect view. She saw Nigel creeping forward, angling himself to take out Charles and Sheriff Baker.

Not happening. The moment he lifted his rifle, Joy fired. The first shot struck his hand. The second hit his shoulder. Nigel screamed and dropped the weapon.

Joy didn't shoot to kill. She shot to protect, to stop evil long enough for justice to catch up.

And she never lowered her aim.

Charles and Dave glanced up toward the loft window. When they spotted her, both men nodded sharply. Even though Dave knew exactly how skilled Joy was with a firearm, moments like this never failed to impress him. Under pressure, with lives on the line, she had not hesitated, and she had not missed.

Joy stayed focused. Nigel was on the ground, cursing loudly and clutching his wounded arm, but she also spotted movement beyond him. Several U.S. marshals were advancing carefully, weapons raised, closing the distance. Relief flickered, but only briefly. This was not over.

Joy slid down the stacked straw bales and hit the barn floor running. Without a second's hesitation, she darted toward the rear door and slipped outside, pulling it closed behind her as quietly as possible. This, at least, she remembered perfectly. Charles had drilled it into her repeatedly: *Never stay where they expect you to be. Make them waste time looking in the wrong place.*

Vernon and Jane were still out there somewhere. She could feel it. They were the kind who preferred shadows, who waited until others did the dirty work before striking. Joy moved low and fast, angling away from the barn and toward the trees. Her heart thundered in her chest, but her steps were measured, controlled. Panic would get her killed. Her destination was clear. The waterfall. Charles had shown it to her weeks ago, pointing out the narrow ledge and the natural hollow carved into the rock behind the rushing water. From the outside, it looked like solid stone but tucked behind the curtain of falling water was a shallow recess, deep enough to hide, deep enough to vanish.

She followed the path through thick brush and tangled shrubbery, using every tree and rise in the ground as cover. The forest here was dense, alive with shadows and movement. It was easy to disappear, but just as easy for danger to creep up unnoticed. Joy paused more than once, crouching behind a tree, listening. Shouts and distant gunfire echoed faintly behind her, muffled by the trees and the growing roar of water ahead. The last stretch was the most dangerous. The trees thinned, opening into a narrow clearing that led directly to the waterfall. There would be nowhere to hide for those final yards.

Joy hated not knowing what was happening to Charles and the others. Every instinct in her screamed to return, to stand her ground beside them, to fight this through together. But instinct was not the same as wisdom. She knew, without a shred of doubt, that the Nortons were after her. She was the prize they wanted, the leverage they believed would give them power, revenge, or both. And as long as she remained anywhere near the men protecting her, she made them targets as well. That, she could not allow.

The more people in town became aware of the Nortons' presence, the faster word would spread. Elkhorn might be small, but its people were fiercely loyal and quick to act. It would only take a few raised voices, a whiff of smoke, or a single frightened messenger before telegrams were sent racing down the line, calling for reinforcements, if that had not already happened.

Joy pressed deeper into the cover of the bushes, forcing herself to think several steps ahead. The Nortons thrived in chaos, in confusion and fear, but they were also careful. They would not linger once the odds turned against them. Which meant time mattered. If she could stay hidden long enough, if she could draw them away from the town and the men standing their ground, the balance would shift. Every moment she remained unseen increased the chance that help would arrive, that the Nortons' escape routes would close. Leaving Charles behind, tore at her heart, but protecting him, and everyone else, mattered more.

And so, Joy stayed silent, hidden, and resolute, waiting for the moment when the hunters would realize, the hunted had slipped beyond their reach.

The forest lay unnaturally still. Only the occasional drip of rain broke the silence, falling from leaf to leaf before disappearing into the moss-covered ground. The thick carpet beneath Joy's boots swallowed every sound of her steps and spared her from the sucking pull of mud, a small mercy in a moment that demanded every advantage she could claim. Each time a branch creaked, or a bird stirred, she froze, listening intently. Her heart hammered in her chest as she strained to identify the sound. The last thing she needed was to stumble, literally or figuratively, into Lydia's parents or any of the Norton men by sheer misfortune.

She kept the waterfall in view, mist rising where the water thundered against the rocks below. Joy drew in a steadying breath and prepared to cross the exposed stretch of ground leading toward it when voices carried through the trees. Her blood ran cold. She dropped instinctively, peering through the brush just in time to see several horses emerging from the forest path. She couldn't see the riders clearly, but she didn't need to. Whoever they were, they were close, far too close. There was no time to run.

Panic clawed at her as she scanned her surroundings, searching for anything that might conceal her. The underbrush was thin here, offering little protection if someone bothered to look closely. Then she saw it. A hollow tree trunk, weathered and split by time, stood a few paces away, wide enough to hide her completely, tall enough to shield her from sight. Without hesitating, Joy darted toward it and climbed inside, her breath shallow but controlled. She grabbed a thick clump of moss from the ground and carefully positioned it over the opening above her head, disguising her hiding place, just as the horses came to a stop only yards away.

Her pulse thundered in her ears. Through small cracks and knotholes in the trunk, she could see everything. More horses arrived, their riders dismounting. And then recognition struck like a blow. Brigham Harrison. Graham. Matt. A moment later, two more horses pulled alongside them.

Charles. And Sheriff Dave Baker.

Joy's chest tightened. Relief and confusion warred within her as she listened, every word carrying clearly in the damp, hushed air. She almost called out to them, and almost revealed herself, when Brigham spoke again. And what he said shattered her completely. The forest seemed to tilt, the ground beneath her vanish, as her world collapsed... once more.

"Charles, good to see you again."

Relief flickered across Charles's face at Brigham's voice, though it was tempered by the strain lining his features.

"Were you able to find them?"

Brigham shook his head grimly. "No. We ran into a few U.S. marshals while searching the woods, but they hadn't come across anyone either. No sign of the Nortons."

Charles exhaled slowly, his gaze sweeping the trees, the rocks, the mist drifting from the waterfall.

"Did you see Joy?" he asked, tension threading every word.

"Not yet," Brigham replied. "Where is she supposed to be?"

"She was meant to run for the waterfall and hide there," Charles explained, his eyes never still. "It was the safest place for her, at least until now. This stretch here is exposed. If she crosses it, she'll need to be careful."

Matt shifted uneasily. "Shouldn't we go look for her?"

Charles shook his head at once. "No. If we start calling out or combing the area too openly, we'll only draw attention to her. That could get her killed." He paused, thinking quickly, then gestured toward a narrow trail beyond the waterfall. "Let's split up. Matt, Graham, check that area over there. We'll circle this side and look for any sign of the Nortons."

The two young men nodded and moved off without another word, their figures quickly swallowed by the trees. Charles turned to go, but Brigham's hand closed around his arm, stopping him.

"Have you told Joy yet," Brigham asked quietly, "who you really are?"

Charles stiffened, then shook his head.

"Not yet. I need to know she's safe, truly safe, before I tell her anything."

Brigham studied him for a long moment, worry and something sharper in his eyes. Then he nodded slowly.

"Just don't wait too long, son. Graham already broke her heart. She doesn't need to hear the truth from someone else, and she certainly doesn't need to feel betrayed again."

Charles swallowed and met Brigham's gaze.

"I won't let that happen," he said firmly. "I'll tell her, as soon as it's safe to do so, Dad."

Unseen and hidden only yards away, Joy heard every word. And in that instant, the fragile ground beneath her gave way entirely.

Joy felt as though a knife had been driven straight into her stomach. Her breath caught painfully in her chest, and she clamped a hand over her mouth to keep from gasping aloud. The air felt too thin, her lungs refusing to cooperate as tears surged into her eyes. She folded in on herself, pressing her face into her palms, muffling the sobs that threatened to tear free.

Her heart shattered. Charles was Graham's brother. The son of Brigham and Darlene. The realization crashed over her in brutal waves, leaving her dizzy and unsteady.

Why had he used the name Gregory? Were Reverend Gregory and Grace truly his grandparents? Had everything she thought was safe, every smile, every promise, every tender word, been built on a lie? Her chest tightened until it hurt. Had he used her too? Had his concern, his devotion, his confessions of love all been carefully chosen words meant to earn her trust? To keep her compliant? To keep her close?

Joy shook her head slowly, silently, as if refusing to accept what her mind was assembling piece by piece. She should have listened to her instincts. She should have trusted her reason instead of surrendering her heart, again. A sharp, helpless pressure built behind her eyes, and for a moment she wanted nothing more than to scream. To release the hurt, the betrayal, the suffocating weight settling deep in her stomach.

Charles had lied to her. He had pretended to be someone else, someone unconnected to the Harrisons, someone safe, someone impartial. Someone who had no reason to deceive her. And her father... How had Pa known about him? How had Max Collins discovered who Charles truly was, and why had he trusted him enough to bring him into their lives? Shame and disbelief warred within her as another realization struck.

How had she not seen it? The resemblance was suddenly unmistakable, the build, the eyes, the set of his jaw. It was all there now, glaringly obvious. But before... before, she had never once imagined they could be related. Her mind had simply refused to go there. Each unanswered question made her feel as though she were splintering apart, her thoughts spiraling faster, darker.

No. This was not the time.

Joy forced herself to breathe slowly, deliberately, pressing her spine against the rough wood of the hollow tree. She wiped at her tears with shaking fingers and clenched her jaw, steadying herself. She could unravel later. Right now, she had to survive. Whatever the truth about Charles, whatever his reasons, his secrets, his intentions, she could not afford to let heartbreak cloud her judgment. The danger was real, immediate, and unforgiving. She swallowed hard, lifted her head, and focused on the present. She would deal with the betrayal, *if that was what it was*, once she was out of this alive.

27

Every Word She Heard

The forest had gone eerily quiet again. Joy waited for several heartbeats, forcing herself to listen, to the rain dripping from the leaves to the rush of the waterfall, before carefully climbing out of the hollow trunk. She crouched low and parted the bushes in front of her, peering through the narrow opening to see if the men were still nearby.

That was when it happened. A hand clamped over her mouth from behind, cutting off her scream before it could form. An arm locked around her middle, crushing the air from her lungs, and she was dragged backward through the brush, her boots scraping uselessly against the mossy ground. Everything happened too fast, too suddenly, for her to fight properly or even think. She was hauled forward and then shoved hard.

When the grip released, she stumbled and barely caught herself before falling. As she looked up, her blood ran cold. Vernon Norton stood before her. His face twisted with rage. Jane was beside him, her eyes blazing with triumph.

"Did you honestly reckon you'd get away with this?" Vernon snarled, shoving Joy violently to the ground. Joy rolled with the fall and sprang back to her feet, her heart pounding but her chin lifted defiantly.

"Get away with what?" she shot back. "Trying to stay alive? I wasn't the one practicing medicine without a license, or stealing and selling babies."

His lips curled in a cruel scoff. "You ain't gonna be breathin' much longer," he sneered. "An' them precious protectors o' yours won't save you this time. Woods are thick with men workin' for us. They'll either put 'em in the dirt or keep 'em tied up till we're done with you."

"Wonderful," Joy snapped, forcing steel into her voice despite the fear clawing at her spine. "Are you actually going to kill me this time, or is this just more empty threats?"

"You arrogant little hellcat," Jane hissed, lunging for her. Joy moved fast, stepping out of reach. Jane's fingers swiped through empty air. "First you go an' steal Lydia's husband," Jane went on, venom dripping from every word, "then you see to it she's tossed straight into prison."

Joy let out a sharp, humorless laugh.

"I didn't steal anyone's husband. And if you're still pretending your daughter is a victim, it's beyond pathetic. She was warned not to return to Deer Lodge. She ignored the judge and paid the price. Maybe you should be more upset that your husband let her walk straight into her own ruin while he was busy burning down my uncle's house."

Vernon's face darkened. "How in blazes did you live through it? Why are Gerald an' Eliza still breathin'?"

"Because I wasn't fighting you alone," Joy replied coolly. "And because good people finally decided they'd had enough of your family."

Jane's lips twisted cruelly. "Heard tell Graham didn't pick you after all," she drawled. "Bet that smarted. What goes 'round comes 'round, sweetheart. You toyed with him while he was still married, an' the minute he was free, he cast you aside like yesterday's trash."

Joy's pulse stumbled for just a fraction of a second. Her thoughts flickered, briefly, painfully, to Charles. The hurt there cut deeper than Graham ever had. But she refused to let them see it.

"So, it seems," she said lightly, her voice steady. Then her eyes hardened. "At least I was only dismissed by a man I thought might court me. Lydia managed to lose two husbands in record time. If she wants another one, she'll have to find him in prison."

Jane screamed in fury and charged again. This time, Joy was ready. She caught Jane around the waist and, using the woman's own momentum, shoved her hard, into the pool at the base of the waterfall. Jane surfaced sputtering, shrieking curses as icy water soaked her clothes and hair. Vernon lunged next. Joy dodged at the last possible moment. His foot slipped on the wet rock, and he went down with a splash, disappearing into the cold water beside his wife.

Joy didn't hesitate. She ran. The Nortons' horses stood tied nearby, restless and snorting. She reached one and grabbed the reins, just about to swing herself into the saddle, when something yanked her backward. She barely had time to gasp before a cloth was pressed firmly over her mouth and nose. A sharp, bitter scent filled her lungs. She struggled, clawing at the arm around her chest, kicking wildly, but her strength drained away with terrifying speed. The forest tilted. The roar of the waterfall faded. And then everything went black.

He caught her before she could slump to the ground, lifting her easily and keeping the cloth pressed firmly over her face as he turned toward his horse. Joy was completely limp now, her body unresponsive. Vernon and Jane, soaked and furious, scrambled out of the water and hurried after him.

"I thought she wasn't meant to leave this place alive," Vernon said sharply, confusion creasing his brow. The man didn't slow.

"Yeah, well, I just went an' changed my mind." He shifted his hold on Joy, making sure she couldn't slip free. "Figure I'll see what kind of ransom she fetches instead. Folks protectin' her strike me as the sort who'd pay real handsomely."

Vernon stopped short. "And just how do you aim to split it?"

The man laughed, cold, humorless. "Split what?"

"The ransom, what else?" Irritation flashed across Vernon's face. The man turned then, his eyes hard.

"Ain't got nothin' to do with you no more."

Jane stiffened. "What d'you mean by that? We're in this together."

"That's where you got it wrong," he said easily. "I was never in this with nobody. You helpin' me was convenient, but there was never any partnership."

Vernon stared at him in disbelief.

"You're lyin'. We did what Pa wanted. Thatcher took up law. We tried greasin' Collins so we could take over—"

"I never meant this to be a family business," the man cut in, flat as stone. "Now get out."

"You ain't gettin' away with this," Vernon shot back. "Nor with the girl!"

He roared and lunged for Joy. He never reached her. An elbow slammed into his face with brutal force, sending him sprawling backward onto the wet ground. Jane screamed in fury and spun toward her horse, reaching for the revolver tied to the saddle. A shot rang out before her fingers closed around it.

Jane cried out and collapsed, struck squarely in the back. Vernon barely had time to gasp before two more shots tore into his stomach, dropping him beside her. They writhed and screamed in agony behind him. He didn't look back. With practiced ease, he swung into the saddle, Joy still cradled in his arms, her head lolling against his chest. The horse surged forward, hooves pounding into the forest floor as he rode away. Behind him, the Nortons' cries echoed through the trees. Ahead of him lay the certainty that, at last, he alone held the prize.

Not long after, Charles and the others returned to the waterfall, several U.S. marshals spreading out behind them. They searched the area thoroughly, calling Joy's name again and again, their voices echoing off stone and rushing water. There was no answer. Instead, they found Vernon and Jane sprawled on the ground near the edge of the lake, soaked, unconscious, and bleeding heavily.

One of the men from town crouched beside them and grimaced.

"We don't have a doctor in Elkhorn. Just a small infirmary and a nurse."

Dave ran a hand through his hair. Worry etched deep into his face.

"Helena has a hospital, and Deer Lodge has a doctor, but it'll take hours for either to reach us."

Charles knelt beside the wounded pair, his jaw tight as he checked their pulses.

"We can't leave them here. Get them back to town. We'll stabilize them as best we can until a doctor arrives."

The marshals nodded immediately. A few of the men secured Vernon and Jane carefully to their horses, binding their wounds as well as circumstances allowed before mounting up. The small procession turned back toward Elkhorn at once, urgency pressing every step. Charles straightened, his eyes scanning the forest again. Joy was gone.

"I'll go with them," Graham said suddenly, his voice tight. "I'll make sure Julia gets on the next stagecoach out of town. If things are escalating like this, she shouldn't stay."

Charles studied him for a long moment, then nodded.

"Do it."

As the riders disappeared down the trail, Charles remained by the waterfall, his fists clenched at his sides, dread coiling in his chest. Joy hadn't been here when they arrived. And that meant only one thing... someone had taken her.

"What are we going to do? Where is Joy?" Charles called her name again, his voice breaking the stillness of the forest, but there was no answer, only the constant rush of the waterfall behind them. One of the marshals suddenly crouched, brushing damp leaves aside and studying the churned earth.

"There was a third horse here," he said grimly, pointing to a fresh set of hoofprints pressed deep into the mud. "And it headed off in that direction."

Charles's chest tightened. "Then she was taken."

Matt ran a hand through his hair, disbelief written across his face.

"Why would anyone kidnap her? This doesn't make sense. If they wanted her dead, they had their chance."

"That's exactly why," Charles replied, dread sharpening his voice. "She's more valuable alive. There are several hunting cabins scattered through these woods. Whoever took her likely knows the terrain and is heading for shelter, somewhere they can hide and wait."

Brigham swore under his breath.

"Then we don't have a moment to lose."

One of the deputy marshals straightened and looked at his superior.

"We should split up. Cover more ground. Cut off possible escape routes."

The marshal nodded without hesitation.

"Two groups. Stay within hearing distance if possible. If anyone finds her, or the kidnapper, signal immediately."

Charles mounted at once, urgency burning in his eyes. He, Brigham, and four of the marshals followed the trail of hoofprints deeper into the forest, weaving through trees slick with rain and moss. Every broken branch, every disturbed patch of earth felt like a ticking clock.

Dave, Matt, and the remaining marshals veered onto a parallel path slightly to the left, scanning the terrain for signs of movement, abandoned camps, or smoke. No one spoke as they rode. Every man there understood the same terrible truth. Every minute they lost put Joy further out of reach.

Joy came to with a jolt as her body was dropped onto something hard. The impact rattled her bones and sent a sharp pain through her back. For a moment, everything swam, shadows and shapes blending together, until the blur slowly sharpened. An old cabin bed. Its sagging wooden frame creaked and shuddered beneath her as she shifted, the thin mattress offering little comfort. The air smelled of damp wood, smoke, and something sour. Before she could sit up, rough hands seized her arms and yanked her upright.

Joy gasped and fought instinctively, clawing and kicking, panic roaring through her veins. He didn't flinch. Instead, he shoved her hard against the wall. The breath was knocked from her lungs, stars bursting behind her eyes. For a terrifying second, she thought she might lose consciousness again. Then she looked at him. Her heart lurched violently. No. It couldn't be.

"You—" Her voice trembled, disbelief cutting through the fear. "You're dead. I saw your body. You died in the fire."

A slow, cruel smile spread across his face.

"I let you believe that, Joy."

The world tilted. "That's not possible."

"I was never in the house when it burned," he said coolly. "We used someone else. A poor fool who'd already made a fatal mistake. It was convenient."

Her shock hardened instantly into fury. "So, you ran. You escaped and hid like a coward, while your family nearly burned and paid the price for your crimes?"

He scoffed, unimpressed. "Don't pretend you care about them."

"Does your mother know you're alive?" she shot back. "Or your brother?"

His expression darkened. "Of course not. They'd have turned me in the moment it suited them."

Joy shook her head, disgust curling in her stomach. She struggled against him again, but he only pressed closer, his body pinning hers with deliberate force.

"You know," he said, his voice lowering, oily and unsettling, "I always wanted you. If you hadn't been such a devoted little daddy's girl, I would've made sure you became my wife instead of your sister. I do love a woman with fire."

The look she gave him was pure contempt.

"I would have never married you. And my sister regretted every second she did. At least she's safe now."

His grin widened, sharp and dangerous.

"Alice is still my wife. And once I find her, she'll be mine again."

"She will never be yours," Joy snapped. "Her husband will lock you up, or kill you, if you so much as touch her."

The grin vanished. His hand clamped around her waist while the other shot up, fingers digging into her throat, forcing her chin up. His grip tightened until panic flared white-hot.

"It doesn't matter," he hissed. "I have you now. Once I recover the gold and money my father hid on your father's land, we'll disappear. Somewhere quiet. Somewhere no one will ever find us. You'll be my little captive while I squeeze your precious attorney and friends for every dollar they're worth." He leaned in, breath hot against her face, trying to force a kiss.

Joy reacted without thinking. Her knee drove up hard into his leg. He cursed, staggering back a step. She sucked in a desperate breath, pain flaring in her throat.

"Nothing will go the way you think it will," she said hoarsely. "You won't find the gold. It's gone."

His eyes narrowed. "Gone?"

"I had Judge Lawson recover it and return it to the banks," she said, defiance blazing. "Then I sold the land. His son bought it. They're building a school there now."

Rage exploded across his face. "You had no right—"

"I had every right," she cut in fiercely. "I'm of age."

The last thread of control snapped. His hands closed around her throat again, harder this time. Joy clawed at his wrists, air vanishing, her vision dimming at the edges. Her heartbeat thundered in her ears.

Think. Move. His fury made him careless. With trembling fingers, she reached into her pocket, wrapped her hand around the small revolver hidden there, and pulled the trigger without even drawing it free. The shot exploded through the fabric. He screamed. The force sent him stumbling backward, his hands flying to his abdomen as blood bloomed dark and fast. He collapsed against the far wall, wailing in agony.

Joy tore herself away, staggering back, dragging in shallow, painful breaths. Her lungs burned, each gasp a battle. She put as much distance between them as she could, her legs shaking violently. The room spun. She lurched for the door and burst onto the front porch, gulping air, clutching her throat. Her vision blurred, tunneled. Somewhere in the distance, hooves. Horses. She tried to call out. No sound came. Her knees buckled. She reached for the wooden beam beside the porch, fingers scraping empty air. The world tilted sharply. And then everything went black.

When Joy opened her eyes, she had no idea where she was, or how she had gotten there. For a moment, she lay still, staring up at the familiar ceiling beams, her mind foggy and slow. Then recognition crept in. Her room. Her bed. The soft quilt pulled up around her shoulders. Grace sat nearby in a chair, her head tilted slightly to one side, hands folded in her lap. She was asleep.

Joy didn't move. Memory crashed over her all at once, sharp and merciless, stealing the air from her lungs. The cabin. The struggle. John, alive. The gunshot. The porch. The darkness. Her heart began to race. How long had she been unconscious? Where was John now? Where were the Nortons? Had they escaped? Had anyone else been hurt? And if they *had* escaped, why was she still alive?

Her gaze drifted back to Grace, and something in her chest tightened painfully. The older woman looked worn with worry, dark circles beneath her eyes, her expression still protective even in sleep. Joy swallowed hard. Then the other truth rose up, heavy, bitter, impossible to ignore. Charles had lied to her. Not just him. Everyone had. The Harrison family. Darlene. Brigham. Even Grace and the reverend, people she had trusted, people she had come to love. No one had told her who Charles really was. No one had given her the chance to decide for herself.

Her throat closed. Slowly, carefully, she turned onto her side and buried her face in the pillow, pressing it tight to muffle the sound that broke free. She tried to be quiet, tried to hold it back. She couldn't. The sobs tore from her chest, raw and aching, shaking her entire body. She felt hands moving around her, heard the scrape of a chair, murmured voices entering the room, but she didn't lift her head.

"Joy," Grace said softly, her hand warm and gentle on Joy's shoulder. "Are you in pain, dear?"

Joy shook her head, her face still hidden.

"Is something troubling you?" Grace asked, her voice full of concern. Joy nodded once. Then she felt another presence, closer, familiar. A hand at her waist, careful, tentative, trying to turn her toward him. She didn't need to look. The moment his touch registered, something inside her snapped. She shoved his hand away with more strength than she thought she had.

"Leave me alone," she choked out. "Get out of this room."

"Joy," Charles said quietly, his voice low and earnest. "Please, look at me."

The sound of him hurt more than any wound she carried.

"No," she said fiercely. "Just leave. I don't want to see you anymore."

"Why?" he asked, pain seeping into his tone. "What have I done?"

She rolled onto her back then, finally facing him, her eyes red and burning with betrayal.

"You lied to me. You all did. Your entire family."

Silence fell, heavy and suffocating.

"You're just like Graham," she went on, her voice trembling despite her effort to keep it steady. "You let me believe something that wasn't true. You let me trust you. Please, just go. I can't take this anymore."

Her words landed like blows. Grace looked between them, confusion and worry etched across her face, but Joy couldn't bring herself to explain. Not now. Not when everything inside her felt shattered. All she could do was close her eyes again, turn her face away, and hope, futilely, that the ache would stop hurting so much.

Graham, standing behind his father and beside Dave, looked utterly taken aback. The accusation had clearly struck him harder than he had expected, and for a moment he seemed at a loss for words.

Charles met his father's gaze, then looked to his grandmother. Grace didn't say a word. She merely tilted her head toward the door, her eyes firm and unmistakably clear in their request. Everyone understood. Reluctantly, Brigham motioned for Graham and Dave to follow him. Charles hesitated, his eyes flicking once more to the bed, to Joy's turned back, before he finally stepped away. Dave closed ranks with the others, his expression tight with concern. One by one, they filed out of the room, the weight of the moment heavy on their shoulders.

Grace sat down on the edge of the bed and gently began stroking Joy's hair, her touch slow and soothing. She didn't rush her, didn't ask questions. She simply stayed, a quiet presence, until the sobs gradually eased and Joy's breathing finally steadied. When Joy looked up, her eyes were red and swollen but searching. Grace patted her cheek tenderly and offered a warm, patient smile.

"Why don't you tell Nana what happened," she said softly, her voice the same gentle tone one might use with a frightened child. Joy swallowed.

"Were you lying to me too?" Her voice trembled despite her effort to steady it. "Did you hold back the truth?"

Grace's brow creased with concern.

"What should I have lied about, my dear?"

The question broke something loose. Joy took a shaky breath and began to speak, about Graham, about the kisses that had meant more to her than they ever had to him, about the quiet abandonment once his divorce was final. She told her how she had tried to make sense of it, how she had blamed herself for believing in something that had never been promised.

Then she spoke of Charles. Of the trust she had given him. Of the way her heart had opened again, only to discover that he was Brigham's son, Graham's brother, part of a family who had known the truth all along. When she finished, tears slid down her cheeks once more, and she turned away, burying her face in the pillow as if she could hide from the ache inside her chest.

"Oh, my dear child," Grace murmured. She clasped Joy's hand and gently pulled her into her arms, holding her with the quiet strength of someone who had weathered many storms. She rocked her slightly, one hand smoothing Joy's hair.

"I had no idea," Grace said softly. "None at all. And I am truly sorry that you were hurt like this. Graham... he has always been impulsive. He follows his feelings without thinking through the consequences, especially when it comes to women. That does not excuse what he did to you. Not in the slightest."

Joy didn't respond, but her grip tightened on Grace's sleeve.

"As for Charles," Grace continued, her voice thoughtful now, "I honestly don't know why he didn't tell you who he was. I wish I did."

Joy pulled back just enough to look at her, pain flashing in her eyes.

"Then why was he using your last name, if not to hide the truth from me?"

Grace sighed and shook her head slowly.

"My guess would be that it had something to do with his work as an attorney. He's always been careful, sometimes too careful. But I can't say for certain." She brushed a tear from Joy's cheek. "Why don't you ask him, sweetheart? Let him explain himself."

Joy shook her head immediately, her jaw tightening.

"No. I won't talk to him again."

Grace's heart sank at the finality in her voice.

"His betrayal hurts more than what Graham did to me," Joy whispered. "Because I trusted him. I let myself believe again. And I promised myself I would never do that twice."

Grace studied the young woman's face and saw it at once, the fierce, unyielding stubbornness set behind the tears. Joy's hurt had hardened into something defensive, almost protective. Grace knew that Charles would eventually have to make her listen if there was ever to be any true closure between them. But not now. Right now, Joy's wounds were far too raw. She softened her expression and brushed a thumb gently across Joy's knuckles.

"Why don't you rest now, sweet girl? It's been a long and dreadful morning for you."

Joy nodded faintly, then frowned.

"What happened to me? Were the Nortons arrested, or did they get away?"

Grace exhaled slowly and chose her words with care.

"From what the boys told me, a man kidnapped you and took you to a cabin in the woods. They followed the hoofprints and heard a gunshot as they were getting close. As you can imagine, it terrified them, they thought he had shot you." She paused, squeezing Joy's hand. "But then they realized it was *you* who fired the shot. You must have injured him and freed yourself. You made it to the front porch before you collapsed.

Charles reached you just in time and caught you before you hit the ground."

Joy swallowed hard.

"A few of the men from Elkhorn had already taken Vernon and his wife back to town," Grace continued. "It appears the man who took you turned on them and shot them. They're still unconscious and being watched closely. A doctor has been sent for from Deer Lodge."

"Will they survive?" Joy asked quietly.

Grace shook her head. "No one knows yet. The nurse did what she could, but it depends on whether they hold on until the physician arrives."

Joy drew a careful breath. "What about my kidnapper?"

"The marshals tried to subdue him, but he fought back. He injured two of them before he was shot and killed."

Joy lifted her head sharply, searching Grace's eyes.

"So... he's dead? Truly dead? He won't come back a second time?"

Grace blinked, startled. "What do you mean, dear?"

Joy's voice wavered. "John faked his death before. He was my sister's husband. We all believed he died in the house fire months ago. Seeing him alive again..." She swallowed. "It was a terrible shock."

"Oh my," Grace whispered, her hand flying to her chest. "That must have been dreadful."

Joy nodded. "I don't intend to tell my sister. John abused her. If he really is gone for good, there's no reason to reopen wounds she's finally begun to heal."

Grace nodded slowly, respect and sorrow mingling in her expression.

"You're protecting her," she said gently. "That speaks volumes about the kind of woman you are." She rose carefully from the bed. "Would you like some lunch? I can fix something. I doubt you've eaten, everything happened before we ever sat down."

Joy shook her head. "Thank you, but I just want to rest." After a moment she added, almost wistfully, "When I'm better, I'd like to explore some more. I heard about a beautiful lake and waterfall up on the mountain. Is it difficult to reach?"

Grace smiled faintly. "If you mean Crow Creek Falls, it isn't difficult, if you know where to go. You follow the trail to the small waterfall first. From there, you take the forest path and keep walking until you hear rushing water. You can't see the falls from the path, but you'll hear them. There's also a cabin by the lake."

"That sounds wonderful," Joy murmured.

"It truly is one of the most beautiful places around Elkhorn," Grace said warmly. "Well worth the walk." She hesitated. "Are you quite sure you don't want anything to eat?"

Joy nodded again. "I'm sure. Thank you, Nana."

Grace squeezed her hand gently, then left the room, closing the door quietly behind her, leaving Joy to rest, and to gather the strength she would need for what still lay ahead.

As soon as Grace stepped into the sitting room, Charles was at her side. The other men looked up from their chairs at once, sensing the tension written across his face.

"Why does Joy think I lied to her?" he demanded quietly. "Why does she believe our entire family deceived her?"

Grace sighed, the weight of it heavy on her shoulders.

"She was hiding in a hollow tree trunk near the waterfall," she explained gently. "When you men stopped not far from her, your father asked whether you had told her yet. She heard everything, Charles. Every word."

Color drained from his face. "I need to speak to her, now," he said, already turning toward the hallway. Grace caught his arm.

"No. You don't."

He spun back to her, frustration flashing in his eyes.

"Nana—"

"Give her time to cool off," she said firmly. "She's deeply hurt and utterly exhausted. If you confront her now, she won't hear a single word you say."

"I'll make her listen," he muttered through gritted teeth. "She's as stubborn as a mule."

Grace couldn't suppress her smile.

"That she is. And yes, you will have to force her into a conversation eventually, but not right now. Let her think. Let her rest. Give her the chance to see that there was a reason you kept your name from her." She paused, then added softly, "She's reacting so strongly because Graham hurt her first."

"I didn't mean to hurt her," Graham protested from across the room, bristling. Grace turned her gaze at him, calm but unyielding.

"I know you didn't. But you can't deny that beautiful women have always been your weakness. And tell me, have you ever truly spoken to Joy about what happened between the two of you?"

Graham looked away, muttering something under his breath. Charles dragged a hand through his hair.

"What if she won't give me another chance? She moved on from Graham once she realized it wasn't love on either side."

Grace reached up and cupped his cheek, her touch warm and steady.

"If she loves you, she won't stay angry forever. And she does love you."

He looked at her helplessly. "How can you be so sure?"

"Because of how she lashed out," Grace replied gently. "From what I can tell, she never confronted Graham about how deeply he hurt her. She made her peace alone and moved on. But with you, she spoke. She demanded answers. She asked you to leave." She smiled sadly. "That tells me her feelings are raw and unguarded. You and Joy weren't guessing at each other, you were officially courting. She trusted you completely, Charles. And that trust feels shattered right now."

He exhaled shakily. "I should have listened to you, Dad. I should have told her from the beginning who I was."

Brigham shook his head. "You did what you believed was right, for your work, and for her safety. I'm not convinced you could have stayed close to her if Thatcher had known who you truly were."

Grace nodded. "Give her time, Charles. Then talk to her, honestly and fully. If the two of you are meant for each other, nothing, not even this, will destroy that." She gave him an encouraging smile, then turned and headed into the kitchen to prepare lunch, leaving Charles standing there with the weight of her words, and his own fragile hope, settling heavily on his heart.

Joy waited until the house grew quiet again before she moved. Her heart still ached, raw and unsettled, and she knew with painful certainty that it was only a matter of time before Charles would try to speak to her. She wasn't ready. Not for his explanations, not for his eyes, not for the way her heart would betray her all over again.

She rose slowly, dressed in warm layers, and pulled on her coat. Each movement felt deliberate, as though she were bracing herself for something final. She paused at the door, listening, then turned instead toward the window. Carefully, she eased it open and climbed out, landing softly on the ground below. The chill air bit her cheeks, sharpening her resolve.

Without looking back at the house, she hurried toward the barn, keeping to the shadows. She stopped at the door and peered inside, her breath held. The barn was empty. Relief washed over her. Brigham had brought her horse, she saw it at once, and gratitude flickered through her chest. She went to the animal, stroking its neck and murmuring softly, as if confiding a secret. The familiar presence steadied her shaking hands. She saddled the horse quickly but carefully, added a folded blanket, and tucked what little she needed into her saddlebags.

When everything was ready, she led the horse out of the barn without a sound. Only once the buildings were hidden by trees did she swing into the saddle. Joy took one last breath and turned her horse toward the forest path. Crow Creek Falls awaited, and for now, it was the only place where she could think clearly, away from heartbreak, explanations, and the man she loved but could no longer trust.

28

A Love That Waits

Dave Baker rose from his chair and gave Matt a meaningful nod, urging him to do the same.

"We'd better get back in the saddle if we want to make it to Deer Lodge before it's fully dark," he said, pulling his pocket watch from his vest. He studied the face for a moment, then sighed. "Joy's been sleeping for over two hours now. I'd hoped to say goodbye, but I reckon that won't be happening." He rolled his eyes with mild disappointment, and the two men headed for the door to fetch their horses from the barn.

"Perhaps I should check on Joy," Grace said thoughtfully, already half-rising from her chair.

Before she could take more than a step, Sheriff Baker reappeared in the doorway, his expression anything but lighthearted.

"Did you forget something?" Brigham teased. Dave shook his head slowly.

"Joy's horse is gone. Is she still in her room?"

Charles was on his feet before the sentence was finished. He crossed the room in long strides and burst into the

467

bedroom without knocking. One glance was all it took. The window stood open.

A low curse left his lips.

"I am going to kill her," he muttered, raking a hand through his hair. "Why does she keep running away?" He turned back toward the others, agitation and worry warring in his eyes.

"Does anyone have the slightest idea where she might have gone? She didn't head back to Deer Lodge on her own, did she?"

Murmured guesses filled the room. Then Grace gasped softly.

"She asked me earlier how to get to Crow Creek Falls," she said. "I told her, of course, but I never imagined she meant to go there immediately."

Charles let out a sharp breath and shook his head.

"She's avoiding me." His jaw clenched. "That girl deserves a good—" he stopped himself, exhaling hard. "Spanking aside, she's reckless when she's hurt."

Everyone could hear it now. Beneath the irritation was pure fear.

"I'll go after her," Charles said at once, already reaching for his coat. "If I don't find her, I'll come back straightaway and we'll search together."

Heads nodded all around. Brigham clapped a hand on Dave's shoulder.

"You and Matt ride home. I'm certain Charles will find her. Once we know more, we'll send a telegram to Deer Lodge."

Dave didn't look pleased, but he understood. This wasn't a matter for marshals or sheriffs. This was between Charles and Joy.

Brigham and Graham stepped outside with them, watching as the men mounted. Charles turned his horse toward the mountain trail without hesitation, spurring it forward. Dave and Matt rode in the opposite direction, toward Deer Lodge, their figures quickly disappearing down the road.

The clouds hung low and heavy by the time Joy reached Crow Creek Falls, their dark bellies swollen with rain. Grace had been right, she never once glimpsed the waterfall from the path, but she heard it long before she reached it, the steady roar echoing through the trees like a living thing.

When the clearing finally opened before her, she stopped short, breath stolen.

It was breathtaking. Perfectly secluded. Sheltered. Hidden so well that anyone who didn't know exactly where to look would pass it by without ever suspecting what lay beyond the trees. She guided her horse toward the small cabin near the lake and dismounted, tying the reins before peering inside. To her surprise, the place was far cleaner than she had expected, as though it were still being used, if only occasionally.

The light was fading quickly now, and the wind had begun to rise, tugging at her skirts and whispering warnings through the branches. There was no barn, but a fenced-in area stood nearby, partially surrounded by trees. It wasn't ideal, but it would give her horse some shelter if the storm worsened.

She unsaddled the horse, carried her belongings inside, then returned to check on the animal once more. There was grass enough to graze and access to the lake for water. That knowledge eased some of the tightness in her chest. She had barely stepped back into the cabin and shut the door when the storm broke.

Rain began softly at first, tapping against the roof, but within minutes it intensified into a steady downpour, wind-driven and relentless. Joy leaned her forehead briefly against the door, whispering a quiet word of thanks that she had arrived in time. She set her saddle in a corner and took a proper look around.

The cabin consisted of a single large room: a bed tucked into a shallow alcove, a fireplace with a sturdy bench before it, a small table with two chairs, a wide cupboard, and a compact stove in the corner. The stovetop was only large enough for a single pot or a coffee kettle, but it was better than nothing.

Joy exhaled slowly. She had hoped the rain would pass quickly and allow her to ride back before nightfall, but the sky told a different story. A pang of guilt settled in her stomach as she realized she hadn't left a note. They would worry. Charles would worry.

She pushed the thought away and opened the cupboard, finding several canned goods, a pot, a pan, and a coffee pot. Tucked behind them was a small tin of tea. Her shoulders sagged with longing. If only she had water, warm tea would have been a comfort beyond measure. At least there was firewood stacked neatly beside the hearth and stove. She built a fire, the flames catching quickly, then checked a narrow closet near the bed. Inside were blankets, several pillows, and a few spare garments. Nothing more. Whoever owned this place had prepared it thoughtfully.

FLAMES OF THE FIRE

As she pulled the blankets free, she discovered lanterns and candles tucked among them. She placed them carefully around the cabin and lit them one by one, their gentle glow pushing back the shadows.

The fire soon filled the room with a welcoming warmth. Joy layered blankets and pillows onto one of the chairs, transforming it into a makeshift armchair, then shifted the bench against the wall and pulled the table closer to the hearth. The raised brick in front of the fireplace would serve nicely to rest her feet. Outside, the rain showed no sign of easing. Through the window, she watched her horse standing calmly beneath the dense canopy of leaves, sheltered and unbothered. That, at least, brought her some peace.

She returned to the chair, curled into it, and drew the blankets close. Exhaustion crept over her at last. She had just begun to relax, her eyelids growing heavy, when the door flew open. Joy gasped sharply, her heart leaping into her throat as she sprang upright, every nerve instantly awake.

Joy's hand reached for the small gun still tucked into her pocket, then froze when she recognized the man standing in the doorway. Charles. He was dripping wet, rainwater streaming down his hair and coat, his boots caked with mud, his saddle slung over one shoulder as if he had ridden straight through the storm without a second thought.

"What on earth are you doing here?" Her eyes widened, her voice betraying the faint tremor she couldn't quite suppress. He shut the door behind him with his heel.

"What do you think I'm doing?" he shot back. "I'm looking for you."

"But how did you know where I was?" She stared at him for a moment longer before understanding dawned. Her jaw tightened. "Nana."

"That's right."

Irritation settled firmly over her features.

"If you think I'm going to talk to you, you're mistaken. I obviously can't ask you to leave, the weather is dreadful, but—"

"I honestly don't care," he interrupted, lifting an eyebrow as his gaze locked onto her face. "Did you manage to get water before the rain started?"

She shook her head. Charles muttered under his breath, rolled his eyes, and without another word grabbed two buckets from the front porch. A moment later, he was stomping back through the mud. Joy watched from the doorway as he reached a small spring near where the horses stood, filled the buckets, and turned back toward the cabin. Halfway there, one bucket slipped from his grasp. His boot skidded on the slick ground, and the next instant he went down hard, pitching forward and landing face-first in the mud.

For a heartbeat, Joy could only stare in shock. Then he pushed himself upright, and when she caught sight of his mud-smeared face, she burst out laughing. One stern look from him wiped the smile right off her face. She bit her lip, schooling her expression into something suitably serious, though her eyes still betrayed her amusement.

Shaking his head, Charles abandoned the now-filthy buckets where they lay and strode straight toward the lake.

Without hesitation, he waded in, then plunged beneath the surface. Joy gasped. She knew exactly how cold that water was.

She rushed back into the cabin, crossed to the alcove, and opened the small closet again. The clothes inside were clearly meant for a man, simple, sturdy garments, including two large nightshirts. She selected a pair of trousers, a clean shirt, and undergarments, laying them neatly over the chair near the door. After a moment's thought, she removed the blanket from her saddle and added it to the pile, so he'd have something to dry himself with.

When she straightened, her laughter had faded, replaced by an unsettling awareness. Despite her anger, her hurt, and her determination not to speak to him, Charles had followed her into a storm without hesitation. And that realization unsettled her far more than she cared to admit.

Charles emerged from the lake with a sharp gasp, the cold stealing his breath. His teeth chattered uncontrollably, every muscle protesting as icy water streamed from his clothes. He didn't linger. Gritting his teeth, he trudged back toward the cabin, retrieved another set of buckets, and headed once more for the spring, this time far more cautiously. He skirted the worst of the mud, keeping to the shelter of the trees where the ground was firmer beneath his boots. By the time he returned, his hands were numb and his shoulders tense from fighting the cold.

Joy stepped forward without a word, took one of the buckets from him, and carried it inside. As she passed, she tipped her head toward the chair near the door, a silent indication of the clothes and blanket waiting for him.

A small, almost disbelieving smile tugged at his lips. Despite the hurt in her eyes and the distance she was trying so hard to maintain, she hadn't turned her back on him entirely. She didn't hate him, not enough to leave him freezing and miserable, at any rate.

Charles took the blanket and clothes, nodded his thanks without speaking, and stepped back onto the front porch. He pulled the door closed behind him, leaving Joy alone with the fire and the soft, relentless drumming of rain, while he changed out of his soaked clothes and tried to steady the fragile hope stirring quietly in his chest.

It didn't take long before he stepped back inside, a blanket wrapped low around his waist. Joy caught only a glimpse before she turned away, yet it was enough. His bare, broad chest glistened faintly from the rain, droplets tracing paths over sun-bronzed skin, and heat rushed to her cheeks so fiercely she feared it might give her away.

Determined not to look again, she busied herself at once. She filled the coffee pot she had found in the cupboard, set it on the stove, and coaxed the fire higher so the water would heat. Anything to give her hands purpose and her eyes somewhere else to land. She heard Charles cross the room toward the alcove to change. Her cheeks still burned, and she resolutely refused to turn around, even when she sensed his return rather than heard it. The floor creaked softly as he dragged the second chair closer to the fireplace and sat, extending his hands toward the flames.

"Thank you," he murmured, his voice low and rough, clearly referring to the clothes she had laid out for him.

"You're welcome," she replied quietly, keeping her gaze fixed on the stove. Some of the anger she'd been clinging to loosened its grip. The simple truth that he had come after her, followed her into a storm, soaking himself just to bring her water, made it impossible to believe he had ever been indifferent. And perhaps, just perhaps, there had been reasons she had not yet allowed herself to hear. She felt him move closer before she saw him.

Then his arms wrapped gently, but firmly, around her from behind. She stiffened at first, startled by the intimacy, but the warmth of him, solid and real, melted her resistance almost immediately.

"Are you still angry with me?" he asked softly, his voice brushing her ear and sending a shiver down her spine.

"Not as much," she admitted, barely above a whisper. "But I still don't understand why you didn't tell me the truth."

He exhaled slowly, then turned her to face him. His fingers lifted her chin, gentle but unyielding, and the moment their eyes met, tears welled up before she could stop them. She tried to pull away, embarrassed by her sudden vulnerability, but he tightened his hold and drew her fully against his chest.

"I never meant to hurt you, Joy," he said, his voice thick with emotion. "I never kept my name from you to deceive you. When your father hired me, he already suspected Jonas wasn't a good man. I didn't know how far this would go, and to protect my family, and you, I used my mother's maiden name. I needed Jonas to believe I was no threat."

Her lashes fluttered as she listened, her heart pounding.

"When you and your sister came to Deer Lodge, I asked my family to pretend they didn't know me. I asked your uncle, my father, everyone, to play their part. I wanted to tell you myself. I just needed the danger to pass first."

Joy swallowed hard. "So, you did all of this to protect us?"

He nodded. "Every bit of it. And when I realized how deeply I cared for you..." His voice softened. "It nearly tore me apart not to tell you. But I was afraid, afraid of losing you, afraid of putting you in more danger."

She searched his face, blinking away tears.

"I'm sorry I jumped to conclusions," she whispered. "I was just so afraid of being hurt again."

He smiled then, warm, understanding, achingly tender.

"After what my brother put you through, I don't blame you. But tell me, what changed? Why did your anger fade away so quickly?"

"You came after me," she said simply. "You didn't let me disappear. Graham barely noticed when I pulled away. But you followed me into the rain, into the mountains... and you fell into the mud just to get water." She tried to keep her composure, truly she did, but when his brow lifted knowingly, amusement flickering in his eyes, a laugh escaped her. Light. Unguarded. Real. He didn't give her time to recover.

Charles pulled her close, silencing the laughter with his presence alone. Her breath caught as his hands framed her face, his gaze burning into hers, and then his lips met hers, slow at first, then deepening with a hunger he had clearly been holding back for far too long. The kiss stole the air from her lungs. It wasn't rushed or reckless. It was deliberate, aching, full of longing and promise. The world narrowed to the warmth of him, the steady strength of his arms, the unmistakable truth in the way he kissed her as though she mattered beyond measure.

Joy melted into him, her fingers curling into his shirt as if anchoring herself to the moment, to him, certain, at last, that this was not infatuation. This was love.

Joy longed to return his kiss with the same fire that burned through her veins, but she stopped herself. Desire was a dangerous thing, especially now. They were alone in a secluded cabin, miles from anyone else, and she knew how easily passion could blur judgment. She would not play with fire.

Long ago, she had made a promise, to God and to herself. She had vowed to keep her heart and body guarded, to remain pure for the man she would one day marry. No matter how powerful the attraction, no matter how real the feelings in this moment, she refused to jeopardize her self-respect, her self-worth, or the quiet assurance of knowing she had remained true to her convictions. It was not worth it. Not for a fleeting moment of passion.

Her mother's voice echoed softly in her memory, calm and loving, as it so often did when Joy stood at a crossroads. *Love brings powerful emotions,* Mama had said. *Beautiful ones, but dangerous, too, if they aren't guided with wisdom. Feelings must be stewarded until marriage, not surrendered to impulse.*

Joy had seen the truth of those words play out in the lives around her. How easy it was to justify crossing boundaries, because others did, because a man insisted, because one believed marriage would surely follow. And yet, so often, those promises dissolved, leaving regret, heartbreak, and wounds that never fully healed.

Her mama had been a woman of quiet strength and unwavering integrity. Joy had watched her parents' marriage with admiration, built on trust, patience, and faith rather than haste or desire. That example had shaped her more deeply than she sometimes realized.

She exhaled slowly, grounding herself. Nothing was worth sacrificing her self-respect for. Nothing was worth disappointing God. And though her parents were gone, Joy believed with her whole heart that death was not the end. She was certain they were watching, still cheering her on, hoping she would choose the harder but holier path.

She wanted to make them proud. So, she steadied herself, even as her heart raced and her pulse betrayed her. Loving Charles did not mean surrendering her principles. If anything, it meant honoring them even more. Because true love, she believed, would wait.

29

Hers Now and Forever

Charles eventually drew back, his forehead resting lightly against hers, a warm, reverent smile curving his lips. The fire still burned in his eyes, but there was something deeper there now, gratitude, respect, and quiet awe. He brushed his thumb gently along her cheek.

"Thank you," he murmured.

"For what?" she asked softly.

"For being strong. For knowing who you are." His gaze lingered on her with unmistakable admiration. "It makes it easier for me to stay true to what I want, too."

Her heart tightened at the sincerity in his voice. Behind them, the kettle began to whistle. Joy reluctantly stepped out of his arms and turned back to the stove, removing the pot from the heat and adding the tea leaves. The simple, familiar motions helped steady her racing pulse. While the tea brewed, she moved to the window and watched the storm rage outside, rain streaking the glass, wind bending the trees as if the mountains themselves were breathing.

Charles joined her again, stepping close, his presence warm and grounding. This time, he didn't pull her into an embrace meant to steal her breath. He simply wrapped his arms around her from behind and held her, protective and patient, as though there was nowhere else, he would rather be.

"Can you see yourself living here?" he asked quietly. She turned her head, surprise flickering across her face.

"Here?" she echoed. "In this cabin?"

He chuckled softly and shook his head.

"In Elkhorn. Or would you rather return to Deer Lodge?"

She considered the question seriously.

"I thought Deer Lodge had become home," she admitted. "But now..." She glanced back at the storm, at the mountains beyond it. "Now I think my heart belongs here."

He nodded, as if he had hoped she would say exactly that. They stood in silence for a moment before Charles gently turned her to face him. Then, without hesitation, he went down on one knee.

Joy's breath caught. Her heart thundered as tears welled in her eyes.

"I love you, Joy," he said, his voice steady but thick with emotion. "You are everything I never knew I was searching for. Will you marry me?"

She closed her eyes for a moment, overwhelmed, not with doubt, but with the weight and beauty of the moment.

"What about your work?" she asked quietly. "Sacramento? Your future as an attorney?"

He smiled. "Would you come with me, if that were the path I chose?"

"Yes," she answered instantly. "Without hesitation."

"And if I stayed?" His gaze searched hers. "If my future was here?"

Her smile trembled, but it didn't fade.

"I would miss nothing, if I were with you."

"So, you love me," he whispered. "And you'll be my wife?"

She nodded, tears slipping free as she laughed softly through them. He rose and kissed her, deeply, reverently, with joy and promise woven into every heartbeat. When he pulled back, her cheeks were flushed, her eyes bright.

"I want to build a life with you here," he said. "A ranch. A family. Horses, land, a home that grows with us."

She stared at him, stunned, and then, radiant.

"You mean it?"

"Every word." His smile widened. "My grandparents want me to buy the cabin. We can add to it. There's land, plenty of it. A barn, gardens, stables... a future."

Her hand tightened in his.

"It sounds like you've thought about this."

"I have," he admitted. "Ever since I saw how much you loved this place."

She leaned into him, emotion swelling in her chest.

"I would love to raise a family here. Close to your grandparents. Close to mine, if they stay. It feels... right."

"Then it's settled," he said softly, pulling her into his arms. "Two weeks?"

She gasped. "So soon?"

"My family will rejoice," he said with a grin. "And winter is coming. Let's begin our forever now."

She laughed and whispered, "Yes."

And in the storm-wrapped cabin, with the fire crackling and the world held at bay, their future took root, strong, faithful, and fiercely loved.

Joy was still stunned, her heart racing as if it had not yet caught up with reality. Then emotion overtook her, and she slipped her arms around his neck, pressing a quick, breathless kiss on his lips, more instinct than intention.

"I suppose that means we're getting married in two weeks," she said softly, a shy laugh escaping her as warmth flooded her cheeks. Charles smiled, unmistakable pride and delight shining in his eyes. He lifted her chin gently, his thumb brushing along her jaw, his lips hovering just close enough to make her pulse stumble.

"Perhaps," he murmured, his voice low and teasing, "we could come up here for our honeymoon."

Her breath caught. The intensity of his gaze made her tremble, and she instinctively tried to look away, suddenly flustered.

"I—I don't think the owner would approve of that," she stammered. He didn't release her. Instead, he leaned closer, his forehead nearly touching hers.

"What if the owner is me?" he whispered.

Her eyes widened. "You want to buy this place?"

He grinned, clearly enjoying her surprise.

"Already did. Before we even came up here." He glanced around the cabin fondly. "I've loved Crow Creek Falls since I was a boy. When I heard the land and the cabin were for sale, I didn't hesitate."

Joy slowly turned, taking in the room again, the firelight dancing on the walls, the sturdy furniture, the quiet promise of shelter and warmth.

"Well," she said carefully, smiling now, "it *is* cozy." Her gaze softened. "Maybe someday we could renovate it a little. Turn it from a cabin into a true home."

His expression gentled, emotion flickering across his face.

"Anything you want. We'll build it together." He kissed her then, slowly, reverent, and full of promise, until her knees nearly gave way. When he finally pulled back, her cheeks were flushed, her eyes bright with happiness.

Certain now, of him, of their future, of the love that had grown strong through hardship, Joy kissed him back, tender and unguarded, before resting her head against his chest. Wrapped in his arms, with the storm fading outside and the fire crackling softly, she knew without a single doubt:

Nothing could undo what they had found in each other.

It was pitch-black outside, yet the rain showed no sign of letting up. It drummed steadily against the cabin, relentless and cold. Joy found herself standing before the window once more, her reflection faint in the glass, worry settling visibly upon her face. They would not be able to return to Elkhorn that night. The muddy paths would be impassable, and the storm far too dangerous to risk. That meant staying in the cabin, with no chaperone present. The thought left her uneasy, her nerves stretched taut despite her trust in Charles.

When he stepped outside onto the front porch, giving her privacy to change, Joy moved quickly. She slipped into one of the nightgowns, her fingers trembling just slightly, then hurried to the bed. She piled on every blanket and pillow she could find, building a careful barrier before climbing beneath the covers herself, pulling them up nearly to her chin.

When Charles returned inside, he paused, a faint grin tugging at his mouth at the sight of her nearly hidden beneath layers of bedding. He stepped closer and sat carefully on the edge of the mattress.

"Will it be all right if we share the bed?" he asked gently. "It's not small, and if we keep the extra blankets and pillows between us, we needn't be close. I promise to stay on my side." He watched her closely as he spoke, noticing the way her cheeks flushed a deep, telltale red. After a moment's hesitation, she nodded, unable to bring herself to meet his gaze.

Rising again, Charles crossed to the hearth and added more wood to the fire. Once the flames caught, he moved about the room quietly, blowing out the candles and lanterns until only the soft glow of the fireplace remained. Shadows danced along the walls as he prepared for bed and finally lay down himself, careful to keep his distance.

Joy faced the wall, her eyes closed, her breathing measured. Charles understood her bashfulness and was careful to give her all the space she might need, determined not to add to her discomfort.

She was certain sleep would not come, not with the storm raging outside and her thoughts racing so fiercely. Yet the long, eventful day had taken its toll. Before she realized it, the tension eased from her body, and unconsciousness wrapped her in its gentle hold.

Charles was startled awake when the woman beside him suddenly bolted upright. Joy gasped violently for air, clutching at her throat as though invisible hands were wrapped around it, trying desperately to tear them away. Her breaths came in broken, panicked bursts, her body rigid with terror. It took him only a heartbeat to understand. She was trapped somewhere between sleep and waking, caught in the grip of a nightmare, reliving something she had never truly escaped.

"Joy," he said softly, his voice low and steady. "You're safe. You're here with me."

She didn't seem to hear him at first. Her struggle continued, her fear raw and unmistakable. Carefully, he reached for her hand, then drew her gently into his arms, holding her close. She fought him at first, her hands pressing against his chest, but after another desperate gasp, her eyes flew open. Recognition flickered there.

Charles cupped her face, his thumb brushing her cheek as he continued to speak in soothing, measured tones. Gradually, her body began to soften. The panic gave way to sobs, and she broke down entirely, tears spilling as he held her firmly, protectively, until the trembling eased and her breathing slowed. Only then did she seem to become aware of their closeness. Her gaze dropped and froze. She swallowed hard.

"Why... why are you not wearing a shirt?"

"I never do at night," he replied calmly. Then, with a faint note of dry humor, he added, "I did keep my trousers on, though."

Her cheeks flamed instantly, the color spreading like wildfire. "Would you like to fall back asleep in my arms?" he asked gently. She stared at him as though he had suggested something utterly scandalous.

"I doubt that's a good idea."

Charles noted the nervous tension still clinging to her, the way her fingers twisted into the blankets. It wasn't only modesty, holding her back. She was afraid to close her eyes again.

"All right," he said thoughtfully. "How about this, I'll put my shirt back on and wrap you in as many blankets as I can find."

"I... I don't know," she stammered, uncertainty clouding her expression. He lifted her chin gently, forcing her to meet his gaze.

"Joy, I want you to feel safe," he said quietly. "I can see it in your eyes. You're frightened to go back to sleep, and I don't want you facing that alone."

After a moment, she nodded. Charles rose quickly, tugged his shirt back on, then returned to the bed. He wrapped her in blanket after blanket, cocooning her so thoroughly that she suddenly let out a small, unexpected giggle. He paused, lifting an eyebrow in question. She ducked her head, embarrassed.

"Isn't this what you wanted?"

"Yes," she said softly. "I only laughed because I thought this must be how it feels when someone's tied up during an arrest."

He chuckled quietly, then gathered her carefully into his arms, holding her close against his chest. Lowering his head, he pressed a gentle kiss to the top of her hair, brief, chaste, and protective. Within minutes, her breathing evened out, the tension finally leaving her body. Not long after, Charles allowed himself to drift back into sleep as well, keeping watch, even in his dreams.

Joy woke early, the faint gray light of dawn filtering through the small cabin window. For a moment, she lay perfectly still, aware of the warmth surrounding her. Charles's arms were still wrapped securely around her, holding her as though he feared she might vanish if he let go. Careful not to wake him, she slowly eased his arms away, unwinding herself from the cocoon of blankets. She slipped from the bed and padded softly across the floor.

The cabin was cold, the night's chill still clinging to the air. She went straight to the stove, coaxing a fire to life before placing the coffeepot on top and adding water. Tea would do nicely, something warm and familiar to start the day.

While she waited for the water to heat, Joy wandered to the window. Outside, the world had been washed clean. The rain had finally stopped, and the rising sun painted the sky in soft hues of gold and pale rose. Every blade of grass glistened with lingering moisture. Beneath the trees, the two horses stood quietly, heads lowered, seemingly lost in their own peaceful thoughts. The sight made her smile. It was so still. So safe.

She was lost in the beauty of it all when suddenly two strong, muscular arms slid around her waist. Joy nearly leapt out of her skin. A startled gasp escaped her as her heart raced, and she clutched at his forearms in surprise. She hadn't heard him get up at all.

Turning quickly, she looked up into his face. Charles was grinning. He must have noticed her reaction, because amusement danced in his eyes.

"Morning," he murmured, clearly pleased with himself. "Have you ever gone fly-fishing before?" he asked casually. Joy blinked at him, her expression shifting into open confusion. At her reaction, he gave a sheepish grin.

"Is that why you bought this cabin up here?" she asked. "For fishing?"

"It's one of many reasons," he replied, watching her with quiet amusement. A faint blush touched her cheeks now, softening her features.

"I've never fished in my life," she admitted. "We lived in Sacramento most of my life, and there simply wasn't the opportunity. And even if there had been, it wouldn't have been considered ladylike." She hesitated before adding, "After we moved to Auburn, the idea of wanting to try it as an adult just felt... strange."

"It's never too late to learn," Charles said gently. "And fly-fishing is far from boring." He held her gaze a moment longer than necessary, something warm and encouraging in his eyes.

"I think we should return to Elkhorn," Joy said suddenly, unease creeping back into her voice. "Everyone will be worried about us, and they might even think we—"

Before she could finish the thought, he lifted his hand and lightly covered her mouth with his fingers. The simple, unexpected touch sent a shiver through her.

"We did nothing wrong," he said quietly. "My family knows I followed you, and I doubt it took them long to figure out why we didn't return last night. Riding back in that storm would have been foolish."

She nodded, though the discomfort lingered. Gently, Charles drew her against his chest, his arm settling around her in an unmistakably protective way.

"It's still very early," he said. "We have time to do a bit of fly-fishing before anyone starts questioning our whereabouts."

She looked up at him, uncertain, but intrigued.

He winked. "I'll go outside to change," he added. "You can change in here."

He crossed the small room to the closet and pulled out another pair of trousers and a clean shirt. The previous owner had left nearly everything behind, and Charles had made use of what was available, for now. Still, as his fingers closed around the worn hangers, a quiet resolve settled in him. One day, he would add his own things to this place. His own clothes. His own supplies. The cabin would no longer feel borrowed or temporary, especially if circumstances ever brought them here again.

With the clothes folded over his arm, he picked up the blanket Joy had handed him the night before. The simple gesture carried more weight than it should have, and he found himself holding it a moment longer before turning away. Then he stepped outside, the door closing softly behind him, leaving Joy the privacy he had promised.

Joy watched him go, still puzzled as to why he had taken the blanket with him. She stepped back to the window just in time to see him walk toward the lake, the early morning light glinting off the water. When he reached the shore, Charles pulled off his shirt.

Joy's cheeks warmed instantly, and she turned her gaze away, though not quite quickly enough. Her heart gave a startled leap as he plunged straight into the lake. She pressed a hand to her chest, momentarily breathless at the thought of how bitterly cold the water must be. It seemed impossible anyone could endure it for more than a heartbeat.

True to that thought, he resurfaced almost at once, climbed out, and reached for the blanket he had draped, over the fence. Wrapping it tightly around himself, he headed back toward the cabin.

Joy hurried to the stove, where the water had begun to boil. She lifted the coffeepot carefully and set it on a plate atop the table, adding the tea leaves before moving quickly to change into her own clothes, her motions brisk and purposeful.

By the time Charles returned inside, she was in the middle of pouring tea into two cups. She handed one to him without a word. He accepted it with a grateful smile, his shoulders still trembling from the chill of his early-morning plunge.

Standing near the stove, he cradled the cup between his hands, letting the warmth seep back into his fingers. It didn't take long before the shivering eased and color returned to his face.

"Are you ready?" he asked at last. Joy nodded. Reaching to the top of the closet, Charles pulled down a fishing rod along with a few small items they would need. He grabbed an empty bucket, then turned toward the door. Joy followed him outside, the fresh morning air greeting them as a new, quiet adventure began.

"I think you'll like this," Charles said. A soft, contented smile bloomed across Joy's face, and she nodded. He showed her how to hold the fishing rod and work the fly reel, explaining the motions with patient ease. She tried a few times while he watched, offering quiet encouragement.

Then he stepped closer. Before she realized it, Charles moved behind her, his arms coming around her once more. He placed his hands over hers, guiding the rod as he moved with her, slow and deliberate. Joy felt the familiar heat rise into her cheeks, butterflies erupting in her stomach all at once. She was certain he was doing this deliberately, fully aware of the effect it had on her. Still, she said nothing, concentrating fiercely on the task at hand even as her pulse quickened.

After a few more attempts, she managed the motion on her own. Turning toward him, she offered a proud smile that made something unmistakable flicker in his eyes. She caught several large trout after that, growing more confident with each cast.

When she glanced over, she found Charles leaning casually against one of the fence posts near the horses' enclosure, his cowboy hat pulled low over his face.

Joy shook her head. There was no chance she would allow him to nap while she did all the work. With a mischievous glint in her eye, she turned back toward the water and cast her line again. It took a few tries, but suddenly the hook caught on a tree branch above Charles's head. Before she could reconsider, she gave the line a sharp tug and then let go. Water cascaded down over him.

Joy burst into laughter as Charles jerked upright, sucking in a startled breath. The moment he saw her drop the fishing rod and sprint toward the cabin, his expression shifted, from shock to something far more dangerous.

Joy reached the door first and grabbed for it, with the intent of locking him out. She was just about to close it when he caught her hand, tugged her back outside, and swept her up in one smooth motion. With a startled cry, she found herself thrown over his shoulder as he charged toward the lake.

"Charles!" she protested, laughing even as she pounded weakly against his back. "Put me down!"

He didn't slow until they reached the shoreline. Then he pulled her off his shoulder, spun her once, and tossed her lightly into the air before catching her again. The sudden movement stole her breath, but relief flooded her when she realized he had only pretended to throw her into the icy water. He drew her close, holding her tightly against his chest, his gaze never leaving her face. The world seemed to narrow to the space between them, sparks crackling in the air long before his lips claimed hers.

The kiss was demanding at first, raw, breathless, almost overwhelming. Then it softened, deepened, and slowed until it became something far more dangerous. Joy felt herself melting into him despite her better judgment. Gently, she pressed her hands against his chest and pushed him back.

"You are stealing my breath, Charles," she said softly but firmly. "And it is best not to play with fire. We need to return to town."

He hesitated before lowering her to her feet, his hands lingering far too long at her waist. The strength of the attraction frightened her. How easily she could give in if she allowed herself to forget everything else. Charles leaned his forehead against hers, exhaling slowly.

"You're right," he murmured. "Playing with fire is foolish. It's easy to forget how quickly a kiss can get out of hand when the pull is this strong."

She met his gaze, her voice quieter now.

"Believe it or not, it's difficult for me as well. Your kisses make my knees weak, and I want to return them. But giving in to too much temptation, especially when we're alone, would lead us straight into disaster." A faint smile touched her lips. "We can survive another fortnight, can't we?"

He nodded, his expression softening, then winked before pressing a gentle kiss on her forehead.

They packed up without delay, making sure the stove fire was fully extinguished. Charles lifted the bucket of trout, and moments later they were on their way back to town, each of them far more aware than before of just how thin the line between restraint and surrender truly was.

Both Charles and Joy came to an abrupt halt as they stepped out of the barn after unsaddling their horses. They had expected to see his grandparents and his father waiting, but not his mother.

And certainly not his sisters. Joy's breath caught as she took in the gathered faces, surprise mirrored on every one of them. Charles blinked, clearly just as stunned.

"Mom," he asked, disbelief edging his voice, "what are you doing here?"

Darlene stepped forward at once.

"The girls and I were in town when Julia's telegram arrived," she explained. "She couldn't leave, she has several patients under her care, but she sent word to the hospital in Helena." Her expression softened, then tightened with lingering worry. "The message frightened me enough that we took the stagecoach and came straight here. I couldn't sit and wait, not knowing whether you and Joy were safe."

Guilt washed over Joy. She stepped forward, hands clasped together.

"I'm truly sorry," she said earnestly. "I shouldn't have left without telling anyone. I was just so afraid the Nortons would come after you next, and I couldn't bear the thought of that."

Darlene didn't hesitate. She crossed the space between them and wrapped Joy in a firm, loving embrace.

"Oh, sweetheart," she said softly. "We know. And we understand."

Joy blinked back tears before turning to face Brigham and Charles's grandparents.

"So... everyone has been caught?" she asked. "What will happen to them now?"

Brigham nodded. "Yes. Everyone involved is either under arrest or dead. The doctor from Helena confirmed that Vernon and his wife will survive. Once they are strong enough to travel, they'll be transferred to Helena and imprisoned. Most of the marshals have already left with Nigel and Thatcher and are on their way there now."

Joy frowned slightly. "But can we trust the sheriff there? His deputy let them out before. What if the sheriff was involved as well?"

Her gaze flicked from Brigham to Charles.

"We can trust them," Charles said immediately. "The deputy was involved, yes, but he pretended to help them. Their release was deliberate. It was the only way to bring this to an end."

Joy exhaled slowly. "Is that why there were so many marshals here?"

Charles nodded. "Yes."

"Well then," his grandmother said, clapping her hands together gently, "why don't we all go inside and have some lunch?"

They had just begun to turn toward the house when Charles cleared his throat.

"Wait," he said, holding them back. The sudden seriousness in his voice made everyone pause. He glanced at Joy, who met his gaze with a small, encouraging smile, then turned back to his family.

"Before we all go in," he said, steady now, "there's something I want you to know. I asked Joy to marry me, and she said yes."

For a heartbeat, there was stunned silence. Then Grace let out a delighted cry and pulled Joy into a fierce embrace.

"Oh, Joy! Congratulations!"

The spell broke all at once. Cheers erupted, voices overlapping, hands reaching out. His sisters surrounded her, offering congratulations through laughter and happy tears. Charles grinned broadly as his father clasped his shoulder with unmistakable pride. Joy stood in the middle of it all, overwhelmed, in the very best way. As she looked around at their smiling faces, warmth spread through her chest. The fear and loneliness she had carried for so long finally loosened their grip. The Harrisons were no longer just Charles's family. They were hers, now and forevermore.

Cathleen and Olivia descended on Joy the moment they returned to the house, their questions tumbling over one another in rapid succession. They had been utterly convinced she was in love with Graham, and now they were determined to know exactly what had gone wrong, and how Charles had managed to swoop in so completely. Meanwhile, Grace drew her grandson aside, a knowing glint in her eye.

"You see," she said smugly, "I told you everything would turn out just fine. How long did it take before Joy was willing to listen to you?"

Charles smiled faintly. "Following her helped," he admitted. "Seeing how upset she was... that mattered. It showed her I cared."

Grace's expression softened into a beaming smile.

"Exactly," she said, satisfied, before turning her attention back toward the kitchen as though the matter were settled beyond all doubt. Charles made his way back to where his sisters and Joy were seated, just in time for his mother to stop short and scowl.

"What on earth happened to your clothes, Charles?" Darlene demanded. "Did your horse toss you into a mud puddle?" She lifted the hem of his shirt for emphasis. The room went silent. Charles felt it instantly, Joy's breath hitching, her lips twitching, laughter barely contained. Before she could speak, he reached for her hand and tugged her smoothly into his arms, raising an eyebrow as he met her gaze in silent warning. It didn't work.

Joy burst out laughing and launched into a brief explanation of events, barely making it through the story for her giggles. By the time she finished, the entire family was laughing with her.

"I warned you," Charles growled, though the corner of his mouth betrayed him. In one swift motion, he scooped Joy up and tossed her over his shoulder.

"No—no—please—don't do anything to me," she whined dramatically, perfectly aware she was in no real danger. And sure enough, both his mother and grandmother immediately began scolding him at once.

"Charles Harrison!"

"Put her down this instant!"

Joy bit her lip to keep from laughing again as he finally set her back on her feet.

"I'm sorry," she said breathlessly, still giggling. "I truly am. But it was so funny."

His lips twitched despite himself. Before she could say another word, Charles framed her face in both hands and pressed a firm, unmistakable kiss to her lips. Her laughter died instantly. Heat rushed to Joy's cheeks as her thoughts scattered entirely. When he pulled back, she promptly buried her burning face against his shirt, mortified and breathless all at once. Charles wrapped his arms around her, holding her close, unapologetic.

"Well," Olivia said brightly after a moment, "I suppose that answers all our questions."

Joy groaned softly into his chest. Charles only smiled.

"So," his father said suddenly, fixing his gaze on his son, "have you given any thought to when you'd like to get married?"

Charles didn't hesitate. He nodded once.

"In two weeks."

The room reacted all at once.

"Wow," Cathleen drawled, arching a brow. "That's... efficient. Talk about a short courtship and engagement. I'm guessing you two are burning for one another, hmm?"

Charles only grinned. Joy, on the other hand, looked as though she might faint on the spot. Darlene shot her daughter, a sharp look.

"That was entirely inappropriate, young lady," she scolded. Cathleen opened her mouth, no doubt to defend herself, but Charles beat her to it.

"She isn't wrong, Mom."

Joy's eyes widened, her cheeks erupting into a wildfire of color.

"My word," she mumbled, mortified. This family clearly took great pleasure in watching her blush. Before the teasing could go any further, Grace stepped in and pulled Joy gently into her arms.

"That's quite enough," she said firmly. "Can't you see how uncomfortable you're making this poor girl?" She glanced at Darlene. "We can have everything ready in two weeks, can't we?"

"Of course we can, Ma," Darlene replied without hesitation. "I'll stay here and help with the planning and preparations. We'll make sure everything is perfect, for Joy and Charles."

Joy managed a grateful smile, still very carefully avoiding eye contact with Charles.

"And where do you plan to live?" Brigham asked then, stepping closer to his son. Charles straightened slightly.

"I'd like to buy this cabin for us, and the surrounding land as well." He paused, then added, "If you're all right with it, Dad, I'd like to start my own ranch."

Brigham didn't hesitate either. He nodded, pride evident in his smile.

"Of course I'm all right with it. I'll help you however I can. Graham has decided to stay on with me and take over the ranch when the time comes."

"What made you choose this place?" Darlene asked, her gaze moving thoughtfully between her son and Joy.

"We both love it here," Charles replied. "Joy likes being close to Nana and Grandpa, especially since their children and other grandchildren live so far away. And," he added, glancing at Joy, "she felt at home in this cabin from the very beginning."

"It's not very large," his grandfather noted mildly. "Once you start a family, you'll need more space."

Charles only smiled. "It's perfect for us, for now. There are two bedrooms to begin with, and it wouldn't take much to add more rooms. We could even build additional space beneath the roof."

He looked at Joy then, warmth shining unmistakably in his eyes. She slipped her arms around him, resting her head briefly against his chest.

"I love it," she said softly. And this time, no one teased her for blushing.

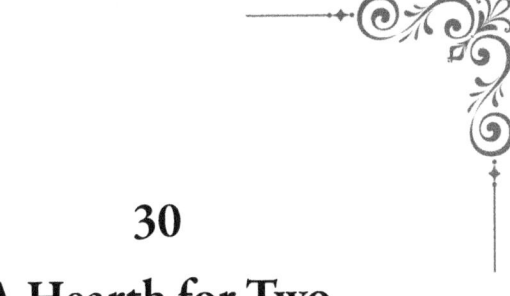

30

A Hearth for Two

The next two weeks passed in a blur. Charles sent telegrams announcing the wedding, making certain that everyone connected to them, family, friends, and those who mattered most, would have the chance to attend. Joy could scarcely contain her happiness when she learned that her sister and her family would be coming, along with her aunt and uncle. When her uncle promised to walk her down the aisle, she had to blink back tears. It made everything feel real.

While wedding plans unfolded, Charles was often away. Along with his father and many of the men from town, he spent long days behind the church, building a guesthouse for arriving family members and guests. Yet despite all the work, he grew increasingly secretive. Joy barely saw him, and whenever she did manage to corner him with questions, he only smiled, infuriatingly calm, pressed a lingering kiss on her lips, and promised that she would find out soon enough. "It's a surprise," he would say, every time.

Elkhorn had its own seamstress, and under her careful hands Joy's wedding dress came together, simple, elegant, and more beautiful than Joy had dared to hope. Each fitting made her heart flutter even more.

As the day drew nearer, excitement slowly tangled with nerves. There were moments when the weight of it all felt overwhelming, so much happiness arriving so quickly, after so much fear and uncertainty. But each time doubt crept in, her future mother-in-law and Nana were there, offering steady reassurance, gentle smiles, and quiet encouragement.

By the eve of the wedding, Joy's nerves were fluttering wildly, but beneath them lay a deep, unwavering joy. Tomorrow, everything would change. And for the first time in her life, she wasn't afraid of what waited on the other side.

"You look beautiful, Joy," her uncle said softly as he offered her his arm to walk her down the aisle. Before they began, he lifted her veil and pressed a gentle kiss to the top of her head. The simple, fatherly gesture nearly undid her.

"Thank you, Uncle Gerald," Joy whispered. Her eyes shimmered with tears, and she realized her hands were trembling slightly. He drew her into a brief, reassuring embrace, steady and warm, before guiding her forward. Together, they walked toward the front of the church.

Charles was waiting there, handsome and composed, though his eyes gave him away the moment they found hers. Graham stood beside him as best man, his expression openly proud. Julia, Alice, Olivia, and Cathleen lined the aisle as bridesmaids, their smiles radiant.

The ceremony itself was everything Joy had hoped for, and more. There was something profoundly moving about being married by Charles's grandfather, his voice steady, his words filled with wisdom and affection. The church was full to the last pew, a gathering of relatives, friends, and townsfolk who had witnessed their journey and come to celebrate its beginning.

When Charles leaned down and kissed his wife, gentle, reverent, and full of promise, a collective *aww* rippled through the church. Laughter and applause followed, and once the ceremony ended, the newlyweds were swept up in embraces and congratulations from all sides.

Not long after, Charles leaned close and murmured something in Joy's ear, reminding her of their plan. He had convinced her to spend a week at Crow Creek Falls, to begin their marriage in quiet seclusion, just the two of them.

When the time came to leave, Joy held Alice tightly, the sisters clinging to one another longer than intended. Alice would soon be moving to Sacramento to be nearer to Dylan's family, and the thought tugged sharply at Joy's heart. She kissed each of her nieces, blinking back tears.

Sensing the moment, Charles took Joy's hand and gently guided her toward their horses. He lifted her into the saddle with practiced ease, his hands steady, his smile soft and full of pride. As they turned to ride away together, Joy glanced back one last time, then forward, toward the life waiting just beyond the small town. For the first time, the future felt certain. And it felt like home.

Joy remained quiet as they rode up the mountain, the steady rhythm of the horses carrying her forward, and inward. Her heart felt full, weighted with memory and gratitude all at once. The past year had tested her and her sister in ways she never could have imagined. She still missed her parents terribly. That ache would never truly fade. And she would miss Alice and her nieces as well. Yet comfort followed close behind the sorrow. Alice had found a good husband, and she would be surrounded by Dylan's family in Sacramento, safe, loved, and supported.

Joy was grateful, too, that her aunt and uncle were now firmly part of her life again, more than ever before. Their decision to settle in Helena, closer to most of their children, brought her a quiet sense of peace. Family, once so fragile and scattered, was finally mending.

A small smile touched her lips as her thoughts drifted to Cathleen and Matt Haven. It had never been a secret how fond they were of one another. Joy suspected it wouldn't be long before their affection turned into something more official. Then there was Dave, and her sister's former mother-in-law. Life had a strange way of weaving people together. Their growing bond had surprised everyone, and the idea of them marrying, moving to Elkhorn, Dave becoming the town's first sheriff while Maureen opened a café, filled Joy with warm amusement. It felt like hope taking root everywhere she looked.

Her gaze shifted to the man riding beside her. Charles. Her heart skipped, fluttered, then settled into that familiar, heady rhythm he always stirred in her. He was devastatingly handsome, yes, but it was more than that. He made her feel safe. Seen. Cherished. It still astonished her how swiftly everything had changed. Only weeks earlier, she had been convinced she loved Graham. Or at least, she had believed that was love. Now she understood the difference. What she felt for Charles was deeper, fiercer, something that ignited her very soul. Her heart raced whenever he pulled her into his arms, whenever his kisses claimed her with a passion that left her breathless and unsteady. She felt blessed beyond measure.

The danger had passed. The threats, the fear, the violence, they were behind her now. Despite the attacks and losses, both she and her sister had survived. More than that, they had been given new beginnings, surrounded by people who had become family almost without effort. Joy had never imagined she would one day belong permanently to the Harrisons. Now, she could not imagine belonging anywhere else.

Through it all, God had strengthened her, especially after the brutal loss of her parents. He had steadied her when grief threatened to break her, hardened her resolve when evil sought to destroy what remained of her family. He had given her the determination and fierceness to protect her sister and nieces, to stand her ground when everything felt uncertain.

Lifting her face toward the sky, Joy whispered a silent prayer of thanks. The wind felt warmer now, though dark clouds were gathering overhead, carrying with them the sharp, unmistakable scent of snow. A storm was coming, but instead of dread, she felt anticipation. There was comfort in knowing she would face it with Charles at her side.

Her eyes returned to him once more, and her heart leapt anew. He had captured her heart swiftly, undeniably, with sparks that sizzled between them. He had never used her, never taken from her what she was not ready to give. Instead, he had earned her love, quietly, steadily, until she realized he had slipped past every guard and settled deep within her soul. This love was not merely physical. It was enduring. Anchoring. And Joy knew, with unshakable certainty, that she would never let him go. Not now. Not ever.

Dusk was settling in by the time they finally reached the cabin. The light had softened into deep blues and golds, shadows stretching long across the land. Joy drew in a quiet breath as she looked around and then stopped short. Everything had changed.

Where there had once been only an open enclosure, there now stood a proper barn, sturdy and well built, offering real shelter. Their horses would be warm and dry through the night, protected from wind and snow alike. A large shed had been added beside the cabin, stacked neatly with split firewood, enough to last well through the coming winter. Joy's gaze lingered there, awe growing with each new detail she noticed. And on the front porch, two rocking chairs. They sat side by side, solid and inviting, facing the land below as if meant for quiet evenings and shared conversations. The sight of them stole her breath more than anything else.

Joy turned slowly toward Charles, stunned. He watched her carefully, a faint, knowing smile tugging at his lips. This was what he had been so secretive about. A home.

Charles lifted her from her horse, an amused, deeply satisfied smile curving his lips. Her wide-eyed wonder told him everything he needed to know, she loved it. Seeing her reaction made every hour of work, every secret kept entirely worth it. He led the horses into the enclosure and the new barn, moving with practiced ease. Fresh straw lay beneath their hooves, hay was placed within easy reach, and water set where they could drink their fill. Once everything was settled, he secured the doors carefully, making certain they would be safe from the cold, and from anything that might wander too close during the night.

When he turned back, Joy hadn't moved. She stood there, taking it all in, her expression one of quiet awe, as though she feared the moment might vanish if she blinked. Charles paused, content to give her a few more minutes. He leaned against a fence post, watching her instead. His heart began to beat faster. He couldn't seem to look away from her, the way the fading light brushed her features, the way wonder softened her face. She was his wife now. The thought settled in his chest with weight and warmth all at once. No more restraint born of propriety. No more stepping back because he must.

Joy nearly jumped out of her skin when Charles suddenly appeared behind her and swept her off her feet. A startled laugh escaped her as she turned her head and found him gazing into her eyes, his expression unreadable for the briefest heartbeat. Then he kissed her, fierce and unapologetic, stealing her breath before she could form a single thought.

Joy returned the kiss without hesitation. The strength of her response caught him off guard, and since he hadn't stopped walking, he stumbled slightly. A delighted laugh burst out of her before she could stop it. Charles shot her a stern glance. Instantly, she clapped a hand over her mouth, her shoulders shaking as she tried, and failed, to suppress her laughter. She tucked her face against his shoulder instead, still smiling, still breathless.

"Behave," he muttered, though the warmth in his voice betrayed him. He carried her into the cabin and set her carefully on her feet. As her eyes adjusted to the dimness, they widened with wonder. Even in the low light, she could see that the interior had changed as well. Before she could comment, Charles crossed the room and knelt to build a fire in the hearth. Flames sprang to life, casting a welcoming glow across the cabin. He moved efficiently after that, lighting lanterns and candles he had placed throughout the space, on the table, along the walls, beside the bed.

As the room slowly filled with flickering light, the cabin transformed before her eyes, revealing thoughtful touches she hadn't expected. Joy stood very still, her heart swelling. Charles turned back to her then, the firelight dancing across his features, and for the first time since they arrived, she realized the truth: This place was no longer just a cabin. It was their second home.

It was a beautiful room. The furniture had been freshly painted, the worn edges softened by care and effort. The bed boasted a new mattress, inviting and pristine. When Joy opened the cupboard, she found it well stocked with food and ingredients, carefully chosen and thoughtfully arranged. The closet now held several pieces of their clothing, neatly hung, and beside it stood a newly added chest of drawers, filled with extra blankets folded with care. There was also a new and larger stove.

The realization stole her breath. She turned slowly to face him, a beaming smile lighting her face. Charles was already watching her, his expression full of quiet pride.

"When did you do all this?" she asked softly.

"I had help from Dad and Grandpa," he admitted. "This was my surprise for you. I wanted to make sure that spending our honeymoon here wouldn't be something you regretted."

Her eyes shone. "It's wonderful," she said sincerely. "Thank you." Rising onto her tiptoes, she kissed him, soft, grateful, and full of emotion.

"Hold that kiss," he said suddenly, almost urgently, and slipped back outside. Joy watched, puzzled, as he closed the new shutters, securing them against the night. A moment later, he returned, the door shutting firmly behind him. This time, there was no hesitation. Charles lifted her into his arms and kissed her deeply, with longing that had been held in check for far too long. He carried her to the bed and lowered her carefully, as though she were something precious. His kiss grew warmer, more insistent, until he felt her hesitate. He pulled back at once.

"What's wrong?" he asked gently, his breath unsteady, worry flickering in his eyes. Joy swallowed, her voice barely more than a whisper.

"I'm scared. What if I disappoint you? What if one day you regret marrying me?"

His expression softened completely. He cupped her face in both hands, steady and sure.

"You will never disappoint me," he said quietly. "And I will never regret marrying you. We'll learn together, how to be husband and wife in every sense of the word."

She searched his face. "How can you be so sure?"

"Because I love you."

The grateful, radiant smile that bloomed on her face undid him entirely. He drew her close again, pressing gentle kisses to her cheeks, her brow, the corner of her mouth, until his lips found hers once more. This time, the kiss deepened slowly, tender and unhurried, filled with promise rather than urgency. Joy slipped her arms around his neck, returning the kiss with trust and longing, her fear melting away as she rested fully in the certainty of his love. And in the quiet warmth of the cabin, with the firelight flickering around them, Joy knew she was safe, cherished, and exactly where she was meant to be.

When Joy opened her eyes, the cabin was still wrapped in darkness. The fire had burned low, casting only faint shadows along the walls. Charles lay beside her, his arm draped securely around her, her body pressed against his bare chest. The steady rise and fall of his breathing soothed her, and yet her heart began to race simply from looking at him. He was still fast asleep.

Smiling softly, she leaned over him and brushed a gentle kiss against his lips before slipping free and rolling to the other side of the bed. Outside, the wind howled against the cabin, restless and wild. Curious, she rose quietly and opened the window, pushing the shutters apart. Snow was falling. She watched in silent awe as white flakes drifted through the darkness, swirling in the glow of moonlight. It felt like magic, quiet, pure, and entirely theirs.

Suddenly, strong arms wrapped around her waist and tugged her backward. She let out a startled gasp as Charles pressed her gently into the mattress, one arm braced beside her head while he reached past her to shut the window and pull the shutters closed once more.

"Are you completely insane?" he growled playfully, his face hovering only inches from hers. "It's freezing out there."

She smiled up at him, utterly unrepentant.

"But it's snowing," she argued. "And it's hardly my fault that you sleep without a shirt." She tried to squirm free, but he caught her easily, pinning her down with effortless strength. His eyes gleamed with warmth and unmistakable desire.

"Oh, I'll remember that," he murmured. Before she could respond, his lips were on hers again, ending the exchange with a kiss that sent heat racing through her. The playful tension melted away as she relaxed into him, her hands finding his shoulders, her heart swelling with emotion. It didn't take long before she was wrapped safely in his arms once more, warmth replacing the cold, love pressing close on every side.

Her heart felt so full she thought it might overflow. It was a love strong enough to kindle warmth in the deepest winter. And it already had.

The End

Epilogue –
4 Years Later

Joy stepped in front of the window and looked out across the yard. She could hear the twins' voices, high, excited, but couldn't see them just yet. Her eight-month-old was perched happily on her hip, babbling contentedly as she responded to her grandmother's playful antics.

Darlene joined her at the window, and together they scanned the grounds, hoping to catch sight of the two three-year-olds. It wasn't long before the stable door swung open and Charles stepped outside, followed closely by his father.

Joy's heart skipped, just as it always did. Even after all these years, her husband still sent butterflies scattering through her stomach with a single glance. The twins suddenly appeared from around the corner of the house, racing toward their father and grandfather. Joy smiled softly. Their daughter was undeniably a daddy's girl, but her son was just as devoted to the men in his life. Even the baby adored her father and grandfather with equal enthusiasm.

Charles exchanged a few words with Brigham, and then, without warning, the two men scooped up a child each, settled them on their shoulders, and took off running toward the house. Joy laughed. Darlene shook her head, chuckling.

"I'm afraid they'll never outgrow these ridiculous games. If my father were here right now, he'd march inside, snatch the baby, and join them."

Joy pictured Charles's grandfather with the baby perched on his shoulders and burst into laughter.

"We should probably get supper on the table," she said, composing herself as footsteps thundered toward the door. She winked at her mother-in-law. The door flew open and the twins barreled inside, breathless and glowing, with Charles and Brigham close behind. The men went straight to the washbasin, but the twins raced to their mother and grandmother instead.

"Daddy and Grandpa raced and carried us on their shoulders!" her little blue-eyed boy announced, his face alight with excitement. He had his parents' eye color but Charles's dark hair.

"Daddy won, Mama," her daughter added proudly. Then she turned to her brother. "And since I was on Daddy's shoulders, I won too."

"Grandpa's older, that's why we lost," her son countered solemnly. Joy and Darlene both laughed.

"All right," Joy said gently, squeezing their round cheeks. "Go wash your hands. You can tell us everything while we eat." She watched them race away, her daughter's red pigtails bouncing wildly. When everyone was clean, Charles crossed the room. Their youngest reached for him immediately, and he lifted her with ease, pressing a kiss on her cheek before handing her to his mother.

Then his attention shifted. Without warning, he pulled Joy into his arms and kissed her, deep, confident, and entirely unapologetic. Instant protests erupted.

"That's gross, Daddy!" their daughter exclaimed.

"Yes," her brother agreed with a grimace. "That's yucky."

Charles only grinned, his lips lingering against Joy's.

"I can kiss your mama whenever I want, and for however long I want." He proved his point with another kiss, just as fierce, before pulling back with a laugh when he heard his daughter whisper loudly, "Grandma... make them stop."

Chuckling, Charles caught Joy's hand and tugged her down the hall, closing their bedroom door behind them. Joy stared at him, stunned, and laughed.

"What are you doing?"

"I'm trying to kiss my wife in peace," he replied solemnly, "without commentary from our offspring."

She giggled and melted into his arms, resting her forehead against his chest.

"I think it's time we escape to Crow Creek Falls again," he murmured. "Just for a few days. My parents won't mind watching the children, they're here more often than they are in Deer Lodge these days."

Joy raised a brow. "Are you certain? The last time we went to the cabin, we had another baby nine months later."

"And wasn't that worth it?" he shot back, smiling. Her expression softened instantly.

"Yes. I wouldn't trade our beautiful daughter for anything. And once Julia has her baby, and Cathleen her second, your parents will have to divide their attention anyway."

"I doubt it," he said lightly. "Maureen will still be hovering over Matt and Cathleen, and now that Julia's father is retired, the Prestons' are practically living in Deer Lodge. My parents just like it here. They love our children."

Joy sighed, thoughtful. "They're lucky. I didn't have that growing up. My grandparents passed when I was young, and we never lived close. Our children are truly blessed. My parents would have been wonderful grandparents too."

Charles pulled her closer, holding her gently.

"Having met your father," he said softly, "I know they would have been." Then his tone shifted, playful, challenging. "So... are you ready to visit our cabin again, or do I need to kiss you until you agree?"

Her eyes sparkled. "I think I need a little more convincing."

Charles didn't hesitate. He closed the distance and kissed his wife until she was breathless, laughing softly against his lips, utterly certain that some sparks never faded, no matter how full life became. And she wouldn't have it any other way.

A Note From the Author

D earest Reader,
     I hope you enjoyed this story. One touched with playful banter, edge-of-your-seat suspense, and kisses that linger just long enough to make your heart race. It has always been important to me to tell stories that could be real, stories grounded in emotion, respect, and genuine connection, while still allowing romance to spark, sizzle, and come fully alive.

Our world has drifted far from what is gentle, wholesome, and sincere. Through my books, I hope to bring some of that goodness back. Evil exists, there is no denying it, but not every man is a villain, and not every touch is something to fear. There is a clear and vital difference between mutual affection, playful teasing, tender embraces, and romance... and acts that cross the line into harm.

Romance can be passionate without being explicit. Desire can burn without being crude. Love can be protective, respectful, and deeply stirring all at once. My hope is that we can once again view friendship and romance between men and women with trusting, childlike eyes, celebrating what is pure and sincere, and reserving judgment only for what truly deserves it. There is beauty in love that honors boundaries, strength in affection freely given, and *something wonderfully powerful about a romance that stays clean... yet undeniably sizzling.*

Thank you for reading my book. If you enjoyed this story, I would be truly grateful if you'd consider leaving a review and exploring my other books.

With heartfelt appreciation,
Rebecca Lange

Did you love *Flames of the Fire*? Then you should read *Wrangling the Demons of Her Past*[1] by Rebecca Lange!

2

New edition!!! (released January 2026)

Leaving the place of her past behind was the only solution. Unfortunately, the demons of her past follow her...

Cathleen Taylor has had enough of relationships and love. After a string of forced and painful courtships and engagements, family losses, and being haunted by the brutal lessons from her uncle on obedience, she escapes to her late aunt's farm in Colorado. But peace is fleeting. Shadows loom

---

and pursue her for emeralds she never knew existed. What is the secret behind the hunt for the green gemstones? Just when she believes she's found solace, two handsome suitors threaten to unravel her vow of spinsterhood, causing Cathleen to grapple with the walls she's built around her heart. As love and danger collide, she has to decide whether risking her heart for a chance at love with the man who pursues her relentlessly is worth it or allow the ghosts of her past to keep her shackled.

About the Author

Rebecca Lange is a devoted romantic at heart. Though she has explored a variety of genres throughout her writing journey, her deepest passion lies in historical fiction—particularly stories set in the 1800s American West and the Regency era.

A passionate advocate, Rebecca uses her stories to raise awareness of abuse, human trafficking, and the devastating impact of drug and alcohol addiction. These themes are not woven in for suspense alone, but as a reminder that such struggles are tragically real—and that victims are never to blame.

She is also a firm believer in women's rights, inspired by the courageous women of the 1800s who fought to prove they were not the property of their husbands but their partners and equals. Rebecca upholds the conviction that violence has no place in relationships or marriage.

Originally from Germany, she was born and raised there before moving abroad in 2002 to serve a mission for her church in Scotland. A member of The Church of Jesus Christ of Latter-day Saints, she now lives in Utah with her husband, their two sons (ages 18 and 20), and two lively Yorkie puppies.

Her writing motto is: *Never Smut, Always Sizzling Kisses, Consistently Closed Door.* Rebecca delights in weaving passion and tenderness into her stories, offering what she calls "sweet and diet spice" romance. Diet spice—what is that, you ask? It's the thrill of longing gazes, passionate kisses, and close embraces that build anticipation without ever crossing into explicit territory. For her, the most powerful love stories are those that remain tasteful and teasing, proving that romance can be both heart-stirring and wholesome.

Read more at https://authorrebeccalange.wixsite.com/bookstolove.